UNAUTHORISED DEPARTURE

Unauthorised Departure

Maureen O'Brien

A *Time Warner* Book

First published in Great Britain in 2003 by Time Warner Books

Copyright © 2003 Maureen O'Brien

The moral right of the author has been asserted.

A CIP catalogue record for this book
is available from the British Library.

HARDBACK ISBN 0 316 85943 5

Typeset in Sabon
by Palimpsest Book Production Limited,
Polmont, Stirlingshire
Printed and bound in Great Britain by
Clays Ltd, St Ives plc

Time Warner Books UK
Brettenham House
Lancaster Place
London WC2E 7EN

www.TimeWarnerBooks.co.uk

For Michael
with even more gratitude than usual

Acknowledgements

With special thanks to Jean-Christophe Rodius who gave me such wonderful help in understanding the French police and judiciary, and especially with recent developments in their organisation. If I've got things wrong that's down to me, not him. And to Alain and Jennifer Belle for correcting my French.

To Hilary Hale, my editor, not just for the title but for an extraordinary feat of lateral thinking when I was stuck. And most of all for her patience.

Every year of my life since the late sixties I've spent time in France. I owe to it, as so many English people do, my appreciation of food, of wine, of cinema, especially *film noir*, based as it has so often been on examples of the *roman noir*, by Simenon, by David Goodis, and others. The Jura is a new discovery – a curious and beautiful region that I have in the course of researching this novel grown to know and love.

French leave: unannounced or unauthorized departure . . .

Shorter Oxford English Dictionary

1

A Communications Problem

You can't escape. You try to hide you'll be hunted out. It won't be clean. It won't be quick. You won't know when. This is payback time.

It came on his email. No sender, and no address. After this they came at funny intervals. No pattern. Sometimes giving more graphic detail, dwelling on what they'd do to him before allowing him to die.

They didn't worry him too much. Let yourself worry about that garbage and your life wouldn't be worth living. It had happened to him before – villains he'd put away, fantasising revenge. Then the threats began to change.

The next one came not on the shiny screen but in an envelope postmarked Portsmouth, a bit of paper, looked like toilet paper, roughly torn, words cut out of a newspaper and pasted on, a kid's idea of a poison pen. But this was no kid:

Mr Bright. You're not the only one fouled up. Your girlfriend done her bit. You tell her take care. It's a small world. Don't just watch your back. Watch hers.

His hand itched to screw it up and sling it. He should send it to the lab but that would mean going through official channels, and attention from above he didn't need. Shopping a corrupt cop and putting him away, as he had done last year, makes you no friends. Friends fade into the woodwork. Enemies bide their time.

He filed it with the others and kicked his desk drawer shut. He jerked his old leather jacket off the back of the chair. He needed a fix of the traffic fumes and fast food smells of Kentish Town Road. He got to the door and his phone rang.

Grant, the new DCI, waved him to the interviewee chair. He signed three documents and put them in his out-tray while Bright sat waiting. Then he looked up. 'Oh yes. John . . .' He opened a drawer, took out a card, read through its message and handed it over. 'This came today.'

Same stuff, only with some unpleasant references to Jude's anatomy. Bright waited a bit before speaking. He sat with the card on the desk in front of him, his head hanging, looking at his hands clasped between his knees. Human hands. A bit small, a bit helpless. In the big view of things this didn't amount to one bean let alone a hill of them. When you'd just over six months ago seen a plane slice through a multi-storey building in downtown Manhattan you knew that we all walk a narrow line just this side of chaos. He sighed.

Grant said, 'Is this the first?'

Bright thought about lying, then shook his head. 'No.'

'How many?'

'Maybe six, over the last three months.'

'Got them on file?'

'A-ha.'

'I'd like to see the file.'

Bright started to get up.

'Don't rush off. All in good time. Did this start after you got Brennan banged up?'

'A-ha.'

'We know who it is then.'

'Well, guv, there's a few possibilities.'

'Yes.'

They didn't need to spell it out. Others had gone down with Brennan. Others with friends in higher places than Brennan. You could lock them up but you couldn't lock up their influence and power. Bright had trusted his old chief inspector. He didn't know Grant yet. He thought Grant was on his side but he wasn't sure. He couldn't be sure of anything.

'You better watch your back,' Grant said.

The echo disturbed Bright, like a breeze lifting his hair. 'I'd need eyes in the back of my head to do that, guv.'

'It's not a joking matter, John.'

'What else can you do? The Met gonna give me an armed guard, are they, to watch over me?'

'Have they threatened your girlfriend before?'

Bright's scar hurt, just below the bottom rib at the back. He shifted in the chair. 'A-ha. This is the second to mention her.'

'What we going to do about this?'

'Take the usual precautions?'

'I can go higher.'

'Don't do that, guv.'

Grant looked at him. 'No . . . ? But—'

'Look, I've had threats before. My old ma in her wheel-chair has had threats through me. Nothing's ever come of them. Some wanker in a jail cell jerking off, that's all it is.'

'This could be different. This was the biggest case of your life. It shut down a big operation. Those guys, you know as well as I do, they're businessmen, John, they're not your small-time loser. They really don't want you around.'

'What you suggesting? I give up the police? Jack it in?'

'Just maybe take some time off.'

'Forget it.'

'You've got leave owing. Take a couple of weeks. Then maybe after that we can think again.'

'That's what they want. They want me off the job. Playing

right up their alley. Come off it, guv. What would I do? Look after my ma's roses in South Norwood? Can you see it? They wanna shoot me in the back of the head the way they shoot innocent witnesses? Let 'em. I'd rather go like that than sitting on a deck-chair in a holiday home with cirrhosis of the liver and Alzheimer's dribble. Given the choice. Which I won't be.'

'And your girlfriend? That what she wants? She's had a taste of their nasty little ways, hasn't she? You want her to get some more?'

Bright's right hand covered his face.

'Have you told her about these threats?'

Bright went to the window and looked at the dust on the Venetian blind. He shook his head.

'You going to?'

'Nope.'

'You going to hire a minder for her?'

'They're not gonna make good on these.'

'Because they never have before? We never had one like this before. We never had a case that took so many down with it. And we don't know how many others that didn't go down. The ones still out there. What would you do if anything happened to her?'

'No. You don't lie down for these bastards, guv, you don't scuttle down a mouse-hole. What's the good? You gotta come out the mouse-hole one day, you can't stay down there for ever, and who's sitting there waiting for you to come out? The big fat cat, that's who. We could all be dead of anthrax next week, there's a war on, so the Yanks say. You want me to go scuttling away? Forget it.' He held his jacket by the loop and swung it over his shoulder. The loop broke. The jacket hit the floor and subsided, slowly. A pathetic sight. Bright bent to retrieve the poor old thing. Pretty ignominious after his heroic speech. The symbolism wasn't lost on him. Or on Grant. They stared at each other.

4

Grant lifted his forearms in a hands-off gesture. 'Okay, okay, only I'm going to file this, right? So you can't say I didn't warn you. And if something happens one dark night, don't say I didn't suggest some options. You want me to send this to the lab?'

'Think you'll find anything on it?'

The DCI raised his eyebrows. They both knew there'd be nothing. No fingerprints, no particles, no DNA.

'Waste of lab time and money.' Bright held out his hand. 'I'll put it in my file.'

'I want the file on this desk before you leave the building today.'

'A-ha.'

'And a bit of advice, John.'

'A-ha?'

'Tell your girlfriend? Put her on her guard.'

He photocopied the file in the afternoon and gave Grant his original. He thought about telling Jude.

But he didn't tell her. He put himself on the late shift so he could spend his days keeping an eye on her. He spent a lot of time in his office, nights, organising investigations, writing up reports, and sleeping at his desk.

Jude got fed up. 'You need a holiday,' she said.

'I can't stand holidays, Jude.'

'You've never spent a holiday with me.'

'That's true.'

'Just think about it?'

He thought about it. He thought about his life: his youthful marriage that had lasted less than a year because his wife couldn't stand his obsession with his job; about Millie Hale, the only other woman that had ever affected him the way Jude did. He'd lost them. He thought about losing Jude, through his own stubborn refusal to give in to Brennan. He thought about the acts of ruthless cruelty inflicted by Brennan and his associates on anyone who got in their way. He ground his teeth at the idea of quitting, crushed. By Brennan or the seditious bastards in the police who took Brennan's blood-money and carried out his orders. Maybe Grant was one of them. Maybe a few weeks of leave was Grant's way of easing him out? Or maybe the DCI was telling him the plain truth. But in the end, which mattered more – the ugly mess of self-serving craphounds issuing the death-threats, or Jude? On leave it would be easier to keep an eye on her, that was for sure: watch her back, if not his own. 'Okay,' he said. 'I'll take some leave.'

2

The Plans of Mice

'So where are we going to go?'

'Go?'

'Yes, John. People go away for their holidays.'

'We're not people. We're staying here.'

'We've got to go somewhere. We can't just stay at home.'

'What's wrong with home?'

'Nothing; it's not abroad, that's all.'

'I don't like abroad.'

'You liked Hong Kong.'

'That was work, Jude.'

'You can't just work all the time.'

'Try me.'

'I have.'

'I've noticed. Wanna try me again?'

'Don't change the subject. You need a holiday.'

'Know what I need? I need you. And this nice house. That's what I need.'

'And that's all?'

'A-ha, that's all.'

'And what about me?'

'Oh, didn't I mention you?'

'Very amusing. *I* need a break.'

'What from?'

'Work. Look at this garden – it's a tip. If I stay here I'll spend the whole time out there fixing it.'

'Good idea. I'll help. My ma's got me well trained. I'm a dab hand with the secateurs.'

'I'm serious.'

'Okay, let's get serious. We've hardly spent any time just here, just on our own, not working, just living. Well, have we?'

'No . . .'

'I'll do a bit of – you know – I'll get this room fixed up.'

'What's wrong with this room?'

'Nothing.'

'Exactly.'

'Well, I'll put my feet up and look at it.'

'Just like now in fact?'

'Just like now.' He put his arm round her and kissed her. Then his other arm round her and kissed her again.

Later she said, 'We could have such a lovely time . . .'

'We're having an excellent time. What could be better?'

'Oh you—! We just go round in circles.'

'As long as we keep finishing up right here that's fine by me.'

'You're hopeless.'

The doorbell rang. Bright said, 'Ah shit who's this?'

Jude, having been on top of him, was gone before he could stop her.

George scurried away and hid under the desk. Bright said, 'I'm with you, George.' He followed the big tabby, parted two slats of the window blind and craned sideways to see the invaders. He recognised the girl but couldn't place her. George leapt on to the desk. Bright stroked him between the ears but George did not relax, tail out straight, nose quivering. Bright, light on his feet, swift and silent as the cat, padded to the door, listening.

There was a funny silence out in the hall. Then a murmur. Then Jude came back in. She looked rueful and amused and embarrassed and a little bit shocked. She raised her eyebrows at Bright and scratched her nose.

Bright, back in the middle of the room, still tucking his shirt in, said, 'Oh, it's you.'

8

The big man with the shaved head held the hand of the girl Bright had seen. He said, 'Lina, this is Inspector Bright—'

'—John.'

'Nice to meet you, John,' the girl said.

He placed her now. 'Saw you at the trial, didn' I?'

'Oh, yes.'

Dan put an arm round her shoulders. 'She was a great support to me, weren't you, love?'

'I hope so.' She spoke in a little girl's breathy whisper.

She looked eighteen to Bright and knockout glamour – the way she stood, the way she tossed the long hair back, the way her short black frock just touched her in all the right places and had cost a thousand quid, or did she just make it look like that? He'd seen women who had paid a thousand and might as well have been dressed by Oxfam. This was class, thoroughbred greyhound class. He caught Jude's eye. She was watching him watching the girl; she was trying for amused and not quite succeeding. 'I'll put the kettle on,' he said. 'Or maybe you'd like something stronger.'

'Will you do me for drunk-driving?' It was meant to come out as a joke but just missed.

'I'm not on duty, mate.'

Jude said, 'He's actually taking some long-needed leave.'

'I'll have a Scotch then. Thanks.'

'Lina?'

'Have you any fizzy water?'

'We drink eau de tap here, I'm afraid.'

'Oh. That's fine.'

'*Which?* did a taste test on several bottled waters and compared them with Thames water.' Jude was nervous, chattering. 'Thames came out top.'

'You're kidding?'

'Want any eau de Thames with this, mate?'

'Dan just has ice.' Jude blushed. 'Well, you used to, I don't know if . . . '

'Drop of dilution these days – Lina's influence.'

'Gosh.' Jude smiled at Lina. 'I could never dilute him.'

Lina smiled back at Jude but said nothing.

Jude squeezed past her and Dan, and escaped into the hall. She heard Dan say, 'Hey, George!' then George shot out of the room and scooted ahead of her down the basement stairs. She heard Dan say, 'He always was Jude's familiar. Never really did more than put up with me.' She stopped on the stairs to listen, heard only silence, and carried on down to the kitchen.

In the living-room, after the silence, Bright said, 'Cheers.'

'*Salut*.' Dan tasted his undiluted drink. 'Good Scotch.'

'O'Leary's.'

Dan laughed. 'Whose?'

'*Which?* did a test.'

'Not Scotch then?'

'Not exactly, no.'

'Very good though.' Dan drank again and paused, added, 'Jude always was mad on *Which?* tests,' and drank some more.

'That right?' Bright bounced on the balls of his feet.

No one said anything else. You could hear Dan swallowing.

Jude came back with a jug of water and a bowl of ice. She poured water for Lina who tasted it and said, 'Mmm, delicious.' Jude and Bright laughed. Lina looked puzzled, then smiled in a baffled way.

'Cheers.' Jude and Bright clinked glasses. Jude wondered if she should clink with Dan, decided not to, and sipped her whisky. 'I think the guy who tested this for *Which?* must have been drunk at the time.'

'It was cheap though, Jude.'

'I could have told them that just by tasting it. Mmm' – she rolled it around in her mouth – 'this whisky is obviously very . . . cheap.'

10

'Dan thought it was okay.'

'He was being polite. Weren't you?'

Dan smiled but didn't answer. This leaky conversation was about to founder on the rocks. Jude's childlike eyes fixed on Bright with a pleading expression. 'You like going on holidays?' Bright suddenly asked Dan.

'Sure. Great drives we had, through France, Italy, Spain. Didn't we, Jude?'

'John doesn't see the point.'

'What do you do there?' Bright said.

'Where?'

'On holiday.'

'Well, you – potter about. You look at things.'

'What things? Monuments?'

'Buildings, mountains, countryside. Where Jude's concerned – plants. People. And yes, I guess the odd monument.'

'Flora and fauna. And eat lovely food and drink lovely wine, and lie in the sun . . .' Jude's voice yearned.

'We can do that here.'

'We can lie in the carbon emissions anyway, down there at the end of the garden, to the regular beat of diesel loco-motives.'

'Bet you don't miss the trains, eh, Dan?'

Dan was looking at Jude and appeared not to hear Bright. Then he came to. 'Sorry, what?'

Bright didn't say it again.

'No. No, I don't miss the trains,' Dan said at last.

Jude flushed. 'How is your new place, Dan?'

'Nice.'

'Loft in Southwark? Can't get more trendy these days, mate.'

'You must come and see it one day.'

'A-ha.'

'Has he made it gorgeous?' Jude brought Lina into the conversation, if this feet-on-eggshells, cat-on-hot-bricks manoeuvring round sensitive topics could be called a conversation.

'Yes, it's heaven. The wall overlooking the river? Dan had them remove it and put in floor-to-ceiling concertina windows. So it's a huge terrace now, or a conservatory, depending on whether you have it open or closed. I've put tree-palms and bamboo in there, it's so light. And he took out one ceiling so that part of the living room is now double height and the bedroom is, you know, galleried? So all the space is kind of all around you all the time and you feel it's all just one lovely whole, you know?'

Her last phrase echoed around for a while and everyone drank and didn't look at anyone else.

Dan said, 'You've made it cosy in here.'

'Yes but it will always feel like your workroom to me.'

'Oh, was this your workroom, darling?' Lina began to circle the room touching things. 'Was this your desk?'

'Yes—'

Jude said, 'My mum's actually originally—'

'—Oh yes, that's right . . .' Dan passed a hand over his smooth scalp.

'She was a teacher. Used to do her marking on that.'

'What did she teach?'

'Kids.'

'Hey, Jude!'

'Sorry. I wasn't being flip. She was a primary-school teacher. She didn't have a specialist subject. She just had what she called "my class". She taught them everything. Would anyone consider sitting down?'

Bright put his hand on the back of Jude's neck. She didn't normally go for proprietary gestures, but found herself grateful. Dan put his hand out in the direction of Lina without moving towards her – the kind of proprietory gesture Jude did not go for – and Lina, smiling gratefully, crossed the room and leaned on him, till he moved his hand

12

up her back to between her shoulder blades to give her a prod in the direction of the couch. He sank into the brown velvet cushions. Lina subsided next to him, touching him all the way down. Bright caught Jude's eye and grinned without moving his face. She felt grateful again.

'Old couch still going strong.' Dan stretched out his legs towards the fire. 'Looks better than it did as workroom furniture.'

'Oh, was this in your workroom too?' Lina began to stroke the velvet cushion as if it were Dan's flesh. Bright covered his mouth.

'We bought it in a junk shop in Mill Lane,' Jude said. 'When we lived in West Hampstead.'

'Nineteen eight-eight.'

'Before we were married even.'

'Really . . . ?' Lina stopped stroking the couch. She held her glass of water with both hands.

'I don't suppose it would look its best in the penthouse?' Jude said.

'Oh I don't know—' Lina looked to Dan for confirmation '—with new upholstery it might have a sort of retro charm. You know? Surrealist almost.'

Dan inadvertently caught Jude's eye. He said to Lina, 'Don't think so, love.'

'Oh? Right . . .'

A fog of puzzlement settled on Jude. Why had they come? Was this a social visit – an overture? Did Dan want them all to be friends suddenly? Or did he have a more practical motive – further sharing of the spoils perhaps? Lina seemed to think so, though her tactlessness was possibly caused by nerves.

At a loss for any other inoffensive subject, Jude started to ask Lina where she'd bought her dress. At the same time Bright proffered more whisky, Dan cleared his throat, and Lina was heard to say the word "commission".

'You've got a commission, Dan!'

'Don't sound so surprised, Jude.'

'I'm thrilled. I'm so thrilled. What is it?'

'It's a small housing development—'

'Still—'

'—They're giving me a free hand.'

'O wonderful wonderful and most wonderful wonderful and yet again wonderful and after that, out of all whooping.'

'Hey?' Bright said.

'It's from *As You Like It*. When Kate was doing it. She got me to hear her lines. I did like it. So I remembered it.'

'A-ha.'

'Who's Kate?'

'Dan! Kate Creech. You remember Kate. Client of mine. Lady Margaret Road?'

'Oh, the actress.'

'An old flame of John's as it happens. Who's your client, by the way?'

Dan sat up as if she'd goosed him. 'Erm . . .'

'It's my father actually.' Lina gave Dan a proud look. 'He has a construction firm.'

A short pause. Jude's eyes caught Dan's and couldn't let go. Neither managed to think of anything to say.

Bright decided to break it up. 'Where's the site, mate?'

'Bermondsey, a factory that's been demolished. A good-sized site, great position.'

'You will be good, won't you, Dan?' Jude meant, *don't get on the wrong side of the client by refusing to compromise, by getting up to your old tricks. Don't spoil it.*

Dan never missed her unspoken messages. An expression of irritation crossed his face. 'I will have another, of this dubious Irish brew, just a small one thanks, and then we must be—'

'I'm very pleased, Dan.' Jude tried to make up for her lack of tact. Lina was not the only one affected by nerves.

14

'Yes, well . . .'

Dan's deflation told her why he had come. To show off: his commission, his girl, his trendy loft apartment, his luck, his survival, his success. She was glad for him. She was pleased, as she had said. But, thus shown-off to, she felt in a false position, as though she should do a bit of parading too, of luck, of love. But it wouldn't be right. If Dan didn't want what she had – the old house, the old sofa, the old cat, the old life, and love, real live love, not just the pretty model girlfriend with the influential dad – he wouldn't need to come here and show off.

'Cheers mate. Here's to the project.'

They raised their glasses and sipped.

Jude marvelled at Bright. He looked sharp, he looked out-for-the-main chance, he looked a little crooked, he looked able to take care of himself in a scrap, a Jack Russell, not a greyhound, no pedigree. He'd never be rich or successful in any way the world understood. He was no intellectual either. But he had this native intelligence as subtle as water. And he committed his heart. She felt overcome for a second with a surge of love. He took care of her. Dan had never done that. She had always taken care of him.

Lina leaned against Dan. Lina the Leaner, Jude thought. The lean leaner. She leaned on Dan now, but some day she would discover she was leaning on air. Or maybe not. Maybe it was a question of balance, of two people together. Maybe, with Leaner leaning on him, Dan might have less to prove. Maybe she'd bring out some strength in him that Jude never could. Together they might achieve perfect equilibrium. Dan turned and smiled into Leaner's eyes and Jude felt a stiletto of jealousy pierce her chest and lodge in the empty space there that Dan had left behind.

Dan said, 'You must come round and—'

'Yes, it would be nice to see the place and—'

'I'll do lunch!' Leaner stood up, chatty with relief, now

that they were about to depart. 'It's great to have your fellah working on the premises.'

'What do you do, Lina?'

'I'm his receptionist and secretary.'

'Oh.' So the leaning wasn't all one way. 'I could never have done that.'

Leaner's face grew pinched and narrow. Her shoulders expressed defeat. 'Well, I never found anything I really liked doing before.'

'Oh yes!' Jude rushed to make amends. 'It's the luckiest thing – I know that – to have work that you really enjoy.'

'So when will you come?'

'Oh. I er . . .'

'Well it won't be soon.' The nasal South London raven croak. Bright put down his empty glass and they all looked at him with a certain alarm. He was a bloke who didn't obey the rules. Things might be said that were not normally said. He wasn't middle class. He wasn't even aspiring middle class. He didn't muck about.

At last Dan said, a little cool, a little polite, a little wary, 'Oh, why's that?'

'I don't want you taking Jude away from me, do I, mate? Not now I've found her.'

Everyone flushed and everyone laughed and everyone stopped laughing. Jude looked at him with a perplexed, slightly cross, pursed smile. He moved close to her and put his arm round her shoulder. 'Nah,' he said. 'Just joking. We're going on holiday. Aren't we, Jude?'

3

Such Sweet Sorrow

It only took her four days to plan the trip and she kept laughing and looking up from her maps and guide books and turning her astonished face to him, saying, 'I don't get it. What was it that changed your mind?'

He was going to tell her the real reason? What for? To wipe that glow off her face? 'You were just gonna go along,' he said. 'You were all ready to get civilised and do the right thing and go visiting their posh pad and eating their posh nosh. They'd have lunch catered by *FISH* of Southwark and Daddy'd drop in to give the ex-wife and her downmarket bloke the once-over, giving me the funny handshake just in case being a copper I could ever be any use to him. No thanks.'

She looked shocked. 'You're a snob!'

'Everyone's a snob, Jude.'

We could have just made an excuse – you know – sorry-something's-come-up.'

'Not me. Got no patience with that bollocks.'

'What bollocks precisely?'

'Making excuses, not saying what you mean.'

'I see. You'd rather travel a thousand miles than make an excuse to get out of a social engagement. Don't you think that's a bit extreme?'

'I suddenly changed my mind, okay?'

Even now, the day before their departure, revisiting the streets of his no-good boyhood, she wouldn't let it drop. 'You were so against a holiday!' she said.

He turned off South Norwood Hill into a cul-de-sac of

17

small thirties semis, and stopped. He turned off the engine and took the key out of the ignition. He tossed the key in his hand. 'I got jealous,' he said. 'All right?'

'Jealous? Of me and Dan?'

'Well, who else?'

'Oh. Lord. How lovely. You couldn't say a nicer thing.' She started to get out of the car but stopped. 'You can't be serious.'

'I am.' It occurred to him now that maybe jealousy had been the deciding factor, but how would he ever know?

She brought her face close up so her eyes crossed a little, like his. She kissed his mouth. 'Oh, don't be,' she said. 'Don't be. Ever.' She got out and opened the rear door. 'Come on, George.' She lifted the basket off the back seat.

George, knowing he was about to be abandoned in an alien place, let loose a howl of terror. 'I know, George. It's awful. I'm so sorry. But you'll be all right, I promise you will. Lily's nice and she'll be very good to you.' Walking up the path she said, 'You can't be half as jealous as I am of George. What if he likes it better here than with us?'

'Too bloody bad. He lives with us, he comes back where he belongs and lumps it. He's a cat.'

George yowled.

'It's okay, George.' Bright patted the basket as his mother opened the door. 'She's a harmless old bird,' he said.

'Who are you calling harmless?'

'Who's he calling an old bird for that matter?' Jude said. 'Hello, Lily.'

Lily leaned forward in her chair in a way that for her was oddly polite, and offered her cheek for Jude to kiss, then she turned her wheelchair with one smooth movement and led the way into the living room, bay window at the front, sliding french windows, open, at the back. Books either side of the fireplace in white-painted shelves, reachable from wheelchair height. It was a pleasant room but George continued to howl.

18

'George, for heaven's sake!'

'Ah, poor wee thing, he knows you're putting him into care.'

'Shall I leave him in the basket?'

'If you want to look at my garden.'

'You bet.' Jude lowered George to the floor and whispered, 'Just for a while, dear old thing. I'll be back.' She followed Lily. George lapsed into silence.

The garden this time of year should have looked depressing, like everyone else's garden. Like Jude's own. But the *Coronilla glauca* spattered the wall with yellow, snowdrops posed elegant in green and white under the white camellia, and close to the window the pale blossoms of the viburnum lapped the terrace in its scent.

'Of course to a professional my poor wee patch won't look much.'

'Lily, it's amazing. You know it is.'

'Well, you have to say that, haven't you?'

Jude smiled. 'No.'

'I don't like to ask your advice for free.'

'I don't have any advice. You could advise me.'

'Och, flattery'll get you anywhere.' Lily rolled out into the garden.

'I'll put the kettle on, Ma.'

From the kitchen Bright watched the pair of them. The wheelchair glided over the grass. Lily pointed, waving her hands, Jude examined plants, talking earnestly, smiling hard. He could sense the strain from here. They wanted to like each other, all right. They did like each other – kind of. But his ma was keeping Jude at arm's length, with a deadly politeness he'd never seen her do before. He had to hand it to her, she was good at it. You couldn't fault her.

He took the tea into the living room. George was curled with his eyes shut pretending to be asleep. Wouldn't open them when Bright spoke to him through the bars of his cage.

Wouldn't purr, wouldn't loosen up and roll over. 'You and my ma should get on fine,' Bright said. 'Two of a bloody kind. Stubborn old birds, the pair of you.' George opened his eyes and gave Bright a look of straight despair. 'Hey, she's not leaving you for ever, old mate. We'll be back. Two weeks. That's my limit. I've told her. Anyway, she wouldn't leave you longer than that. You know Jude. It'd break her heart.'

The women came back in with determined smiles. 'Ooh, tea,' his ma said.

Ooh tea? She didn't talk like that; she was acting like Jude was the bloody Queen.

'Lily's an amazing gardener,' Jude said, her expression wild and sad.

'Jude's a kind person,' Lily said, pouring the tea.

'Jude never says what she doesn't mean. Any more than you do, Ma.'

Lily handed him his mug with an old-fashioned look. 'How's Kate?' she said, shamelessly. 'I haven't seen her in a while.'

'She's okay, Ma. Sends her love.'

'Hasn't been to see me lately.'

'She's going away,' Jude said.

Lily turned her head. 'Kate Creech? Do you know her?'

'Yes, I do her garden. She's an old mate.'

'Oh.'

One up to Jude, Bright thought.

'She'd have taken George for me if she hadn't been offered this job—' Jude stuck her face into her mug of tea. Imply that Lily was second choice for cat-sitting? She'd bite her tongue off rather than do that. But it was too late to take it back now.

Two up to Jude, Bright thought.

There was a bit of a silence.

'Where's she going?' Lily asked stiffly.

20

'Filming a telly series in Donegal.'

'She usually lets me know.'

'They didn't tell her till the other day. Very short notice. Less than a week to get ready. Costume fittings and stuff. She says the actress they really wanted must have dropped out and she was next on the list.'

'Och, she'd be joking. She's too modest. Of course she'd be their first choice. She's a marvellous actress, Kate is.'

'Yes, I know.' *And I know you like her more than me,* Jude wanted to say, *and that John was in love with her once and that you wanted him to stay with her and that you'd much rather he was with her than with me, but I can't help it if it didn't work out between them; it was before my time.* What she said was, 'Shall I close the windows and let George out of his basket?'

Lily smiled – 'Yes' – but looked nervous.

Jude shut the french windows and got down on her knees, speaking to George in a reassuring murmur. She opened his wire door. 'There you are, George, it's okay, look.'

George crouched for some time, shoulders hunched, then he crept out on his belly and slunk, low to the ground, into the darkness under the sofa.

'It's no use trying to coax him out,' Jude said.

'He'll have to emerge eventually to eat.'

'Anyway, the minute we're gone, he'll probably leap out and be all over you. Cats – you know – don't like to parade their relationships in public, don't like to make people jealous. He won't sit on John when I'm there but he's all over him the minute I'm gone.'

Lily said in a huffy tone, 'How does he manage when you're both there?'

'If we're side by side he thinks about it a lot, then stretches across both laps. So neither of us can take offence.'

Lily's smile was stiff, confronted with the image of Jude and Bright side by side, on the same sofa, in the same house, rather suggesting the idea of them side by side in bed.

Oh lord, Jude thought. Anything I say . . . 'Actually, I think the sooner we go the better. Less painful all round. Then you and George will be able to work it out. Just keep talking to him.' She hunted in her jeans pocket for a tissue.

'I had a cat when I was a girl,' Lily said. 'She was a wee blackie, not a big bold stripy like George. I was way fond of her. She was run over. That's why I never would have another.' It was the most sincere she'd been yet.

'Come on.' Jude touched Bright's arm. First time she'd ever laid a finger on him in front of his ma. 'We should go. I'm sorry, Lily, you must think I'm completely daft.'

'No,' Lily said. 'We can't help who we love. Can we?'

Bright thought he'd be in tears himself in a minute. 'See you then, Ma. See you, George. You take care of my ma, okay?'

They opened and shut the living-room door fast, George being liable to scoot out of the front door in panic. Bright slid into the downstairs loo for a pee. Jude and Lily were alone in the hall, marooned in the sudden silence, Jude wiping her tears, unable to think of anything except George, Lily groping for a safe subject.

At last Lily said, 'He works too hard. It'll do him the world of good getting away, because all he ever does is work and when he's not working he's looking after me. I feel bad about it but he won't be told. I don't know what you did to persuade him. He hates abroad.'

'She pestered me. She's a nag. Like you.' Bright had reappeared unnoticed, a trick of his trade. 'Take care of yourself, Ma.'

'Me and George'll be fine!' Lily said. 'Don't you fret.' But she didn't look at Jude.

4

To Arrive is Better
than to Travel?

Bright the traveller was a complete surprise to Jude. She
and Dan had always studied the yellow Michelin maps,
deciding their route on the little roads, whether to go
Portsmouth–Caen or Dover–Calais, how long they could
afford to stay away, whether they should camp or could
manage small hotels. But Bright had left everything to her.
'Shall we go by the tunnel?' she'd asked.

'Yeah, fine.'

'Do you fancy the Luberon?'

'Sure.'

She'd got out the big map of France and spread it on the
kitchen table. Bright went on reading the *Independent*. 'Shall
we go Reims–Chaumont–Dijon?'

'Mmm.'

'You know, I'd really like to take a look at the Jura on
the way south – what do you think?'

'A-ha, right.' He did insist on driving: 'No offence, Jude,
but I can't stand being the passenger.' And he wouldn't let
her pack the car when they got home from Lily's: 'Don't
wanna advertise to the neighbourhood we're going away.'

'But, John, they'll know anyway. They know everything
in this street.'

'Nah. We'll pack tonight and throw it all in the car when
we're leaving.'

'In the dark at five a.m.?'

'A-ha.'

'You don't trust anyone.'

'I'm a copper.'

'Mmmm. Maybe you'll relax a bit abroad.'

He said nothing to that.

He zoomed across London, five a.m., in the dark, tackling the suburbs south of the river – a foreign country to Jude – like the driver of a black cab. But when the big, safe city was left behind, nothing but fields lapping the motorway, mist floating in the pearly dawn light, he got nervous as a cat and, approaching the Eurotunnel, silent, tapping a rhythm on the steering-wheel, then whistling silently between his teeth as he manoeuvred the car on board, his knuckles white when they closed the doors, his eyes flicking everywhere, geared up for ambush.

Off the shuttle, however, clear of the terminal at Calais, he changed. Unfazed by driving on the right, but surprised by everything else: the hazy sunshine – 'How can it be this different? We've only crossed the Channel!' – the *péage* on the motorway – 'What's this peeje business? You mean they fine us for driving?' – the price of petrol – '*How* much? Be worth the fare over here just to fill up' – he did seem to relax. He first whistled, then sang in a light pure tenor, *Sous les ponts de Paris*. 'You do speak French,' Jude said. 'You lied to me!'

'Nah, that's my ma, taught me that when I was a tadpole. She's a Scot. They teach them things there. They don't come out of school worse morons than they went in.'

'You're a constant surprise to me.'

'I'm hoping to keep it that way, Missis.'

He did.

They came off the autoroute at Reims. He worked out the euros – 'Ten quid all that way. Not bad!' – was bowled over by the cathedral, coming at it head on, and by the statue of Joan of Arc on her horse – 'Christ, she was really here. How about that?' – but in the crowded restaurant

24

where they ordered the *plât du jour*, he grew uneasy again. 'Change places,' he said.

'Why?'

'Just do it.'

Jude got up, bewildered. He moved to a seat between her and the other tables, where he could see the whole restaurant but not be seen himself.

'What's this in aid of?' she said.

'The bloke over there.' He indicated a lean, broad-shouldered man eating his lunch in a corner.

'What about him?'

'He was on the Eurotunnel. He was next to us in the queue.'

'Well, so what? Lots of English will be going down south and taking this route. Do you think he's following us?' She laughed.

Bright gave her an odd look. He nearly spoke, then didn't. Soon after, the man got up and left without looking at them. Ten minutes later they were back on the A4. But he wasn't happy, she could tell. Nor was she, bored with the endless sameness of the autoroute.

He cheered up when, at Chalon, she directed him on to a minor road that undulated round the Champagne country like a creamy ribbon. He saw his first vines and his first Champagne château – 'You mean that's like, *the* Mumm's, for real?' But soon he went silent again. Jude, happy to be gliding among the lovely hills, was content to be quiet. Then the bare vines, cross-stitching the hills in regular patches like brown tweed, distracted her with their beauty, and suddenly they hit one of the roundabouts the French are crazy for, with five roads out of it, and Bright was saying, 'Come on, Jude, which road?' with a sharp edge on his voice.

She panicked. Somewhere north of Dijon, that was all she knew. A crossroads in the middle of nowhere and the pair of them in the middle of their first row.

'Where now? Which way?'

'Oh God. Oh hell.' His anger froze her brain. The map blurred, meaningless.

'Come on, Jude! I can't just keep going round this bloody thing.' He screeched the car to a halt off one of the roads. Three cars drove past. 'That bastard Volvo's been behind me ever since Reims.'

'Volvo?' she said. 'What Volvo?'

'It's got Brit numberplates.'

'So what? What are you talking about?'

'Thought I'd lost it when we came off the motorway.' He watched the big grey car sail over the hill, out of sight, then grabbed the map from her. 'Here, give it here. Where are we? What road were we on before we fouled up?' He studied the map for thirty seconds. 'How did you manage this? We're miles off course!'

'Kilometres,' she murmured but he said nothing, thrust the map back on her lap, U-turned, tyres squealing, circled the roundabout again and spun hard left.

'I'd have worked it out if you hadn't got cross with me,' she said after a while.

'I don't like being lost in the middle of nowhere. I don't like not knowing where I am.'

'Why can't you just enjoy it? It's beautiful. It's Burgundy. Nuits-St-Georges is just over that way. You've never been here before.'

'Shoulda stayed on the bloody motorway.'

'I'm a good navigator as a rule. But if you get angry with people they fall to pieces, of course.'

Neither spoke again for a quarter of an hour. Then Bright gave a short laugh. 'Anyway, at least I've shaken off that bastard Volvo.'

She didn't answer. She couldn't. Their little world was coming apart. It was getting on for tea-time. She was dying to stop but couldn't say so. Under the wonderful viaduct of

Chaumont, round the great fortress walls of Langres, through the ancient village of Pesmes, she directed him in terse short statements – 'Left here, right there, there's a fork ahead, take the right' – demonstrating her navigation skills, at last, too late. A big roadside sign welcomed them to the Jura. But she couldn't rejoice.

He said, 'Maybe we should stop soon. Maybe we're just tired.'

But she still said nothing. They had each been mistaken in the other. She should have known. This holiday was a disaster.

At Vaudrey the hills began, thick with forest. They drove on, always towards more hills. 'We gotta stop soon, Jude. We can't go on driving all night.' They passed hotels, all closed, this out-of-season season. Miserably they drove on through the darkening woods, up over a high open plain where suddenly, out of the trees, it was day again. Then they came down a heavenly green valley, scooping around a fairytale château, towards Poligny.

Zigzagging down the hill into the small country town, Jude knew there'd be only one hotel and that would be closed. But no. True, there was only one, but it was a Logis de France and it was open. The street was too narrow to park. Bright drove on round the corner and put the car in the square.

It was an old coaching inn, the sort of place Jude and Dan had always stayed in, modernised in a mish-mash of French rustic styles, with a conservatory out at the back, and an odd high counter stuck in the middle like a *guichet* at a railway station, where a couple nearly as old as the place itself stood to welcome them. Asked did they want a *grand lit* Jude automatically said yes, then her heart drooped. Well, too bad. For this one night they would just have to sleep in one bed. Bright came in with the night cases and they trudged up the oak staircase carpeted to half-way up the walls. The old man led the way, pressing the *minuteries* to give them dim light along the corridors.

The room was familiar to her from years of holidays in France, just big enough to hold the high French bed and eighteenth-century armoire, the shower and loo squeezed into a corner behind a flimsy partition, brown and orange wallpaper-roses splayed over every surface including the door panels, the smell of clean linen, late sunlight slicing through the slats of the shutters, the pleasure of the shower to come and a bed for the night. She smiled wide at the old man. 'It's fine.'

He gave her the key. 'Vous prenez le petit déjeuner, Madame?'

'Do we want breakfast?' she asked Bright.

'What – now?' he said.

She did not find this amusing and told the man yes, please.

Bright dropped the bags on the floor and made no comment on the room. She said, 'Do you mind if I shower first?' Very polite. He shook his head, no.

Even in her state of misery the shower felt good. When she came out he was naked. The sight of him naked flooded her with desire, as always. And with tenderness. But this evening also with a sadness that overwhelmed her. He walked by without looking at her. She slumped on the bed. Outside now the sun had nearly gone.

It was a mistake to have come. Had been a mistake to persuade him. Well, she had learned her lesson: *it's always a mistake to persuade people against their will.* She pulled on her jeans and a clean sweater, she brushed her hair. Should she wait for him? She called at the bathroom door, 'I'm going down for a look round. I'll see you out front, okay?' She waited, listened to a long pause. The water had stopped running; he had heard her.

'Sure.' His voice was muffled, maybe by the face-cloth.

She listened for more, but that was all he was going to say.

28

Outside in the narrow main street the sunshine had gone but not the light. Small stone houses with steep roofs stood higgledy-piggledy round the square, hairdresser, hardware shop, *boulangerie-pâtisserie,* just closing, no one outside the cafés in the evening chill. Hills rose up all round, vines at their feet, forest up their slopes, the last of the sun reflected on the eastern peaks. She shivered on the corner, turned, and Bright was coming towards her, walking with his athlete's spring. His hair, fresh from the shower, stuck up in dark spikes that seemed to express the energy that sizzled up through his strong legs, his wiry body, straight out of the top of his head. She waited. He put his arms round her and they stood clinched on the narrow pavement while people walked round them. She said, 'John—'

'You're hungry. We're hungry. We gotta eat. I asked the guy where to go.'

'How?'

'Sign language. Even I can speak that.'

The restaurant was done out as a Swiss chalet, the walls decorated with mountain scenes, men in hunting gear, so jolly you expected them to open their painted mouths and yodel. They ordered *gigot d'agneau* and a *pichet* of the local wine. They were the only customers. The waitress suggested the *vin jaune du Jura* as an aperitif. 'It's advertised everywhere,' Jude said. 'They're very proud of it.'

'We'll try that then, love,' Bright said to the waitress, in English.

The wine was indeed a disturbingly bright yellow. They lifted their glasses, toasted each other, and sipped warily. It had an oily texture and a faint flavour of petrol.

'Perhaps it's an acquired taste,' Jude said.

Bright checked the menu. 'It's thirty-three quid a bottle. I don't think it's a taste I'll be bothering to acquire, somehow.'

The restaurant started to fill. A man by the window took

out a newspaper. It was last Sunday's *Independent*. Now that he was reading it, his face was out of sight. Jude sensed Bright watching him out of the corner of his eye. Then a woman came from the *toilette* and sat at the same table. She picked up the culture section and began to make loud comments on the book reviews, which the man ignored. Jude grinned at Bright. He half-grinned back. His attention returned to her. And to the meal.

The *gigot* was seasoned well, with garlic and rosemary, but tough. The beans were done in the French way, tossed in olive oil, with a hint of garlic too. 'See? We were hungry. People always fight when they're hungry,' Bright said.

'Is that so?'

'Yup. Do you love me again now?'

'No.'

'I was out of order, Jude.'

'You were.'

'But you gotta shout back.'

'What do you mean?'

'Don't play the martyr. It's the pits.'

'I play the martyr?'

'All that suffering. I'm not worth it. Just tell me to fuck off. You'll feel better, I'll feel better, quick shout, all over, back to business as usual, no bones broken.'

Jude drank her wine. *Did I do that with Dan? Suffer in silence? Suffer cheerfully, which is worse. Never complaining. Just understanding, in what must have been an infuriating and devastating way?* She saw herself from the outside suddenly. She blushed.

'What's up?' he said. 'I upset you again?'

She shook her head. 'I might find it hard to shout,' she said. 'Shouting's not my style.'

'Give it a whirl. You might even get to like it. I'm not going to fall down dead, am I, just 'cause you tell me to piss off?'

30

Tears filled up her eyes. She wiped under her bottom lashes with one finger. He said, 'Jude . . .' He wanted to say she was the best thing for him since Millie Hale, but that would hardly help. He felt sad that all happy things have sadness at their heart and that we all learn to accept the sadness, accommodate it, live with it. He wished just then that he and Jude were eighteen, meeting for the first time, falling in love for the first time. He closed his hand around hers and she turned her face to him. She smiled, her eyes washed clean, a comforted child. Her honesty pierced him like needles. It made him dishonest, wanting to keep her from hurt.

She saw in his face a tender expression, just for a second, that she had not seen before. It struck her that he was afraid of losing her. She was surprised, and touched.

They nuzzled together that night like small animals in the dip in the middle of their old French bed. Jude woke only once. He was cursing the bolster. 'It's like a Japanese torture. How can anyone sleep on a bastard thing like this?'

Almost unconscious, she got the big square pillows out of the wardrobe and buried herself in sleep again, with his arms round her. She felt safe.

5

Room at the Inn

Bright opened the window, then the shutters. Below, the English couple from the restaurant came out of the hotel with their cases. She shouted orders while he calmly went on packing the car. They drove off, heading north. Bright took a deep breath. It was a damp dull morning but not cold. He looked up at the hills over the ancient lichen-covered roofs. He discovered that he felt happy, but uneasy, missing something.

Jude came close. She was warm and damp from her shower. She put her hand on the back of his neck. He shivered with pleasure, turned and held her tight, but the uneasiness did not go away.

The dining area was separated from the main foyer by a screen of plastic greenery. Only one table was set and there was no sign of life. 'Are we too late for breakfast?' Bright said. He was whispering.

Jude laughed.

The old lady came from the door on the other side of the staircase. 'M'sieu-dame, bonjour. Qu'est-ce que vous désirez?'

Jude said, 'Do you want coffee or tea?'

'Eh? Er – coffee.'

'Café au lait, s'il vous plaît.'

'Pour deux?'

'Oui.'

She came back with two glasses of orange juice, a basket with thick slices of French bread and two croissants, and a small glass dish of jam. Bright plastered his bread with butter and took a bite. 'This butter's something, all right. No salt in it. No E-type yellow dye either. You not eating?'

32

'I'm waiting for the coffee.'

Madame brought a jug of coffee and a smaller jug of frothy hot milk. Jude poured. She poised her nose over the cup and sniffed, then dunked her croissant and ate. Bright watched her pleasure with pleasure. He wondered why he had ever disliked the idea of holidays.

After breakfast they packed and paid and stowed the cases in the car. Pollarded plane trees bordered the square. There was no market today, but small groups of people stood talking in the sun. 'This is a proper place,' Bright said.

'What do you mean?'

'Well, it looks like it's got a life.'

A few hardy types sat outside the Café du Centre but the day was not quite hot enough yet for Jude and Bright; they went inside. The café, a long narrow room, bar down one side, tables down the other, opened out to a big square space at the back, with kids at every table, average age perhaps fourteen, mostly boys. Some of them worked at their books, two or three lounged with an arm draped round the neck of a girl, a few grouped round the video game.

He noticed that most of the kids were smoking and that they didn't make trouble; they kissed cheeks in greeting, even the boys; they treated each other with courtesy. He couldn't imagine a crowd of teenage lads in England as civilized as this. And then it dawned on him what it was he was missing: he wasn't picking out the suspicious characters, he wasn't sussing out criminal intent; he'd even stopped looking over his shoulder for the agent of the London death-dealers. He was observing life around him like an ordinary human being, not like a cop, and not, as he had been the last few months, a cop with death-threats stalking him. The discovery gave him an eerie sensation, as if the ground was sliding out from under his feet.

Jude said, 'What's the matter?'

'Nothing!' He grinned. 'Weird, isn't it?'

Jude bought apples and tomatoes at an *alimentation* in a street off the square. A few shops down, she found Bright spellbound outside a *traiteur*. 'Look at this!' he said. 'It's better than Harrods food hall.' They went inside and joined a loosely organised chatting queue. Pâtés, salads, pies, pastas, beef bourguignon, confit de canard . . . Bright stared like an eight-year-old in a toy shop, and settled on the pâté Comtois. 'Let's have some of that.'

They walked past the school, a handsome eighteenth-century building three floors high with a mansard roof. It was eleven-thirty. Hordes of young people flowed out, and Jude and Bright were swept towards the square in their slip-stream. They bought a *ficelle* from the bakery in the square where the schoolkids draped themselves on benches, smoking like vivisection beagles.

'We could stay here,' Bright said.

'We'll never get down south if we stay in every nice place.'

'Have we gotta go down south?'

'Oh . . .' Jude's open freckled face creased with perplexity. Bright said, 'No, no, forget it.'

'Are you sure?'

'Yeah, sure,' he said. Then, after a short pause, 'Maybe we'll come here on our way back?'

Jude laughed. 'The man who never wanted to go abroad.'

They had their picnic on a high plain above Plasné. The sun was hot now. Bright couldn't believe it: 'This a heat-wave, or what? But Jude said no, it was often like this in the spring, in France. He decided to enjoy it, lie back and *not* think of England. The pâté had bits of runny cheese in it, excellent with the bread and the wrinkled yellow apples that looked too old to eat but were juicy and sweet. They drank water, resisted the temptation to drink wine, and set off again. Bright put Motown on the CD player and they bowled over the plain to 'I Heard it through the Grapevine', then on a narrow road that wound between fields and copses, heading always towards the hills.

A sign at a junction announced Le Cirque de Ladoye. 'It's shown on the map as a circle of rocks,' Jude said. 'There's a lot of them in the Jura apparently, *cirques de* this and that.'

They could see nothing, just hills, forest, fields, the odd farmhouse, but they parked on the wide grass verge and walked to the viewing platform. They found themselves on the edge of a precipice, protected only by a wire fence from plunging into the deep green valley circled by a wall of sheer grey rock. Valley was hardly the word; its walls were precipitate, vertical, its floor, with the winding road and river, hundreds of feet down. A small red car lay in the treetops far below. 'Oh, I see. That's what they do with their used cars,' Bright said. 'Just like everywhere else – sling 'em over the edge into their beauty spots.' His mind was busy with the scenario. Was the car stolen? Had it been driven over the edge? Had people been killed? Had it been done deliberately? He didn't want to start thinking like this again. His policeman's mind had been enjoying its respite in the sun.

As they got back in their car a minibus arrived and five or six small boys tumbled out accompanied by a chic blonde woman. Bright said, 'Wonder what else gets thrown down there. Convenient, innit, for getting rid of anything you didn't want?'

Jude said, 'You make me shiver sometimes. You can't leave crime behind, even here.'

'Crime's like that, Jude.'

'You're not a criminal but you might as well be. You think like one.'

'You gotta think like them to beat them.'

'If you think like a criminal you might as well be a criminal.'

'A-ha?' He just wanted to drop the subject.

But Jude wouldn't let him. 'So why aren't you one?'

He side-stepped.

'The old ma. She'd never forgive me.'

'Is that all that stops you? That someone else would disapprove of you?'

It was no good. He had to take her on. 'Why are *you* good, Jude?'

'Because I think it's better for everyone, society, whatever, if we all abide by the principle of do as you would be done by. Enlightened self interest.'

'Right. You scratch my back I'll scratch yours. That's pretty much the way the villains work it.'

'That's just self-interest without the enlightened bit.'

'No, Jude. The villains is another world. It's another society. It's the parasites on the cow's back.'

'A parallel world.'

'That's it – the underworld.'

'You fight it,' she said, 'but you sympathise with it.'

'I understand it. I gotta.'

'You actually *like* it, though.'

'It's my job. It's what I do best. I'm good at it, for Chrissake.'

His vehemence halted her. She reflected. 'I suppose anything you take the trouble to understand you end up having sympathy for.' But she didn't sound convinced.

'A-ha. Tell you what – I could do with a cuppa. Think they've heard of tea round here?'

They got out of the car stiff-legged in a medieval village called Château-les-Mînes. Their half-joking, half-rankling argument faded. This ancient stone world, unchanged for a thousand years, silenced them. Birds chattered after them down the narrow village streets, to the ruins of the abbey that teetered on the edge of a sheer escarpment overlooking the valley of the river Seille. Bright said, 'If you could see this far in England you'd see the sea. Here it just goes on and on.'

'There is an awful lot of France.'

'It's like you can't get off.'

'Do you want to get off?'

'No, but it's weird, innit?'

The church clock clanged three. Beyond the churchyard, in a little sunny square, they found the café. It was closed. Bright said, 'Jude, I gotta tell you – this place – it's the most – it's the – the – well, it's the nicest little place I've ever seen.' They studied the village notice board. Potters and *caves de dégustation* advertised themselves, but no hotel. 'We gotta leave here then?' He sounded truly sad.

'First Poligny, now here. You just like the Jura.'

'And you don't?'

'I'm keen to get down south, that's all. To the sun.'

'We got sun here. Would you think this was March?'

'I mean the real sun. You ain't seen nothing yet.'

He squinted into her eyes, very close. 'Hey, Jude? What's the hurry? One more night wouldn't hurt, would it?'

She began to relent. 'I guess the next town might have a hotel.'

'That's it. Stop one night, come back and have another look at this place tomorrow.'

Back in the car Jude looked at the map. 'Neufchâtel,' she said, 'right in the centre of the wine region. You never know, it might be as nice as this.'

'What? Not possible.'

The road snaked down the valley, through vineyards, the vines, this time of year, serried rows of gnarled, dead-looking stumps. 'Hard to believe they're ever going to grow anything,' Jude said, 'leaves, grapes, that sort of thing.' A few men and women were working among the rows. 'See how hard they prune them – right back to the old wood except for three little twigs, two very short, one about a foot long.' The workers threw the prunings into rusty old oil drums that lay sideways on metal legs, two flaps on their upper side standing open, from which smoke rose in hazy snakes. Jude craned to get a decent view. 'I guess they spread the potash back on the soil,' she said, 'to feed the vines and encourage the fruit.'

Bright said 'I can't stop thinking like a cop? You can't stop thinking like a gardener. See?'

Jude gave him a level look. He gave her his no-smile smile. 'Okay.' She grinned. 'I get the point.'

They came down into Neufchâtel. Château-les-Mînes, up there on its cliff, seemed close enough to touch, but was as far removed from this place as Paradise from sinful earth. Neufchâtel was non-stop traffic, with not a café to be seen. They turned right into a long dull street. A few motorbikes parked outside the Hôtel Sanglier suggested that it might be open. The place did not look inviting. But they were tired. Jude's bladder was making urgent demands, and it was that time of day when the British need tea. Bright parked on a piece of wasteland opposite.

The bar was the usual thing, counter on the left, tables to the right, widening to a larger room at the back where a few young people, school age boys and girls, played bar billiards. There was also a table-football game which two boys played without passion. A large boar's head bared its fangs high on the back wall. Jude passed under it to the *toilette*, which was large and clean and tiled in Prussian blue.

Bright had managed to order tea in her absence and was pleased at having made himself understood. 'Sign-language again?' Jude said.

'Matter of fact, I said "tea".'

'That was original.'

'I thought so, yeah.' He was engrossed in watching the game of darts which a young man was playing against himself, registering his two scores on the electronic score-board squeezed between the bar and the front wall. Each time someone entered, the darts-player had to stop and wait till the door was closed again and the person had passed.

Jude and Bright sat on high stools at a small table. A few customers, all male, stood around the bar in desultory conversation. The barman, probably the proprietor, was dark, with a long narrow face and small miserable brown eyes. A grizzled old farmer-type came in. He had bandy legs and used a stick. He was dressed in a dark green hand-knitted jersey zipped up the front, and a hunter's cap. He stared at Jude and Bright: they were strangers. Jude wished him *bonjour* but he went on staring at Bright whose back was to him, until Jude nudged him and he turned to be greeted too. This satisfied the old man, who nodded, then went to the bar and took out a small grey money purse to pay for his glass of wine.

The darts-player stopped to let in another extremely elderly man wearing a beret, a rarity in France these days, and carrying a shabby tartan shopping-bag. He too stared at the strangers, through round specs with brown rims. When Jude wished him *bonjour* he approached rather alarmingly as if to kiss her then found he didn't know her, and grinned, showing a mouth overfull of crazy horse-teeth. The rounded toes of his boots turned up. His old mac hung loosely from his coat-hanger shoulders.

The atmosphere was quiet, afternoon-cosy, subdued. Bright and Jude felt self-conscious, as though they had wandered into a family gathering, uninvited guests, their presence perhaps causing constraint. They spoke in hushed voices. 'They've known each other all their lives, these blokes,' Bright said. 'Those kids playing pool? They're all at school together. And these old blokes were all at school together. The same school. They live next door to each other.'

'They even look alike,' Jude said.

'They're probably related. Though they might not admit it.'

'They might not know. For sure.'

'Long winters in the Jura. Nothing much to do.'

'No industry to speak of, just wood-turning, waiting for the wine season to come round again.'

'These old guys have never been anywhere else.'

'They must have fought in the 'thirty-nine war,' Jude said.

'Oh yeah, that's right. Two wars, probably, these old guys.'

'The Jura was a great centre for the Resistance.'

'Was it now?'

'They must have some stories to tell.'

'Yeah, if you could only understand a word they said.'

'But these kids won't be here all their lives,' Jude said. 'Some of them will go away.'

'Wouldn't blame them either. You'd go mad growing up here.'

'Oh, I don't know . . . peaceful life.'

'People don't have peaceful lives, Jude. Wherever they live. It's patronising to think they do.'

She was taken aback. By his insight, and by her lack of it. 'You're quite right,' she said.

The tea-bags had the yellow label of a company that had cornered the European market, a brand never seen in England. 'Don't think I'll be ordering tea here again,' Bright said. Jude agreed. They smiled and paid. Everyone bade them *au revoir, m'sieu-dame*.

Outside, the afternoon sun was almost hot. Neither the village nor the hotel tempted them to spend a night but they were reluctant to get back in the car just yet. They wandered down the street, a hotch-potch of periods and styles. The little houses were connected by ancient barns, most now used as garages or workshops. Only one still had hay in its *grenier*, a tractor below. This village stood on the edge of a rural existence, not only in space but also in time. The quiet was not peace but a sulky brooding. This street fitted nowhere, gave no sense of joining past and future, just a sense of encroachment – of town into country and country into town, of a place in the process of losing one identity without replacing it with another.

The street ended in a narrow stone bridge, the river flowing under it, a natural stop to development, a boundary, encircling the town. They leaned on the stone parapet, the sun hot on their backs. Over the bridge the road forked, the fast, straight route skimming alongside the river, the other curving gently upwards around shallow hills of vines, trails of smoke rising towards the cliff where Château-les-Mînes elegantly perched.

'You still want to go back up there again tomorrow?' Jude said.

'Where would we stay? The one horse inn? Bates' Motel?'

'It's not that bad, is it?'

'Thought you wanted to get on down south.'

'Well, but there's no rush. We don't have a timetable.'

'That's right! We don't . . . First time in my life, Jude. I can't get used to it.'

They strolled back along the time-warp street. A small low-slung tabby flickered across their path, giving Jude a pang, and disappeared over a wall. Outside each front door a handsome iron manhole cover was set into the pavement. 'What would they be for?' Bright said. 'Coal?'

'Wine?' Jude said. 'Nearly all houses in France have a *cave*.'

They studied the tariff stuck up in the window of the hotel. The usual price, shown in francs and euros, about twenty-five pounds for a double room. They peered through the windows into the dining room which appeared gloomy and vast, and was empty. 'It would be, this time of day,' Bright said.

'The hotel might not be open – I mean *as* a hotel.'

They looked at each other. Bright shrugged. 'What the hell? If they're not open, we move on.'

41

They ventured back into the bar and were struck afresh by the sense of things frozen in time. Six or seven men still lounged round the counter. The kids still played in the back room. Even the darts player was still absorbed in his solo game, pausing patiently to let them pass. Everyone turned and greeted them again, now with puzzled looks. Jude asked if they could have a room for one night. The man behind the bar hesitated. The young people round the pool table carried on unaware, but round the bar Jude felt a strange hiatus, as if they were all holding their breath. 'L'hôtel est ouvert?' she said.

The barman came out of his spell. 'Oui, oui' – he sounded reluctant – 'oui, nous sommes ouverts. Oui.' He did not appear welcoming. He did not smile.

'Vous êtes sur? Parce que—'

'Si, si. Mais nous n'avons qu'une chambre.'

'Nous n'avons besoin que d'une.'

She thought at first that her feeble attempt at a joke had sounded offensive. But the man next to her at the bar, a small man in his thirties with rimless French specs, gave a quiet laugh. The others smiled. And at last the barman–proprietor also attempted a smile and offered to show them the room, indicating that it would probably not please them and that they would no doubt decide to move on.

Bright asked Jude, 'What was the joke?'

'He said he had only one room. I said we only needed one.'

'One room? It's a hotel.'

'Only one ready, I suppose he means. Time of year, I guess.'

The man took a key from the board behind the bar. They followed him through the arch, past the *toilettes*, into the cavernous square restaurant, tables all set for dinner with white cloths, little pots of artificial flowers and candles, under a vaulted ceiling – the room they had seen through the front window. Double doors to the left opened on to the narrow hotel entrance. The man murmured that they couldn't use the door leading directly into the bar because of the dartboard, which was new.

They went up one flight of stairs, the carpet worn almost through in places, but clean. Several doors, either side of the landing, were all closed. The man had pressed the *minuterie* at the bottom of the stairs. It proved necessary, a window to the rear of the building giving strangely little light, the landing dissolving into darkness at the front. The next staircase ascended as though to the heavens. The double-height window was filled with sky, filtered through an antique net curtain, white, starched, clean, like the table linen downstairs. The man opened a door.

The room, in the eaves, was more Scandinavian than French, yellow-painted walls, a nineteenth-century bed with a white bedcover, a polished wood floor with white bedside rugs. The bathroom too was bigger – and classier – than the usual partitioned corner found in most French hotels of this class. It was not what Jude had expected from the atmosphere of the rest of the place. She did not express her surprise to the proprietor; politeness restrained her. She raised her eyebrows at Bright, though.

'A-ha,' he said. 'This'll do, all right.'

Jude told the man it was a very agreeable room and yes, they would take it, please. He nodded in a resigned way, and gave Bright the key. 'Vous désirez le petit déjeuner?'

This time Bright didn't say, 'What, now?' He grinned.

Jude said yes, they would want breakfast, and asked if it was possible to have dinner tonight. A shrug, *Yes, of course, from seven o'clock*. They trooped down the stairs again, and again Jude was struck by the gloom and the chill of the first-floor landing.

They crossed the road to the oblong of weedy grass to fetch their cases from the car. On either side, behind high walls, mansard roofs were just visible through trees. At the far end a picket gate opened on to fenced off woodland, dark and dense.

They brought in their bags and Bright, pointing, asked if the car would be okay where it was. Again, the shrug, *yes, of course, why not?* This time the attempt at a smile almost succeeded. All the blokes round the bar still stared, with the benign fascination of people watching animals in the zoo.

6

Brief Encounter

After trying out the bed and finding it satisfactory in all respects they had a shower and then went out to explore the hidden depths of Neufchâtel. They turned down an alley that brought them to the back of the hotel. Jude looked up at the street sign and laughed. 'This little street is called Little Street.'

'Somebody put a lot of thought into that.'

Opposite the small back-yard of the hotel an old stables had been converted to *chambres d'hôte*. The conversion was recent, and stylishly done. Jude said, 'I can't see mine host doing this, can you? Do you think he employs a designer or something?'

'Not likely, is it? He looks a mean bugger. But you never can tell. Mean buggers are easy to con. If he thought there was something in it for him . . .'

Petite Rue took them to the massive iron gates of the château. But a sheet of solid metal filled the spaces in the ironwork, and the walls were so high it was impossible to see anything of the house except the four towers at the corners of the grey slate roof. 'Keeping the riff-raff out,' Bright said. 'Don't think they're crazy about the neighbours, do you?'

They came to the cemetery, a neat, walled square with three or four cypresses and gravel walks, right under the cliff of Château-les-Mînes. 'The dead people get the best view in the place,' Bright said.

'If you keep on like this,' Jude said, 'I'll have to start defending poor old Neufchâtel.'

45

The lane opened out to a grassy space shaded by trees, next to the river where a small weir rushed the water on under a bridge, alongside the château grounds. They followed the curve of the river back to the main road, and dodged across between a truck and a tanker to the modern side of the town. A children's playground, a sixties-built school, and the *mairie* dating from the thirties, all faced another main road, wider and busier than the first. 'This is a strange place,' Jude said.

'No heart.'

'That's right! No heart.' She turned to him.

'Unlike you,' he said. They stood in the traffic-wrought street between a phone booth and the public *toilettes* in front of the soulless *mairie*, and kissed. Two little girls leaned over the fence of the playground watching. When they came out of the kiss, the little girls said solemnly, 'Bonsoir.'

'Bonsoir,' Jude replied.

'Bonswah, love,' Bright said. And to Jude, 'Can't imagine a London kid behaving like that, can you?'

'You just spoke French.'

'Christ, so I did. How was it?'

'Brilliant.'

'Thought so.'

'Do you think it might be time for a drink now?'

'Well, there's not much more to this place, is there? Apart from the traffic. There's no end of that.'

'Back to the hotel?'

'Haven't seen anywhere else we could get a drink. Have you?'

Sitting outside the hotel in the last of the sun, a couple read different bits of last Sunday's *Observer*, oddly echoing the pair in the Poligny restaurant last night. Bright stopped, hesitating. Jude grinned and led him to the table farthest from

46

the couple. He sat sideways as though keeping an eye on them. Jude whispered, 'So English of us.'

'What?'

'Not to acknowledge that we're all English.'

He took some time to take in what she'd said. 'Oh,' he said. 'That's what we're doing, is it?"

The man lowered his paper to take a drink. He was nothing like the man from last night. He was young, with peeling sunburn. He wore denim shorts and a sweaty T-shirt. He leaned forward and kissed his girlfriend. She had pale red hair and was dressed exactly like him.

'You're worse than Dan,' Jude said.

'What d'you mean?'

'He used to go into hedgehog mode if he saw another English – duck, hide, walk in the other direction – *Can't sit here, they're Brits!*' It was the first time she had mentioned Dan on this holiday. She had been careful. But at least she had got Bright's attention back. He nodded. Though he employed habitually a series of masks, none of them now, Jude believed, hid his feelings from her. 'Sorry,' she said.

He gave her a sideways squint, not exactly a smile. 'Bound to happen. Can't avoid it for ever. Walking on stepping-stones.'

Jude nodded. A small sadness had descended on them. The landlord came out like its embodiment, morose as ever, to take their order. Bright said, 'Scotch on the rocks,' which brought an expression of hopeless terror to the man's face.

Jude said, 'Deux whiskies, s'il vous plaît, avec glaçons.'

Bright grumbled, 'I thought Scotch on the rocks was universal language.'

'Obviously hasn't reached Neufchâtel.'

The gloomy man brought their drinks and they ordered *salade Jurassienne* from the blackboard followed by *côtelettes d'agneau*, with a carafe of local red. They clinked glasses, the sadness slunk away, and the well-being flooded them that goes with the heat of the sun, and the aperitif to a good meal. The sheer unlikeliness of their being together, and being here, on a kind of honeymoon, struck them suddenly. They smiled in the conspiracy of mutual under-standing and said, 'Cheers,' together, meaning more, meaning they were glad to be here, glad to be here together, and that this was the start, not just of a holiday but prob-ably of something more that neither of them was willing to look at closely or to put into words. Bright sipped his drink. 'Well,' he said, 'he makes a mean Scotch on the rocks for a bloke who's never heard of it.'

A blond boy brought their first course, a seventeen-year-old Adonis, shy, not a trained waiter but doing well. He was clever, too, trying out his English. He'd been to London with his school last year, he told them. His face lit up: 'Camden Lack!'

'You been to Camden Lock?' Bright's tone expressed unbe-lief.

'We live near there.' Jude smiled.

Bright's head turned swiftly towards the English couple but they seemed absorbed in each other.

The boy smiled back into Jude's eyes in a way that quite disturbed her. When he went back to the kitchen Bright said, 'You're blushing.'

'I'm not used to the way blokes look at you here. I'd sort of forgotten.'

'Come on, you fancy him.'

'Of course I do.'

For a moment he looked dismayed but then he gave her his particular smile, without moving a muscle of his face, except, she had discovered, a slight contraction of the skin under his eyes. 'Shit, Jude,' he said, 'I'm crazy about you.'

Her face, open as a child's, beamed at him, eyes shining, 'Oh, God,' she said, 'don't say things like that, I might swoon.'

The *salade Jurassienne* was a meaty mix of raw ham and a sausage that was probably wild boar, with *carotte rapée*, *céleri rémoulade* and fleshy lettuce, a home-made mayonnaise adding zest but not drowning, as if anything could, the strong coarse flavours of the rest. Bright was surprised. 'Fancy that miserable sod coming up with nosh like this.'

When the blond boy brought their lamb chops Jude asked him what was in the sausage.

'Ah . . .' He flushed and scratched his head.

She suggested 'Sanglier?'

'Yess, yess, what is in English?'

One of those conversations followed that are pointless, since the translations are instantly forgotten, but that pass the time pleasantly and are full of good feeling, of crossing bridges, forging links.

The cutlets came done to a crisp outside, bright pink in the middle, flavoured with rosemary and garlic, and fried potatoes, also done with garlic and a mixture of herbs. 'I think I'll just live on lamb chops while I'm here,' Bright said. 'Tough as old boots but it doesn't seem to matter.'

The wine was inoffensive and went down smoothly. 'Nice medicine,' he said.

'You are a scream.'

'You amuse easy, thank God.'

The English couple paid the boy, nodded goodbye to Jude and Bright, got on their bikes and rode off down towards the river. Bright watched till they were out of sight. When they were gone he moved his chair next to Jude's and took hold of her hand. They leaned back, contented, a little woozy from the wine, idly regarding the big house opposite with its square of formal front garden and its divided staircase curving up to the front door. It looked deserted. 'But,' Jude said, 'with all the shutters closed, how would you know?'

'A-ha. They could be living the life of Reilly behind there.'

'I bet there's one old lady living in a couple of rooms at

the back and the rest of the family have all gone.'

'A-ha, all waiting for her to pop her clogs so they can get their hands on the house and the dosh.'

'There you go again. Instant crime.'

'That's not crime. Just human nature.'

'Not all human nature. Are you waiting for your ma—?'

'Hey hey, don't bring bad luck. I got the point, okay?'

The boy came out to collect their plates They ordered decaf. 'What will you do when you leave school?' Jude asked him.

'I will go to Paris. To the Sorbonne. I want to study European history.'

'Oh, good luck.'

Three boys arrived on two motorbikes, roaring to a halt inches from Jude and Bright. Taking off their helmets, they said, 'Bonsoir,' just as everyone did here, then carried on a joking exchange with the waiter, dense with incomprehensible slang, prodding and goading him, till, flushing, he went back into the hotel. They flashed their eyes at Jude and Bright, not knowing how much had been understood, and, laughing, they jostled each other into the bar.

'Puppy dogs,' Bright said. 'Wagging their little tails.'

'You were like that once. A Jack-the-lad.'

'I was better.'

'You thought you were.'

'A-ha. Thought I was the bee's knees in those days.'

'I think you're the bee's knees now.'

'That right? Well, look, as it happens, I've got a room booked in this hotel. How'd you like to come back with me after dinner?'

'I'll think about it.'

A man had come out of the bar as the boys went in, a glass of red wine in his hand and many glasses of red wine, it would seem, already inside him. He sat down at a table near the door, talking continuously in a low voice, except when a heavy truck went by. Calling the drivers killers, murderers, he shouted, 'Les petits chats aussi ont le droit de vivre.'

'Oh, hear, hear,' Jude murmured.

'What's he on about?'

'His cat must have been run over by a truck. If you run over an animal you're a murderer. At least I think that's the gist of it.'

The man lifted his glass to them and they lifted theirs in return. Bright murmured, 'Don't encourage him, Jude, we'll have him on our backs all night.'

'How uncomfortable that sounds.'

'He's a drunk.'

'I don't think he's just a drunk. I think he's what they call disturbed.'

'In other words a bit of a nutter. All the more reason not to encourage him.'

'That's such a mean attitude. Heavens, we're only here for a night—'

The man lurched to his feet, held the edge of the table to steady himself, and looked to be on the point of coming towards them. At this moment the bar door opened and a woman came out. At sight of her the man subsided into his chair again and held his hand out to her in an imploring gesture, uttering some kind of plea. She pacified him, touched his hand a moment and shushed him, indicating tenderly that he was disturbing the guests. The man now made a penitent gesture at Bright and Jude, lifting his glass again, then sinking into himself, murmuring, and sometimes wiping his eyes.

The woman turned to them and smiled. Bright sat up like he'd been goosed. The smile exuded not just warmth but a heat you could warm your hands at. She was not particularly tall or beautiful. She was, rather, on the short side. Her cheeks and lips were full and smooth, her breasts large and round. There was a general roundedness about her, though she was not in the least fat or even plump. She moved with a graceful sway, coming towards them. She was not European in origin, not African either. Mixed Asian and European perhaps. Her hair was a deep brown without red in it, straight and worn very plain to her shoulders. You wouldn't pick her out in a crowd, but close up she was curiously impressive. Tiny black dots speckled her face either side of her nose, emphasizing the dark honey colour of her skin. She introduced herself: 'Hello. I am Mariela. You are English, yes?' She spoke slowly, enunciating each word and hesitating shyly in case she was getting it wrong. When they said they lived in London, she sighed. 'Oh I love go to London. I see all the movies, *Briff Inconter*, my favourite. I cry very much.'

'*Brief Encounter*?' Bright said. 'That's an old one.'

'At home, where I come from, we see only old ones. Black and white old ones. My favourite. I say always my favourite because when we learn English in the school we must write all the week, My Favourite Place, My Favourite Poem, My Favourite Person. My Favourite Movie.' She laughed, a deep husky laugh that came straight from her stomach. Her voice had the relaxed throaty huskiness of Italian or Greek women.

'Where is home?'

'Mauritius. You hear of it?' She looked doubtful. And when they said yes, of course they had heard of it, her face broke into another dazzling smile. 'Is beautiful place.'

'Yes, I'm sure it is.'

What are you doing here in this dead-and-alive backwater of rural France? Jude was working out how to put this question tactfully when Bright said, 'So what you doing here then?'

She pointed to the hotel. 'I come with him.'

'Who?'

'The *propriétaire*. Louis.'

52

They digested this information. The doleful man who had shown them their room and this exotic creature? There must be at least ten years between them, if not fifteen, and even more disparity in their expectations of life, their dreams, their hopes. 'He's your husband?' Bright said.

'Ha.' Her smile combined indignation, bitterness, weariness and resignation. 'He say me we marry. But . . .' She made a small movement of her mouth, indicating that men sometimes renege on their promises.

'How did you meet?' Jude said.

'He come in my country for holiday. I am working in bar. He very nice there, in my country, very sweet. He ask me for date, he buy me nice thing, he meet my mother.' Her eyes filled with tears. 'My mother poor, very poor. He buy nice thing for my mother. He bring flowers to her. He is so good with us. He say my mother, "I take Mariela in France to my home. We will marry there. You will come to Mariela after." My mother say, "Yes, Mariela, he good man, you marry him." So I come France. I know Paris, movies, songs, I am always singing French song. And I come here.' She laughed her husky sad laugh, subtly combining contempt for the place, for her own gullibility, for the man who had duped her, for life as it really is and the dreams that drive us on.

Bright said, 'You been to Paris yet?'

Her expression said, What do you think? And they all laughed. She stood up. 'You take a little drink with me?'

'Well . . .' Jude and Bright looked at each other.

'Sure,' Bright said.

'A little digestif. A *marc* perhaps?'

'Brandy,' Jude said.

'Yeah, I got that.'

'Sorry.'

'Mark'd be good, Mariela. Thanks.'

'It is not *de Bourgogne* you understand, it is *marc du Jura*.' She indicated, again with one of her complicated facial expressions, that the Jurassiens admired everything Jurassien above all things, but that she, objectively, begged to differ. She went back into the bar.

Bright and Jude raised eyebrows to each other. Bright shook his head and sighed. 'Bloody hell.'

Jude said, 'No wonder poor old Louis looks depressed.'

'She'd be a handful at the best of times.'

'She's a terrible flirt.'

'Oh, you noticed?'

'She even flirts with me.'

'Yeah, she can't help it. It's the way she gets by. Poor kid. How old d'you reckon?'

'Twenty four? -Five?'

Mariela came back with a bottle of local brandy and three small thick glasses. It was only as she sat that they realised she was a little tipsy. She poured in a way that looked reckless but she filled each glass absolutely equally and did not spill a drop.

The man in the corner called out. She held up a warning hand to him. 'Emile!' she said in gentle admonition, and he subsided again, muttering gently, his eyes on a distant horizon.

'What's up with him?' Bright said.

'Ah, *pauvre* Emile. His little cat die.'

'Oh . . .' Jude's eyes filled with sympathy. 'Yes, we thought so.'

'A big truck, was it?' Bright made a graphic gesture. 'Ran it over?'

She looked at Bright and away, and gave a quick glance at Emile. She smiled sadly and made a slight gesture with her head that could mean yes, could mean no, anyway implying that the story was a little more complicated than a simple road accident. She had an amazing gift for implying subtleties too complicated for words. In any language.

Jude said, 'So, has your mother come to join you?'

54

She gazed at them with eyes like a hungry dog's. She was not flirting now. Her mouth closed in a line that made her older than mid-twenties, older than time. She shook her head: no. She swallowed some brandy.

'You can go back to see her, though, can't you?'

'He not give me money.'

'To go back home?'

'To go anywhere.'

'You mean—?'

'No money.'

Jude and Bright looked at each other. There are dedicated professional martyrs in this world and Mariela might be one of them. But all that youth and juice and joy, and all that pulling power, that sexual energy, going nowhere, imprisoned in this inbred backwater, deprived of the means to spread her wings? It did not bear thinking about. But if she served in the bar, surely money was coming into her hands constantly. Couldn't she just raid the till?

She wasn't stupid: she watched their faces, she followed their thoughts. 'I work in bar. I serve. But he take all money from me.'

The wildness in the girl made it possible to believe anything. She seemed to be on the brink of some crazy action. But this could be a scam, Jude thought. Maybe she found gullible tourists all the time, told them her sad tale, persuaded them to cough up money for air tickets back to Mauritius. Gullible? Bright was a hardbitten Cockney cop, hardly scam material. Still, Jude knew how vulnerable he was to women. And how women sensed this softness in him and went right for it. He was on the point of offering this girl money, she could feel it.

He said, 'Look, love, if you need—'

Mariela laughed. She shook her hand from side to side, palm facing them. 'No, no. When we marry I have one half of all, no?'

'You're getting married then?'

'Yes. He bring me here for marry me, yes?'

'Yeah . . . And you're sure that's what you want, are you?'

She leaned towards them. 'My mother think I marry. My mother want very much.'

'Your mother would want you to be happy,' Jude said.

The bar door opened and Louis the long-faced proprietor stood staring, not at them, just vaguely across towards the shuttered house. Emile the drunk lifted his glass and drained it to the dregs. Mariela sensed her fiancé's presence though her back was to him. The animation drained from her expression, leaving her face blank and dull. He said something to her, low and quick, that Jude couldn't catch.

Mariela replied in English, carefully enunciated. 'I drink with my English friends.'

His face set, mulish, enraged, helpless. Emile laughed in a spiteful way and said something unintelligible. The landlord came towards Bright and Jude, but walked past them to the table vacated an hour before by the English cyclists. He wiped it with a cloth and walked on, turning into the other entrance, presumably to the kitchen. They had been tensed, all of them, for violence, and only recognised this now that they relaxed. He carried a black atmosphere with him and left trails of black mist behind him. He did not appear to be an evil man, just enveloped in an evil fog.

Mariela sighed and finished her drink. 'Okay . . .' Her husky voice lingered. Her smile dazzled them again. She stood up. 'You want more *marc*? I leave the *bouteille*.'

They shook their heads. Bright said, 'Listen, love. You should go back home. Or go to Paris or something. Get work there.'

'No *carte de séjour*.'

'What's that?' he said to Jude. 'Papers?'

'A permit to stay, therefore to work, I guess.'

'She could get the guy on abduction. Just report him. Where's the police station in this place anyway? Don't they have one?'

Jude floundered, in French that was not up to the task, to convey these suggestions.

'My mother think I marry – *alors* – I marry! I wait. Then he marry me. Then I go.'

Jude and Bright just managed not to exchange a glance. But she picked up their thoughts anyway. 'You not believe?'

Bright said, 'Look, love, he's got what he wants; why should he—?'

She smiled. 'No. I no give what he want . . .' She made a slow gesture with her right shoulder, lifting it and moving it forward, rolling it back, then lifting the left shoulder in the same slow movement. She laughed, a husky gurgle with a higher-pitched edge to it.

His eyes fixed on her, holding her in his strange opaque gaze, Bright said, 'Why hasn't he married you? Why won't he? What's stopping him?'

Jude started to translate but Mariela made a small gesture to say she had understood. '*Sa famille*,' she said.

'His family, right? What family? Mother? Father?' He didn't say, Wife, kids? She was in no mood to appreciate the joke.

'Mother, sister, brother,' she said.

'Older? Younger? Married? Single?'

'Brother younger. Sister older. No marry.'

'They're not a family that goes in for marrying then?'

She was quick to pick up meaning. She smiled her subtle smile and shook her head.

'They well off? Got money?'

She raised her hand, palm down, and rocked it from side to side. '*Comme ci comme ça.*'

'They live here?'

'The mother live here. Always.' She raised her shoulders

57

and simulated a shudder. 'The brother, young one, he live Grenoble.'

'What's he do?'

'*Je sais pas.* In a – desk?'

'*Bureau*? Office.'

'Office. Yes.'

'And the sister, in Nogent, also in office.'

'They might give you money to go back home.'

'They offer.'

'They've offered you money?'

'Oh yes! They want buy me. They think I am *putain*. But I say no. I am not *putain*. I am *fiancée*. He promise marry. He must marry, no?'

Bright leaned forward. He said, his nasal Cockney intimate as a purr, 'Mariela? Go home. Cut your losses, take their money. Go. Home.'

Bright's gaze pierced her sad armour of confidence. Her smile failed her. She wavered.

Jude backed him up. 'Your mother will understand. She will be happy to have you home again.'

'No. My mother come here when I will marry. I want my mother will come here. We are very poor at home.'

Then the bike-boys came out, slightly drunk, acting up, not for the benefit of the foreign guests this time, but for Mariela. She turned to them, laughing. A tall handsome boy with a pony-tail asked her if she'd like to ride with him on his little motorbike. She laughed, stood up, collected their empty glasses and swayed back to the bar. As she passed Emile he held out his empty glass to her. She shrugged and poured him a generous measure of *marc*. He thanked her and told her she was a good woman, she was always good to him. He toasted Bright and Jude and said again Mariela was a good woman, a good human being, and she was always good to him. And, he said, he was good to her too. *Don't forget that.*

Then Mariela came out of the bar in a red woollen jacket

and a bright shawl. She shouted, '*A bientôt*', jumped on the back of the boy's bike, and both bikes vroomed off in the direction of the main street. The proprietor stood at the door watching them go. Emile tried to focus on the man's face. His head rolled drunkenly. He murmured soothing words, excusing Mariela's conduct.

'What's he saying to old Louis?'

'That they're young.'

'Christ. That should cheer him up.'

Louis now said something to Emile, a few words, swift and sour, snatched his not-quite empty glass and made a small but vivid gesture with the back of his hand: *get the hell out of here*. Emile gave a shrug that involved his whole body and rose to a dignified posture. He walked straight and slow towards Jude and Bright. He leaned on their table and spoke, in a solemn mumble, an imprecation, a warning, a curse perhaps, shaking his head and his right hand. The proprietor made a threatening move. Emile put up his hand: *okay I'm going*. He wished Bright and Jude *bonne nuit*, and paced away down the street towards the river, in a perfectly straight line. The landlord stood bent over Emile's table a moment, then collected up the glass and the water carafe and went back indoors.

'Phew,' Jude said.

'See what I mean about peaceful lives?'

'I feel sorry for Louis. He goes out there, has a holiday romance, brings back the girl of his dreams, and his family are horrified.'

'What's his family got to do with it? The bastard.'

'She's a silly girl, John.'

'She's playing a dangerous game.'

'Dangerous?'

The blond boy who had served them hurried out of the kitchen entrance. He looked into the bar through the glass. He said, 'You have seen Madame – Mariela?'

'She went off for a gangbang with your mates, mate,' Bright said.

'Excuse me?'

Jude said, 'Elle est partie il y a – dix minutes?'

'Partie? The boy tried to hide his distress. 'She is with the – boys, yes?

'Yes.'

Bright pointed in the direction they had gone.

'Thank you.' He shook their hands like a good French boy. 'Goodbye.' Then he put on his crash helmet, revved his bike and sped off.

Jude said, 'I feel exhausted by all this passion and longing.'

'It's past your bedtime.'

'Did you say earlier you had a room here?'

'I did, yeah.'

The air was chill now, darkness falling. They drained the brandy and went back in through the bar. Three or four men stood at the counter. A girl and two boys played pool at the back under the twin-shaded lamp. They looked like an Edward Hopper painting, the scene given haunting significance by the harsh light, the sharp wedges of shadow, the green of the girl's dress, the classic poses. Fixed in time.

A last drink might have been nice but there was no sign of Louis and they felt awkward, intruders on a family crisis, not members of the wedding. So they said *bonne nuit* and went through the big dark square dining room and up the stairs to their room.

7

A Little Night Music

It was so quiet he couldn't sleep. Each time he dropped off a small sound jerked him awake, a dog barking, a cat yowling, a distant car. Some people talked in low voices in Little Street, probably just left the bar. Also, his curiosity was aroused by the small-town goddess Mariela. She was quite something, must have turned this backwoods place on its head. Dangerous. If you have a weapon you should know how sharp it is, how it works, how to use it. She flaunted her lyrical sensuality as a baby might brandish the bread-knife, thinking it a toy, unaware of the power of the jeal-ousy it could arouse.

Jude, irritatingly, slept peacefully at his side. His thoughts strayed to his own jealousy. Of Dan, from whom she was not yet divorced. He feared the possessiveness he now felt for Jude. He wanted all of her: her body, her spirit, her life, even her house, which seemed a part of her, even her cat. George liked him, and this was a source of pride to him. Ludicrous. He resented this state of subjection. He didn't understand what he was up to. *Where's this journey heading? What's the destination?* Marriage, kids – his lifelong picture of hell on earth – suddenly did not look too bad. In fact, he felt a pull towards them that scared him: to be thus attached means need; need means danger.

He heard voices again in the street at the back. And his sense of danger attached itself to the sounds. This was idiotic. But he got out of bed – Jude didn't stir – and went to the window. The shutters were closed. *Shit. What'm I going to do? At home you can go somewhere – down to the kitchen,*

make a cup of tea, eat a banana, watch a late-night movie.
What can you do stuck in one room with a person you don't
want to disturb, but who pisses the hell out of you by
sleeping soundly on? He wouldn't sleep for hours now,
perhaps all night. He became desperate to get out of the
room, anywhere, he didn't care where. He groped around
on the chest of drawers to find the room key. He found it.
The key to the hotel front door was on the same ring. He
pulled on his jeans and a sweater, opened the bedroom door
silently and closed it without the slightest click behind him.
He thought about locking it, decided against, and started to
creep down the stairs.

Half-way down the first flight it struck him as laughable
to be creeping downstairs in a hotel. *I'm paying to be here,*
for Christsake. But he still felt like a schoolboy raiding the
midnight fridge. He pushed the *minutière* on the pitch-black
first-floor landing and got the dim light that clicked away
the seconds, hoping it would last till he reached the bottom.
Maybe he could still get a drink? But his lack of French
bothered him. He didn't mind looking the idiot – sometimes
he used that to his advantage, it was good now and then
for clever-clog criminals and power-struck colleagues to
think he was thick – but he did mind *being* the idiot, as he
was here. What time was it anyway? He squinted at his
watch. Quarter to midnight. They didn't keep Brit pub hours
here. Probably shut when the last punter went home. He
listened at the foot of the stairs. There wasn't a sound from
the bar. So he opened the main entrance door and went out.

The bar was closed, the hotel in darkness. The night was
chillier than he had expected. He crossed the road to the
wasteground where the car was parked. There was no light
here either, the lamp near the car out of action and no spill
from the street-lamps this far off the road. The grass was
icy and dew-damp to his ankles, his feet bare in trainers.
He opened the car door and leaned in to get his jacket,

draped on the back seat. He sensed a movement, a presence. He looked round. No one. The sound, if it was a sound, the movement, had come from the woods at the far end behind the picket gate. It was very dark down there. He stood still, waiting. A London street he could cope with; the countryside unnerved him. He heard nothing, saw nothing, now. Some animal, he guessed, stoat, weasel – wild boar? How would he know? – waiting for him to leave, to get on with its night's hunting.

He put on his jacket and didn't feel that much warmer. This was not his faithful old leather bomber jacket that had kept him warm through the coldest nights for years; this was a holiday jacket, cotton, linen, something. He felt a right pillock in it. What had come over him? The vision of the holiday self, dashing, carefree? You shouldn't believe the commercials. He couldn't recognise himself. No weight on the shoulders, no armour, no protection, none of that comforting leather smell, and the pockets in the wrong place, so that his whole stance was altered. He put the collar up and walked fast to the crossroads. There, he turned right because they hadn't gone that way before dinner – it might hold more interest than the rest of the town.

Interest? He did not meet a single soul, not even a late-night dog-walker. A car passed, two trucks ripped apart the peace of the night, that was all. It seemed later than midnight. Empty streets. No people. No traffic. Kentish Town at three a.m. was livelier than this. After half a mile of high walls with trees above, he passed a farm that had become incorporated into the suburbs, and five or six detached turn-of-the-century villas on the other side of the road. A sign showed NEUFCHÂTEL with a diagonal line crossing it out, meaning this was the end of the town, village, whatever the hell they called the place. Another sign, next to it, announced the start of COMBRANS. Neither place seemed big enough to constitute a whole town. Then came a level-crossing, with

Combrans railway station over to the left. Next to the railway station stood a white building with a red, white and blue sign: GENDARMERIE. He knew what that meant. There was no sign of life, however. Round here they didn't expect crime in the middle of the night. Their criminals, if they had any, must keep social hours. Not like the villains on his home patch.

He went over the level crossing. The houses petered out, and after a few hundred yards a sign showed COMBRANS also crossed out with a diagonal line. The smallest place he'd ever been. He was in the country again now. Lanes snaked off the main road into darkness. He could hear water gurgling, a stream somewhere, owls hooting. His sense of panic receded. He started to feel calm again, cheerful even. Maybe he could sleep now. He half fancied the country lanes but did not even marginally fancy getting lost. He turned back the way he had come, keeping to the main road.

Approaching the hotel, tired now, looking forward to the big bed and Jude's warm body, he thought he'd better check the car, make sure he'd locked it. His eye caught a movement in the darkness. This time there was someone, coming through the picket gate from the woods, a dark shape emerging from the trees. A bloke, he thought, carrying something. A bag? The man saw him. Bright expected a *bonne nuit*, they were all so polite round here. But it didn't come. He was on his guard, ready to duck, ready to tackle. But the man hesitated, then turned away, walking with swift small steps across the road. Bright got that shiver at the back of his neck: *This bloke's up to no good.* He viewed all life with suspicion, Jude had told him, saw criminal activity everywhere. This was the copper's disease, he knew it, the dark side of the job, his second nature. It made her sad. Anyway, he was on his holidays now, this wasn't his manor. And the guy wasn't after him; he was a poacher after a

64

rabbit. That's what the small-time villains did in the country, right? Poach things. Good luck to the bloke. Nice work if you can get it. But he sneaked a look at his watch: copper's habit, he couldn't help it. Ten to one, near enough. He'd walked for nearly an hour. He checked the car. It was okay.

Sticking the key into the lock of the hotel door he wondered, what if it didn't work and he had to wake the house? The place was fast in slumber. He'd had occasion in his job to wake many a sleeping house but here it would be embarrassing. He had a sudden picture of the luscious Mariela, round soft breasts caressed by her flimsy night-dress, dark crotch almost visible through the filmy fabric, coming out of her room in alarm to check out the intruder. That was something he wouldn't be telling Jude. It was biological, but so what? It made him sad sometimes, the male-fantasy continuum. Every man within a mile of here fantasised about Mariela, some not involuntarily either. Many a bloke in Neufchâtel would be sending himself to sleep tonight with visions raunchier than his. The key worked, knife through butter. No Mariela, then. Well, a bloke can't have everything. Actually, come to think of it, the blokes round here, fancying a change, as blokes do, would not be fantasising Mariela tonight; it was Jude they'd be arranging in the positions of their desire. That blond lad who'd served them might fantasise Jude all his life. The drunk too, Emile, if he had any fantasy-life left in his poor pickled brain; he'd ogled Jude tonight as much as he had the landlord's lady. Bright used the little light on his car key to find the minute-switch. It wanly lit up the stairs. The French were frugal with light. Weird.

He shut the door softly and padded up the stairs two at a time, quiet and quick as a cat. At the landing window he lifted the lace curtain and looked down into the little street behind the hotel. The moonlight frilled the edges of the roof tiles. A real cat slithered like its own shadow off

65

the backyard wall out of sight into the street, and another shadow moved. The owner of the shadow stayed in the lee of the wall, invisible. But the moon showed the shadow's progress, swift and silent, along the street in the direction he and Jude had gone this evening, towards the château and the cemetery. The plan of this little place was laid out in his mind, like one of those old maps with pictures, little castles, churches, farms, familiar to him as though he'd been here all his life. The shadow had gone. No movement now. He heard something then, here in the house. His heart thumped. A key in the lock, turning, as quiet as his own. *Christ!* He felt like a kid caught out in mischief, spying, eavesdropping, stealing, even. The minute-light had gone out.

On his cat's paws he sped along the landing and up the top stairs in a few seconds. The minute-light didn't go on again. The person knew the layout well enough not to need it. He kept still, on the top landing, the way coppers did, fast heartbeat, shallow breathing, listening.

Nothing. No creaking floorboards to give him the direction. No footsteps. His fellow night owl was barefoot, maybe. He visualised Mariela's bare foot and he slapped his naughty mind down. He might, just then, have heard the slightest sound, not exactly a click, but a change in the silence that told him a door had opened somewhere on the landing below, then another change in the silence to tell him the door had closed again. That was all. He breathed out, all his held breath. He could move again. He hadn't dared to think what he'd have said if the person had come up here to the top landing. He laughed now, silently, a bit hysterical, the kid up to no good who'd just escaped being caught.

He opened the door dead slow, dead silent, so's not to waken Jude, saw that the light was on, and came face to face with her. She was sitting up, her chestnut hair tousled, her big breasts stretching the silky thing she wore for bed.

Her expression didn't change as he came in and she didn't speak. She just sat there watching him. Guilt and fear gutted him. But, hey, just a minute here, he'd only been for a little walk, for Christsake; he hadn't done anything wrong.

He felt defiant. He felt a pillock, wondering how to play this in the face of his accuser. Come on, he was a grown-up now, wasn't he? He could do as he liked. If he wanted to go for a walk at midnight that was his business, he didn't have to account for every move he made. He grinned. This was uncharacteristic for a start. *Why can't I act natural?* This was the way suspects must feel, facing him. He'd never understood that before. Not the way he understood it now. He was damned whatever he did, or said. He went to the point: 'I should have left you a note or something.'

'Oh yes? Saying what?'

'I couldn't sleep. I went out for a walk.'

'I see.'

'There was nowhere to go, in here. I didn't want to wake you up. You were deep asleep.'

Jude sat without moving, her face closed against him.

He went close and sat on the bed next to her knees. She didn't shift her legs to make room for him. He was perched on the edge. He didn't dare touch her yet. She'd shake him off and he didn't want that. 'Jude?' His purring, coaxing tone – got her every time. But not this time. 'Come on, Jude, it's not that serious. I just went out for a walk. Yeah, I should've left you a note. I'm sorry, I'm really sorry. But I'm here now, I'm back.'

'Oh fuck off,' she said. 'Fuck off, please.' She lay down. Her resentful back curved away from him.

'Oh shit.' He groaned. 'I go out because I can't sleep. So's not to wake you. And now what we got? I'm going to be wide awake all night and so are you. I tell you what – I feel like a kid caught scrumping. By his ma. Don't behave like my mammy. You're not my mammy. Are you, Jude?' She didn't respond. 'What'd I tell you yesterday? Don't do this silent suffering thing on me. I can't stand it. I can't.' He got out of his clothes and into bed. She didn't open her eyes. 'Jude?' She turned the other way, her back to him again, implacable. She reached up and turned off her light. Childishly he switched his on. He said, 'I could've done this to start with, switched the light on, read the guidebook, put the telly on, woken you up. So I'm fucked if you're gonna lie there in the dark sulking away at me all bloody night just 'cause I went out instead. Christ, Jude – what've I done that's so fucking terrible?'

'Sulking!' she said, turning, facing him, upright in an instant. 'Sulking? How dare you. I wake up, you're not there, I think, are you in the bathroom? No, you're not. You've gone. You've just disappeared into the night. How was I supposed to know what had happened to you? Anyway, gone for a walk, my arse!'

'"Gone for a walk my arse"? What does that mean?'

'Who goes out for a walk at midnight? It's bollocks. You bastard. You bastard.'

'What else would I be doing? The bar was shut when I got down there. Not that I'd've gone in there with all those incomprehensible Frenchies gassing away. Taking the piss out the English pillock. That woulda done nothing for my insomnia.'

'Oh and I wonder what would?'

'Would what? What you talking about, Jude? What's going on here?'

'Don't come all aggrieved innocence with me. You're not an innocent, you're a cynical bastard copper that's used to deceiving people and I should never have got involved with you, it's a terrible mistake, I'm always making awful mistakes, one after another. I was wrong, I was wrong.' She paused and said again, in a low mournful grieving voice, 'I was wrong.'

68

Bright couldn't think of a thing to say. All this tragedy because he'd gone for a walk? She was jealous, that was it. And his fantasies about Mariela made him guilty. Well, he had to face it head on. 'Are you jealous?' he said. 'Is that what this is about? You think I went out to meet— someone? I'm in your company the whole evening but somehow I manage to make an assignation behind your back, right? Arrange to meet someone at midnight? To what? Have a quickie on the billiard table downstairs? Or maybe up against the back wall of the hotel? Or, hang on, I've got a better place – back seat of the car, how about that?' Each minute change in the expression of her face told him yes, she had envisaged all these unlikely scenarios. 'What do you think I am?' he said. 'Some teenage sexual athlete? And who's my partner in all this adolescent shagging in the middle of the night?'

She turned her face away.

'As if I didn't know,' he said.

She lay down on her side again, curled away from him, as far as she could go without falling off the edge of the bed.

He groaned. 'Come on, Jude, it's not likely, is it? Use a bit of common sense. You must think I'm a fuckin' superman. You've got me shagged out my brains, woman. I'd have to have supernatural powers to go doing it with anyone else. Anyway, you fancied that little lad who served us tonight. Don't tell me you didn't, you were blushing as red as your gorgeous hair, you harlot. Don't tell me you weren't. I was a bit jealous myself, I have to admit, but not so's I'd think you were gonna creep out in the night for a quick shag with him behind the bike sheds. Or maybe you did! How about that? Maybe this big tragic act is to cover your guilty secret, my woman. Hey? Is that right? You been at it in the little back street while I was out? Hey? With Little Boy Blue? Hey?' He was spooning her now, pressed, all his front, against her warm back, his knees tucked into the warm fleshy corners of the backs of her knees. He moved his hand down her thigh over the silky stuff of the short slip-thing she wore in bed, and down to firm flesh, thick over the bone but no fat: she was a gardener, worked hard all weathers out of doors, she was fit and strong and gorgeous, her thick firm flesh of a texture and temperature that turned him on every time he touched her. 'Jude?' he said, coaxing, and he knew she could feel his hard-on now. In spite of her resentment she pressed her arse and her lower back against him, she couldn't help it. She was breathing faster. He brought his hand up under the silky stuff and caressed her belly. Her muscles jumped and quivered and she caught her breath, and he stroked her belly in circles that started to include her pubic hair, just a touch and then away, a touch and then away, till she started to move her pelvis to rise and meet his hand and his fingers penetrated the hot crack and found the juice that she always had there for him and the soft flesh of a heat that each time gave him a fresh shock. His breathing too was fast, he didn't know if he could hold on, he was excited with her like he'd never been before, he'd never had to coax her before, use his power on her. He felt her clit hard, engorged, moist, hot, the circles got slower, more concentrated, don't rush, keep it controlled. God, he could hardly bear it, she was circling her pelvis in time with his fingers, and lifting her lower body to press harder against his hand, and then she started to come with a cry he hadn't heard before, bucking up to him with a strength that could lift a man, crying out, in waves that took her over, lifting her, carrying her, so that he was hardly there, she was gone into some ecstatic region of her own. He was almost numb with amazement watching her as her contractions slowed, deepened, quietened and her cries softened and deepened to long slow groaning, then sighing with voice in it, then small moans of love and satisfaction, and she half-opened her eyes

70

and turned to him and pulled his cock and put it into her and pressed against him till he was buried inside her to the hilt where the wet heat was extreme and he said, 'God, be careful, Jude, I'm only human,' and she thrust and thrust against him with deep harsh noises saying, 'Fuck you, you bastard, fuck you, fuck you, fuck you,' and they started to come together, trying to keep it quiet because this wasn't home, this was a strange place, where even now like good English people they mustn't be overheard.

They lay afterwards, sweat between his body and hers, holding each other as if by holding on they could keep this incredible loving for ever just like this. She kissed his eyelids. He kissed the corners of her mouth. The tips of their tongues met in peace. Their lips met soft in the kiss of peace. Her face was wet, at first he thought with sweat, but no. He wiped the tears with his thumb. He said, 'I've made you cry.'

'It's just coming like that. It makes me cry. I don't know why.'

She'd come like this before with someone else. He suffered a pang of jealousy, hard, sharp, but he put it away from him. She had come like this with him now. With him from now on. 'Jude, you're a phenomenon to me. I can't believe my luck. Honest, I can't.'

She hugged him tight, her face hard against the side of his head. 'I'm sorry,' she whispered.

'Listen' he said, 'don't be. That was the fuck of a life-time. It can't get better than that.'

'I can't have a fight with you every time. I couldn't bear it. I can't stand fighting.'

'You never know – you might get to like it.'

'Never,' she said in a friendly way. 'Get off me, I've got to go and pee.'

They jostled each other in the bathroom, their cooling bodies touching, parting touching: kissing bodies. She put her arms round his waist from behind while he pissed, pressing her hands over his nipples, and he gripped her fingertips in his armpits. He'd never felt like this, even with— Never. Had he? With anybody. He had not known it was possible.

'I've never been jealous like that,' she said. 'I was like a mad person. I could see you making signs to her behind my back, having a quick word with her, passing through the bar, overcome with passion and plotting to go off with her, realising you'd made a mistake with me, I wasn't what you wanted at all, and you were getting her to come to England so that you could be together, you'd fallen in love just like that and you couldn't bear to be apart and you were . . . Oh God.'

'I gather we're talking about the landlord's lady, are we?'

Jude covered her mouth and nose with both hands and made a sound between a groan and a laugh.

'Well, it's true,' he said. 'I can tell you now. We're going off together. I just came back up here to pack. You daft cow.'

They went back to the bed and dropped down on to the creased sheets together, he on top of her. He put his arms round her and she clasped him tight. 'You daft cow,' he said.

He rolled off her, pulled up the bedcovers, and lay down. Spooning her warm back again, sliding into sleep, he wondered that a simple fuck, things done with others a hundred times, could lift you into realms you hadn't been before. Same actions, more or less. What was the difference? *And don't tell me "love" – that's bollocks. Love's an extra, love's the consequence. Or maybe when it's this great, that creates love, adds up to love. Is love?* It was hard to imagine loving without this alchemy, this changing of dross into gold by the magic touch. *The magic touch.* Breathing in her smell and the complex smells of sex and the two of them together, feeling different heats of the different parts of her flesh, cool buttocks, warm between the shoulder-blades, hot and damp under her hair which smelt of chestnuts which was strange because it was the colour of chestnuts and . . . swooning into sleep, he got it – the alchemy was all these things, heat and cool of flesh, and compatibility of rhythm, and humour, humour! And each other's smell and the extra, the something extra, the magic that happened between the fingertips and the other's flesh. How could you account for that?

Breathing, without knowing it, in the same slow rhythm as Jude, he slept.

8

Bliss, Was It?

The next morning gleamed as pearly as any morning in high summer. In the night, rain had fallen and the drops, not yet dry, still refracted and reflected the light, so that it almost hurt Bright's eyeballs to gaze on all this sparkle. He stood at the window breathing deep. From here you couldn't see Château-les-Mînes but he looked forward to his second visit there. Jude had woken when he opened the shutters. He'd enjoyed opening the shutters. It made him feel French. Not that he wanted to be French, not in the least, but the fantasy of the moment pleased him. He wondered briefly if his brain was undergoing a softening process, brought on by being on holiday. He suggested this to Jude. Jude said, 'Your brain could do with a bit of softening. Don't worry, it'll harden up again the minute you go back to work.'

Breakfast was laid in the vast square room, not so dark this diamond-sharp morning, blades of light cutting the gloom. They moved cups, cutlery and napkins from a dark corner to a table by the window. When the landlord appeared from the kitchen they almost flinched with guilt. Jude explained that they had moved for the sunlight. He nodded without expression, put down the basket of bread and croissants and asked if they wanted coffee or tea. There was no sign of Mariela.

'She'll still be in bed,' Jude said. 'She gets up at noon every day and lounges around in her dressing-gown till four when she has a leisurely bath with lots of bath essence, then she gets dressed and eventually appears in the bar to do her night's work. And her night's drinking. And her

74

night's flirting with all these poor hopeful men.'

'You liked her when she was talking to us last night.'

'It's called charm. She has that effect on everyone.'

'You're still jealous, Jude.'

'I'm not. How do *you* think she spends her days?'

'Hung over, like you said. Just like you said. Only I don't know when she finds time to carry on all these affairs.'

'No. I was wrong about that. She can't have affairs because she's got to get married – to our friend here.' Jude smiled up at the saturnine man who placed their coffee on the table without smiling back, seeming indeed barely to notice that Jude had smiled at him.

Bright had a momentary impulse to ask how Mariela was this morning, but he resisted. The man looked sad enough, plodding more heavily than yesterday, back to the kitchen regions. He made good coffee anyway. As Jude said, 'You wouldn't know this breakfast had been prepared by—'

'—a miserable bastard like him?'

'Yes. Praps he has help in the kitchen.'

'Don't think your under-age boyfriend'd be up at this hour, do you?'

Jude licked a croissant crumb off her upper lip and Bright grabbed her legs between his knees under the table. She cut short a groan of pleasure when the host came back. He asked if they were checking out today. She said yes.

They paid the bill in the bar which was already open but empty this morning. They loaded the cases into the boot and set off.

Château-les-Mînes was even more lovely on this luminescent day, the views of vines and forest and winding roads glimmering in a mist still rising from the earth. Again Bright suffered the hollow emptiness in his stomach where the knot of tension had lodged for as long as he could remember. Again the sensation disturbed him. Frightened him, even.

75

He gripped Jude's hand harder. She said, 'What's the matter?'

He put his arms round her outside the church and pressed his forehead on hers. She held his back in a strong grip, making him safe again. Fear – this kind of psychological panic, fear of the unknown – was unfamiliar to him. The fear itself frightened him. He told himself it was the sudden relaxation that caused it, being on holiday, leaving the threats behind. But maybe the cause was love? Love was softening him up, undermining his lifelong survival skills, making him vulnerable. He pulled out of her embrace.

'What's the matter?' she said again.

'I dunno. It's being on holiday. Makes me shaky.'

'Let's have lunch.'

'Hey, that's my line.'

'I'm a fast learner.'

'I've noticed,' he said.

She sensed his withdrawal from her. It made her feel that the solid earth beneath her feet had been sucked away leaving her floating without anchor in wide empty sea, out of her depth and without direction. She'd caught his shakiness; she sensed he was not telling her the truth. 'What's really the matter?' she said timidly, 'Can't you tell me?'

'No,' Bright said, 'I'll be okay in a minute. Gonna look for a restaurant. See you under the clock here at noon?' And he went off down the steep street.

Jude wished she didn't soak up other people's emotions like sponge. On this unseasonably hot spring day, it was as though the sun had gone in, the ancient streets of Châteaules-Mînes grown dark.

She wandered first sadly, then more happily, found a tiny house, like a child's invention, constructed of stone, a monument to the *vignerons* of the district. A little cat in a garden came running to her. With a wrench she discovered that George had actually left her mind for a whole hour, nearly a whole morning. The little cat jumped on the wall to be caressed, rubbing her face with its face, walking back and forth, arching its back to her hand, tail in the air, chirruping.

It was nearly noon. 'I have to go, little friend,' she said in French. The cat followed her some yards along the wall but when she turned to look back it was sitting with one leg up, having a wash. A lesson for me, Jude thought, if I could only learn it. *Let things go. Be glad of the moment. Don't want more. Don't want everything at once.*

Standing outside the church in his holiday jacket he looked defenceless. Like the little cat, he touched her heart. But she didn't show it. 'Is there a restaurant?' she said.

'Yup.'

'Oh, good.'

'It's closed till May.'

'Oh, drat.'

'But the caff's open. Might have food.'

The café was open but almost empty, just a couple of locals at the bar inside. They sat outside, in the sun, and ordered a ham baguette. Bright asked for one of those little beers in a wine glass he'd seen a bloke drinking last night. Jude described it to the waiter. '*Un bock,*' he said.

'So that's what a *bock* is! I've read about it. Simenon talks about *bocks* a lot. And doesn't T. S. Eliot? Isn't it in—?' She saw his quizzical squint and stopped.

He said, 'Yeah, yeah, I've heard of T. S. Eliot. I know he's not the plumber, I'm not gonna find him in the *Yellow Pages*. Christ, Jude.'

'Sorry.'

'That's okay. Lots of things I know about that you don't.'

'I know. Oh shit.'

'Don't get in a state about it. Doesn't make me feel bad. Only it makes you feel bad. And that makes me feel bad.

'Cause that's snobbery and I don't like snobbery. Okay?'

He was angry and she knew it. And he'd hit the mark as usual. Snobbery. People like us and people like you. Reading Eliot didn't mean you were cleverer than people who hadn't, who didn't; it just meant you had different tastes, different pastimes, different appetites. But were these differences reconcilable? she asked herself. Were these gaps crossable? If you couldn't pick up references, how did you have a conversation? He hated not being able to speak French. But in English too his language and hers were different. You could learn French. Of a sort. But it would never be your native tongue. A bit of you would always be translating.

'Jude?' he said.

Her round blue eyes came back to him. 'What?'

'There's lots of blokes you know who could quote you miles of T. S. fucking Eliot, and you know what? You wouldn't like these blokes. And you wouldn't fancy these blokes. Will you stop worrying? It's like you're trying to find fault with this. With us.' He meant *find fault with me* but he didn't say it.

Their sandwiches arrived, filled with succulent raw ham and this thick fleshy lettuce you never seemed to get in England. And the little beers, ice cold, sparky, light. And the sun was shining. They'd be okay.

Jude said, 'I know—'

He said, 'Eat.'

She said, 'Okay.'

He said, 'Bet you haven't read Proust.'

She looked a bit surprised. 'No, I haven't. I keep meaning to but I've never got round to it.'

'I have,' he said.

'Oh, yeah!'

'I have.'

'Why?'

'Why not?'

78

'Well . . .' She laughed. 'I don't know anyone else who's read Proust.'

'Just me?'

'Just you.' She laughed again. 'All of it?'

'First three books. I got bogged down in the third one. Felt like I was doing time. But up till then I was really enjoying it. Great stuff. Millie used to explain the bits I didn't get. It was a bit like reading an investigation report, the way he went into all these little details – you know – the people – like you do when you're into an investigation? Every little thing they say and do and don't say and don't do and their expressions and their body language, the whole shebang. He'da made a decent copper if he hadn't spent his life in bed. He knew all about snottery, as well. How it rules the world.'

Jude wanted to cry, for a concatenation of different reasons that she couldn't separate into their different strands. The strand that she pulled out of the tangle was that he'd read Proust for Millie Hale, his past great love. 'How did you come to read it?' she forced herself to say.

'A little contretoms like this one, one day. She says something and I don't get it. What was it now? I know – Albertine. That's it. She's surprised I know the name of these roses, Albertine. She thinks I'm this ignorant copper, see. Just like you. And she says something about Albertine, this character in Proust, and she gets all embarrassed, just like you. So I read it. To surprise her. And after a bit it wasn't to surprise her, it was because I liked it. But it did surprise her all right. When I told her. You jealous?'

Jude nodded. Her eyes were full of complex tears, not enough to fall. She was smiling. Kind of. 'I'm jealous of everything before me. But especially her.'

'Well, there you are then.'

'What does that mean?'

'It means we're quits.'

'You being jealous of Dan?'

'You can't change the past,' he said.

'No.'

'But you can change the future.'

'Yes.'

'So you see – it'll be all right. If you stop worrying at it.'

'You take my breath away,' she said. 'You move so fast. You leap from one logical step to another.'

'I've always been light on my feet,' he said.

She shook her head. She was smiling without sadness now, just with amusement and the sort of excitement he filled her with. The excitement he liked to fill her with.

He said, 'We could go back and have a siesta now. Isn't that what hotel rooms are for?'

'We haven't got a hotel room any more. We checked out.'

'Ah shit. I forgot. We're orphans. We got nowhere to lay our heads.'

'We could check back in again.'

'Yeah, great – hey there, Mushur Misery, we're checking in again for an afternoon shag.'

'Why not? None of his business.'

'You're a shameless hussy.'

'Is that what your ma would say?'

'A-ha.'

'Well, it's true.'

They found a field a little way up the road behind a high hedge, a meadow on the edge of a copse. Naked in the sun, on the picnic rug, the air warm on their flesh, they thought they might expire from bliss. 'Not bad for a couple of home-less orphans,' he said. Her lips looked bee-stung. His hair was wet. She rubbed it with a towel, her legs wrapped round him from behind. She kissed the hollow between his shoulder-blades and leaned her face against his back. She had no words to express the ecstatic happiness she felt. All well with body and soul. Nothing left over for the taking of notes. Nothing but this drowsy fulfilment that would convert in a few minutes to weightless energy, effortless strength. She wanted to say, 'I love you.' But she didn't. The words would alter the moment. And she desired no alteration.

He said lazily, 'Well, this won't do, Missis. Lying about in a field all day. What now?'

A few cars had gone by, down in the lane. This one stopped. A car door slammed. Voices.

'Christ.' Bright scrambled for his clothes. He threw Jude's frock to cover her, but when a French policeman appeared at the gate he found himself clutching his T-shirt and jeans over his crotch. 'Christ,' he said again, and he started to laugh. She'd never seen him laugh like this, bent double, helpless, like a kid. She held her frock in front of her and bit her lower lip. If she started to laugh too, they would become hysterical. A second policeman appeared. Two policemen. Gendarmes. In those funny hats, pillboxes with brims. Climbing over the gate into the field. Serious expressions. This was surreal. Surely you couldn't get arrested for fucking in a field? In broad daylight? In France?

The gendarmes stopped a few feet away. They said, in French, naturally, '*Put your clothes on, please.*' The French was a surprise because the situation had the air of farce and in farce the police spoke English with a terrible French accent like Clouseau. The men turned away, solid backs in well-fitting uniforms, arms folded. Jude was blushing. All over. They put their clothes on, Jude holding Bright upright while he struggled with laughter and his jeans. By the time they were dressed and she was folding the rug his laughter was under control. 'For Christsake,' he said, 'are we getting arrested for shagging in a field?'

She said in a small voice, 'Nous sommes prêts, Messieurs.'

The policemen turned. The smaller, plump one held a small piece of paper. He read from it. 'Monsieur John Brikkt?'

'A-ha, that's me.' Bright suddenly gripped Jude's wrist. As suddenly, she knew what he was thinking: his mother. *Something has happened.* These guys looked serious. 'Whadda they want? Ask them.'

'Qu'est-ce que c'est?' she said. Her French, limited as it was to tourist encounters, flew off into the sunshine. She could see it diminishing as a bird flying away becomes a dot in the sky, then invisible.

The plump policeman asked Bright to go with them.

Jude asked, *'But where? And why?'*

'Monsieur?' the man said, in a manner that you wouldn't argue with.

Jude struggled on: *'Is it his mother, in England? Is it that something has happened? An accident – incident – perhaps? I beg you, monsieur. His mother is an invalid.'*

They were now in single file, struggling back through the grass towards the lane, a tall thin gendarme, Jude, then Bright, with the small plump gendarme in the rear. 'What's it about?'

'They won't tell me.'

'Is it Ma?'

'They won't say.'

The tall policeman helped Jude over the gate, although she was the more agile. They waited for the plump one to get over. He opened the rear door of the police car for Bright.

Bright said, 'We've got our own car, thanks, mate.'

The gendarme held out his hand for the keys.

Bright said, 'Hey, hang on a bit here, what the fuck's going on? Tell them I'm going nowhere till I know what this is about. Who do they think I am? What's happened? Tell him fuck off, get stuffed.'

Jude's French was just about up to: *'Monsieur, we cannot go with you if we do not know what is happening. An explanation? Please?'*

The plump gendarme spoke slowly and clearly. *'We have*

*some questions to put to Monsieur Brikkt. That is all that
I am able to tell you at this moment.'*

Jude said, 'It's no good. They won't tell us. They want to
ask you some questions, that's all they'll say.'

'Has something happened to my ma?'

'It is not then his mother, in London?'

The tall gendarme shook his head in a curt gesture. Any
moment now, Jude felt, he would be manhandling Bright.
If that happened, she knew, there'd be no answering for the
consequences. 'John—' She saw his eyes turn red. Literally
red. It wasn't a trick of the light. His face was white, his
mouth was a tight thin line, he was a missile ready for take-
off: it was count-down time.

She said to him, in a steady quiet voice, 'We have to go
with them. Whatever it is, we mustn't make it worse than
it is, we just have to go along with it until we can get it
sorted out. I'll come with you. We can get the car later.' She
conveyed this idea to the gendarmes as best she could.

They nodded. The tall one got in the back with Bright.
She sat in the front with the plump one, who drove.

The day had not become dark. The sun was still shining.
The vines and the hills were still beautiful. The *vignerons*
still burned the vine prunings in their rusty incinerators and
the smoke still rose in blue and stately columns into the air.
But everything had changed. They were gliding into a dream-
world where anything was possible. They would never, for
instance, get back to the car again, to the field where they
had made love, to that place and that moment in their lives.
She recognised panic. Indeed, the car smelt of it, pungent,
acrid, hot. Nobody spoke till Bright – she could hear that
he had conquered his volcanic eruption of rage – said, 'Where
are they taking us? The why bit can wait. Just ask them
where?'

'Combrans,' was the answer.

'Where is Combrans?' Jude asked them.

Bright said, 'I know where it is.'

'How?'

He didn't reply.

'Where is it?'

'Other side of the tracks from Nerfshattle.'

'Why are they taking us there?'

'The police station's there.'

'How do you know?'

Again he kept his mouth tight shut.

They drove down the main street of Neufchâtel in silence. At the crossroads they did not turn right towards the hotel and the river, they went straight ahead, over the level-crossing, past the railway station, then turned left down a narrow road to the gendarmerie. The boys in blue. Same the whole world over. Jude was keeping herself calm, holding herself together, panic beating its wings in her stomach, her chest, her throat.

The car drove down the side of the police station and stopped in front of it. It was not a large building. It looked like a small block of council flats, four storeys high. They told Jude to stay in the lobby.

'*No*,' she said. '*I want to stay with him. Please.*'

They ignored her, marching him ahead.

He said, over his shoulder, 'How am I gonna understand what they're saying to me?'

She called after them, '*He does not speak French. Please allow me to translate for him.*'

But they took him away through the doors to the inner sanctum. All she could do was sit on the metal bench and wait.

9

His Own Medicine

The three of them trooped down a corridor, small offices off to left and right, all the doors open, gendarmes at their desks, into the office at the end: yellow-tile floor, shabby white walls, scratched metal desks, old maroon swivel chairs. Same high design standards as Kentish Town HQ.

Was he here as a witness or a suspect? They didn't read him his rights. But they weren't polite either. He didn't know how they worked things here. Until he did, the best thing was to look dumb, keep stumm, and try to work out how serious the situation might be.

The office had three desks, one computer. A young gendarme whacked at the keyboard, recording what was said. The file on the screen was headed ENQUETE PRELIMI-NAIRE – preliminary what – inquest – inquiry? – PROCES-VERBAL – no need to translate that.

The tall gendarme asked the questions. The plump one stood by the door. In case he made a run for it? They asked and asked. He shrugged and shrugged. 'I don't speak French, mate,' he kept saying. 'It's no good, I don't speak French.' At last the tall one gave up, hustled himself and his stooge out of the room, and left him alone with the young cop, who ignored him. He had a lot of paperwork. Looked like they had it worse here than in England. Bright sat and watched.

He was good on the computer, using only two fingers but quick. A fresh-faced country lad, smooth-skinned, not stupid, a nice picture over his desk, a painting of Provence: an old garage, *Garage Raoul*, with an ancient petrol pump and an old chair. The desk opposite had a farmer driving his cows along a lane and a big photo of dogs with their tongues out: the plump cop, no question. The desk in the corner where the tall one had put his hat just had a map of the district and a calendar.

Ten minutes, and they hadn't come back. This was interesting. This was what he'd do with a suspect, not a witness: leave him to stew a bit, so he'd come to his senses, agree to talk, incriminate himself. But what did they suspect him of? What was he supposed to have done? His palms sweated. Should he tell them he was a cop? What were the rules here? They followed the Napoleonic Code. He had a sinking feeling that this gave them a bit more leeway than the Brit police. What were his rights? Did they have to get him a lawyer? He didn't know if he needed one. *They gotta get me an interpreter, that's for sure. But how will I know if he's translating right? I'm a babe-in-the-woods out here. I should've known better – don't go abroad.*

At last they came back. A big bloke shambled in after them. He looked bleary, scratching his head, rubbing his face, as if to wake himself up. He saw Bright, came right up to him and shook hands. 'Hello,' he said in English. 'I am Michel Breton. I will translate the questions of the officers, and also your answers. This is okay?'

'Thanks. What's this all about then?'

'I regret – I don't know.' Breton had brown eyes with gold specks. He looked humorous, kind and solid, the sort of guy you could depend on. *Beware.*

The gendarmes began afresh, Breton translating. 'Are you Mr John Bright of London, England?'

'Yup.'

'You arrived in Neufchâtel yesterday afternoon and engaged a room at the Hôtel Sanglier?'

'Yup.'

They showed him the hotel slip he'd signed yesterday. 'This is your signature?'

'Yup.'

'This is your address?'

'Yup.' Strictly speaking, it was Jude's address. His official address was still his one-room flat in Hornsey Lane. But he wasn't going to give them more than he had to.

'The woman who accompanies you is not your wife?'

'Is that any of their business?'

A short discussion followed. The tall gendarme shrugged. Breton's eyes crinkled. 'No. It is agreed this is not yet their business.'

'Not *yet*? Listen, mate, can you get them to tell me what this is about? Maybe I can help them, but not while they keep me in the dark. What's happened?'

Breton put this to the officers. Their answer was short and to the point: '*We're asking the questions.*' He didn't need the translation; it was the reply he'd have given himself. In their place. The place he'd always occupied. Up to now.

'What is your employment please?' Like they'd read his mind.

Unh-unh. No way he was going to tell them that. Not yet. 'Look,' he said to the rumpled man, 'I need to know if I'm here as a witness or a suspect. If I'm here as a suspect I need a lawyer. Where I come from they read you your rights before they take you in for questioning. I wouldn't know if they've done that or not. I gotta know where I stand here. I'm not saying another word until I do.'

The tall gendarme made a speech, down his nose like he was General de Gaulle. Breton reduced it with tact to: 'For now you are a witness only. When you will become a suspect, you will know it.'

Maybe the *when* was a mistake in translation. Like hell. He sighed. 'Okay. Ask.'

'You have not answered your employment.'

'I work for the government.' He looked at de Gaulle. 'Like him.'

'Civil servant?'

'That'll do.'

'You have dined at the hotel last evening?'

'Yup.' *The hotel.*

'While you are dining, Mademoiselle Mariela Joubert has come to your table to speak with you?'

So it is to do with the delectable Mariela. I might have known. 'That's right.'

'What have you said to each other?'

'She introduced herself. Said she was the er – fiancée of the – owner? – of the hotel. Gave us a brandy on the house.'

'What else has she said to you?'

'Talked about old movies. Why?'

'Anything else?'

Bright shrugged, damned if he was going to disclose a word that might do her harm. Or himself either, if they were thinking of fitting him up for something. 'Nothing I can remember. Just chat.'

The gendarmes did not look happy with this answer, but moved on. 'Did you see her leave the hotel after the dinner?'

Ah. Now what should he do? This was trouble for somebody. She'd gone off with those lads. Then what? What if there'd been some rough stuff? 'Listen, mate, I don't want to implicate anyone here. If something's happened to the girl, or to someone else, tell me. Because even if I am just a witness like he said, until I know, I'm exercising my right not to co-operate. They got that?'

The crumpled man translated. The tall gendarme became enraged, strutting in the small space, voice up an octave, dignity offended, feathers ruffled. The stooge tried to calm him down. The argument batted on, Breton keeping out of it, letting them strut and exclaim. But when he suddenly raised his voice, Bright was surprised to note, they shut up and turned to him with deference. They listened while he made a short speech. De Gaulle shook his head, sighed, checked his watch, then, with a sour look at Bright, gave Breton permission to speak.

'Under our regulations the Gendarmerie have only charge of the investigation during the first few hours. They have informed already the district *section de recherches* – that is the judiciary police. I believe it is like your CID. The *recherche* officer is coming now from Lons-le-Saunier to – ah – pursue the investigation. They will await his arrival.'

'Well, that's great. Please tell them I'm very pleased to know that. But they still haven't said what my position is. I mean, can I get up and go now? Why – am – I – here?'

'We must await the officer of judiciary police.'

'And they got the right to do that – just keep me here?'

'It seems that they have.'

'How long?

'The *police judiciaire* can keep you up to forty-eight hours.'

'You're joking.'

'After that they can apply to the prosecutor to keep you for twenty-four hours more.'

'Before that they have to decide I'm a suspect, do they, or can they drag any innocent tourist in off the streets and subject them to police harassment?' He sounded like a thousand bods he'd brought in for questioning himself in his time. He saw the funny side but felt no urge to laugh.

'If the *police judiciaire* will decide that you are a suspect, you will then be permitted to have a lawyer.'

'Well, that's big of them. Christ. Look, mate, did you see Jude out there – the lady who's not my wife?'

'Yes.'

'Can you tell her what's going on? Can you ask her to phone Ted Adams for me? He's a—' *Don't say he's a lawyer, you don't know if you can trust this guy.* 'He's a mate in London. Can you do that? Can you do it without telling them?'

Breton spoke on a different note. 'The young officer speaks English. Just a little. I know him.'

Bright laughed.

'But I will try to do as you want.'

'Thanks.'

Breton shook hands again. Plump-cop opened the door and took him out. Tall-cop sat down at the desk with the map and started to fill in report sheets. They left Bright sitting on the scruffy maroon swivel chair like a chained dog.

When the pass-door opened, Jude stood up. Only the big shambling man came out, however. The door clicked shut behind him. She sat down again. But he came straight over to her. 'I am Michel Breton.' They shook hands. 'The police have called me in to interpret for your friend.'

'Oh. What's happening? What is it about – do you know?'

'I – do not know.'

She didn't believe him. Such a small place. Everyone must know. Except her and Bright. 'Why are they detaining him?'

The man looked at her with sympathy but didn't reply.

'Oh God . . . What should I do?'

'He has asked that you contact a friend in London. Adams?'

'Ted Adams. Yes. He's a— Yes. He's a friend.' *I don't have Ted Adams' number. Who'd know it? Anyone at Kentish Town HQ will know it. God, I don't know if John's told them he's a policeman. And I mustn't tell them in case he doesn't want them to know. I'll ring Niki Cato.* John had given her his sergeant's number months ago: "Cato'll always know how to find me." *He'll know what to do. Of course!* 'What have they been asking him?' she said to Breton. 'What has he said?'

'They are asking about the hotel yesterday evening. He has refused to answer more questions.' Breton hesitated. 'They have asked, are you his wife?'

'What on earth is that to do with them?'

Breton smiled. 'This is what he replied also.'

'If it's about the hotel, why aren't they questioning me too?'

'I do not know.'

'I need to get to the car.'

'I will ask.' Breton talked to the desk officer who picked up a phone.

Jude went out to the car park with her mobile. Thank God, there was a signal. She called Cato's mobile: John wouldn't want this broadcast to the Kentish Town CID room. Not yet. Not till he knew where he stood. She got the message-voice. Why was no one ever there in an emergency? 'Niki, it's Jude. Can you call me?' She gave her mobile number. 'John needs to contact Ted Adams. It's really urgent. Thanks.'

The big interpreter man came out. 'The car has been returned here, to the gendarmerie.'

'How? Towed?' This alarmed her more than any of the strange events so far. 'Where is it now? Am I allowed to have it?'

'They say the *police judiciaire* will decide. I am sorry.'

'Where are they?'

'They will arrive soon from Lons-le-Saunier.'

'What should I do? I couldn't get hold of the friend who knows Ted Adams' number.'

'International enquiries perhaps?'

'Oh, yes! God, why didn't I think of that? I'm in a panic. I can't think straight.'

'I will try. One moment.' He went back inside the building. Outside a block of flats opposite, identical to the gendarmerie block, children were playing, kicking a yellow ball. The place had the air of a barracks. Of course, she recalled, the Gendarmerie were a branch of the army. They lived and worked in these concrete boxes next to the railway

91

line. If only she knew more about how things operated here. If only her French were better. She did not follow the big man back inside. Out here she had air and sunlight at least.

Breton came out and handed her a memo page with Adams' number.

'Oh *merci*, *merci*.' She dialled it. Adams' phone rang and rang. She didn't know if this was his office or his home. Whichever it was, he wasn't there. But all at once, listening to the empty ringing, she knew who to call: Kate Creech. Adams had acted as her solicitor once. She got the message voice again, but Kate always checked her messages. She repeated what she'd said to Detective Sergeant Cato, almost word for word. One of them would get back to her, some time soon. She sagged now. All she'd done was call a few people; she felt as though she'd climbed the Matterhorn.

Breton still hovered. 'Perhaps you must stay here tonight?'

'Yes, I guess that's so. But if this case – whatever it is – involves the hotel I can hardly stay there . . . Is there another hotel?'

'I am afraid not.'

'Oh, well, I'll have to think about that later, when John comes out.' Her phone rang. It was Kate Creech. 'Jude! I thought you were in France!'

'I am.' Jude told her what she knew.

Kate laughed! 'A-ha! As he might say. The boot's on the other foot. He's getting a taste of his own medicine at last!'

'Kate—!'

'Jude, it must be hell, I know. But relax. It's obviously nothing to do with him. It'll all be over in an hour and you'll be off down south. But I've got a break now till the next scene. I've a big costume and makeup change but I can keep calling Ted while they work on me. And give me Sergeant Cato's number as well. I'll keep calling him too. Don't worry, Jude. It really will be all right.'

As she said goodbye to Kate, the automatic gates swung

open and a big black Peugeot drove into the car park, followed by another. Policemen spilled out, in a different uniform from the gendarmes, with flat peaked hats, not the képi that the gendarmes wore. They swept into the gendarmerie like a troop of SAS.

'They are the judiciary police from Lons-le-Saunier,' Breton said.

10

Alarm and an Excursion

He came in like the cavalry. The gendarmes jumped to attention. He had a face like a good-humoured rat – wide mouth, little glittery eyes – and a hard body you'd be wise not to fool with. He said *bonjour* and held out his hand for the paperwork, no time to waste. Plump-cop stood at Tall-cop's side, passing the papers. Rat-face placed his hat on Tall-cop's desk, then sat in his chair. They kept their backs to Bright and talked in low murmurs. Every now and then one of them turned to look at him. He sat with his arms folded across his chest and his legs stretched out, his you-don't-scare-me posture, familiar to him from years of observing nervous interviewees. He tried to act natural. It was impossible. You can't walk with the boot on the other foot.

In unison they stopped murmuring and the gendarmes parted so that Rat-face had a clear view. He stared at Bright, then he got up, very slow, very relaxed, came round the desk and parked his backside on it. 'Miss-TAIR Brikkt. GOOD day. I am Ad-JUT-ant Poupard. I am the chief officer of the IN-ves-TIG-ation.' That was how he talked. He thought it was great. He thought it sounded like English.

Bright stayed in his I-don't-care-if-you're-queen-of-the-Belgians pose, and didn't change his facial expression either.

'You will please ans-WER my quer-IES now, thank you.'

Bright's posture changes. He sits up. He leans forward. He pokes a finger at the rat face. Not on your life. YOU will ans-WER MY quer-IES now, like what the fuck am I doing here for starters. Like hell. He didn't move a muscle.

Alienate a self-important official like this one and you could be in really deep shit. He might talk funny English but he wasn't a man to mess with. And he was in charge. 'Look,' Bright said, very reasonable, 'like I've been telling your guys here, I need an interpreter. I – don't – speak – French.'

'You have not necessaRY the interpr-ETer. I speak Eng-LISH.'

You speak Eng-LISH? You could've fooled me. He didn't say that. 'That right?' he said. 'Well, then, you'll understand this then: I don't. I don't speak Eng-LISH. I don't speak anything. Not till someone tells me what's going on and what my status is: suspect or witness. You got that?' He kept a very pleasant expression on his face all the time he was speaking, and a very genuine tone to his voice. 'My girlfriend has contacted my lawyer in London and he will shortly be in touch. I will be taking his advice. Until then I'm afraid I just have nothing more to say to you, mate. Sorry.'

Rat-face stared at him. He had quite a decent line in stares. He was good, really good. Nearly as good as Bright. 'Ve-RY well.' He took his backside off the desk, slapped down his handful of papers, and rapped out some French to the tall gendarme, who gave orders to his stooge who went running out of the room. Tall-cop took his de Gaulle hat and followed at a steady pace. The young one stayed at his desk. He was recording every word for posterity.

Adjutant Rat-face, still staring at Bright, took a deep breath; his nostrils flared. Bright had never seen nostrils flare so splendidly. 'Ve-RY well . . .' He spoke ve-RY slow-LY-. 'Good.' Then, like a flash, he plucked his hat from the desk, strode to the door, opened it, and said, 'You will go with me please.'

'Go with you? Go with you where?'

'To see something.' He put his charming head on one side and smiled.

'To see what?'

'Please?'

The 'please' was a formality. No doubt about that. This was not a multiple choice question. And Bright didn't want to make a thing of it. Curiosity, anyway, had always got the better of him, all his life.

Jude saw the pass-door open again. A police officer marched through first, a hard man, an officer of the *police judiciaire*. Behind him came Bright and the plump gendarme. Bright wasn't rushing, he was taking his time. The foyer was thick with police; Jude couldn't get to him or even catch his eye. The hard man was now in charge, she could see that, and that they were not bringing Bright out to let him go. She turned to Breton, the interpreter. 'Can I just have a word with him?' she said. 'Will you ask them? Please?'

Breton, nervous, asked the tall gendarme. He waved him on to the hard man who gave a brisk shake of the head. No discussion. Breton returned. 'They regret they must say no. They must go quickly.'

She barged through to the hard man and spoke in French. '*Excuse me, Monsieur. Where are you taking him?*'

His eyes rested on her. They registered no expression.

The tall gendarme explained, she was the *amie* of the witness. The hard man shook his head and sailed on, the tall gendarme in his wake. Bright had already been moved past her, out of reach.

The plump assistant took pity and turned to her. '*It's not far,*' he said.

'*May I come?*'

His smile was apologetic. '*We will return soon.*'

They all moved off. Jude caught them up in the car park. She ran round the little throng to the hard man again. '*May his interpreter Monsieur Breton go with him? I have spoken with our lawyer in London and he says he should have an interpreter with him at all times. So that there will be no misunderstandings. Later.'*

His cold eyes swung round to Breton, who stopped in his tracks. The tall gendarme explained that Breton was the interpreter.

'*He has been questioned?'*

'*But yes, Adjutant.'*

Here they turned their backs to Jude, and the sound down. Then the hard man gave a sigh, shrugged, and moved off. The tall gendarme beckoned Breton who, looking hunted, followed the little gang to the car.

Walking away between the tall gendarme and the judiciary officer, Bright appeared small, vulnerable. Jude was very scared. Not knowing the ways of the French police, she didn't know if this treatment of a witness was normal, or seriously threatening. She watched the police put him in the black Peugeot and pile in after him. She watched the two cars move off and the automatic gates close behind them. Then she went back into the foyer and sat down once more. To wait.

They put him in the back again with the tall gendarme. He didn't like the smell of the guy, industrial strength aftershave with undertone of mothball. They swung out of the automatic gates, drove alongside the station, turned left at the level-crossing, then right, into one of the lanes he had not explored last night. High walls, glimpses of mansard roofs, nice houses standing in gardens, meadows between the houses, then a bridge over a river. The river was in spate, willow fronds sweeping the water, ducks racing. Over the bridge the road ran between the river and dense woodland. A nasty low-level anxiety, unattached to his own predicament, started to prickle his skin. He got intuitions. He was getting one now, an absolute knowledge of what they were taking him to see.

The cars stopped at the familiar police-tape across the lane. The adjutant got out of the car in front, went down the bank and disappeared among trees. Nobody in Bright's car moved. Or spoke. He wished someone would open a window. The adjutant reappeared, coming up the path, in front of him a boy with dark hair in a short ponytail and eyes like a frightened horse. He was one of the bike boys from last night. He was the one who had ridden off with Mariela on the back.

The adjutant opened Bright's door. He got out of the car. He and the boy stood face to face. The adjutant asked the boy a question. The boy nodded. The big interpreter guy said, 'He has identified you as the Englishman who was at the hotel last night. Do you recognise him?'

Bright squinted at the kid with compassion. 'I think he was one of the boys who was there.'

Another police officer took the boy's arm dragged him away.

Rat-face gestured to Bright with his chin to follow him. They set off in single file on the designated path down the riverbank, fresh smells of grass and water under the trees. He hoped they'd already done a thorough search of the area. It went against his grain to contaminate a crime scene.

A small clearing down by the water. One tree in the clearing. Thick undergrowth all round. Trodden-down grass. A bright blue rope snaked her neck, her shoulders, her upper body, binding her to the tree. She had slipped down, her lower body splayed on the ground. Her head lolled forward so he couldn't see her face. He didn't want to. He didn't want to see the rest of her either but he couldn't avoid that. The short red dress was ripped apart, her body exposed, just as he had fantasised last night, the skin like pale brown satin, the torso short, rounded, the slight mound of the stomach, the breasts round too, with dark aureoles round the nipples. Her pubic hair had not been shaved. Dried blood, or so it appeared, crusted her skin between the thighs and smeared her legs, caked the grass between her legs. Her toenails were painted bright red.

He felt the surge of anger he always felt at a scene like this, at the waste: of beauty, of youth, of hope, of dreams. Mariela's dreams. She'd chased trouble in a perpetual circle so you wouldn't know which was doing the chasing, trouble or her. Trouble was her lifelong companion. And death hadn't parted them. She was already more trouble in death than she'd been in life.

'Turn YOUR-self TO me please.'

He had forgotten his own problems at the sight of her but he knew his expression would give away nothing. His face had never given him away in his life. When he was moved his squint, often barely noticeable, would intensify, so that you couldn't see even where he was looking, never mind how.

'Do you re-COG-nise her?'

Bringing a suspect to a crime scene to look at a corpse was way out of line where Bright came from, against the rules. But he knew the temptation: to shock, to get a spontaneous reaction. He'd done it himself once or twice. He took a long time answering. 'I can't see her face. But the girl who talked to us last night outside the hotel – Mariela – was wearing those clothes.'

Rat-face motioned the interpreter, Breton, to go back up the path. The man didn't move. He couldn't: he was stuck, a nightmare-victim who couldn't wake up. He could not shift his eyes from Mariela's corpse. Rat-face rapped out one of his orders and the man came awake, turned and stumbled up the path.

The cars were still in the lane. The motorbike kid was still there, hugging himself round the waist with both arms, holding himself together.

Rat-face again brought Bright face to face with the boy

and said, 'When you have last see her? Was she with this boy?'

Again he didn't want to implicate the kid but this was a suspicious death and to him it looked a probable homicide. The man and the policeman were at war inside him. The copper wanted to pursue the investigation; the man wanted to run a mile. But there'd be no running. There was no escaping what had to come, for anybody. This was what murder did – it left no bystanders: whatever your life had been before, it would not be the same from now on. 'About ten forty-five, eleven o'clock last night. She left the hotel on the back of a motorbike driven by one of three boys.'

'This boy?'

'I believe so. Yes.'

This French cop might not obey the rules but he knew what he was doing. He had this kid in a state so flaky, so frantic, he'd spill information like vomit. The information he threw up might be a cascade of lies. But anything was better than stalemate. He shoved the kid into the front car and got in after him.

Bright got in the second car with the two gendarmes. Breton, the interpreter, was already on the back seat, his hands squeezed between his knees. Bright could feel his big body trembling. His reaction was pretty extreme. But the police showed no interest in his responses. The guy must have a good alibi for last night.

The cars backed down the lane to the bridge where there was room to turn, and the adjutant's car went ahead. Bright had under five minutes to decide what to do. Maybe Ted Adams would have called back with some advice. If not, he'd have to make up his own mind. He rubbed his face. His own hand was none too steady. *How in hell did I get on this side of the fence?*

100

11

Spilling the Beans

Jude stood outside on the steps. Seeing Bright get out of the car she held up the phone and shook her head: *no calls.*

Bright groaned. *They're never there when you need them.* So. No lawyer. Well, that was one factor out of the equation. They marched him on, wouldn't let him speak to her. Why was he putting up with this? He'd had enough. He'd follow his instincts, to hell with the consequences. He'd seen the body. He knew the score. *No more arsing about.*

Rat-face was in the office, barking out orders, taking phone calls. Not every day he got a homicide; he was making the most of it, preparing his TV appearances. He pointed at the chair. Bright sat. He wouldn't get the guy's attention for a while. He could wait. He kept an eye on the interpreter, who sat in the corner looking ill.

At last the important adjutant was ready. He parked his backside on the desk. He liked to do his questioning from a height, emphasising the wrong syllables from close up. 'Very well,' he said. 'You understand now this is a serious matter? You are ready now to answer, perhaps?'

'Am I a witness or a suspect?'

'For the moment you are a witness.'

For the moment. He ignored that – for the moment. 'In that case I'll answer.'

'I will begin again at the beginning.' He jerked his chin at the young cop perched at his keyboard to call him to attention. There was no need. He was poised, all ears, and two fingers at the ready. 'Your name please?'

'John Bright.'

'Your address?'

He gave Jude's.

'Your occupation?'

'I'm a copper.'

'Excuse me?' The man looked like Bright had said he was a handbag or a lettuce.

'I'm an inspector with the CID. The Criminal Investigation Department of the Metropolitan Police. In London.'

Bright watched their expressions change. He enjoyed it. The adjutant pulled himself together fast. Bright had to give it to him: nothing fazed the guy for long.

'You have identification?'

He fished his ID card out of his pocket and handed it over. The Adjutant treated all reading matter like used toilet paper. He held it at a distance by one corner. Bright nearly asked the interpreter, can he read? But he resisted the urge. He'd given up being funny. Being funny wasn't so funny any more. He said, 'Give me a pen and a bit of paper and I can write down who you can ring up and check with, okay?'

The request was granted. Bright thought about giving them Grant, his DCI, but he didn't know him well enough, or trust him enough. He wrote the name of the superinten-dent, her personal number at HQ and her fax number. As he finished writing a cold drop of doubt trickled down the back of his neck. Grant wasn't the only colleague whose solidarity he doubted. A lot of people whose noses he had got up one way or another would be not unamused by his predicament now. A lot of cops have a lot of reservations about a cop who shops a cop. Even clean cops don't like cops who expose dirty cops: Loyalty Rules OK. He thought his superintendent was a straight-up copper but even she—*You never know*. Behind the face was always another face.

Anyway, what was he thinking of? His being a cop wasn't about to get him out of this hole. Being a cop didn't stop you being suspect numero uno. The adjutant needed to get someone for this. And a cop-shopper would suit him fine. Especially a cop-shopper who wasn't French. Who wasn't from round here. The adjutant was the type of cop who likes results. All cops like results. Some like results at any cost. He was maybe one of those. But he'd move with caution. Wouldn't want to upset the Metropolitan Police. He marched out of the room with the memo pad Bright had written on.

No one spoke while he was gone. The air was thick with thinking. The plump gendarme stood at ease, hands behind his back, legs akimbo, studying Bright as if he was a dissection specimen. The interpreter's eyes quivered with unease. The young cop kept grinning and covering his mouth with his hand.

The adjutant came back. He kept his eyes off Bright. He told the others to go with him and they all left, except the young one, who stood to attention until they'd gone and then sat down again at his computer.

At last Bright was alone – more or less – to do a bit of thinking of his own. No question, this thing had panicked him. Being in the suspect's chair had taken him right back: he was a lad again, up on sus, cheeking the cops, wriggling out with a warning, escaping a record by the skin of his shiny young Cockney teeth. Never thought he'd be back there again. And not even able to speak the language this time round. He sifted his problems, wadded up his thoughts, into separate bundles, and came out with: *get the priorities right*. Okay, he was sorted. He was ready now.

In they trooped. Rat-face stood in his most adjutant-like pose. 'I have leave message for the Madame Superintendent. We wait for confirmation of your statement—'

'Sure. Now listen. I'm gonna fill you in on a few things.'

The man went rigid. He didn't like being interrupted; it spoiled his flow.

'I'm gonna give you the sequence of events of last night.

The deceased's movements up to the last time I saw her. Okay? Because I don't know when she died and I don't know what the cause of death was yet and I suspect you don't either yet because the post-mortem has probably only just begun and that's if you're lucky – well, that's if it's anything like my neck of the woods. But I have seen a few corpses in my time and I don't think she ended up like that without some help. Whatever happens, you gotta get her movements straight last night. So I'm gonna give you my observation of the sequence of events last night as far as it goes. You wanna record this?' He was going for the rat-faced adjutant, he was going like daggers, ack-ack-ack-ack-ack.

The adjutant was on his back foot, blinking, not getting a word in. He nodded at the young typing-whiz, who was on his front foot, ready for the off.

Bright went on. 'Okay. We sat down to eat outside the hotel about seven thirty, quarter to eight. A kid served us, nice lad, blond, spoke English. When we were on to the coffee, this girl comes out – young woman – your victim. She has a word with the drunk who's sitting just outside the bar, table on his own, shouting at the traffic about cats and God knows what. She has a word with him. Nice. She's nice to him. He likes her too. Okay. She comes over to our table and she stands there and basically tells us her life story. The fiancé who runs the hotel, miserable sod, comes out a few times like he's keeping an eye on her. She doesn't take a blind bit of notice of him, ignores him. He goes back in. She speaks English. Not bad. Tells us all about her fiancé's family and how they won't let him marry her but how she won't leave because he's got to marry her like he promised. She goes back in the bar. Next thing, three lads who've been in there an hour or so come out and jump on their little motorbikes, and she jumps on behind. I identified one of these kids up there at the scene. I remember him because he's a serious looker and because of the ponytail, okay? He's the one who gave her a ride. But I don't know if I could identify the other two because I never saw them before in my life and at the time I had no reason to take much notice. Anyway there's enough people in the bar to corroborate, and they'd know them. Everyone knows everyone round here. Okay. She goes off on the back of that boy's bike. The two bikes drive off together. The fiancé comes out to the door of the bar. Says something nasty to the poor old drunk, stands there worrying, then goes back in. Then about twenty minutes later, say ten thirty, the nice blond lad who served us comes out. He asks where Mariela is and we tell him. He gets on his little motorbike and goes haring off down the road in the direction they took. The direction was towards the centre of the town, the crossroads. That is the last I saw of any of these people except the fiancé, the hotel guy, who served us breakfast this morning about nine o'clock. After breakfast we packed and drove up to Château-Thing where you found us this afternoon. That is my statement. And I'm giving it to you because, like I said, you gotta get a clear picture of that poor girl's movements last night. A proper factual picture. You gotta question those bike kids, especially the blond one who served us – he's not a member of the gang – find out where they took the victim, when they last saw her, whether they got witnesses – apart from each other – to their movements.'

The adjutant opened his uptight rat-trap of a mouth and spoke. 'We have questioned the boys. Thank you for your valu-ABLE advice.'

'Don't mention it, mate.'

The interpreter sweated a bit in his corner, pulled a tissue out of the box on the window-sill and mopped his face. Bright was sweating, himself, only he didn't look it. *He had been out in the night.* A man with a bag had come out of the woods and crossed the car park towards the hotel. The man had seen him. He'd heard someone let themselves into the hotel with a key. Mariela? Louis? Someone else? He'd seen a shadowy figure creeping away along the little street close to the wall. But he'd keep all that for now. He wanted some endorsement from his bosses back home before he divulged a speck of evidence that could be turned against him. He needed the word from Ted Adams. *Oh Christ. Jude. What if they've questioned her. What if she said— She wouldn't. She knows better. But what if they tricked her into saying more than she wanted. Shit.* He couldn't believe this – here he was, just like a thousand idiots he'd questioned, himself obstructing the police in their investigation, lying, at least by omission. In spite of this, he could not bring himself to say that he had been out last night, maybe at the crucial time. Not to the rat-faced adjutant. He couldn't. He'd wait. And trust in Jude. But he sweated.

The young gendarme gave him the printout of his statement. Bright read it through. It was a right mess. Gobbledegook. There was a knock, and an even younger gendarme put his head round the door. He looked twelve years old. He said something to Rat-face, who spat some words at the interpreter and left the room.

The interpreter said to the two-finger typist, 'I must go through the statement with you to help you make corrections.' The young cop blushed. Like all the local lads, he was in awe of this Breton, even though the man looked a shambling wreck.

'They'll be putting it into French later, right? I want Jude, my – you know – out there – to check it through, make sure they got it like I said it. And I want the English one faxed through to my lawyer as soon as we got a version we agree on. Right?'

The man looked exhausted. 'I am not a policeman. But naturally I will do my best.'

106

12

Pleasant Professions

The big crumpled man reappeared in the doorway. He asked her to go with him. She followed him through the pass-door, down a shabby corridor. She assumed he was taking her to Bright. But when he took her into the office there was no one there but the tall gendarme, and his small plump assistant.

'*Sit down please*,' the tall one said, in French.

Jude sat.

'*You speak French!*' he accused her, as though she had tried to conceal this.

'*Only a very little.*'

'Do you wish that I should translate?' the crumpled man asked her.

'Thanks. Yes. Can they tell me what all this is about?'

He put this to them and got a curt response. 'They say they will decide what to tell you and when. You will please answer.'

'I am a British citizen. I need to speak to a lawyer. That would be my right in England. I don't know what my rights are here, but as I have no access to a lawyer at the moment I'd like to call the British consul. Or somebody.' Jude had been practising during her long wait.

A discussion ensued. She caught a few words. The tall cop then turned on her. His voice rose an octave: '*If you are innocent you should have no objection to answering a few questions, you are not under arrest after all.*'

She refused to be cowed. '*Innocent of what?*' she said. She spoke to the interpreter. 'Can't they see how stupid this is? I don't even know what's happened. I don't know why they're holding my – John. I'm not going to say anything. I'm sure—' Her voice was rising too. She stopped, and started again. 'I'm sure that's the right thing for me to do, in the circumstances.' Fear must not get the better of her; it had to be safer to say nothing.

The door opened. The hard man came in. The gendarmes got into a huddle with him. She couldn't catch a word. She wasn't meant to. This was for French ears only. At last the translator turned to her. But he said nothing.

The hard man leaned on a desk, folded his arms and fixed her with his eyes. They were not nice eyes. The two gendarmes also fixed their darkling gaze on her. The hard man spoke. 'There has been A death. The young wom-AN – the fiancée – of the propri-ET-or of the Hôtel Sanglier. She is dead.'

Jude felt pins and needles, to the crown of her head, to the ends of her hair, to her finger and toes. Mariela? The vibrant girl? With her love of films and her romantic dreams and her determination to get married to impress her mother? The flirt. The cause of lust and hot desire that filled the air like a sharp odour, like a heat haze, creating a micro-climate pulsating with disaster. They had joked this morning about how she wouldn't get up till noon. Had she been dead then? While they were having breakfast under her bedroom? Jude said, 'Mariela?' And then she said, 'When? When?'

'Why do you ask *When*?'

Jude said, 'Because she was talking to us last night. Because we didn't see her this morning at breakfast and . . .' She shook her head from side to side. She had already forgotten her decision not to speak. *Get your cool back. Get control.* She had been jealous of the girl. She shivered. She wasn't jealous now. She said, 'How did she— how did it happen?'

The hard man gave a brusque shake of his head meaning that it was none of her business.

'Do they suspect foul play?'

The hard man looked mystified and it occurred to her what an odd expression this was, medieval perhaps? She amended it to, 'unlawful killing.'

'Why should you think this?'

'Because it appears to be a police matter. You have been questioning my friend Mr Bright for more than two hours.'

Her mind was back in harness, galloping. They had taken Bright somewhere. To see the body? Where else would they have taken him? They suspected him of killing her? Surely not. That wasn't possible. What motive could they impute to him? He'd met her for a few minutes over dinner. Her racing mind hit a jump and pulled up short. *Oh God. He went out last night. I was jealous because I thought he had made an assignation with her, gone out to meet her. But I was mad. Wasn't I? He convinced me I was mad. He convinced me. Don't let these policeman see what's going through my mind. Please.* Her thoughts scudded across her face. She knew this but hoped her loyalty to Bright would hide her dread. *I know I was mad last night. An idiot. He convinced me because he was telling the truth. He couldn't have convinced me any other way. But why has it happened now, this death? Why last night? Why when we were here?* 'Why are you questioning him?' she said. *Do they know he's a policeman? He might not have told them. I mustn't speak out of turn.* She said, 'Surely you don't suspect him?'

The hard man said, 'Do you know where was Mis-TER Bright yes-TER-day night?'

'With me, of course, at the hotel.'

'The whole of the night?'

The question she dreaded. Why had she not kept her mouth shut completely? It would look so bad now, if she refused to answer. But she had to refuse. There wasn't time to give thought to this. 'I have said, I will answer no questions. I want to call the British consul. Do you have the right to keep me, or John, here and question us without legal representation? The idea that we could be involved in some way is simply silly. We didn't know this poor girl. We arrived yesterday to spend one night. We didn't even mean to stay, we're on our way down to Provence, but John – we – wanted to have another look at Château-les-Mînes and the hotel had a room so . . .' Every innocent thing she said – that it was John, for instance, who'd wanted to stay – held the taint of guilt. But that was before he'd even seen Mariela. Wasn't it? She said now to the translator, 'Look, I have nothing to hide. And John has nothing to hide. We're innocent tourists who've got caught up in something that's obviously nothing to do with us. It isn't fair to expect me to say anything, when it seems they want to accuse us. But I'm going to say this: I didn't hear or see anything suspicious last night. She drove off from the hotel on the pillion of a boy's motorbike. Some other boys went along.' She remembered now the nice boy who had waited on them. He had been disappointed that Mariela had gone, perhaps breaking an assignation with him, and he had raced off after the others. It was not her place to reveal this, and she didn't. 'Other people must have told you this. There were several people still in the bar at the time. That's the last I saw of her. She didn't serve us breakfast this morning. We thought she must have overslept after her late night. We checked out of the hotel and went up to Château-les-Mînes. That's it. *C'est tout*. We're tourists. We're on holiday. That's all.'

The hard man smiled down at her while she said all this. 'What is his *métier*, your— *copain*?'

'I told you – I will answer no questions.'

'He has said he is a DE-tective IN-spector. This IS true?'

She thought fast. There was no way they could know this, if Bright hadn't told them. Was there? If he'd told them, there was no reason for her not to speak. She asked the translator quick and low: has he told them? He said yes before the hard man could stop him. 'Yes, he is,' she said. 'With the Metropolitan Police. Haven't you phoned or faxed to verify? Why not? Surely you can verify such a simple fact?'

'Are you a police also?'

She smiled for the first time in some hours. 'No. I'm a gardener.'

'Ah. A pleasant profession.' The smile he attached to this remark was particularly unpleasant.

'He's a detective inspector with the Criminal Investigation Department of the Metropolitan Police. He has several commendations for his handling of cases. His last big case was connected with an international crime syndicate. He put one of the biggest London gangland bosses in prison. No one had ever succeeded in bringing a case against this man before, because witnesses were always killed before they could testify. I know there were accounts in the foreign press. Didn't you read about it? The man in charge of that investigation was John.'

The crumpled man translated. The eyes of the plump gendarme bulged: he had read newspaper accounts, it was obvious, of this classic case, in the course of which, Bright had disclosed police corruption at high rank and put himself in considerable personal danger of losing not just his career but even his life. Plump Cop turned his round eyes on his master.

His master's face remained impassive, giving no clue to his thoughts. His arms remained folded across his chest. His mouth held on tight to its sour expression. Of course, Jude realised, Bright's battle against police corruption might not endear him to policemen here any more than it did to many at home. Loyalty was the watchword. You did not shop fellow officers no matter what evil they perpetrated on the world and on their own organisation. But in this case, the corruption had been so disgusting that Bright had not suffered too much backlash, especially from the rank and file. He had kept out of the case a lower-ranking officer who'd had a hard choice to make. This was widely known in the police ranks, and had given Bright a name for fairness. However, the facts, as always, had been carefully selected for public consumption. Bright's clemency in the matter might not be generally known.

'Yes, it was reported here.' The hard man was not impressed. 'He betrayed fellow police officers, I believe.'

'He put justice first,' Jude said.

He ignored her. 'You will stay please in Neufchâtel until the examining magistrate is appointed. He will decide whether you may depart.'

'Where shall we stay?' she asked the translator. ' Is there really no other hotel?'

'You could stay in my house?'

'We don't know you. And if you're connected with the case—'

'No, no! I am a teacher of English. I am director of the *lycée* here. I was simply called in to interpret, that's all. I will be happy if you will accept my hospitality. It will be only for one night perhaps. The examining magistrate will commence his enquiries tomorrow. He will not detain the two of you longer than is necessary. It would not be polite.'

'Thank you. It's kind of you. I'll see what John thinks. Will they release him now?'

A knock interrupted his translation. A young gendarme opened the door and handed a fax to the hard man. He read it at arm's length, perhaps more to do with his eyesight than distaste for the message. He handed it to the tall gendarme who read it slowly, and read it again. The hard man's mouth set in a harder line. He snarled at the interpreter, '*Venez!*' and marched out of the room.

The door slammed open, and almost slammed shut on Breton. Rat-face strode to the desk and played with files and interview forms. He did this for some time. Then he looked up and, surprise, surprise, there was John Bright, still sitting in his office. 'You may DE-part.' He squeezed the words out between his small teeth and immersed himself again in his paperwork.

'Why?' Bright said, leaning back in his chair.

'The Metropolitan Police have verified your identity.'

'How do they know I'm not someone else impersonating me?'

That got his attention – for a second or two. 'We have faxed to them your card of identity with photo.'

'Who did you speak to?'

'Your Madame Superintendent at your headquarter.'

Breton held the door open. Bright stood up. His legs felt weak and stiff as though he'd been sitting for weeks.

'But you will please stay in Neufchâtel tonight.'

'Oh yeah? Like where for instance? The Wild Boar Hotel?'

Breton repeated his offer of a bed for the night. Bright hesitated. Breton said, 'Your – Jude – has accepted.'

'So do I then. Thanks, mate. Okay with you? Officer?'

'L'addresse, s'il vous plaît?'

Breton started to reply but the keyboard cop didn't need to be told; he'd already typed it out. Rat-face gave Breton a sideways look.

'Where's my car?' Bright said.

'It will be returned to you. Perhaps tomorrow.'

'PER-haps TO-morrow? ThankYOU. Off-IC-er.'

Rat-face suspected the piss was being taken but couldn't put his finger on precisely how. He ignored them as they left the room. Well, he was a busy man.

Through open doors, in offices down the corridor, Bright saw first one, then another, of the motorbike boys, hunched at the side of a gendarme's desk. No sign of their being let go. Ten minutes later he was out in the forecourt. And Jude was waiting in the sun. She came to him but didn't hug him.

He knew why: the force-field around him crackled with complicated reactions. For the moment he was forbidden territory. To her. To anyone.

Breton scratched his head and leaned sideways, like Jacques Tati. 'I do not either have my car. We will walk? It's okay? It is not a long distance, just . . .' He made a vague gesture in the direction of the railway station. They followed him out of the narrow gate to – temporary – freedom. The ground under Bright's feet rocked as though he'd been twelve hours on a boat.

13

Teacher's Pets

'They have released you because you are a policeman?'

'They released me because they've got no evidence against me.'

'But also because you are a policeman, I think.'

'Right. Adjutant Rat-face could find himself in deep sh— in big trouble.'

'You can become an international incident.'

'They took hours to verify your identification,' Jude said. 'How could it take so long?'

'Perhaps one or two of my superior officers were having a bit of a laugh?'

'That's a comforting thought.'

'No means out the question: "Who? John Bright? No, mate, never heard of him. Guy's obviously an imposter." No one'd ever know.'

'You could be languishing in the Bastille for years.'

'The prisoner in the iron mask,' Breton said.

'Those motorbike lads were still there, just sitting by the gendarmes' desks.'

'Yes, I have seen them.'

'Not letting *them* go, are they?'

Jude said, 'They were the last to see Mariela, I suppose.'

'Well, that's the Big If, isn't it?'

'What do you mean?'

'Well, if they weren't the last to see her, then somebody else was.'

'Oh.' Jude looked appalled. 'I hadn't thought.'

'Hey, mate?'

Breton peered round Jude to look at Bright. 'Yes?'

'The blond lad – served us at the hotel last night – he went off after the other kids on his bike, maybe quarter of an hour after? I didn't see him round the old johndarmerie. His parents got influence or what?'

They were at the main road. Breton held them back for a car at the level-crossing, then led them over. He still had not replied.

'Well?' Bright didn't let it drop. 'Why wouldn't they be questioning him, the blond lad?'

Breton took his time answering. 'This boy is not yet found, I believe.'

'Jesus.' Bright and Jude turned slowly to each other.

Breton turned off the main road into a lane. 'My house is this way. Not far.'

This was the way the police had driven him to the crime scene. Breton lived down here? He made no reference to this, and nor did Bright. 'That blond kid. They think he's another victim or what?'

Breton looked sick. 'Who knows? They are searching for him. They question the other boys. Nobody has seen him.'

'You know him, do you?'

'I know all of them, of course.'

He's their teacher,' Jude said.

A teacher? It fell into place – the deference of the gendarmes, the way they trusted him: Breton was Authority of the first order. The one authority figure you never got out from under. But they all seemed to like him. Bright had never in his school-days in South Norwood met a teacher he liked. The concept was outside his experience.

Just before the bend in the lane and the bridge over the river, Breton pushed open a big iron gate between high walls. The house was a four-square detached stone building, the garden a shady enclave: long grass, wild flowers already showing, clumps of iris in bud, Jude noted,

116

one or two dark purple ones, the earliest, already in flower.

Breton went up three steps and opened his front door. 'It's not locked?' Bright said.

'No. I do not lock my door.'

'As a cop I gotta advise you that's not a good idea.'

'In this village it is not necessary.'

'In this village a girl has just been murdered.'

'Anything of mine, anybody who wants it may have it.'

'That include your life?'

Breton didn't answer, just gave a slight smile. In an English house such as this, the stairs would go straight up out of the hallway. Here there were no stairs, just three doors, one to the left, one to the right, one at the back. The floor was terracotta tiles, faded to a dusty pale pink, the walls the colour of parchment, the plaster rough and pitted. Some coats hung on a peg-rail as old as the house, opposite an iron table with a lamp and some junk mail. A painting of a woman in Edwardian dress hung over the table, a pure stern beauty with severe eyes. 'Who's that?' Bright said.

'Ah. My – grand-grandmother? My mother's grand-mother.'

Breton opened the door on the right to a dining room: a long table, four rush-seated chairs, Boule cabinets in the alcoves, dark paintings above of rural scenes, a musty damp smell, in spite of the Godin stove that glowed dimly and the lamp that hung over the table on an elaborate pulley and chains. Its curving copper curlicues held a white glass bowl surrounded by four smaller bowls, each with a bulb of feeble wattage.

'Please, sit.' Breton made one of his vague sloping gestures, then left the room by double doors at the back.

Jude and Bright sat side by side, clasping hands in the grimy light. 'Think he's gone for his cane to give us forty whacks?' Bright whispered.

'He's not that kind of teacher.'

117

'How do you know?'

'I can tell.'

'Oh, can you? Think anyone else lives here?'

'I don't hear the patter of tiny feet. Do you?'

'Not exactly lively, is it?'

'It's better than the gendarmerie, John.'

'You reckon? It gives me the creeps.'

'It's so kind of him to take us in.'

He's keeping an eye on us. He knows all the johndarmes here. He was their teacher. They trust him. Why d'you think they let him bring us here?'

'Even if that's a joke it's in bad taste.' Jude pulled her hand out of his.

Bright had no time to reply. Breton came back with a bottle. 'Our *vin jaune*,' he said. 'The pride of the Jura.' The evil yellow brew they had drunk on their first night.

Inwardly groaning, they smiled as he poured the precious gold liquid into little thick glasses. He took one sip with them. 'I must attend to my kitchen,' he said. 'Please help yourselves to the wine.'

They sipped. It didn't taste as bad as their first time. Jude said in a stiff way, 'Where did they take you, the police?'

'To view the body.'

'Where?'

'Edge of the river. Just down the lane here.'

'What did you think?'

'Looks like a sex crime but you never know.'

'Oh poor girl. Poor girl.'

'A-ha. Did Cato call back?'

Jude blinked at this callous dismissal. 'No. Nor Ted Adams.'

'Christ.' Bright took out his mobile.

'Kate did, though. She said Ted and Maggie have gone away for a week.'

'Great. Hope they're having a better time than we are.'

Jude still looked stricken but he had to get some advice. He took the phone outside.

Cato's wife answered. 'He's out on a surveillance, John. They've been on it three nights. He hasn't been getting in till after eight in the mornings. That's nine where you are, isn't it?' She was a Geordie like Cato. Her voice comforted him though her news could not. 'Couldn't they get him on the radio for you?'

'No, it's okay. He can give me a buzz when he gets in. If he's still awake. Don't bother him. Just a detail. Thanks, love.'

He tried Ted Adams, just in case. The answering machine said he was away but his partner would deal with anything urgent. No partners, thanks. Not for this. Not yet anyway. He went back into the house.

'Couldn't raise anyone,' he said.

Jude said nothing and didn't look at him. Bright felt ill. He needed to talk to her about serious stuff and he couldn't do that here. His nerves were shot to hell by today's events. He couldn't control his reactions, couldn't get the tone right. He needed Jude to be kind to him, not treat him like something that had crawled from under a stone. At last he poured another glass of the *vin jaune*. 'Doesn't taste so bad today.'

She nodded but still said nothing.

'Maybe we acquired the taste after all,' he said.

'Or maybe it's just a better example than the one we had at that strangely Tyrolean establishment in Poligny.' She spoke in a making-conversation voice. But she was speaking; that was something.

Breton took knives and forks and napkins out of the sideboard drawer. The napkins were thick white linen elaborately embroidered, the knives and forks solid silver with ivory handles. In the middle of the table he placed a heavy silver cruet. He disappeared again to the nether regions.

'And this guy doesn't lock his door?' Bright whispered.

'It's all been in his family for generations, I suppose.'

'What you've always had you don't value? You believe that?'

'Maybe he's religious. Unattached to worldly goods.'

'He's some sort of a nutter all right. But he's a generous nutter.' Bright leaned forward. 'I don't think he's a police snout, Jude, honest I don't.'

Her mouth tucked in at the corners. She flicked her eyes at him.

'Jude,' he said.

They clasped hands again.

Breton came back bringing another bottle from which he was wiping dust with a damp cloth. He took the corkscrew, the old fashioned kind, wooden handle, spiral bodkin, from the sideboard drawer, and lovingly coaxed out the cork. He put the bottle on the table, and from the Boule cabinet he took three stemmed rummers, thick glass with faults in it, short heavy stems.

He did all this without speaking, with a dutiful reverence for the ritual. Jude and Bright were kept silent by his silence, and by their precarious truce, by gnawing hunger brought on by the kitchen smells. And by a sudden sense of bitter exhaustion and dread.

The schoolmaster came and went, bringing bread in a silver basket, a carafe of water, painted plates, chipped and cracked but probably eighteenth century. Then he brought in a big iron pot. He lifted the lid and ladled out platefuls of a thick, rich, dark stew. He poured the wine. Bright stuck his nose in the glass. A deep, complex, mellow, heady smell. He sipped. 'Bloody hell. I thought I wouldn't be able to tell the difference. But I never tasted anything like this before.'

Breton sat down and handed round the bread. '*Bon appétit.*'

The flavour of the stew was as rich and dark as its colour. Jude said, 'Mmmm . . .'

Bright said, 'Aw-wuaugh.'

No one spoke or looked up for a while. Then Jude said, 'What meat is it?'

'Venison.'

'It's incredible.'

'Hunting is a big activity in this region. Almost every man hunts.'

'You kill this yourself?' Bright said.

'No. I am a pacifist where animals are concerned. But not fish. I am the enemy of fish. In that I catch and eat them.'

'Why make an exception of fish?'

'I don't know. They are cold-blooded? They have no expression in their eyes? An animal – a mammal – can look at one more expressively than a human being.'

Bright said, 'You don't like killing it but don't mind eating it.'

'Evidently, yes. And you?'

'Same here. Not big on killing things.'

'I shot my dog. Last year.'

Bright and Jude both looked at him.

'He was too old, too sick.' The schoolmaster dabbed his mouth with his napkin. His eyes were full of tears. 'He knew what I was about to do to him. He accepted. He forgave me. Forgave. I could see in his eyes. He is buried in my garden. I planted a new iris over him.' He smiled. 'It is not doing well.'

Jude said, 'Irises don't like a rich soil. Oh God, I'm sorry—'

But the schoolmaster smiled with more conviction. 'Of course. You are a gardener.'

'I notice you like irises.'

'Yes. My mother was growing them, some pure white and some lilac blue, when I was a small boy. She wore dresses of the same colours. In my mind, my child's mind, I have associated the two, in a Proustian sense, perhaps.'

121

'Great stew,' Bright said. 'You cook it yourself?'

'Oh. Yes.' The schoolmaster sipped his wine and lowered his head.

Bright's interruption had sounded, had indeed been, brutal. Why had he cut off the man's tender remembrance of things past? Jude felt cheated, as well as shocked. She wanted to pursue Breton's irises, and his mother. Was he gay, she wondered, living alone, cooking well, doing things so *comme il faut*, loving flowers, disliking hunting? What a lot of sexual stereotypes she was listing. She blushed to find herself capable of such a bundle of clichés.

'You knew Mariela?' Bright said.

The man's face drooped as though a stiffening substance had been removed from beneath the skin. 'I hoped to divert us from this subject.'

'Can't be done.'

'No . . . Yes, I knew her, of course. We are a small place. The bar of the Sanglier is where one meets everyone. She has been an enormous shake-up in our town. We have seen no one like her here before. Here one is correct in public. We live our lives behind closed doors. Our public life, social life, is calm, polite. Naturally sometimes two men will quarrel. And these quarrels can last a lifetime. Here we have known one another since schooldays and before. Our histories are . . .' He made a complicated knotting motion of his fingers . . .'

'Intertwined?' Jude offered.

'Yes. Intertwined.'

'You know anything about her? Apart from the stuff she told us last night?'

'What has she told you?'

'He found her in Mauritius, promised her the earth, brought her back to marry her but his family say no, so she's stuck, he gives her no money, so she can't leave, and she won't leave anyway till he marries her. That about right?'

'Yes. Of course we all know this story. She tells everyone. It is bad for Louis because, as I say, we live privately, we pretend at least that our neighbours do not know our intimate secrets. Louis was a popular man in the town. Now he is not on a good term with many who were his friends. They become his enemies. And with his family, it is difficult. She has made a big storm in our little teacup. Oh yes.'

'What did you feel about her?'

'Like every man, including, I imagine, yourself.'

A quick frank glance flashed between Bright and Jude. She remembered afresh that he had gone out last night. He remembered how mad with jealousy she had become. The glance said, *we have things to talk about but not now*. The schoolmaster, catching the glance, said, 'I apologise. Such things should not be said in the presence of ladies.'

'I'm no lady,' Jude said. 'She was flirting even with me. It was her natural way. Her way of getting through life. Making life work for her.'

'It has worked against her now.'

Bright said, 'You know all the people round here. You got any ideas about this killing?'

'I do not think it is intentional.'

'Oh yeah? Why's that?'

'Why do I think this? Because of the way she— the way the body—' He turned to Jude again, then looked at his hands on the table. He lowered his voice. 'It appeared to be a— sex play of some kind, no?'

'Maybe. But we don't know yet whether she was trussed up like that before she died or after, do we?'

'Ah. No . . . I had not thought . . . . No.'

'And who was she having sex games with? There must be some gossip, little place like this?'

'I have not heard any.'

'You must've.'

'I am afraid not. Being the prof, you know, I am not taken

123

into their secrets. I am a little outside, a little isolated.'

'Like a parson.'

'Like the priest, yes.'

'They tell you what they think you wanna hear.'

'That is precisely what they do.'

'No one ever use you as a confessional then?'

'No. They have the priest for confession.'

'What, even now? Twenty first century and all that? Age of disbelief.'

'Here, most people pay lip service to the Church. At least Christmas and Easter, weddings and – funerals, yes. They may not believe but they—'

'Hedge their bets. Right.'

'It is not as secular a society as in England. Not in rural France. Not yet. The Catholic Church has a stronger hold here, I think, than the Anglican has in England.'

'That wouldn't be hard. So if someone had something to tell, they wouldn't tell you, they'd tell the priest.'

'They would not tell me.'

'And yet you seem to me just the sort of bloke that people would tell things to.'

'No.' He shook his head with a sad smile. 'No. Even when I was a boy they did not confide in me. I was outside their secrets.'

'Why was that?'

'I don't know. My mother did not permit me to play with the other boys outside school times. She did not invite them. My parents were older than the general age of parents. This house was a mysterious place for the boys. They have climbed in to steal apples from the orchard and my parents would chase them away. So, you see . . .'

'Yeah . . .' Bright did see. Poor sod. Nothing worse. And clever too, cleverer than the others. That wouldn't endear him either. 'So you haven't heard any talk? You know. Gossip. About weird sexual practices for instance?'

'I never heard anything. As I have said, I am the school-master. I have taught many of the people here. Almost all. They like me well enough. But they never quite completely forget their old relationship to me.'

'Must be lonely,' Jude said.

Again Bright flashed her a glance. She saw it but ignored it. Her childlike eyes turned their compassionate gaze on the teacher.

He shrugged and poured out the last of the bottle. 'I work too much. I do not have time to be conscious of my solitude.'

Before Bright could shoot in another question, she said, 'You speak such beautiful English.'

'It has been my lifelong study. My passion, from when I was a boy.'

'How did it begin? Your passion.'

'The English language is rich in nonsense, nursery rhymes. My mother taught me nursery rhymes.'

If Bright wanted to know about flirting he was getting an eyeful now. Jude's flirting was an example to all women. It didn't look like flirting at all. Her voice lowered a bit, she gave her whole attention, turned just a little, physically, towards the guy, opened the amazing innocent eyes and fixed them on his face. No smiles or simpering or wriggling, so straightforward, the impression was of nakedness, which came into the man's thoughts unbidden. And the man felt bad, undressing her like that, a woman so honest, so good, so intelligent, so sympathetic. He recalled his first sight of her in Kentish Town police HQ. He had got locked into her eyes and had undressed her at first sight. He allowed his thoughts no further down that road. The teacher was still going on about his mother teaching him nursery rhymes.

'See saw Marjorie Daw, Johnny shall have a new master. He shall have but a penny a day Because he can't work any faster. Such a mysterious story. What is Marjorie Daw? As a child I was thinking, *March to the door*? Such a sad story: a man who is slow, losing his job, pushed out of doors? I pondered very much about such matters.'

'It's true – nursery rhymes are mysterious.'

'Bloody good stuff,' Bright had drained his glass. He now picked up the bottle and studied the label. 'Christ, this is twenty years old. You bought it twenty years ago?'

The schoolmaster gave his slight smile. 'Not I. I think, my father. Just before he died.'

'Where's it been since then? You got an actual wine cellar?'

'The *cave*, yes, of course. Every French country dwelling has a *cave*.'

'I wouldn't mind a gander at that. I've never seen an actual wine cellar before.'

'A gander?'

'Goosey goosey gander, where shall I wander? Upstairs, downstairs and in my lady's chamber.' Bright said this with his smile that was no smile.

Breton was mystified.

Jude said, 'It's slang for a look. That's all.'

'Another mysterious rhyme.'

'A friend of ours, an actress,' Jude said. 'She says, in the English language, if you can't understand what it means it's bound to be something dirty.'

'Oh.' Breton's face reddened. 'Yes.' He gave a self-conscious laugh. 'This is certainly true in the case of Shakespeare.'

'Is that right?' Bright said. 'No one told me that at school. I might have taken more notice.'

'The naughty hand of the dial is now upon the prick of noon, for example.'

'A-ha? What's that?'

'*Romeo and Juliet*. When the boys are teasing the nurse.'

'You got me there. You know your Shakespeare a damn sight better than I know mine. I should have had a schoolmaster like you.'

126

Jude smiled. 'Yes. You must be very good at your job.'

'Can I have a gander at your wine cellar then?'

'Ah, tomorrow perhaps. There is no light in there. In the dark a torch is necessary and you would not – gander – well. If you don't mind?'

'Aw, come on, let's have a look now. I'd get the general impression.'

Breton shifted, awkward, uneasy.

Jude felt sorry for him. She looked at Bright – why was he insisting like this? And caught a fleet, squinting glance. Warning her? Inviting her complicity? Her complicity in what? And with a shock she understood. *Of course! He's working! He's working this man like a suspect. Working him over. Questioning him. Investigating him. This man who has helped us. Who has invited us into his house. Given us hospitality. How can he do that? He's a cop, always a cop, a cop through and through. Suspicion runs in his veins like blood.* She hated him with a fierce burning hatred that took her breath away. Her eyes swept across his and back to the teacher. She said, 'It's late. You've been wonderful to us today. I don't know what we'd have done without you. You've given us a delicious meal, exquisite wine. I, for one, am exhausted, I can't keep my eyes open another minute. Would you mind if I went to bed?'

'Of course. I will show you the room, the *chambre d'amis.*'

Bright lowered his eyes. Refused to look at Jude. Refused to stand when she did. Went on sitting at the table, drawing circles with his knife on the cloth.

'John? Are you coming?'

'No. I'm gonna help his nibs here with the washing-up.'

'It is not necessary—'

'Come on, mate. You've done enough for us. 'Bout time we did something for you. A bit of washing-up ain't much, but it's all I can come up with at the minute.'

'Please—'

But Bright was on his feet, collecting up the plates, piling them deftly. 'Just point me at the kitchen.' Without waiting, he was through the double doors at the back of the room. 'Okay,' he called, 'I got it!'

The teacher hesitated, not knowing which way to move. Jude liked his old-fashioned courtesy, and his gaucheness, engendered perhaps by too much solitude. She smiled at him. 'Leave him to it,' she said. 'He likes domestic tasks. He'll be happy doing it.' She was nettled by Bright's behaviour but hoped not to show it.

Breton too seemed put out, but he smiled also. He leaned and held out an arm in one of his Tati gestures to lead her through the double doors into a smaller room with cane furniture, low bookshelves and a big desk piled with papers.

'Ah, this is the room you use for every day.'

'Yes. My mother was calling it "the morning room", in English, you know. But I eat my meals here, work here, everything.'

'Your personality is in here.'

'Yes. The rest of the house belongs to my – antecedents.'

She felt comfortable in this room, reluctant to follow him into the passage where a stone staircase with fine iron banisters curved up to the floor above. Beyond, she saw Bright in the kitchen, a dimly lit, narrow space, barely changed, it seemed, in two centuries. Bright was running water. He didn't glance their way as the teacher preceded her up the stairs.

14

The Ring of Truth

Bright waited till he heard the floorboards creak upstairs. He left the sink and, alert for any sign of the teacher coming down again, crept to the door under the stairs. He lifted the iron latch and pushed. An open-tread rough wood staircase descended into the dark. A torch hung on a nail. He lifted it off and listened again. Voices. They'd be having a cosy chat about irises or nursery rhymes. Could go on for some time. He hoped. He stepped into the darkness.

The torchbeam showed rough stone walls, an earth floor below. The wooden treads were narrow and too close together; he went down sideways. At the bottom, along the wall, was a wooden manger that horses must once have eaten from. Opposite, a work-bench, with a vice and other tools. Saws, four or five of them, and hammers of various shapes and sizes, hung on the wall near a stone arch. Next to him, at the foot of the stairs, a closed door.

He heard a sound. A creak? The rustle of movement? Where had it come from? The other side of this door? Outside? Or above? He stopped still, listening. Nothing. He felt unnerved. *Come on, pull yourself together, either his nibs is still upstairs getting chatted up by Jude, or he's down and you'll just have to face it out.* He dragged his concentration back and put his ear to this door. He heard nothing. But what if the sound he'd heard had come from there? He didn't have much time.

The knob, a smooth cold oval, turned with a slight rattle, loose. He pushed; the door didn't move. It was locked. He stooped and shone the torch at the keyhole. The beam went right through. There was no key on the other side. He heard another sound. This time he was certain it came from above.

He took the stairs two at a time, hand and foot, ladder-mode, and hung the torch back on its nail. He pushed the door open. There was no one in the kitchen. He latched it quietly and sped back to his washing-up. The teacher came down from upstairs and stood behind him, leaning at an angle and rubbing his head. He wanted to ask Bright something? Tell him something? Bright waited but nothing came, so he said, 'Listen, mate, what's gonna happen tomorrow?'

'I don't know. I think the examining magistrate may come?'

'Come from where?'

'Perhaps from Dole. Dole is our local capital. Capital of the Franche-Comté. However, Dole is just a sous-préfecture. The préfecture is at Lons-le-Saunier.'

'What's that mean?'

'Perhaps they will send a magistrate from Lons-le-Saunier, I do not know.'

'And this magistrate, what powers does he have?'

'He examines the case. He – I believe – decides how the case will proceed.'

'He's the organ-grinder, the local cops are the monkeys, right?'

'I'm sorry? Oh – yes, I see. They are – at his disposal, yes.'

'How do they like that?'

'It is the custom, I suppose. It is normal for them.'

'So who's this guy who was in charge today? He's not a normal johndarme, is he?'

'Ah, no. He is an officer of the *brigade de recherches*.'

'This brigard thing – that's like the CID, right?'

'I apologise, I am a little ignorant of these matters.'

'Not half as much as I am. Anyway, in a case that looks

130

like a suspicious death this magistrate is automatically called in?'

'I believe so.'

'And he's part of the judiciary or part of the police?'

'Of the judiciary. He is the *juge d'instruction*. Examining magistrate is the closest translation.'

'Why don't they have local johndarmes to investigate serious crime?'

'Again, I do not know. I have never asked myself these questions.'

'Well, you've never had to up to now, have you, mate?'

'I came down to say to you – the police will telephone here, this house, tomorrow morning. They wish you to remain here until that time.'

'What time do you reckon?'

'I think this may depend on where the examining magistrate is coming from. What distance he must travel.'

'We're an hour later than England, right? I'm wondering if I'll get time to phone my superintendent before the circus starts.'

'I hope so.' Breton seemed anxious now for the conversation to be over. 'Is there something that you require for the night?'

'Er – glass of water?'

'But certainly. Help yourself please.'

Bright took a glass from the plate rack over the sink and filled it at the tap. The teacher told him the guest room was at the top of the stairs, the bathroom over the front door, then shook his hand. 'Good night. Sleep well.'

The stairs turned once and then again. The doorway facing him showed a vertical crack of light. There was Jude, fast asleep, being devoured by a bulbous duvet, her red curls all spilling over the big square pillow. His breath caught in his throat. Things couldn't be that bad while he had Jude. Could they?

He found the bathroom. The john was a hundred years old, chipped white china with pink flowers on it. Nice. The teacher was still downstairs, he could see a light and hear small movements. He wanted to know more about the guy but couldn't go down there again. He wished he hadn't got himself a glass of water before coming up. He went back to the guest-room.

He stood watching over Jude for a minute. Then he pulled off his clothes and slid in beside her. He felt her warmth but didn't snuggle up to her. He didn't want to wake her with his chill. She snored quite lightly, like a cat purring, he had discovered that. He lay and listened. He heard the teacher creak up the stairs, along the landing, open a door, silence for a while, another door, sounds of running water, the rattle of a closing door. Silence again. The usual creaks and cracks of a house settling on its haunches for the night, that was all.

He was in trouble. He told himself it was not serious. It couldn't be. In the morning it would be cleared up. But being a policeman was no defence against suspicion. He knew only too well that cops commit crimes too, worse crimes – or better, depending on your point of view – because they know how. He also knew how the average police mind works: find a likely culprit, put all your energies into amassing evidence against him, ignore evidence in his favour, ignore evidence against other suspects, ignore lack of motive, even. Lack of motive was no barrier to his becoming the prime suspect here.

Look at it from their point of view, the coppers here. For them he's perfect. God's gift. He's seen talking with the victim, and a few hours later she's dead. Why does it happen the night he comes to town? He checks out of the hotel next morning. Could have been gone, far away by the afternoon, if the gendarmes hadn't chased him down. And – his throat closed with sudden panic – he had gone out, alone, last night. As yet, no one knew this. Except Jude. Had she mentioned it to anyone? He had to ask her, warn her— He almost shook her to wake her up. But shame curled him into a foetal ball, facing away from her. Sweat broke out all over his skin, coating him. He threw off the duvet, hugging his knees to his chest, staring into the dark. He was seriously going to ask Jude to conceal a fact from the police to protect him? He was going to ask Jude to lie? No. Just to keep stumm. But he had to find out what they had asked and what she had said. He needed to talk to her. But couldn't wake her. And couldn't sleep, sleeplessness a major feature of this holiday, rarely experienced at home.

He clung to the edge of the bed to avoid rolling into the central valley. It was no good. He swung his feet out and levered himself off the edge, wincing at the bounce and twang of the springs. Jude stirred but turned over, her breathing hardly changed, insomnia not a problem for her.

You couldn't even look out of a window without opening the shutters, a major operation, having to open the windows first, those French window-locking devices, a vertical bar operated by the handle, fixing both windows in place. Efficient but noisy. A swarm of buzzing insects in his head, in his limbs. Perhaps he'd visit the john again. Somewhere to go. Something to do. At least he could put a light on there, better than sitting staring into the stifling black fur of darkness in here. He opened the door with caution. The handle rattled like all the handles in this house, but he was good at silent entrances and exits. He waited, half hoping Jude might wake of her own accord. She didn't. He pulled the door to, but did not shut it.

The shutters were open on the landing window. The moonlight shone in like a blessing, like forgiveness, like hope. His panic was calmed by the stream of white light. Clouds would soon cover it, the clouds that were now, edged with dazzling silver, creeping towards the moon. Down in the garden cypresses pointed up like long black fingers, and fruit trees squatted here and there. Nearer the house, the vegetable beds were marked out between grass paths, with rows of tent-shaped canes, ready for beans to climb. Looked like a nice garden. Jude would like it. Lily would like it. How were Lily and George getting on? His tension loosened a little for the first time this nightmare day. George and Lily and gardens and Jude, this was the direction for his thoughts to take, the route to follow back to sleep. He turned round to go along the landing to the bathroom.

The teacher was standing watching him.

Bright was good at frights, at coping with them. It came with the job. But this was a sharp one. It cut up through him, zinging like piano wire. Heart battering, sweat pouring from his armpits, he nearly ran down the stairs, but instead put his hand on the banister and steadied himself. *Enough*.

The teacher said, 'You also can't sleep, like me.'

He looked to have just come out of his bedroom but maybe he'd been there all along? Watched Bright creep from the room and stand looking down at his garden? 'Couldn't stand the dark in there,' Bright said. 'We don't have shutters in England.'

The teacher padded along the landing. He wore his dressing-gown. Bright was in his Y-fronts and nothing else. The sudden sweat was drying and he shivered. He crossed his arms over his chest.

The teacher said, 'And in London there is always orange light and always noise.' He made Bright's paradise sound like hell.

'Too right, mate. I'm not used to this. It's weird. All this dark. And the silence. How can you stand it?'

'In London, it was I who could not sleep. Let us go down and drink something, yes?'

'Sure. Hang on.' Bright slipped inside the room, Jude still

134

purring in her mighty sleep, and grabbed the first thing to hand that felt like clothing off the arm of the chair. It was his sweatshirt and jeans. Thank Christ. Naked is not good to face the enemy. As he hopped about, getting into his jeans on the landing, he thought, Why the enemy? He's been helping me all day. He comes across as a good bloke. So why does he scare me?

Breton whispered, 'I will go down and—'

Bright put out a hand. 'No, mate. Hang on. I don't know my way around down there. Wait for me.'

'Yes, of course.'

Bright struggled into his sweatshirt, getting his head out into the open again as fast as he could. It was his guilty conscience that made him fear the guy. He'd snooped around his house, poking his nose where he had no right. He, the cop, was the enemy, not the teacher. He'd got it the wrong way round. But the uneasiness persisted. Following Breton down the turning stairs he was glad the teacher was not behind him. Or too far ahead.

In the kitchen Breton said, 'What shall you take? A tisane?'

'No, thanks, mate. A whisky if you got it.'

'I have it. But whisky will not help you to sleep.'

'No, but it'll make being awake a bit more tasty.'

'Tize-tee,' Breton murmured. 'A bit more tize-tee.'

'You taking the piss?'

'No! Of course not! I wonder – may I ask? Will you come to the school and speak to my students?'

Bright, halted at his heels, was taken aback. 'Me? What for?'

'You speak – Cockney – is that right?'

'Yup. I guess.' Bright sounded a little huffy, like any English person accused of an accent. 'South Norwood's not exactly within the sound of Bow Bells, but you got the right general area.'

135

'Yes! It would be good that they should hear this way of speaking. Do you say – streetwise?'

'Streetwise? What I used to think I was before I landed in this mess? Streetwise, yeah. Trouble is, round here, there's not much in the way of streets to be wise in, right?'

The teacher watched his lips, shrugged and smiled. The open fridge lit his face, the unlined face of a good man, a calm, quiet man, a man without much drama in his life. Why didn't Bright believe it? And how was he going to see behind that locked door in the cellar without staying up all night? He couldn't, that was the answer. Unless— 'Look,' he said. 'Seeing as how we're up anyway, you wouldn't like to show me your wine cellar now, would you? You know, pass the time?'

The teacher hesitated. 'It's late. You must be tired, no? After this troublesome day.'

'Troublesome. You're right there. But, like I said, I've never seen a real wine cellar. How about it?'

'I shall happily show you tomorrow.'

'But if the cops keep me all day tomorrow I won't get another chance.'

'But I said already to you, it will be better in the daylight.'

'It's a cellar, mate! What's the difference, day or night?'

'Ah. Here, at the rear of the house, my *cave* is not a cellar, it is at the garden level.'

'Well, whatever, I wanna see it. Won't take a sec. Eh?'

'The ice will melt.'

'What you got down there – a torture chamber?' Bright gave him a horror-movie grin.

The man stopped arguing. He slowly opened the door to the cellar and took hold of the torch. He directed the beam down the precipitous stairs. 'Be careful,' he said. 'There is no hand-rail.'

Bright thought, I must be a nutter, going down a dank cellar miles from home with a big bugger twice my size armed with a torch that in a ruck would do all right as a weapon in the middle of the night on his territory that he knows like the back of his hand *leaving my girlfriend upstairs so if anything happens to me she's alone in the house with him*. He went dry-mouthed at his own stupidity. *Irresponsible asshole that I am.* But he was here now, as usual trusting in his own ability to come out of a scrap alive. His life-threatening experience last year in Hong Kong had shaken him. He wasn't invulnerable after all. He measured the teacher for a throw. Bright's centre of gravity was lower, an advantage. He prepared himself, staying well behind as they reached the bottom of the stairs. Bright was glad he'd been down here before. At least he knew the layout.

But the teacher plodded steadily ahead across the earth floor, his shaggy head almost touching the roof beams, to the stone arch by the workbench. He circled the torch slowly around, across the soft grit floor, up the damp stone walls, over shelf after shelf of wine, brown wood shelves, floor to vaulted ceiling, filled with dusty bottles. The room smelt like toadstools, a dank dark foresty smell. Chill.

Bright whistled. 'Bugger me!'

'What?'

'Just an expression. You wouldn't want to teach it to your students, believe me. I've never seen this many bottles of wine outside a wine shop. Where they all come from?'

'These are all Jura wines. My father – laid it down, I think you say. He would buy the good wine of the year and keep it. It's normal to do this, I think, not only here but in all of France.'

'It's fantastic, mate.'

'Well, it is good for me, because I simply like to drink the wines and am not so interested on buying them.'

His English gets worse when he mentions his pa or his ma. Bright had noted this at dinner and noted it afresh. 'You like your pa?'

'I'm sorry? Am I like or do I like?'

'Take your pick.'

'I am not like. He was not a large man. He was thin but strong.' He looked at Bright and said in a surprised way, 'Like you.'

Bright raised his eyebrows. He felt uneasy under the man's gaze.

Breton went on looking, considering. Then he looked away. 'Did I like? No. I did not. He was a pedant, a pedagogue. In his opinion a child was for training. To be obedient. To be good. To be in fact what he wanted. In fact naturally I became deceitful. My mother and I, we invented our own world, we concealed our world from him. This was sad for him actually because he became alone, isolated in his own house, excluded.'

'So your ma didn't like him either?'

'He was somewhat – you say – in her power.'

'Why? Sex? Money? What?'

'Both, I imagine. She had money and he did not. This gave her power, naturally. And also he was in love with her.'

'And she wasn't, with him?'

'No. She did not like him. Because of me. Because of his severity to me.'

'So why didn't she leave? Take you and piss off?'

'Where would she go? This is her town, all she has known, her family is here since always. And that generation, good Catholics, they did not leave. Marriage was for life. They – do you say – make the best of it? They—' He gestured, out of words.

'Put a good face on it?'

'Yes! This is a marvellous expression, no? Put a good face on it. Yes. This is what my mother did. Put a good face on it.' He drew a picture in the air with the torch, painting a face with the line of light. 'Good. You have seen enough wine for now?'

'That why you never got married?' Bright said.

138

The teacher turned slowly. Bright got worried again. He'd felt easier while the guy talked about his parents, safe ground, familiar territory. Breton was still staring hard. 'It may be a reason,' he said.

'Sorry, mate. Didn't mean to poke my nose in. Just wondered—'

'But, my goodness, I am forty-five years. This is not so old. There is time to meet the right person, don't you think so?' He moved in front of Bright, headed for the stairs, and started up.

Bright stopped below, in the dark, at the locked door. 'What's in here then?' he said. As he spoke he tried the handle. It turned easily in his hand. And the door opened. The door that had been locked an hour or so ago. The shock zipped through him from head to foot. He was glad to be in the dark, unseen.

The man stood on the fourth stair a moment, then came back down. Bright stood off from the door to let him get in front with the torch. He swooped the beam over a slatted bench with clay pots and seed trays, watering cans, over bunches of onions and garlic and hanks of raffia, hanging from the beams.

Bright got his breath back. 'Jude'd like this all right.'

'Yes. It is agreeable. My garden room.'

The torch was not so necessary in here because a blade of moonlight cut the darkness in two. 'You left your outside door open,' Bright said.

'Oh. Yes.'

'That leads out to the garden, right?'

'Yes.' Breton crossed the room. Bright followed him. The teacher stood in the doorway looking out. Bright joined him. He moved out on to the stone slabs outside. Again Bright went with him.

'Big garden.'

'Yes. Almost one hectare.'

139

'You do all the work?'

'Yes. It is my pleasure, my relaxation. Sometimes my students come to help. To harvest the fruit and so on. I – I think you say – pay them in kind?'

'A-ha.' The night air was cool, almost cold. Owls called to each other, near then far. He heard a cock crowing in the distance. Funny. They were supposed to do that at dawn, weren't they? Dawn was not close yet. Funny too, now that they were in the open air, he felt no sense of danger any more. Why? He was still with the big man, who now had nasty-looking tools at his disposal and was still on his own territory. The man himself had relaxed, was that it? The air smelt good – fresh, watery, grassy, clean.

The teacher said, 'The ice will have melted, I think.' He made one of his angular gestures, guiding Bright back inside the cellar. He pulled the door inwards. It didn't creak or scrape on the stone paving outside. It moved smoothly. The teacher closed it and bolted it on the inside.

His cop's eyes now adapted to the dark, Bright sucked up the details of the garden room like an industrial Hoover. He saw nothing suspicious, nothing out of place. But he knew that something here was not as it seemed. And now that he was shut inside the house once more, his hackles rose: danger felt close again. Why?

He nipped across the room, through the inner door to the foot of the wooden stairs. The teacher hesitated, hovering near the shelf where the seed trays were. Then he turned and came through to join Bright.

Bright watched him close this inner door. Less than two hours ago it had been locked. And between Bright going to bed and coming down here again it had got itself unlocked. Somehow. By someone. By the teacher? Or who? *When I saw him on the landing upstairs, in his dressing-gown, he looked like he'd just come out of his bedroom. But what if he'd been down here and just come back up? If I'd've come out a few minutes earlier, what would I have seen? Him coming up the stairs in the dark?*

In the kitchen, in the light again, dim though it might be, Bright knew in his bones that Breton had some connection with the death of Mariela. The man might not be directly involved but he maybe knew someone who was? He knew something about it, for sure. Maybe he knew everything about it? And he wasn't saying. Why?

The teacher said, 'The ice is not melted. Not completely.' He opened a cupboard and took out a bottle of single malt. It was only a quarter full. Not enough to send Bright to sleep. Not tonight.

'Serve yourself, please.' The teacher ran water into an old battered aluminium kettle. He took a jar from another cupboard. When he unscrewed the lid a comforting sweet aroma escaped.

'What's that?'

'*Tilleul.*'

'Tea earl?'

'Lime flowers.' He put a handful of dried cream-coloured flowers and crisp glaucous leaves into a mug. 'Good for sleeping. You have not changed your mind to take a tisane instead of whisky?'

'Nh-nnh.' Bright shook his head. *No, I have not changed my mind. Not about your tease-ann. Not about you. And not about this house. You're implicated somehow, mate. This house is implicated somehow.* 'Nah,' he said. 'Thanks. I'll stick to the poison I know.'

'Poison?'

'Just an expression.'

'You will speak to my students?'

'Nah, mate.'

'But why?'

'Not cut out for it. You're a teacher, you got the gift of the gab. I can't do that.'

'"Cut out for it". "Gift of the gab". Street-wise language. You see?'

Bright's lifelong loathing of teachers rose into his throat for a moment, threatening to choke him. That was the reason he didn't trust this bloke: he was a teacher. What more reason would you need? 'Yup,' he said. 'I see. Taking the piss again.'

'But I assure you—'

'Yeah, yeah. You're not taking the piss. But that's how it feels to me. I can't stand up in front of a gang of kids so they can take the piss out of how I talk. I don't do that. I don't do lectures. Okay?'

The teacher was taken aback. 'Yes. Sure. Okay.' He made a placating gesture. 'I apologise. I did not think—'

'That's okay. It's okay. Only don't ask me again, right? Cheers. Anything else I can do for you . . .'

'No . . . No.' Disconcerted, Breton wandered to the window. Bright followed him. He did not hear that Bright had followed him because Bright did not want him to hear. He stood sipping his tisane and looking out into the garden and he jumped when Bright said, in his lulling tone, 'You know something about what happened to Mariela. You're hiding something. You're protecting someone. Aren't you, mate?'

The man's eyes met his, in a long look. Bright realised there had been no honest look from him before, the crinkly-eyed, smiling expression a trick, a spurious intimacy, a pose, an act, a teacher's way of appearing benign, getting what he wants without cracking the whip. *Cracking the whip.* Just an expression. A picture of Mariela's body trussed up, hands bound, crotch violated, came to him and made him sick.

The teacher said at last, 'You are a good policeman I am sure. But you have no jurisdiction here.'

'Either you did it or you know who did and you're protecting them.'

'This is nonsense.'

'They didn't check your alibi.'

'I do not think they know yet when she died.'

'Where were you last night between about half-ten when I last saw Mariela, and getting to the school this morning?'

'Last evening I was in the bar at the Hôtel Sanglier when you have arrived there. I ate my meal there, inside in the restaurant. I returned to the bar and stayed there until it has closed. I was there when you and Jude went to bed.'

Bright felt like a pupil whose report said "could do better". The teacher smiled. 'Yes. You did not see me. But I saw you. In a small place a new person is noticed. To you we are just a bunch of locals, not interesting enough to differentiate, indistinguishable one from another. Yes, I was in the bar, watching Mariela become drunk as she did every evening, tormenting Louis, her sad – fiancé – as you call him. Chatting to you. Chatting you up, I think it's the correct expression? As she always did with a new man. Probably causing Jude to be angry. Making trouble between you? And then driving away with the boys on the scooters. My students. And Louis wanting to follow her but he cannot leave his bar, for the reason that this is his livelihood, and because of his humiliation. This happens many nights, you know. It is normal. I stayed in the bar until perhaps eleven thirty, perhaps a little later, then I walked back here to my house.'

'On your own?'

'No, happily. I was accompanied by Jacques and Olivier Buchon who live a little farther down this road, closer actually to where Mariela was found. They came in to take a last glass with me. They frequently do so after the bar. One glass and then they have departed. I read a little then I have gone to bed. This morning I wake, I go to the school, I do my everyday tasks, then at noon the gendarmes telephone me and request that I come to the gendarmerie to speak

143

with them. They tell me what has occurred. I am shocked but of course not precisely surprised. They ask me questions, the questions you ask now, Jacques and Olivier too, separate from me, and I answer. I answer them as I answer you.'

'You're the one who told them about me and Jude?'

'Ah. All the people who were there last night will tell them about you. Of course. It is always good to blame the stranger, no? This is the reason I am happy to interpret for you, because I know it is easy to blame you.'

With his command of English and his articulate flowing speech he had diverted Bright's question into another channel as a boy will dam a stream to change its direction. This tactic itself was of the utmost interest to Bright. *A-ha, you're a good chap, a nice bloke, you speak English good, mate, and I bet you speaka da French even better, and I bet you been winding all these blokes in this town round your little finger since God knows when, but that's not what I asked you.*

Bright did not speak these thoughts. He let a silence stretch till it was taut but he did not take his eyes off Breton's face. His unfocused squinting stare disconcerted the man: at which eye should he direct his frank unassuming smile? Bright waited till the smile began to disintegrate, then he started to talk fast. 'Now listen,' he said. 'Earlier tonight when you were upstairs with Jude I went down to your cellar. Yeah, that's right. The door at the bottom there, the door to your garden room? It was locked. There was no key in the lock. And just now – an hour or so later? – we go down and the door is not locked. How do you account for that?'

The teacher's face crinkled into an embarrassed, puzzled, amused grimace. Then he laughed. His laugh was a high-pitched boom, awkward and exaggerated like his movements. 'Oh dear. When you saw me – upstairs just now – on the *palier*, the – landing – outside my bedroom – I had

144

been out. Into the garden. I am – *gêné* – embarrassed – because every night I do this. I go out, with my torch, I collect snails and put them in the snail box – you know? To feed on bran until they are cleansed sufficiently to eat? And then I – ah – piss? – on my, I think you say, compost heap? It is the best thing for the activation of the bacteria in the *mélange*. I am sorry. It is not the thing to tell a stranger who does not understand. My father has done this also, every night. It is normal, I assure you. Also, I enjoy at night to come out in my garden and – ah – absorb the aromas of the *herbes* and the leaves and all that.' He laughed again. 'I am sorry I do not have a more sinister explanation for you.' He reached into his pocket and took out an old key, black metal with a handle like a an open clover leaf.

Bright regarded him for some time, his gaze blank. 'Why was the door at the bottom of the stairs locked when I went down before?'

'But that's normal, no? To lock a house?'

'Not round here. Not for you. So you say. And if it's normal to lock a house, why wasn't it locked just now?'

'Well . . .' Breton appeared nonplussed.

'It wasn't just not locked, mate, but the outside door was open as well! What's all that about? That normal too, is it? Leaving your back door open all night?'

The man's face had dropped, bewildered.

'Well? Come on, what's your explanation? Gotta be one, hasn't there? Leaving your house open at a time like this, Mariela raped and murdered just up the road?'

Breton now appeared concentrated in thought. 'I have no explanation. I can only think that I was – do you say lost in thoughts, lost in thinking? I was thinking of Mariela and this evil affair, and also of you and Jude and of the police. And I have had a little more wine than I am accustomed to take because you have dined with me, and so I am perhaps not aware of what I am doing. That is all I can—'

145

'You do this every night, that what you're telling me? Go out, catch the snails, piss on the compost, come back, lock up. Right? Every night?'

'Yes, most nights.'

'So it's your routine. You could do it in your sleep. You go through the motions wherever your thoughts are, no matter how lost you are, how much you've had to drink. You go through the motions, mate. You do not forget to lock up.'

The teacher shrugged. 'I agree. You are right. But I did forget. Obviously I did forget. It has been a shock, this terrible incident. It is my only explanation. I have no other.'

'Well, I have another.'

'I am sure you do.'

He's treating me like a fuckin schoolboy. He's patronising me, the arrogant git. Well, let him, that suits me fine. 'Someone was in that garden room down there. Hiding out. Whoever you think killed that poor girl was in that room. Locked in. The outer door, the door to the garden, bolts on the inside. So if anyone tried to get into that room, either from the garden or from inside the house, they wouldn't be able to because the person in there would have the key. After you got me off to bed you went down there to warn this person. He cleared out in a hurry. He left the key on the bench with the plant pots. You retrieved it just now, while I was waiting for you by the door. And now when I challenge you, you produce it out of your pocket, bingo, like a rabbit out of a hat. Now I can guess who that person was. And I agree with you, I would like to protect him too, because he's a nice lad, and a clever lad, I bet he's your best student, your little teacher's pet, and he deserves better than to be led up the garden path, if you'll excuse the expression in the circumstances, by a tart like Mariela, because whatever you might think about Mariela and, believe me I thought she was a cracker of the first water, mate, just like the rest

146

of you, she was an incorrigible irredeemable unrepentant tart. I don't know what she got up to with those lads but she had them wired up like fairy lights and she thought she was clever enough to keep it under control, use 'em to get old Louis worked up enough to defy his family and marry her, use 'em and lose 'em, but she was too stupid to know what she was dealing with. You know what adolescent lads are like – testosterone times ten. You can only mess with them so far and then – you've had it – bomb's gone off and blown up the whole village, your whole little world. He was in that garden room down there. You were protecting him. You still are. Now look, you're right. This is not my jurisdiction. Personally, I think she was asking for trouble, and she got it. But she got some more that she shouldn't have got, she got some sick git that she hadn't bargained for. And maybe it wasn't just one lad, maybe it was a major gang-bang down there on the riverbank. Or somewhere else, eh? Maybe here in your cellar? And maybe you knew. Maybe you watched. Maybe you like it. Maybe, maybe. I don't care. But I am under suspicion. I been set up – even to be the prime suspect, maybe. I'm gonna be under investigation for this crime. There are people in the Met who won't mind that one bit and won't lift a finger to help me and will even leak this to the tabloids to jolly things along. And that's my whole life on the line, my job, the lot. I don't like that. I am not involved and I don't wanna be involved in your stinking little inbred small-town drama. So whoever you're protecting, I don't give a toss if you hand them in, give 'em up, grass 'em or what, but *get your cops off my back or I will tell them what I have found out here.* You hear me? You following me? You hear what I'm saying to you? You get me off the hook. Thanks for the whisky. Don't think it would pass the *Which?* test but welcome in the circumstances. Now I'm going to bed.'

Well, that was sensible. That should improve things.

What's the matter with me? I'm off my stroke. I'm out of my depth. That bloody schoolmasterish stare. The kindly gaze from high to low. Patronising git. But what possessed me for Christsake? He dragged off his clothes and clambered in next to Jude. She murmured and her breathing changed but she didn't wake. He never knew anybody sleep like Jude. It must be her life in the open air.

He lay there on his back, listening. He listened for a phone being used, Teacher-man going out, anyone coming in. But he heard nothing.

He listened to Jude's breathing. He needed to wake her up, get his arms round her, her arms round him. Tell her to get out of here tomorrow before they took him off somewhere where he couldn't protect her. *Just get out.*

He heard the boards creaking. Teacher-man going to bed, pissing in the bog this time, not the compost heap – he heard the lavatory flush. It was a good story, the compost heap. Maybe it was true. He saw a circle, a gold circle, turning. He tried to catch it but the gold turned to fire and he tried to stop it with his hand but the flame burned the ends of his fingers and the ring wouldn't stop burning and wouldn't stop turning. The ring of truth.

15

Take a Sad Song

Jude was up before him. She stood next to the bed. 'You'd better get up. They're coming for you at eight.' She was dressed and she looked grim.

'Jude, listen—'

'You have to hurry.'

'What is this?'

'Nothing, just you must be quick, that's all. They'll be here in ten minutes.'

'Christ, woman, are you fighting with me again? Now? I don't believe it.'

She brushed her hair at the mirror. It sparked red in the light from the window.

'Jude?'

She wouldn't look at him. 'How could you do that? What you did last night?'

'What did I do?'

'You treated this man – who had been so kind to us – who is our host, for heavensake – like a criminal, like a suspect. You were *working* him, like someone you'd pulled in to question off the street. How could you behave like that? I was shocked and ashamed. I just wanted to disown you. I still do.'

He said nothing. He got out of bed. He stood close to her. He watched her in the mirror, and himself tousled and hung-over next to her. She met his eyes in the mirror and her eyes showed him no softening, just staring hard and cold like she had really finished with him. And he had no time now to deal with this, to change anything. He picked up a towel and went out of the room.

Showered, shaved, he found no one in the bedroom. He packed his stuff and hers, watched his hands, touching her blue frock, her bras and pants, trying not to shake. He left the bags in the room. He went downstairs. Jude wasn't in the kitchen, she was in the sunny room next to the kitchen, the one with the cane furniture and the desk. She was eating breakfast. She didn't look at him. He went through the dining room and out of the front door. He keyed in Cato's home number. No signal. *Ah Christ.* He went back in. Jude was clearing her breakfast things. 'Where's Teacher-man?' he said.

'Gone to teach. He left half an hour ago. He said we're welcome to stay as long as we like.'

He poured some coffee into a bowl. 'Where's his phone?' He found it in the clutter on the big desk. He dialled. Drank his coffee waiting for Cato to pick up.

Cato was half asleep. But got the gist. Said he'd get to work on it straight away, find a lawyer, come himself if Bright needed him. 'I'll let you know later this morning, guv, what I've managed to put together.'

'Thanks, mate. Think I'm going round the bend.'

Jude was in the kitchen washing up. Bright went in with his coffee and a piece of bread with jam on it, some blackish jam that even in his knotted fog tasted good. 'I haven't got time to make this up with you, Jude.'

'I don't think there is enough time in the world,' she said.

'But you've got to get out of this house.'

'I'm sorry?'

'If they keep me in custody – and it's possible, believe me – you gotta be somewhere else.'

'Like where for instance – back at the hotel?'

'What about that hotel we were at in Polinny? That was a nice place. Go there?'

She turned away again. Wiping the surfaces with a cloth. Martyr-woman through the centuries, didn't even know she was doing it.

150

'*Jude!*' He mustn't touch her, that would be dynamite.

But she stopped and turned round. 'You're a policeman,' she said. 'Always a policeman. You have no trust.'

'I trust you.'

'Up to a point. People are potential suspects to you. All human activity is potential crime. It's a horrible view of the world and I can't live with it.'

'Jude, put this on hold till I'm out of the johndarmes' clutches. You're in a state. So am I. Wait. Till I get out. Don't let this be the end, girl. I can't stand it.'

'We're not suited, John. I was thinking for hours last night.'

'You were asleep last night.'

'I was asleep till you came to bed after creeping round his house spying on him. From then on I was wide awake, believe me.'

'I believe you. I can tell. It's all rehearsed, this. I can hear it. Lying there in bed making up the speeches, getting the words right. Not fair, Jude. This – man – has – at – least – harboured – whoever – killed – that poor girl. I know it. And he knows I know it – that's the bad part. So don't be around him when I'm not. Go. And don't tell anyone but me where you've gone.'

'It's a form of madness,' she said, 'it's paranoia. I'm not going anywhere.'

'Jude, I'm begging you. If this is the end, I'll never ask you anything else. Listen, I'm gonna tell you something. Maybe I shoulda told you before. Before we left London, I was getting threats.'

'Threats?'

'Putting Brennan away – well – you had a taste of his medicine, you know how he gets his jollies, and how wide his network goes. And putting a bent copper away – that's worse. I got a few threats. That's why I took some leave, okay? Didn't want to take them that seriously but you never know.'

Her face went stiff. 'That was happening to you and I

151

didn't know? You didn't think you should tell me a thing like that?'

'I didn't want to scare you.'

'Thank you. How kind. What you mean is, you didn't trust me. Like you don't trust anyone. We were living together, for Christsake, John.'

'It's not nice living with that stuff hanging over you. I'm used to it but you're not, I just thought—'

'So why are you telling me now?'

'You gotta understand that life is not nice. It's not full of lovely civilised middle-class people who only want to do you favours. I'm trying to tell you why I am the way I am, and why you gotta take care of yourself. I know this stuff better than you, Jude. You're too NICE. Just please believe me and do what I say. Just this once? You can end it if you want, but please just this once do what I say. Last thing I'll ever ask you, maybe.' Knowing it was blackmail but anything to make her say yes.

She didn't say yes. Her face remained stiff.

The doorbell jangled through the house. Bright picked up his jacket. 'Ask someone to fly out here to be with you. Kate, maybe. Anyone. Or just go somewhere else and get me on the mobile when you've got there, okay? And – don't – tell – anyone – else.' He flung open the front door. The plump gendarme started to talk but Bright pushed past him out of the house. A young cop tried to open the car door for him but Bright yanked it open himself and threw himself in the back. The plump gendarme hurried in after him. The young cop jumped in the front and started the car. Bright's own car turned in at the gate. The police car swerved round it. Bright didn't even look back.

16

And Make It Better?

Jude finished the washing-up. She didn't know what else to do. She put things away and washed all the kitchen surfaces. Her brain was on hot-spin cycle. She had to decide what to do next. She couldn't think in this dark house.

The kitchen door was bolted top and bottom. The bolts were ancient, caked with dust and rust, so stiff she could barely budge them. But she would not let them defeat her. She pulled the door by its handle and banged the bolt with the heel of her other hand. Rust showered her hair. The bolt shot free. The bottom one was easier – she kicked it loose. When she pushed the door open it scraped the stone of the balcony outside and the crusty hinges screeched.

She went out and stood on the narrow balcony over the garden, her hands gripping the cool iron of the balustrade. The hazy sun cut diamonds of dew on the grass. She went down the stone steps. The iron rail curved under her hand. Snail trails shone silver in the slanting light. Her feet in sandals were drenched, treading down the grass, trickles of water between her toes. She breathed the damp morning air.

She had felt it all her life, this lightening of her spirit, no matter how bad life might be, just walking into a garden alone in the early morning; it was the reason she had become a gardener, she supposed. Her gran's garden in Otley, where the brick path took you on a curving journey between big plants, taller than herself. The ladybirds, bees, butterflies. The smells.

In a sunny corner invisible from Gran's house she'd made her own secret garden. She found all the plants that had seeded themselves and, with the trowel she took from the shed without permission, she dug up the little seedlings and replanted them in her purloined patch. She discovered by trial and error that without water her transplant operations would fail. She lugged the watering-can from the garden tap and watched her patients respond to her aftercare. She waited till Gran snoozed on the couch after lunch to raid the flower-beds and perform her clandestine operations.

But Gran must have known all along that her innocent granddaughter was an infant thief. Later, she taught Jude another magic way to make new plants: she took off a dried poppy head and shook it like a pepper-pot, showering seeds. After this, Jude began to filch seed pods from other gardens besides Gran's. She sowed them in her secret garden and found out for herself the times of sowing and growing, ripening and dying away.

Gardening had begun as her secret vice; it still gave her rushes of secret delight, even now, this lovely morning in the midst of these terrible events. She stood under an apple tree and thought of the apple tree at home and of George. She wanted the warm dusty clean smell of him, his growls of pleasure as he rubbed his face on hers. He sat under the apple tree, the embodiment of optimism, certain that this time he would catch that bird, teeth chattering in anticipation, tail waving, advertising his presence to the birds who ignored him. Was he okay with Lily? Yes. Cats are pragmatists, making the best of what they've got. He'd be on Lily's lap, charming her to bits.

Lily didn't like her. Lily was jealous. Well, it didn't matter now. Jude loved John, but it wouldn't do. At this moment she knew with a fervour that surprised her that the person she wanted was Dan, her husband Dan. And he was hers no longer. She had given him away. He belonged to Lina the Leaner now, and the trendy Southwark loft. The lofty heights. A new life, not to be shared with Jude. Sorrow

154

swelled her throat. She sat on the seat under the tree. It was scabby with grey lichen, and rickety, still a little damp with dew. She turned her face to the tree and stretched her arms around it. It wasn't the tree she was hugging to her; it was Dan and her life with Dan. The sorrow came out of her eyes and wet her face, all the emotion of this stupid holiday pouring out.

The crying fit didn't last long; she wasn't a crier. She let go of the tree, rubbed the bits of lichen and tears off her face and her arms. And as she swept the scraps of bark off her knees into the grass, all at once she was hit by the truth: that the Dan she wept for, longed for, was not the real Dan; he was the Dan of her fantasy, the Dan she imagined when he wasn't there. The real Dan was a leaf in the wind, a frail being, not to be leaned on at all. What a mess she had made. They had made. Together. Taking years to get it just right: their particular mess. Perhaps every marriage was some sort of mess, nothing else possible, considering human fallibility? So did it follow then, perhaps, that she and John were just a different *kind* of mess?

She put both hands over her stomach because that was where this idea seemed to strike – just under her heart. It occurred to her that all the emotion Bright aroused in her, all the anger, the rages against him, stemmed from one big emotion: fear. Fear of a new commitment, fear of loving him, fear of trusting him. And the reason her emotions with him were so intense? Simply because their relationship was of such great importance that she could not bear anything to go wrong with it. She could not bear for them too to get it wrong.

And because of this she had rejected him, alienated him and, worse than all this, left him to face his ordeal alone. What was she going to do? Wait for him to be released and go back with him? She knew she would wait. She hoped he knew that too. She'd go back to the house and phone the gendarmerie to tell him so. She'd go back to Poligny as he'd suggested and wait for him.

But even now anger still worked inside her. Seeing the house from here, its peaceful grey stone, peeling grey shutters, how many hundred years old – two, three? – Breton's family there for generations – how could John have convinced himself that the place was a harbinger of evil and evildoers, that she was in danger here? It was nonsense. You had to trust, to know who to trust, to trust your own instincts. The teacher was a good man, she knew he was, and the only reason John could not see this was that years of looking for evil in his job had corrupted his mind so that he saw evil in every innocent act, saw evil everywhere. She turned her head. It was just instinct – she had not precisely registered a sound; perhaps a movement had flicked at the corner of her eye? Ten metres over to her right in the long grass the blond boy who had served them at the hotel stood, like a bird on a branch, poised between fight and flight, staring at her.

He seemed more startled than Jude. Certainly, she recovered first. She sized up his alarm. Like a feral cat he had to be reassured that she was no danger to him. She must stay calm, make no sudden movement. 'Bonjour!' She smiled at him. 'Vous souvenez-vous de moi? Vous nous avez servi à l'Hôtel Sanglier avant hier.' She gave the details of their encounter because he looked nonplussed. Scared even? 'Ça va?' she said. In fact he looked odd, dishevelled, as if he hadn't slept all night or had slept rough. His blond hair had not been combed, his sweatshirt was crumpled, his face was pale and his eyes were bloodshot.

He still did not speak; he hovered, more like a cornered animal than the boy she had liked so much the night before last. She asked him again, 'Ça va?' with more concern in her voice, and took a step towards him. This movement frightened him. He took a step one way, then the other, staring around. She thought, Oh, my God, this is to do with the murder. He— *He*—? No! This was the way John Bright thought. She had to keep faith in her instincts. There was no way this boy with the angelic face was a wicked person. If he were somehow involved, it was by accident. He was terrified and posed no danger to man nor beast. He needed help and there was no one to give it except her. 'Je peux vous aider?' she said.

He shook his head in a despairing and desperate way but didn't speak.

'Vous cherchez le professeur? Monsieur Breton?' she said.

Again he simply looked at her.

'Il n'est pas chez-lui. Il est déja parti pour l'école.' Then she thought, Oh bloody hell, I've just told him I'm here alone. I shouldn't have done that. Then she thought, But I haven't. He doesn't know that the police came for John. Then, seeing the boy, so beautiful, so young, so innocent, she again felt it silly and disloyal to harbour suspicion of him. This was no criminal, no murderer; this was just a frightened child. What he needed was help and refuge, not a silly woman scared out of her wits. And he looked as though he needed food too. She told him to come back to the house with her and she would give him something to eat.

The look in his eyes at the mention of food was pathetic to behold.

'Suivez-moi.' She smiled and set off through the grass back towards the house. When she turned he was following, like a dog many times beaten but who yet hopes for mercy and anyway has nowhere else to go. He looked around and behind him every few yards. At the house he headed for the cellar. But Jude went up the steps to the kitchen door and waited. He hesitated. He gave another look round, then sprinted up and came in after her. As she shut the kitchen door, Bright's warnings came back to her. Because of this, she did not shoot the bolts. She must leave herself a means of escape. Just in case.

She told the boy to go into the morning room and sit at the table. He did not obey, hovering instead close to her in the narrow kitchen. She found bread in a big stone crock and cheese in the fridge. She poured the remains of the breakfast coffee into a pan. 'Café au lait?' she said.

He nodded.

She added milk to the pan and lit the gas. The boy's expression when he smelt the coffee would have made her laugh but the sense of fear and doom he gave off was no laughing matter. And close to, when she handed him the food, the odour he gave off was pretty serious too. A rancid, panicky smell. She knew then for certain he was in a bad fix, because only last year she had been there herself. That was how she recognised the smell. Fear for your life. Fear so bad it spurted out of your very pores.

He broke the bread with his hands and stuffed a large piece into his mouth. She gave him a knife, a sharp little Sabatier with a blackish steel blade, to cut the cheese and, at this moment, pressed close together in the narrow space, they were both struck by the realisation that he was, as far as she or anyone knew, a killer, and that he was wielding a lethal weapon within inches of her.

They stared at each other. Jude stood very still. The boy began to shake. His grip on the knife tightened, the muscles in his arm knotted. Jude reached forward to take the knife from him.

17

It Takes One to Know One?

The adjutant sat in the front, the plump cop drove, but the de Gaulle character had stayed at home. Bright was grateful for the smallest reprieve. They did not take him to the gendarmerie. At the end of the lane they turned right, out of the village, off into the countryside, slopes of vines, fairy-tale castles, a horse on a hill, outlined on the sky.

He found he couldn't speak. But he was working on it. They hit a roundabout and swerved up on to a main road. He said, 'Where are you taking me?'

'To the préfecture at Lons-le-Saunier.'

He put a lot of patience into his voice. 'What for?'

'The prosecutor will decide how will the case proceed.'

'Will he be the officer in charge?'

'No.'

'Who will?'

'I will.'

Oh, great. So the teacher had got it wrong. After that Bright spoke no more. He heard Jude's words to him, he saw her face. He didn't know how they had come to this. What had he done in his life bad enough to bring him here? The threats in London came back to him with force. For a mad five seconds this chaos was a fulfilment of those threats. But he pulled himself away from that brink. In real time there was no way the two nightmares could be connected. But somewhere in the darkest corners of his mind the conviction lingered and would not go away.

They were coming into Lons-le-Saunier. The outskirts were not pretty. A Ford dealership flanked a roundabout with a

159

power station opposite. They took the left fork and swung off past garages, small factories, the industrial zone, then alongside the railway into the town. At the *gare* they veered right into a street where tall grey houses looked down on them, dignified and serene. A pair of big iron-barred gates stood at an oblique angle on a corner. The car slowed, stopped, the gates swung slowly open. Bright thought he might throw up. This was it. The préfecture of Lons-le-Saunier.

They drove through the gates into a courtyard with prison-high walls all round. The gates rolled shut behind them. The adjutant was out almost before the car had stopped. The plump cop opened the door for Bright and tried to scurry across the car park after the boss-man. But Bright, going dead slow, forced him to slow down. He was in no hurry to see the inside of the préfecture. The outside was fine by him – another dignified grey building, only three floors high but massive, two rows of windows with grey shutters then a row of mansard windows all along the brown-tiled roof. The entrance was in a new extension, tacked on at the far end. The adjutant marched up the steps. The doors flew open at the sight of him. Bright followed with the plump cop panting at his side.

The adjutant did some business with the man on the desk, signing them in, then pushed the lift button. The big lift took them down below. Bright panicked. *Oh Christ they're gonna put me in a cell.* 'Listen, Officer, I got rights here. I gotta have a lawyer. That's the law the world over. I need a lawyer. Get me a lawyer. NOW.'

'I have a lawyer for you.'

'What language does he speak?'

'He speaks English, of course.'

You let them take one step, then they take another, and step after inevitable step brings you here: in a French dungeon, about to be interrogated, with a lawyer you've never seen in your life, for a crime you're not guilty of. His head was leaving his body. He couldn't breathe. But on he went, step by step, in the wake of a French cop determined to have him for some French bastard's crime, down a wide stone corridor, to a waiting area with black padded leather seats. The plump cop took his arm to sit him down. His legs would not bend of their own accord: he had to give them instructions in order to sit.

He put his head into his hands. Just the touch of his own fingers on his own eyelids was enough to tug him back to real life. He pulled in some deep breaths and let them out long and slow. He lowered his hands and opened his eyes. The adjutant stood in front of him. 'May I present Maître Lunel, your lawyer.'

The guy was four foot six, in a black suit, a big briefcase gripped over his crotch in his two little hands. He looked about fifteen. He stuck out a hand to Bright. 'How. Do. You. Do,' he said. He enunciated well.

Bright said nothing. He was going to say nothing from now until he knew he had to speak. But he shook the little guy's hand. It wasn't his fault he'd been dragged into this French farce. They said tragedy and farce were never far apart. Well, here he was – living proof.

The little lawyer sat next to Bright on the black leather bench. His toes pointed straight down to touch the ground. They missed by a centimetre. He dug an arm into his brief-case. This was the briefcase of a much larger man. Bright thought he might start to laugh. He knew if he did he would not be able to stop. So he swallowed the rising hysteria, rubbed his hand over his face. The little guy said, 'May I do somsing to elp you?'

Bright said, 'Would they run to a cup of coffee round here?'

'Pardon?'

'Coff-ee?' Bright mimed, lifting an imaginary cup up to his mouth three or four times.

161

'Ah. Yes! I am sure! Excuse me.'

He wriggled off the bench and went to the big mahogany horseshoe-shaped enclosure that housed six officers with computer terminals. He stood on tiptoe and had a chat. He came back. 'Yes. He will take. Bring.'

'Thanks, kid.'

A woman in uniform brought it. Gave it to the lawyer, who gave it to Bright. It was really bad, bitter, with cold milk, the only bad coffee he'd had in France. He just felt glad that at least his feet touched the ground; he didn't have to concentrate on pointing his toes like his little friend the lawyer.

The lawyer enunciated again. 'Mistair Braht, I will translate for you. Is okay?'

'Is okay, mate. Thanks.'

Another uniformed officer marched up to them and gave instructions to the lawyer. The lawyer slid off the bench again and clutched his briefcase to his crotch. 'Mistair Braht. We go now to ze prosecutor.'

Back along the corridor they marched, behind the uniformed officer. They went up in the lift again, this time to the first floor, and along another corridor to big oak double doors where the officer halted and knocked. The doors opened.

A pale man in rimless specs sat behind a big desk. His secretary, who had opened the door, led them forward then sat at her place near the window. Her desk was normal size; her boss's desk took the three of them easy, standing along its front.

The prosecutor glanced at Bright over his specs. 'Asseyez-vous, s'il vous plaît.' They sat, in a little row facing him – the lawyer, then Bright, then the man in uniform. After this he spoke only to the lawyer, in French, through lips that barely moved. How did he do that, all those nasal honks and complex *grrs* at the back of the tongue and those narrow *yuhs* squeezed out of the ears?

162

The lawyer, translating, asked him to confirm that he was John Bright. This was just as well because he was beginning to wonder, himself. And that he was also a detective inspector of the Metropolitan Police. Just now he had grave doubts about that too, but he didn't say so. Was he at the Hôtel Sanglier, etcetera, etcetera. All the same stuff. Nothing incriminating. He answered yes, yes, yes. The lawyer read out his statement in English. He confirmed it was his. He asked the lawyer to check that it said the same thing in French. The lawyer confirmed that it did. 'I'll have to take your word for that, won't I?' Bright said. The little lawyer looked scared. The prosecutor gave Bright another gimlet glance over the rimless specs. Then he took a breath and dived into a torrent of French.

He'd changed his tone and his facial expression. Whatever he was saying, it was serious: different from what had gone before. The stream stopped. The lawyer turned slightly to Bright to translate. 'Mistair Braht, you have been seen outside the Hôtel Sanglier at fifteen minutes to one o'clock on the night in question. This information has come this morning. The time of the death of the victim is perhaps one half-hour before. You have not said to Adjutant Poupard this information. Do you wish to say something now?'

Well, here it was. Who'd grassed him? The teacher? Jude? The bloke he'd seen near his car? No. Not him. Whoever he was – poacher, thief, murderer – he'd been up to no good and would say nothing. Bright bet the information had come without a name. No one would want to admit being out that night. Well, he didn't know what to do now. He was out of inspiration. But, hell, that's what lawyers were for, wasn't it? To advise their clients. He turned and looked down at his lawyer. 'What do you advise?' he said.

The lawyer gave the question solemn thought. 'You may say nothing. Or you may deny. There may be evidence to corroborate this testimony. There may be not.'

'You advise say nothing?'

The lawyer pulled a little face, harder to interpret than his English. Not a lot of use to a suspect in need of advice.

'Who grassed me?'

'Please?'

'Who gave them this information? Who is it says they saw me?'

'They are not obliged to say you this.'

'I know, I know.' All of a sudden his position became clear to him. He'd been waiting, that's all, in a house over a chasm that had been shored up with props. A rock shifted. The props gave. The house imploded, rolling down, earth, stone, props and all. Well, he figured he had nothing more to lose. He stopped looking at, or talking to, the lawyer. He looked at the prosecutor. He talked to him.

'Okay. Yes, I was out. I couldn't sleep. I went for a walk.' He gave him the times and the route he had taken in detail. He told him about the man on the wasteground: 'I was by my car. It was a quarter to one. I did not mention this before as I felt it might damage me unnecessarily. Now that it has been reported, it's no use me keeping quiet about it. Or about this: I went back into the hotel. I looked out of the landing window. Someone was creeping along the little street at the back. Petty Roo? And while I was watching that, someone let themselves in down below through the front door, with a key. I don't know who it was. It was about five to one by then. My girlfriend Jude Craig can confirm the time.' He said to the lawyer, 'You got that?'

The lawyer swallowed, his Adam's apple nodding over the perfect knot in his tie. The prosecutor listened to the lawyer saying it in French but he watched Bright. And he went on watching Bright for a good minute after the lawyer had finished. Bright felt his scalp creep. All over his head, he thought, his hair might be moving. He tried to remove all trace of his slight squint. He could normally do this at

164

will; now he had no idea what his eyes might be doing –
rolling in their sockets maybe. At the same time he was
flooded by a feeling of relief that made his knees wobble.
Just because he'd talked. He'd seen this reaction in suspects
all his life when they finally decided to spill. Now he understood. For better or for worse, you handed yourself over to
Fate. All responsibility was over. You had no further need
for strength. You'd handed over responsibility. And all this
time he was staring back at the pale prosecutor and trying
to look expressionless.

At last his ordeal by glassy stare was over. The prosecutor made a short speech to the lawyer, which the lawyer,
interpreted to Bright: 'Thank you, that is all for the present
time. You will wait please. You will be informed soon of
the – the—'

'Yeah, okay, I get it: while they decide whether they're
gonna charge me or not.'

The lawyer slid off his chair and gave a little dip of his
head, almost a bow. Bright resisted the temptation. The
lawyer and the prosecutor bade each other a tight-lipped
goodbye, and Bright felt the prosecutor's pale eyes on him
all the way to the door.

They put him in a cell. A cell. He couldn't believe it. It was
no bad cell as cells go – he knew – he'd seen a few in his
time. It had a bed, and even a lavatory that flushed. He had
no window but then, hey, what the hell, you can't have
everything, as the legless man said to the armless woman
trying to dance the polka. They hadn't taken his belt or his
money or his watch. It was twelve noon. Three hours had
passed in here. He'd paced. He'd lain down. He'd even tried
to sleep. After last night he needed to. But sleep had gone
a long way away. He shut his eyes but he couldn't shut his
brain. He thought about Jude, wondered where she was,
what she was doing. Had she taken his advice and gone to

Poligny? She ought at least to be told where he was. Praps they'd let him phone.

The *kerchonk* of the lock, and the door opened. A guy in uniform beckoned him. Back at the mahogany enclosure his little lawyer waited. This time the lift took them to the second floor and an office half-way down the corridor.

Different floor. Different office. Different bloke. Not in uniform. And not in a suit. In shirtsleeves, with his jacket on the back of the chair. He stood up when they showed Bright in. 'Thank you for coming, Mr Bright. Or rather Inspector Bright, as I understand?'

The guy spoke English. Proper English. Bright felt the clots of fog begin to dissolve. He breathed out.

The bloke put out his hand and Bright shook it. He looked like a film star. Not a pretty film star and not that big, hardly taller than Bright, he just had that gold-plated look, like he knew the score and nothing surprised him, the Robert de Niro type. He was younger than Bright but not so as you'd notice. He did not look like a cop. Not like any kind of a cop.

'Do sit down, Inspector.'

Bright sat.

And the film star sat. On the other side of the table. 'I am Judge Folin. The *juge d'instruction* in this case. Ah – examining magistrate, I think is what you would say.'

'You're a JUDGE?'

'I am.'

'What's happened then? Is this an arraignment or what?'

'Ah no. Please. Not at all. I am a member of the judiciary, yes. But we do things differently here. May I explain? You have been kept for twenty-four hours on what we call *garde à vue*, that is, kept for questioning at the discretion of the officers of the Gendarmerie and then the police.'

'These guys in the Foreign Legion hats are not police?'

'The Gendarmerie is, strictly speaking, a branch of the

army. Their ranks are army ranks: captain, lieutenant, adjutant for instance, colonel. This last year the police ranks
also have been renamed, to co-ordinate with the
Gendarmerie. It is called streamlining, I believe. The judiciary police take over quickly in a case such as this. In such
a small place, a village like this one, with no préfecture, no
brigade de recherches—'

'Sorry, you just lost me.'

'Ah, yes. You have CID, we have *brigade de recherches*
– judiciary police. But we do not have the concept of detective as such. Any officer of the judiciary police may investigate a crime. On my behalf as it were.'

'On your behalf?'

'Ah yes. The prosecutor has appointed me to investigate
this case. Normally I would hand it back to the officer who
began the investigation. In this instance Adjutant Poupard.
I would be in charge, but from here, not on the spot. It is
eccentric of me to investigate the case myself in a – I think
you say "hands on" – fashion?'

'You mean he's off it? The adjutant? He's not running it
any more? You are? Sorry, I . . .' Bright shut one eye in a
grimace of pain. Was there such a thing as a headache
brought on by relief?

'Yes. For a number of reasons. You will understand many
of them without my going into details. But my personal
reason is that this was my village. Not true, actually.
Château-les-Mînes was my village, but Neufchâtel is where
I went to school, where I had my friends, my social life. A
crime here intrigues and, well, bothers, me. So . . . I will go
there myself to co-ordinate the investigation.'

Bright couldn't believe it. Rat-face was off the case. Over-
zealous in the course of duty being one of the reasons, he
wouldn't be surprised. Maybe his luck was on the turn. 'A
guy in uniform investigating a murder,' he said. 'I couldn't
get my head round that.'

'Ah, yes. Until recently the judiciary police wore plain clothes like your CID but since last year they are obliged to wear uniform.'

Bright breathed blank astonishment. 'Why?'

Folin shrugged. 'A good question. Of course crime has increased ten times since then, in the cities especially, but . . .' He gave a more elaborate shrug. He smiled. His smile was matey, conspiratorial. 'Our democratically elected government knows best, of course. Who are we to question their wise decisions?

'Now, before I question you, I will tell you the information that we have, because as a police officer, a detective inspector no less, you will suspect when I hide information from you.' He smiled.

Bright almost responded, but stopped himself. He was being subjected to a charm barrage here. The guy was winding him in, and they hadn't even started yet. This we're-in-the-same-boat-we're-buddies stuff; Bright had done it himself countless times but this was the first time he'd been this end of it. Folin grinned again, like he was reading his thoughts, and again Bright nearly grinned back. What a good method of interrogation it was. If he ever got out of this and took up policing again he'd have more faith in it.

'Now. I have your statement here. I have read it. This is a small place, a village. The inhabitants all know each other. Of course. Probably they all know who has done this and when and why. But they will not tell it to me. They will protect their own, like a big family. You as the outsider are the perfect scapegoat. You could also be guilty, but I am not inclined to believe this. You come with your girlfriend, a very attractive woman I understand. You are happy together, on your vacation. You reserve only one night at the hotel, you meet the victim only once, for a short time. If the murder had been brutal, quick, violent, perhaps I might think yes, you have had a – an encounter – something has been said or done to provoke

168

violence which has progressed too far. But this elaborate tying with rope, perhaps ritualistic, perhaps sex games, followed by such brutal violation? No, no, I do not think so.'

'What you saying here—?'

Folin held up his hand. 'For the moment please allow me . . . I have also this morning spoken with your superintendent in the Metropolitan Police. She is a charming woman, no? She speaks highly of you. And she has reminded me of your gangland case. You did remarkable work on that. I congratulate you. I followed the case in your *Daily Telegraph*. Excellent crime reporting, though its politics are not my own. Also its foreign news. Excellent. I read it to discover what is happening in my own country sometimes.'

Bright was just being seduced here, sucked in, like a babe in arms. He couldn't hold out against this bloke. He was a wizard. He sat back and folded his arms and watched the performance. He even found himself grinning back. The conspiratorial grin. Just what the guy wanted, and here he was giving it: take me baby I'm yours.

'This is another reason the prosecutor and I thought Adjutant Poupard not quite right for the investigation. He also knew of your London case. He has strong feelings about – "shopping"? – a fellow officer. I, not being a member of the police, have no prejudice in these matters.'

'I'm quite glad to hear that.'

Folin gave him the grin again. 'Inspector Bright, it seems to me that I would be foolish not to use your exceptional talents to help me find the perpetrator – or perpetrators – of this nasty crime. What do you say?'

Bright actually laughed. 'I got to give it you, Judge. You're good. You could give me lessons. Keep suspect number one in your sights at all times by convincing him you don't suspect him, he's in the clear, he's even on your side. I mean, anyway, what's he got to lose?'

169

'Inspector, you have been a police officer too long. You see conspiracy everywhere. You suspect everyone.'

Bright's smile dropped away. Where had he heard that recently?

'I appear to have touched a nerve,' Folin said. Observant with it.

Bright nodded, couldn't even speak. No little jokes on this subject. Not since this morning.

'Now, I will read you your statement and you will please tell me if it is correct.' He did, and it was. 'Do you wish to add anything?'

'Not yet.'

'Good.' Folin said this like it was the end of the conversation.

'But I want to ask something. Who grassed me up? Who told the police I was out for a walk that night?'

'It was an anonymous note. Left at the gendarmerie. No one saw by whom.'

'When?'

'Very early this morning.'

'Okay. Thanks.'

'You have an idea who this anonymous caller may be?'

'Yes. But I'm not saying. Not yet.'

'I hope you will become more willing to communicate with me as time goes on.'

'You mean you can keep me here?'

'Oh yes.'

'You're *going* to keep me here?'

'I'm sorry – yes.'

'You haven't charged me with anything.'

'No. Of course. I have no evidence.'

'You can say that again.'

'Yet.'

'How long can you keep me without charging me? Don't you have any laws here about this kind of stuff?'

'Yes. We do, Inspector. Of course. No, this period, as I said, is called *garde à vue*.'

'Guard in view, right?'

'Yes. The prosecutor has given his permission to keep you for another forty-eight hours.'

'Oh great. And after that?'

'If the case is not solved, I can apply for another twenty-four, and so on.'

'For ever?'

'I hope to eliminate you from the investigation before eternity becomes a question.'

'Oh well that's fine then. Jesus. And if someone digs out my lawyer from wherever he is – my English lawyer I'm talking about – he'll be allowed to tag along, will he?'

'Of course, yes.' Folin leaned forward. 'You see, Inspector, I cannot let you go because by your own admission you were out at the time of the killing, and I cannot charge you because I have no evidence against you. Therefore until I find evidence to convict the killer—'

'—Or killers.'

'—quite so – I cannot eliminate you.'

'The stuff I gave the prosecutor this morning . . .'

'Yes.'

They looked at each other. They both knew. 'Just as the anonymous information that you were out at the time of the crime, so with your information that other people were also out at that time. And, you see, also, of course, you did not reveal your movements until you were absolutely constrained to do so. And then your statement about these others seems rather – convenient? And again is not supported by evidence.'

Bright sighed. 'Yeah, yeah. So how does it go then, now? How does this investigation proceed?'

'I am here to gather all evidence and to evaluate it and to reach a conclusion.'

'The police line up the suspects for you?'

'Yes, some. But I can call anyone to speak to me, not on suspicion, you know, just to tell me their story. And also anyone can call on me to tell me what they know. I am at the disposal, as it were, of all parties.'

'You get a lot of cranks?'

'Cranks? Ah, yes, eccentrics. A few. But, you know, I evaluate. For instance, the family of an accused may all come to speak to me. They are interested parties, they are going to lie sometimes, concoct alibis and so on, but I, I evaluate. Sometimes as you know it is only in the lies that people tell that we can understand what it is they wish to cover up.'

'Sure. So what now? They take me back down to the cells? Are you serious?'

'I can do that just now because the circumstantial evidence is against you. You were seen out in the middle of the night. By more than one person, Inspector. The anonymous note is not our only – "tip". It was a confirmation of previous information.'

Previous information? Where from? Who else had grassed him? When? Before the johndarmes came for him in the meadow? Had to be. But it would have to wait. There were more urgent questions to be settled now. The film-star judge was laying out his problems, in a manner that was detached and sympathetic at the same time.

'So you had opportunity, Inspector. Motive? Well, who knows? Perhaps you had met this Mariela before, and arranged this trip to meet her again?'

'Last time I was in France, Judge, was on a school trip to Calais in 1970 or thereabouts. And I've never set foot in Mauritius. I don't do abroad as a general rule.'

'So. No previous relationship with the deceased, you say. But perhaps we will discover other motives in your background. I don't believe so, but it's possible . . .' Folin got up and came round the desk. He pulled another chair close to Bright and sat. He leaned forward. 'Inspector. I am serious, what I have said to you: I would prefer that you stay of your own free will and assist me in my observations.'

'So was I, saying you get to pick my brains and keep me under surveillance at the same time, right?'

'Precisely.' Folin grinned. 'Yes.'

'Stay of my own free will in a police cell. Are you kidding?'

'Of course not in a police cell. I decide where *garde à vue* is to be. It will be in the place which I believe to be appropriate to the investigation.'

'That right? Okay. Can I go and stay at the Hôtel de France in Pollinee?'

'I would prefer to have you closer to me, if you don't mind.'

'What about my girlfriend? Can she stay where she likes? Can she go back home?'

'I would prefer that she too stay here in this region but of course I have no reason to keep her. She is not under suspicion, not at all.'

Bright fell silent, just for a moment, thinking, coming to a decision. Then he said in a casual way, 'Cause I want to get her out of the teacher's house.'

Their eyes met.

Folin, aware of Bright's decision, that an agreement had been reached, also spoke in a casual tone. 'Oh yes? Why is that?'

Bright, knowing to the letter the inference Folin would draw, said, 'Well, we can't go on cadging off him. He's given us enough hospitality. It can get embarrassing, you know.'

'You are uneasy to accept his hospitality?'

Bright said nothing.

'It is a large house, no? Plenty of space.'

Bright thought a moment. 'A-ha. Plenty of room, it's not that. It's – a bit spooky.'

'Spooky?'

'Nothing changed in a hundred years, everything the way

173

his parents left it.' His slight squint increased as his eyes changed focus. 'He's got an amazing wine cellar, though. Calls it his carve.'

'Yes? Well, I must take a glass of wine with him.'

'Good idea.'

'You think so?'

'Yeah. His carve is definitely worth a look. Not just the wine bit, the whole thing.'

'In that case I will take a look at it.'

They looked at each other and nodded slow.

'Renew my old acquaintance,' Folin said.

'You know him? Breton?'

'He was my teacher.'

'Is there anyone within a hundred miles of here whose teacher he wasn't?'

Folin smiled.

'Taught you your English, did he?'

'Yes.'

'So, he's good.'

'Thank you. Yes. But he was young then, not yet the director of the school at that time. He was just a humble prof. A very good man, in my recollection.'

'That right?'

'Oh yes. Much respected. Dedicated to his students, to his work.'

'Nothing much else in his life?' Bright said, speaking slowly.

'Not at that time, it appeared.'

'Not now either. It appears.'

'You must correct my English also.'

'Not me, mate. You're better at it than I am.' Flattery could work both ways and Bright was keeping his options open. The guy had led him into hostile remarks about a man he'd respected from a lad. That wasn't wise. Folin was a lawyer, not a copper. And Bright knew just where he'd like

174

to shove most of the lawyers he'd met. It was only being in this dodgy position had led him to trust the guy this far. This was way far enough. No further. Not if he could help it.

'Perhaps we will call at the prof's house so that you can pick up your bags?' Folin said.

'Where am I going?'

'I will stay at the Hôtel Sanglier. I would be happy if you would stay there also.'

'The Hôtel Sanglier? You're kidding.'

'It is the most convenient place for my centre of operations. We cannot crowd the gendarmerie with our numerous officers and machinery, plus those whom I will interview too.'

'I'm gonna be on gardy-voo at the Wild Boar Hotel?'

'Yes.'

'This'll teach me not to go on holiday. Jesus Christ.'

'I'm sorry, Inspector Bright.'

'No, it's good of you, Judge. I appreciate – you know . . .'

'No, no, no, it's nothing.'

'Can I call my girlfriend?'

'Of course.'

'Just to let her know what's happening.' He dialled Jude's mobile. It rang. The Voice told him this mobile might be switched off and did he want to leave a message. He was puzzled. Jude was mad with him, but switch her phone off? Why would she do that? 'She's always forgetting to switch it on,' he said. Feeble or what? Her bloke's in the Bastille and she turns her mobile off? Some girlfriend.

But Folin didn't comment. He took a soft leather jacket off the back of his chair. 'You can try later,' he said. 'Or you may accompany me now to the teacher's house and perhaps we will find her there.'

Down the wide corridor, door after open door, the motorbike boys sat, each in a separate office, just the way they'd been at the gendarmerie, each at the side of a cop, handcuffed, heads hanging, asleep or nearly asleep. They looked young, worn out, pale, sick. Bright was shocked. 'You can keep them like this? That's legal here?'

'Until they tell the truth, yes. The gendarmerie in Combrans has only one cell. They could all be in that one cell together. Here the officers can keep them under observation at all times.'

Bright shook his head. It was barbaric.

'Yes, we do not treat our suspects gently. I worked on a case in London once. I raided a grand house with your CID. They were so polite! Calling the culprit "sir", telling him, "we have permission to search your premises"! We would pin him to the wall and tear his place apart. They had all the evidence to convict him ten times over! How will anybody ever confess if you are so sweet with him?'

'A-ha. Our hands are tied all ends up these days. And the CPS – you know – Crown Prosecution Service—'

'—the equivalent of myself?'

'Right. It gets harder and harder to bring a prosecution, let alone get a conviction, it's soul-destroying, I mean it. Still . . . you got any evidence against these kids?'

'Just about as much as we have against you.'

18

House and . . .

Folin drove back to Neufchâtel by a different route, purring along in his sporty silver Merc. To Bright it was not just a different route, it was a different world. The sun was shining for a start. Had it been shining when they came to Lons this morning? He doubted it, but he wouldn't have noticed then if there'd been two suns in the sky. Folin took a narrow wiggling road up into rolling country, green, with the short-cropped grass that just seemed to grow that way on these rounded limestone hills. They slowed down through little villages with *cave* and *dégustation* adverts on old stone barns and farmhouses. Ducks, geese and hens pottered about in gardens. Then came the neat rows of sloping vines and, up above them, Château-les-Mînes, the cause of all his trouble – if he hadn't wanted to go back there they'd have been in Provence by now – poised on the edge of its cliff, with the furry brown roofs of Neufchâtel below.

They progressed through a flat grey street of flat grey houses, to the crossroads, and there was the Hôtel Sanglier fifty metres down on the right. People stood outside, chatting in clumps. They stopped to watch as Folin swung the car into the wasteground car park. Bright felt their stares like sandpaper on the skin. Folin said, 'We will walk from here to the prof's house, yes?'

Bright's anxiety came up into his throat again. He was anxious to see Jude. And anxious *about* seeing her. Was she serious about ending it between them? He did not know her well enough to be sure. This holiday had shown them that they didn't know each other at all.

'We will go this way,' Folin said. The people watched them in silence get out of the car, and make their way through the picket gate at the far end of the wasteground into the woods. Then the talk started up again, distant now, in the street behind them.

It was dark on the narrow path, the high wall of the shuttered house to the right, water trickling in a ditch to their left, under the thick-packed trees. Bright was glad to get out into daylight again, five minutes later, through another little gate, a narrow iron one, into a lane. Folin turned left. It was only now that Bright understood where they were: this was the road along the river. In fifty metres or so they'd reach the crime scene. Folin said nothing. Clever bastard, he was. Bright said nothing either. The time for spontaneous reaction was past.

There was heat in the sun and its light spread like honey around him but Bright's constricted heart could not open to warmth or light. He had to see Jude; he dreaded seeing Jude. He found himself almost praying that she'd gone to Poligny out of harm's way till this mess was sorted.

They came to the crime scene. Just police tape now; no cops examining the riverbank, no trussed-up bloody corpse. Folin paused. He looked about with his hands in his pockets like a tourist. 'The adjutant brought you here, I believe.'

'Too right.'

'You disappointed him. You did not pass out. You did not vomit up your breakfast. And, most unexpectedly, you did not break down and confess.'

'Asshole.'

'I did not hear this.'

'Thanks.'

'But you may have some interesting thoughts for me about the scene.'

'They brought your teacher too, to translate for me. He didn't pass out or confess either. But he looked pretty sick.'

178

'The normal reaction, no? For those who see such things for the first time.'

'Sure.'

Folin walked on. They came to a small stone house with a steep red-brown roof behind the usual high hedges. Folin stopped again. 'The house of Jacques and Olivier Buchon. It is they who discovered the body, early yesterday morning.'

'How early?'

'Dawn.'

'Normally up at dawn, are they?'

'The insomnia of the very old. They were old when I was a boy. I was surprised to find that they are still living.'

'One's got teeth like a horse, right? Carries his ma's old tartan shopping bag?'

'Still? Yes. That's Jacques, the older. You have seen them.'

'Yeah. The other one wears a hunting cap and a green zip-up jumper.'

'Olivier, yes.'

'They were in the bar the afternoon we arrived. Couldn't speak for later. They're your teacher's alibi.'

'And he is theirs.'

'They went back to his place that night. He says.'

'Just so. They say so too.'

'Thought they might.'

They crossed the river over the narrow bridge. Folin stopped to watch the ragged water chase over the stones. 'Was it more . . . ?' He made a gesture.

'In spate?' Bright said.

'Thank you – in spate – the night of the killing?'

'I didn't come this way the night of the killing.'

Folin gave a small nod and a small smile, acknowledging that Bright had swatted his transparent little trick.

'But when they brought me to the crime scene yesterday,' Bright said, 'the water was higher than it is now. Why?

179

Haven't you found the foreign object that was used to rape her? You think it went in the river?'

Folin ignored both questions and crossed the bridge. Bright stayed watching the water a moment, then followed.

The high hedges of the teacher's house were just ahead now. Folin got there first. He rang the bell at the side of the big gates. No one came. He turned the handle and the gate swung back. The drive was empty. Bright said, 'My car should be here. The police returned it this morning.'

Folin stopped on the front door steps. 'I will telephone. The forensic examiners may have taken it again. Or perhaps Miss Craig is now using it.'

Bright said nothing. Folin pressed the doorbell. They heard it reverberate inside the house. No one came. He tried the big front door. It was locked.

'He said he never locks it,' Bright said.

'Perhaps recent events may have caused him to change his custom.'

They went round the back, through a narrow gap between house and hedge. The hedge, some evergreen with small round leaves, smelt bitter, as they brushed by. Under their feet the path was overgrown with weeds. Folin reached the back of the house first. He gasped. 'I had forgotten how beautiful these gardens may be.'

Even Bright's heart expanded, a painful movement of a muscle he was trying to keep from reacting to anything at all. The garden lay peaceful under a golden mist of light, blossom budding on the fruit trees and flowers glittering in the grass.

They walked side by side through the cool grass to the *cave* door.

Bright said, 'He does lock this one. So he tells me.'

Folin, using a tissue, lifted the latch and pushed. The door opened easily.

Bright said, 'But he contradicts himself.'

Folin went inside. Pitch darkness after the outside hazy day. Bright moved out of the doorway and a shaft of light showed them the earth floor of the garden room, some sacks, stacks of wooden boxes for storing apples, rolls of string, tools. Keeping to the edge of the room Folin felt his way to the inner door. He turned the handle and pulled, then pushed, then rattled it back and forth. No good. They were locked out of the rest of the *cave*.

Bright went out again into the sun. He couldn't get enough of the warmth and the light. It was never like this in England. Never. Even the brightest, hottest day never had this depth to it, the accumulation of sunlight over months and years, the earth sensing the sunshine as its due, its natural element, even this early in the year. It was like food to him just now, good wine, something the body needed, to give it life, strength. Something like the way he needed Jude.

Folin came out of the garden room and joined him. Bright was looking up at the balcony that ran along the back of the house. 'These steps must go up to the kitchen,' he said.

Folin went ahead, up the curving stone steps to the kitchen door. It had once been painted grey but the paint had cracked and peeled, showing dry old wood of a different grey beneath. Folin, again with his tissue, pressed down the handle and pulled. The door moved, stiff, grinding on the stone of the little balcony. They shifted round it.

The kitchen was a well of darkness after the blessing of the light outside. But you could see it was empty. You could feel it was empty. The whole house told you it was empty. There was no one home. There was now a more urgent question for Bright than the teacher's cellar. 'You said you'd phone about my car.'

'Ah yes. What car is it?"

'A Golf GTI, three years old.'

Folin raised his eyebrows. 'Ah yes, a good little car.'

181

Bright's anxiety was making his scalp cringe; the put-down barely grazed him.

Folin shut down his phone. 'They know nothing of your car since it was returned here this morning at eight o'clock.'

Bright stood. He stared at something. At nothing in the room. At something in his head. But all he said was, 'We came here to look in his carve.'

'Yes. Show me please.'

Opening the door in the kitchen on to the stairs that went down to the cellar, his anxiety was a high-pitched humming in his veins, in particular the veins at the sides of his eyes pulsated, from looking and listening too hard, from a concentration too acute. The circle of dim cold light from the torch patterned the floor, a circle within a circle within a circle. The teacher had told him it was better down here in daylight. It wasn't. And then a voice said loudly, 'Bonjour?'

Folin jumped, just as Bright did. They turned, and a big shape filled the doorway at the top of the stairs. 'Monsieur Bright, c'est vous?'

Folin recovered. 'Monsieur le Professeur?' He went to the foot of the stairs but did not go up. 'Bonjour. Je suis Folin. Je suis le juge d'instruction—'

'Folin? Auguste Folin de Château-les-Mînes?'

'Oui.'

'Vous étiez un de mes élèves, non?'

'Oui.' Folin shrank a little and hung his head like a boy.

'What's he saying?'

'The *professeur* reminds me that I was his student in the past.'

'Good old Mr Chips.'

'I'm sorry, Mr Bright,' the teacher said. 'We will speak English now. Auguste has learned well from me, I am certain.'

Bright cut through the jokey tone. 'Where's Jude?'

182

'She is not here?'

'My car's not outside.'

'But the police—'

'They brought it back this morning. She didn't say where she was going?'

'No.'

'She didn't phone you at the school?'

'No.'

'She didn't leave you a note?'

'I will go up to see.'

They ran up the stairs after the teacher. He switched on lights, searched the kitchen surfaces. Bright noticed the dishes hadn't been washed, grey water stood in the sink, dishes visible in it, bits of food floating on top, dissolving bread and crumbs of cheese. His stomach knotted. No note in the kitchen. Or in the dining room. Or in the parlour on the other side of the hall. Ghosts moved when the door opened on the cold dank air imprisoned in there, but there was no note. And nothing inside the letterbox.

'You got an answering machine?'

'Ah. Yes.'

Breton pressed a button and they heard his voice, then a series of clicks and whistles, the usual thing. A male voice, thin and reedy, spoke for a short time and clicked off. That was all.

'Who's that?'

'Olivier Buchon. He and his brother live up the lane. The next house.'

'I remember,' Folin said.

'They would come here this evening to eat with me but naturally in this circumstance they wonder if . . .'

'Yes . . . They dine with you each week on the same day?'

'Yes. As they have also in my father's time.'

Bright felt these centuries of tradition like a fine cold pain inside him. At this moment he hated these stagnant lives that didn't change or see the need to change. He also wondered what the old guy had really rung for. At this moment he didn't care. 'Listen, can we look upstairs?'

Breton nodded. 'Of course, yes. Please.'

He was about to go up with them. Folin had to ask him to let them go up alone. Bright could see this embarrassed the urbane judge. But the teacher meekly stayed below.

Folin opened the door to each bedroom and the bathroom, Bright by his side. The room he and Jude had slept in was empty all right. She'd stripped the bed and folded the sheets. The good guest. His bag stood in the middle of the room.

'This is her bag?'

'No.'

'It is your bag?'

'A-ha.' *She's left my bag. If she went to Poligny she'd take both bags. Wouldn't she? She's gone home then? On her own? In my car?*

'You are – puzzled?'

'Erm . . . I'm puzzled, yeah.'

'She has taken away her bag and not yours?'

'Looks like it.'

'You – quarrelled?'

There was no point lying about it. Bright moved his head slightly to one side. He didn't need words.

'May I ask why?'

'I'm a copper. It's a problem for her.'

'Why?' Folin lifted his shoulders in an astonished way and they stayed up, almost to his ears.

'Apparently I was treating your schoolteacher like a suspect. She got upset.'

'Well, you were his guest.'

'A-ha.'

'The quarrel was not from – jealousy?'

'Jealousy?' Bright looked at him. He used his squint to

184

give him distance. This was not a subject he wanted to pursue. Not in public. Not now. 'No.' Folin wanted more but he wasn't going to get it. 'We haven't looked at his wine-carve yet. He interrupted us.'

Now Bright went first. All the time he was thinking, Go off in my car and leave my bag but take her own? Jude wouldn't do that. She was angry, sure. But even so, she'd fix something up with me, wouldn't she? I mean, how many couples split up on holiday? They wait till they get home to sue for divorce, don't they? Jude wouldn't do this. Not the Jude I know. Thought I knew. Thought.

Breton hovered in the hall. They trooped after him down the cellar stairs again. *Upstairs, downstairs and in my lady's chamber.* He was getting a gander now all right. Why did he feel in this house that wherever he was, something crucial was happening somewhere else? That he was always just too late or too early? That whatever, whoever it was – this presence he sensed – had just gone as he arrived? It was like that now in the cellar. The first time down there the teacher had disturbed them. Now there was nothing. Natch. Just the ranks of wine bottles in their old wooden racks, the earth floor with their footprints all over it, and the locked door to the garden room where they had already been.

'Nothing,' Folin said.

'And if there had been anybody they'd have been out of here by now and far away, right? While we were upstairs.'

'But—'

'They'd only need a key.'

The French guys looked at him in a pitying way. The paranoid English cop, suspecting all these nice countryfolks of god knows what. Well, it's understandable, he's had a tough time lately. And now his girlfriend's done a runner, which does not show him in a good light either, right? But they're kindly giving him the benefit of the doubt because he's under a fair bit of strain what with one thing and

185

another. He said to Folin, 'Can I phone this hotel at Pollinee? Where Jude might've gone.'

'I will phone,' Folin said. 'If I may, Prof?'

They processed back up to the morning room where the phone was. Folin dialled and they all waited. He asked a question, then another, then said thanks and rang off. 'She has not arrived there and has not reserved a room.'

'A-ha.'

'Inspector Bright? I advise you please not to distress yourself. She may have gone for a drive somewhere and intends to return here for you. This is the most reasonable expectation, don't you think so?'

'She left in a hurry.'

'Yes? You know this?'

'She didn't wash up.'

The three men went through to the kitchen. They stood solemnly at the sink, gazing thoughtfully at the murky water with bits of soggy bread floating on it. 'Jude wouldn't have gone out leaving a mess like that in someone else's kitchen,' Bright said.

'Perhaps someone has been here since she left. Perhaps it is this person who has left in a hurry.'

Bright looked at Folin. The guy wasn't daft. They both turned to the teacher. Breton shrugged. 'Yes, but who?' Very puzzled, very innocent.

'Is there anyone who has access to the house?'

'Well, anybody, everybody. I leave open the front door.'

'Not today you didn't.'

'But today it was not I the last to depart; it was Jude, no?'

Bright shut his eyes a second. 'How would Jude know how to lock your door?'

'There is a – a small *bouton* below the handle inside. If this is pressed down the door will lock when one goes out.'

'Did you leave your carve door open this morning? The outside door.'

186

Breton didn't answer Bright; he spoke to Folin, his English a little less good than usual. 'I think, yes. I leave open sometimes the outside door to the *cave*, for my gardening, you know? Sometimes I forget also to lock the inner door down there, Mr Bright knows. But—' He stopped. He changed tack. 'How have you come in?'

'By the kitchen door.'

'The kitchen door? Here? No!' Breton swung round. 'But this door is never used! I have never opened it in all of my life!'

A spontaneous reaction. For the first time. It justified Bright's sense that Breton's persona was a careful construct, the real man crouching inside it, hidden like a hedgerow animal.

The teacher went to the door but Folin gently stopped him, moving faster than Bright had expected from his usual languid air. He put his hand on the man's arm and murmured to him. Breton stood back. He was running his hand through his coarse grey hair and breathing a bit fast. This door being opened had unnerved him, knocked him off his perch.

Folin examined the bolts, the handle, the specks of rust on the floor. 'No one will touch this door for the present, please.' With his tissue he pushed the door. It creaked and its bottom scraped the balcony again.

Bright drank the sudden sunlight like water. And the dazzling garden. He knew immediately, now, who had opened the kitchen door, and why she had opened it. He pushed past Folin and ran down the steps.

19

. . . Garden

He ran down the path between the vegetable beds, rows of bean canes, rows of spinach, seed rows marked out with string, big clumps of iris at their corners. Folin sprinted easily behind him. They reached the grass, and the fruit trees just coming into flower. Round the trunk of an apple tree a seat was fixed, faded to the grey-green and verdigris of the lichen-encrusted bark. Jude would sit here. She'd like this. Centuries of gardening the same way. Not like an English garden, though he couldn't put his finger on why: the mixture of flowers and veg maybe. In England, now, gardens were for show, to look like they did on the telly, all decoration. Not here. Here they liked food, so they grew stuff to eat; no objection to the odd clump of flowers but flowers were not the point. He looked at the bench as if she might have left an impression of herself sitting there. But it was just an empty bench. He touched it a moment. It was warm, but that was the sun.

They opened the shed in the far corner, an old lean-to. A rampant ivy was holding it up and at the same time tearing it down, killing it in its close embrace. Bright resisted the comparison with human relationships. He examined the place with his cop's suction-pump eyes: door nearly off its hinges, leaves and the debris of years piled on the floor, rusty spades and forks propped in a corner, an old zinc watering-can. No markers of any kind, no smell of recent disturbance or habitation.

The teacher puffed up behind them. 'When I was a child

this was our garden shed. But, perhaps twenty years ago, I began to use the *cave*.'

They each took a different route back to the house, Bright and Folin along the side walls, the teacher down the middle path. In the big square garden there was no refuge but the shed for someone to hide.

In the kitchen again, Bright asked Folin, 'Are there any other hotels, maybe not Pollinee; some other place she might go?'

'There is Lons-le-Saunier, where you came, you know? There is Dole.' Folin went back to the dining room and got on the phone.

The teacher said, 'There is the whole of the Jura, Monsieur. There is the whole of France. You said you were going south. Perhaps she has begun her journey there?'

This reasonable little speech came across as pure malevolence. Bright hated the man so much, the hatred must be mutual. He said, 'Why don't you use your kitchen door?'

The man recoiled. This was a sore subject. So Bright pursued it. 'Seems the obvious way out to the garden,' he said.

'Not for me.'

'Oh, why's that?'

'My implements, my boots etcetera. They are down in the *cave*. We were always using the *cave*.'

'Your mother too?'

The man almost swerved away. 'My mother?'

Yes. That was the sore nerve. He'd got it. Instinct. All alive-oh. The sorer you are, the surer you are. 'Your mother, yes. Did she use this door?'

The man swallowed. His eyes were wild, like an animal frightened and about to bolt. 'My father. The day he— died, my— mother closes this door and it is not opened again. That's all.'

Bright watched him. His discomfort was excessive for

189

such a simple little tale. He intended to ferret further, but it would have to wait.

Folin came back into the kitchen. 'I have telephoned to Lons to the préfecture, also to Dole and to Besançon. The word will go out. We will institute enquiries. Nothing to worry about I am sure, but we will discover if the car has been seen. Or your friend Miss Craig.' He shifted his attention to the teacher. 'You saw her this morning?'

'Yes.' Breton seemed still shaken by Bright's attack. 'Just for a small moment. I was ready to go out. She has come down the stairs. I have told her where to find the coffee and so on.'

'Has she said she might go somewhere?'

'No. I said I would return for lunch. She said she hoped to see me when I return.'

'She has not spoken of going for a little tour, close to here?'

'No. But I was *pressé*, you know, a little late. We have not had much conversation.'

They lapsed into French. Bright didn't care: Folin would give him the gist. Or as much of it as he wanted him to hear. He needed the time to calm himself down. He was getting hysterical. There was no doubt that something wrong had happened here, but it didn't necessarily mean harm to Jude. Maybe she'd gone off to help somebody else. She was like that. Her heart was too big. She'd gone to drive someone to a station or airport or hospital somewhere. Hospital. Christ. He interrupted the French flow. 'Hospitals—'

'Of course.' Folin gave him that look, with his head on one side and the small lift of his shoulders. 'Our first enquiries, naturally.'

Bright bounced on the balls of his feet, rattled the change in his pocket. Bloody euros. He hadn't got the hang of them yet. Any more than he had of the language or the customs of this alien place.

'You must have patience, Inspector.'

Bright hissed through his teeth. 'Am I allowed to make a phone call?'

'Of course.'

He used the teacher's phone. Cato answered right away. 'How you getting on, guv? They charged you yet?'

'Listen, mate. I'm worried about Jude. Keep an eye out, will you, case she comes back?'

'What do you mean?' Cato dropped the jokes. 'She's on her way home?'

'I dunno. She's gone and the car's gone. I don't like the look of it.'

Cato knew him. He knew that if Bright was worried he had reason. But he said, 'Guv, you're in a fix, your nerves'll be a bit shot up, you know. You could be overreacting—'

'Yeah, yeah, I know, and I don't understand a word they say and yeah, I'm paranoid, I'd be crazy not to be. See – if she's gone home, the first thing she'll do is get George from my ma's. But I don't wanna call my ma and get her in a state—'

'No. Right. Okay, guv. When did she leave?'

'Some time this morning.'

'In your car?'

'In my car.'

'With her luggage?'

'With her luggage.'

Cato whistled. 'See what you mean. Well, even driving like the clappers she's not going to get here before tomorrow morning, is she, guv?'

'No. No.'

'John, listen, if you want me to come out there—'

'Yeah, yeah, Cato, I know. Thanks a lot, mate. I'm not ruling it out, believe me. I'm not ruling anything out. But I'll hang on and see how it goes.'

'I located Ted Adams. It's not a vacation, it's a case. He'll

191

come as soon as it's over. The weekend, he thinks.'

'Thanks, but for now my own troubles are the least of my worries.'

'But if they've got you in custody you won't be free to—'

'I just don't see Jude doing a runner on me. Whatever else she is, she's faithful.'

'Guv, she wasn't exactly being faithful when we first came across her.'

'Oh yes she was.'

'Well, not to her old man, was she?'

'Yes she was. In her way. And don't you ever think anything else. I'm telling you, mate. She's faithful all right. She might hate my guts but she wouldn't leave me in the lurch like this. It just ain't Jude. So don't you go thinking—'

'Okay, guv, yes. Right. You leave it with me. I'll have an eye kept on her house just in case. Let me know if—'

'I will. I will, Cat. Thanks.'

Cato's slur on Jude's character had jerked him out of his paralysis. He'd told Cato no more than the truth: Jude would never, whatever their quarrel, have left him to fend for himself in this situation. But Folin was right too: he had to calm down and get this in proportion. Maybe she had just gone off for a drive. Stuck in this mausoleum on her own, no news of him, no way of getting news to him— 'Judge? Do we know if Jude phoned the police station this morning?'

'She has not.'

Of course, Folin would have checked. 'The nice place up on the hill? Château-the-Mines? She might go there again.' *Without washing up first? With her own luggage but not mine?* The questions nagged like a sore tooth.

'I have set in motion enquiries all around. There is another "nice" place close to here. Beaumes-les-Messieurs, very ancient, beautiful. Perhaps she has gone there, it's possible.

192

I have contacted there. You know, an English car, it's unusual at this time of year. It will be noticed. I think we will have news of her soon.' His voice took on a reassuring tone. Bright tried to look reassured.

The teacher opened the fridge. 'Will you take some bread and cheese with me?'

Folin hesitated a moment. 'Thank you, Professeur, but we must go. If you have any news you will inform me? Anything you wish to say to me, you may call any time. I am here to listen.' Folin held out his card to the teacher. He paused for a fraction of a second. 'You must be worried about the missing boy, your pupil, no?'

The teacher put down the baguette and the plate of cheeses. He wiped his hands on the cloth that hung on the handle of the fridge. He took the card and studied it. 'Yes.' He lifted his head and looked at Folin. This seemed an effort, but he looked the judge straight in the face. 'Je suis très, très inquièt. Et tous ses collègues étudiants, et ses parents. Je ne peux pas croire que ce garçon soit l'auteur de ce crime.'

'Non, non. Il faut trouver le garçon, c'est tout. Il pourra tout expliquer, j'en suis sûr. Il ne risque rien. Ni de moi, ni de la police.' Folin spoke with great emphasis, not loud but forceful, insistent. 'Vous comprenez, Professeur?'

'Oui, oui, je comprends. Merci.'

Folin shook hands with Breton. Bright did not. They went down the path and out of the big gates into the lane.

'You think he knows where the kid is?' Bright said.

'It's at least possible, no?'

'He knows. Any use hanging about a bit?'

'He will not make the risk, I think. I have asked him to come to me at the hôtel this evening when he comes from the school. His house will now be discreetly watched, Inspector. I have taken your advice, you see?'

He led Bright down a cart track off the lane, heading back towards the village. In a field, two horses stood close

193

together, side by side, nose to tail. One was a foal, almost full-grown. Its mother flicked her tail back and forth over her big child's face, chasing off the flies. The two men stopped a minute to watch. The mare watched them back with idle eyes, incurious. They were nothing to her. Different worlds. But we all inhabit the same world, Bright thought. *No, we don't.* He had no more idea what went on in Jude's head than if she were this big gentle horse. He had thought he did, but it was illusion. This knowledge gave him nausea, a physical sickness in his stomach.

The next house was a medieval castle with grey slate roofs, a round tower at each corner, and a dovecote in the garden, with all these little holes for the birds to fly in and out. This was a different world all right. The garden walls were high and the hedges higher, like everywhere round here. You could only see the tops of things. The tips. Bright was struck suddenly by the myriad meanings of the word tip: tip of the iceberg, tip as in dump, tip as in betting – get a good tip, a tip-off like he got from his snouts. Did they have that in French – five meanings, maybe more, for one word? He didn't ask. His mind was taking silly journeys, diversions from the main event. All he knew was, he was seeing only the tip of the iceberg in this tip of a town and he could do with a few tips as to what in hell might be going on. 'Where we going?' he said.

'The hotel. For lunch. And for arrangement of my head-quarters there.'

'Trojan horse, right?'

Folin gave him a sideways flick of the eyes, taking his measure, but he said nothing.

The wall of the garden of the house with the towers and the dovecote was still on their right, they hadn't got to the end of it yet. 'This is a big place. Lord of the manor?'

'It belongs now to a design and architectural business.'

'But it was the lord of the manor once upon a time, right?'

'In this part there were many little lords of many little manors. He was not a big one. The lord of the château in Neufchâtel was bigger, though only in comparison. He also was just a little one in fact.'

Bright liked the way Folin talked. It gave him pleasure, listening to him. The lane ended here, in forest. And the high stone wall ended too. Over its corner a weeping pine of immense height drooped its branches loaded with cones. It smelt like a vigorous bath oil, reminding him of rough towels and steaming green water. And Jude. Was there anything that didn't remind him of Jude?

Folin went ahead, apparently into a solid wall of trees, through a narrow kissing-gate, on to a path. The thickness of trees hemmed them in on both sides. After five minutes they crossed a little wooden bridge. The path curved to the right. Bright could hear the gurgle of water and just glimpsed the shine of a stream, deep in a gully hidden by twisted roots and vegetation. Lush grass caressed their ankles as they walked. Then another gate swung open at Folin's touch, and Bright saw the hotel straight ahead, facing them across the road. They had, somehow, in the woods, joined the path that came out into the wasteground car park.

'The bloke I saw the other night when I came out for a walk? When I was getting my jacket out the car and this bloke suddenly appeared, like from nowhere? This is where he came from.'

'Bloke?'

'Oh – er – man.'

'Ah. That man came through this gate?'

'Well, either that or he was already lurking.'

'I'm sorry? "Already looking"?'

'Er – no. Lurking. Hanging about.'

'Hanging?'

'Waiting around, just – you know—'

'Hiding?'

195

'Well, not exactly.' Bright rubbed a hand through his hair. 'Lurking . . . It's . . . Yes, it's kind of hiding, kind of waiting, but it's . . . Ah Christ.' He gave up.

'Will you spell it for me?'

Bright spelled it.

'I will check my dictionary. It is obviously a useful word.'

'It is in my job, mate, believe me.'

'Where was your car that night?'

'Er . . . Here. Just here.'

'You remember so clearly?'

'Yup. I parked just under the lamp so it'd light the car but not show up the inside too well. Just in case anyone got tempted, you know?'

'Tempted?'

'To break a window and have it away with the old clothes and the parking change.'

'Inspector, you will have to use less colloquial language for me. My brain is very tired already with so much English.'

Bright gave his no-smile smile, and his squint intensified. 'Do my best. But when I came out later I discovered that the lamp wasn't working so I needn't have bothered.'

'So this man who was – loorking – perhaps, or who came from the gate perhaps – he spoke to you?'

'No. Weird. I thought that at the time. They all say bonswah round here. But he didn't.'

'Yes. You can describe him?'

'I didn't hear him approach, so I didn't take him in that well. I didn't see his face. He was average height, not fat. He wore a dark jacket, dark trousers, but it wasn't a suit, the jacket was an anorak type of thing. He was carrying a bag. Not a briefcase, a shopping-type bag, soft, something in it but I couldn't say what, something lumpy, not papers or books. Could have been food. You know. Something lumpy.' Bright gestured, describing something like a bag of fruit or vegetables.

'A rabbit perhaps? At night, a man loorking, a bag – it could mean a rabbit. But no gun, no?'

'Gun? I don't think so. Could have concealed it as he passed me. But I don't think so. He was walking too easy.'

'And I think it would be a different sort of bag.'

'Yeah?' Bright had a flashback to the horse-teeth Buchon brother coming into the bar with his funny tartan shopping-bag. He described it to Folin.

'But you were not able to see for sure that it was this bag?'

'No way. Too dark. And anyway I didn't look that close. Didn't know then it was gonna be matter of life and death, did I, Judge?'

Folin smiled. 'You saw anything else before you have left the car park that night?'

'No.'

'Has anyone come out of the bar? Or gone into the bar?'

'The bar was closed. The hotel was dark. I didn't see anyone. This bloke – man – with the bag – he coulda gone into the bar maybe. He coulda been the individual slinking down the little back-street a few minutes after. All I know is, he crossed the road, that's all. I checked my watch like a good cop. It was getting on for ten to one. I checked my car. I didn't look to see where he went.'

'If we find him, he can confirm this part of your statement.'

'Maybe he already did.'

'The anonymous note? No. This note does not say you were here in the car park at this time.'

Bright stood still. 'Where does it say I was?'

Folin slid him a glance and shook his head, refusing to say.

'Anonymous letter-writers aren't famous for sticking strictly to the truth,' Bright said.

Folin didn't reply. They crossed to the hotel entrance. They could smell the lunch from here. 'Ah, rabbit, I think. Louis' vintners' casserole of rabbit is very good. It is worth coming back to Neufchâtel for this alone. You will enjoy it.'

Bright needed Louis' rabbit stew like a smack in the mouth. The idea of eating just now brought on the nausea again. But he couldn't get in a car and go on a Jude-hunt. No car, no freedom, and anyway no point: the gendarmes for miles around had it covered. 'Louis' cooking rabbits,' he said, 'when his girlfriend's just been raped and killed?'

'Life goes on. The hotel is his *métier*. Also, this is my headquarters. My officers will need food. All people need food. Many people in the district eat at the hotel. Meet at the hotel. Drink at the bar of the hotel. It is the central place.'

'I see. Good for the gossip.'

'You have it. The best place for me. So I request that Louis will remain open.'

'Like he had a choice?'

Folin smiled.

'When it was just me and Jude, he only had one room.'

'Really? He tellls me he has employed extra staff now.'

'That'll cost you.'

'I am providing employment, no?'

'Where's he get his rabbits?'

They both smiled. Folin was learning to tell when Bright was smiling. Nothing much changed in that thin tense face. You had to read the signs.

They sat at a table in a dark corner, far from the window, with a view of the whole room. 'So Louis does the cooking himself, does he?' Bright said.

'They tell me Mariela did not cook.'

'That's no surprise.'

'You did not like Mariela?'

'Oh, I did, mate. I liked her a lot.'

'Ah, just in that way.'

'No. Not "just in that way". In every way, if you want to know. She walked on the wild side all right. But she was a good girl.'

Folin raised his eyebrows but said nothing.

The dining room was hushed. Five other tables were occupied, three by blokes, looked like locals, eating alone, not communicating; two by couples, tourists, who talked in hushed voices, overcome by the atmosphere of the place.

A little thin woman with arms and legs like sticks scuttled over with her order pad. Folin ordered and she scampered away again. She made another entrance with a basket of bread, a carafe of red wine and another of water. Folin poured some wine. Bright drank. It went straight into his bloodstream like a transfusion. Then she brought the stew on thick white plates.

Bright started to change his mind about eating. He'd never seen a gravy that dark wine-brown, or been seduced by such a rich wine-smell. Even the venison at the teacher's house last night didn't come up to this. The meat was in big tender succulent pieces, on the bone. Little onions and strong-flavoured mushrooms added their individual tang and sweetness and texture. He ate spellbound, hardly speaking. At last he said, 'I see why you decided to run the investigation yourself now.' He dipped the bread in the last of the sauce and wiped it round his plate. 'And why you picked this as your HQ.'

'Ah yes! Louis' father cooked the traditional dishes of France. Louis has not changed. In this he is now an anachronism. Good food is harder to find in France now. There is not food such as this in Lons-le-Saunier.'

'Maybe you should keep Louis on gardy-voo for the rest of his life?'

Folin, pouring the last of the wine into their glasses, paused. 'The possibility has of course occurred to me.' He went on pouring.

'Has he seen her?'

'The body? Yes.'

'And?'

'He—' Folin held up a hand to demonstrate tremor.

'Trembled? Shook?'

'Very much, yes.'

'He cry? Yell? Throw up?'

'Nothing. Just confirmed it was Mariela and – shook.'

Just then, one side of Louis slid round the kitchen door. His skin looked grey. His one visible eye fixed on Folin and Bright like the eye of a bloodhound in despair. Then the half of him slid out of sight again.

Bright did not look at Folin. 'You ask him if he was out that night? If he got back about five to one?'

'Naturally. And naturally he tells us he was inside the hotel all evening, all night.'

'But he's got no alibi?'

'No.'

'You'd think he'd go out looking for her when she didn't come home, right?'

'He says it is normal for her to stay out late. He is accustomed to that.'

'Where I come from The Husband is the first place you look.'

'He is not her husband.'

'You know what I mean. He's the one with the motive. Not those lads.'

'Until "those lads" begin to talk, I cannot eliminate them.'

'Why aren't you talking to Louis?'

'I am letting him – you say "stew"?'

'Like his rabbits.'

'Under my eyes here day after day, he will make a mistake. If he has done it. If he has not, of course, he will simply continue to cook and we will continue to enjoy his food.'

'Too slow for me.'

'I leave the more direct method to my police officers.'

'I'd rather be one of them.'

'A question of temperament, no?'

Bright shrugged. A heaviness descended on him, mental as much as physical. 'Normal for you, is it?' he said. 'A big lunch like this?'

'Of course.'

'And work in the afternoon?'

'A little rest, a little sleep, just twenty minutes, and I am good.'

'Twenty minutes where?'

'In my chair? At my *bureau*.'

'Your burrow?'

'My office. My desk. Or I go home for lunch. Whatever is convenient.'

'Who's at home?'

'Ah. I am recently alone. Divorce.' He shrugged and sighed. 'This is the reason I sleep at my desk these days. And eat too much for my lunch. You will have dessert?'

'No, mate. God.'

'But a coffee? *Deux cafés, s'il vous plaît?*'

The little bundle of sticks, her spine rigid and her movements sharp, snatched up their plates and their cutlery and the bread basket and scuttled away through the pass-door to the kitchen. She was the kind they'd say lived on her nerves.

'Who's she?'

'I do not know. You did not see her the other day?'

'No. She must be the extra staff. You're getting your money's worth. Listen – the blond lad – the one who's missing—'

'Ah yes. Franck de Genares. His parents will come to see me at two-thirty.' Folin's mobile rang. 'Oui?' He listened and asked, and listened and gave instructions. He put his phone away slowly. 'Your car?' he said to Bright. 'It was seen.'

20

Affairs of the Heart?

They say it happens when you drown: your whole life passing before your eyes in an instant. But it happened to Bright now. Folin touched his shoulder to get his attention and he had no idea how much time had passed or where he had been.

'Drink some coffee, Inspector.'

The coffee was hot. It burned his mouth. 'Where?' he said.

'On the edge of Combrans just beyond the *gendarmerie* is a *lôtissement* – a group of new small houses?'

'The pink estate. Saw it this morning.'

'A boy from there, walking to school, saw a black right-hand drive Golf GTI with English numberplates. He remembers two numbers, one letter: a V, a 4 and a 3. He did not see well who has driven the car but he thinks it was a woman.'

'Thinks?'

'They ask him why he thinks so. He says she is wearing a *chapeau de dame*.'

'Unh?'

'A woman's hat.'

'A hat? Jude? Inside the car?'

'A *chapeau de paille*. Straw hat. She has such a hat?'

Oh Christ, the holiday clothes. They'd joked about the straw hat. The tourist hat. I look like an English lady on holiday, she'd said. But why wear it in the car? Forgotten she'd got it on maybe? That was possible. Leaving in a hurry. But leaving in such a hurry, she'd think to put her hat on? Maybe she had her hands full, carting out her luggage, her

202

head the obvious place to carry a hat? How on earth would he know? 'Yes,' he said. 'She's got a straw hat. Was she alone in the car? No one with her?'

'It appears she was alone.'

'What time was it?'

'The boy was late for school. Very late. Close to nine thirty.'

'Where's it go, that road? Up to a roundabout, right?'

'One direction is route N83 for Lons-le-Saunier or Poligny, the other to the Lyons autoroute.'

'It's a pay-ardge, right?'

'Yes.'

'Would there be a record? If she'd paid?'

'My man has gone now to question the people who work the *gare de péage*.'

'They couldn't keep records of every car.'

'No. And entering the autoroute the *péage* is not manned. One simply takes a ticket—'

'—from the machine, yeah. Unmanned. Shit.'

'No, but again an English car, and so early in the year. Somebody may remember. It's a chance.'

'It's a chance, yeah.' She had not just disappeared into the blue. She had been seen. Or at least the car had been seen. *If it's been seen once, it can be seen again. There's the start of a journey here.*

A uniformed cop called Folin into the bar. Bright sat on at the table. A thought shot into his mind like an arrow. A thought he had been keeping at bay: There's not just one person missing. There's two. The blond boy and Jude. He heard her say *I've been thinking all night. It's over.* She fancied the blond kid. He'd flirted with her. There are women, apparently happily married, who suddenly meet a bloke and wham bam just go off with him, D. H. Lawrence mode, without thinking twice . . . Even in these circumstances . . . Even Jude . . .

'Inspector?

Again the sensation of coming from a long way away. A slight dizziness; his brain was revolving slowly inside his skull.

'I have arranged for you a room in the hotel. It is not the room in which you stayed before – I think you would prefer another?'

Bright would not prefer another but he nodded. 'Fine.'

'You are in the room next to mine on the first floor.'

'Same floor as mine host.'

'As Louis, yes. He is across the – landing?'

They exchanged looks: much understood; nothing said.

'An officer will bring your bag here. We will examine the contents together, if that is okay with you? Now I will show you to your room and we will have a short break.'

Bright shut his eyes.

'Inspector, if there is one word of your Jude, you will be informed immediately, I swear to you. But for now you must have patience. You must.'

'Sure.' Bright exhaled hard. 'Yeah. Thanks.'

This room was at the front. The window overlooked the street and the wasteground where his car no longer was, and the big red brick house with all its eyes closed – shutters closed – an image of death. He turned his back on it.

He looked at the bed for some time, then lay down on it, then got up again and paced round the room. He opened the wardrobe, an ancient thing, creaking door and a smell of imprisoned air and feathers. He found a blanket and two square pillows, took out the pillows and threw them at the bed. The bed-head had curlicues on its corners. It matched the wardrobe: the satiny mid-brown wood that Jude called French wood. He lay down again.

The room was dark, the wallpaper busy with dark brown and orange flowers. Even the panels of the door were

204

papered. Just like the hotel in Poligny. Would she go back to Poligny? They'd been happy there. He wanted to remember that, but she wouldn't want to. No. She wouldn't go back there, unless she was taking the same route home. Would she go home? She wouldn't go on down south, would she? Alone? But maybe she wasn't alone. Here it came – the question he didn't want to face: would she go down south with the blond boy? *I don't even know her well enough to know that.* But one picture kept coming: Woman in Straw Hat in English Golf GTI. Blond Boy Hiding in Back; or even in the boot until they're clear of the Jura, out of harm's way. Why would the blond boy need to be out of harm's way? *Because he's guilty of* . . . Bright hauled the bolster from under the bedcover and flung it on the floor. He arranged the pillows, then got up and dragged the blanket out of the wardrobe. Lying down once more, he pulled the blanket over him, for comfort rather than warmth. He didn't even take his shoes off.

The blond boy's face when he heard Mariela had gone off with the motorbike boys. The blond boy jumping on his bike and roaring off after them. Did he know where they would be? Was there one place they always went? The spot by the river where she was found? Was that their regular place? Did he catch up with them? Did they kill him too? Was it the blond boy's body these police were looking for? Or had the blond boy fled? Fleeing didn't mark him guilty; it just marked him scared. What if the boy had seen the killer – or killers – and then they'd seen him?

The police thought the motorbike boys had done it? That was the obvious assumption. He'd give anything to be able to question those boys, last seen handcuffed in the prefecture at Lons-le-Saunier. To question anybody, come to that. To do something. *They might as well have* me *handcuffed to a gendarme's desk as lying here helpless. Come on, hold on, Folin's being as good as gold. Thank Christ he took over the case from that bastard adjutant. You gotta keep faith with Folin.* But the lack of activity was killing him, squeezing the breath out of his body. He gasped for air, sitting up and holding his chest. He sweated, not with heat. On the contrary, the room was cold. This was a panic attack. Not a heart attack. *Not at my age. Couldn't be. Could it?* He crossed his arms over his chest and tried to breathe. His shoulders came up; the air wouldn't go down to his lungs, stayed trapped in his throat. His lungs were shut off, closed down. He stood and went to the wall and raised his arms and put both his hands flat on the wall and lowered his head and, that way, breathing into his back, he forced air into himself. His old wound stabbed him sharp in the back below his bottom rib. He preferred the pain to the panic. Panic like this was new to him. He never wanted it to happen to him again.

Waiting. That's what was doing it to him. Waiting. He'd never been able to wait even for a bus. Kicking his heels while someone else carried out an investigation: this was his nightmare. To have only Folin's account of the questioning, the interviews, the witnesses, the forensic discoveries, the conduct of the case. No control. No decisions. No activity. How could he bear this? His hands curled into fists. Elbows against the wall, he beat the horrible French wallpaper silently, banging silently on the wall as in a nightmare – or a padded cell – where you scream and no one can hear you. And Jude was crying out now and no one could hear her, either. He wanted to beat the truth out of the teacher-man. He wanted to beat him even if no truth came out. He wanted to clout him round his big smug head till he bled. 'Ah, Christ.'

He came away from the wall and sat on the bed with his hands over his face. He got up and went into the little shower room that was hardly a room, just a hardboard partition with a loo and a sink and a shower, barely space to move.

He ran cold water and splashed his face, his head, then drank from his cupped hands. Held his hands there, wet, over his nose and mouth. Cold water dripped down his neck, off his face and his hair. He looked in the pockmarked mirror. He was still there. He looked the same. More or less. He'd hold it together till he knew where Jude was. The rest could go to hell. There was a knock on the door. He jumped, and the breathing problem threatened to hit him again. He kept his eyes steady on his face in the mirror. Told himself, *You'll be okay.*

'Inspector?'

Bright opened the door.

Folin said, 'The parents of the missing boy have arrived to speak to me. You would like to accompany me?'

'What – sit in?'

'Sit in?'

Bright spelled it out. 'Be present for the interview.'

'You don't want to?'

'Christ, Judge—' Bright grabbed his jacket off the bed.

'Good. And also you have been perhaps the last person to see him, you know. The parents surely will be happy to hear some news of their son.'

21

The Horse's Mouth

Folin was using the top floor as his centre of operations. His officers were in the room where Jude and Bright had slept. You had to pass it to reach the interview room. Folin turned his head to look at Bright. Bright let no expression cross his face.

The door of the interview room was open. You could see the oblong of darker carpet where the bed had stood. A desk and four hard chairs had been brought up from the dining room below. Harsh light came from the window, and the sharp noises of the street. Two chairs had been placed opposite the window. A man and a woman sat there, upright and motionless. When Folin and Bright came in their heads turned in unison and Bright got the impression of a couple in perfect communication without the need of speech. They were twinned in appearance too: both tall, thin, straight-backed, mid-forties or a bit older, elegantly dressed.

Folin introduced them. 'Monsieur and Madame de Genares.'

They nodded gravely to Bright, so he nodded back. He sat on the other side of the room with his back to the window. Folin talked to them in French. Bright watched them. They remained upright and grave. They might have been discussing world events, the bombing in Afghanistan perhaps, rather than the disappearance of their son and the possibility that he had killed, or been killed. They showed no personal involvement. They nodded, they shook their heads. They seemed impenetrable. Bright wanted to shake them, but that was the mood he was in. Instead he concentrated on their body language. People who are lying, their faces show little expression, they sit very still. That's one way you detect liars. But these two – their stillness seemed natural. They were tense all right, but maybe more from being here, involved with a murder investigation, police prying into their nice private lives, than because they had something to hide.

Folin said, 'Monsieur and Madame de Genares speak a little English. Will you tell them of the last time you saw their son?'

Bright described the evening outside the hotel. When their brows furrowed Folin translated. They listened without a spark of reaction. Bright said, 'You must have been worried when he didn't come home.'

They looked to Folin who said, 'No. It seems not. Franck has his own part of the house with its own entrance. They and Franck, they keep different hours. Until Professeur Breton telephoned them they did not know he had not gone out to school as usual.'

'Can I speak to them or you want me to keep stumm?'

'Please,' Folin said, with a graceful gesture of his hand.

'Do you have other children?' Bright said.

They shook their heads. She looked to her husband and then to Bright. 'We breed horses.'

He looked twice at her. She wasn't being funny.

'It needs much time,' she said. 'Much work.'

He got it. That lovely lad – Franck – was an accident. A nuisance. Rage came up and hit him in the throat. He said, slow and clear and in his best English, 'Your son was in love with Mariela – the victim. Did you know that?'

They shied like a pair of their own thoroughbreds, nostrils flaring, heads back, away from this distasteful subject.

'He was crazy about her,' Bright said. 'He was very distressed when we told him she'd gone off with the boys.'

They continued not to look at Bright, both concentrating on the same corner of the room. They wanted to hold hands, he could tell, but they wouldn't while they were being watched.

'Have any of your neighbours seen him?'

'No,' Folin said.

'Any relations – grandparents, aunties, uncles he might have gone to?'

'Our families are in Paris. We have telephoned. He is not with them.'

'We are checking,' Folin said. 'And they have an apartment in Paris. That is being watched also.'

Bright had a vision of a Paris apartment. Something out of a movie. The boy and Jude there alone, a bed in a big dim room, the two of them on it. He said, 'He's a clever boy,' like he was making conversation. 'He has a future.'

They looked down their horsy noses like he'd spoken ill of the dead. How dare he speak with familiarity of their son.

He said, 'This teacher, Mister Breton – he seems to have a close relationship to the boy.'

'He is a good teacher. He thinks well of our son. He has devoted himself to Franck's study of languages. Professeur Breton has inspired him.'

'You ever think the teacher was maybe a bit too close to him?'

They looked to Folin for help. Like they hadn't understood. But they had understood: that was clear as glass. Folin translated. Bright had to give it to him. He didn't turn a hair, just made the suggestion in a neutral tone with a bland face.

Again they curled back their lips in horsy contempt for this nasty notion. They shrugged ever so slightly: *So what if the teacher was a little too close? What harm would that do to anyone?*

'You think Franck can take care of himself, that it?'

They gave him a high-handed stare that was meant to

wither him. Then they spoke to Folin in French. Bright didn't need a translation: Who is this nasty little English creep and by what right is he questioning us, two upright French citizens who have done no wrong?

But you have done wrong, you creeps, you've left that kid to fend for himself and not even noticed when he's missing from home for a night and a day. And they wouldn't have noticed after another night and day if— 'How long would it have been,' he said 'before you noticed he was missing? If there hadn't been a murder, that is.'

The man spoke in French to Folin, ignoring Bright. Folin said, 'They would have noticed on Sunday. They have a family lunch each Sunday. The boy always comes.'

'Nearly a week.' Bright nodded, gazing at them. 'Have they searched?' He directed the question at Folin. 'These two. Have they looked for him? Have they searched his room? Have they searched their house and their grounds and their stables? Have they checked to see if he's hidden on their estate anywhere? Could they be hiding him from you?'

Folin repeated all that, more politely, in French. The man raised a hand in a weary way as if to say of course they had searched, 'Et nous n'avons rien trouvé.'

'Yes and they have found nothing.'

'Thanks, I got that.'

The woman's face showed a quiver of something, Bright didn't know what. Conscience maybe? Not pain. They wouldn't show their pain till they got home. And even there maybe they wouldn't. Just then, observing the woman, he got something; nothing definite, just an intuition: that she might never show her husband what she felt. *She's been broken like a horse. She can't show love for her son, because this man has her in hand. If we could get her on her own, we'd find out more, find out something anyway.* He couldn't say this to Folin in front of them. They understood more

English than they cared to admit: they'd lose face, speaking it badly. Bright subsided. No point probing further with the husband here: they'd get nowhere. He said to Folin, 'Have you been to their house?'

'My officers are searching now. Monsieur and Madame de Genares have kindly allowed us full access to their house and grounds.'

'Where do they live?'

The husband didn't wait for the translation. He shot out, 'Château-les-Mînes,' like Bright was a spittoon.

'Lovely place,' Bright said. 'Is he impulsive? Your son. Franck. Is he the type to go off – like fall in love and take off – with a woman he'd just met? An older woman. In her thirties, say. That sound like him?'

Folin got the point. He explained that Bright's girlfriend had disappeared too. Bright knew, because the woman shot him a quick look from the side of her eyes. But it was the husband who replied, shaking his head irritably. Folin said, 'Monsieur de Genares thinks it unlikely that Franck would have run away with— with your friend or with Mariela. Franck has never been impulsive.'

'The lad I saw haring off after Mariela was.'

Folin ignored this. He stood up and so did the thoroughbreds. They shook his hand and said their au-revoirs. Very gracious, very polite. The man did not shake Bright's hand or even look his way as they went out of the room. The woman gave him a solemn nod. No hint in her eyes admitted the moment of truth he had seen. *But if I could get you on your own, Madam . . .*

When Folin shut the door Bright said, 'He's jealous of her. Wants her all to himself. She's had to make the choice – her son or him.'

'Why do you say this?'

'Just a little glimpse. You wouldn't have seen it, you were talking to him. You'll have to get her on her own. She'll tell

212

you stuff you'd never get out of her in front of him.'

'I cannot force her. She is not a suspect.'

'Right.' Bright paused. 'You might find she comes to you.'

Folin smiled at him. 'I do not think I have your gifts of observation.'

'Well, you're the bloke in charge. It's easy for the onlooker, right?' *You stroke my ego, I'll stroke yours. Flattery cuts both ways.* 'Well, then. What next?'

'Next I will check my messages.'

Messages. Jude. The car. Bright's stomach clenched like a fist. He turned to the window. The horse-couple came out of the hotel. They didn't look to right or left or hesitate in any way. They crossed the road to the wasteground and the husband unlocked a beaten-up old Land Rover. She waited while he unlocked her door. He waited while she got in, then shut the door on her. Very solicitous. Very polite. He got in and reversed into the road. A truck had to brake for him. The Land Rover turned left along the street that led to the main bridge over the river and the road up to Château-les-Mînes.

Folin put down his phone. 'Your car has been seen again.'

Bright's mouth went dry. 'Where?'

'In Poligny.'

'Yes!'

'On route N83 going north. At about ten minutes before ten this morning. Driven by a woman. No passenger. Driving fast.'

'Fast?' *Not stopping then.*

'Again, it is two boys who notice. They are outside the school.'

'Having a smoke.'

'Probably.'

'The hat? She still wearing the hat?

'They don't know.'

'They were asked?'

213

'They have been thoroughly questioned. They recalled the same digits of the numberplate.'

'They describe the woman?'

'I'm sorry. They were interested only in the car.'

'Nothing? Jude has this hair, curly, colour of chestnuts, you know, this dark red?' Bright couldn't go on speaking.

'I'm sorry, Inspector.'

'Why do they remember it was a woman at all? If they didn't look at her?'

'We all notice only those things that interest us.'

'How old are these kids?'

'Twelve years.'

'Fourteen, they'd be able to describe the woman. If it was Jude, believe me they would.'

'I believe you.'

Bright covered his eyes with his hands. Not for long. An officer came in from next door with some papers. Bright said, 'Anything else new?'

'These are the *procès verbal* forms, the depositions from all the three parents of all the three boys on the motorbikes. Ah yes, I see – their sons are each one at home in bed before midnight on the night of Mariela's death.'

'There's a surprise. You believe them?'

'No. But of course I hope to discover that their stories are true.'

'You questioned the boys personally?'

'Not yet. They are still on *garde à vue* at the préfecture. Still telling the same story, that they fooled around a little bit with Mariela in that place at the river but that she became tired of the game and so they went home.'

'They left her there on her own?'

'She told them to go.'

'Oh yeah!'

'One of them will decide at last to tell the truth, I think. Then he will be brought to me here.'

'They got any legal representation?'

'Only one has an advocate. In this part of the world we do not have many criminal lawyers. They have to come a long distance. It is difficult for the parents to arrange. This lawyer who has come for Gérard Touzet will persuade him to speak, I think.'

'Our guys generally tell them keep stumm. Silent. Dumb.'

'Thank you. I understand stumm.'

'You have the right to silence here?'

'Yes. But anywhere it is the same. If you exercise this right it is seen as an admission of guilt, or of guilty knowledge. It is a delicate balance, no?'

Bright was in the same boat as those lads. He needed Ted Adams: Ted could at least hire a car, drive round looking for Jude. 'Listen,' he said. 'Put me on gardy-voo with one of your cops. We could drive round looking for Jude. Then I'd have a reason for living. I can't stay cooped up here, man. I'm doing no good! Standing round listening to people telling lies in French. If they do it in English I can get them to cough but here I can't. I'm the spare prick at the wedding. I'm going out my mind. Let me out!'

Another uniform knocked and came in with a ring binder. He and Folin exchanged rapid-fire French. Bright turned back to the window. It was all he could do not to jump out, second floor or not. As he turned, one of the shutters on the big red house over the road opened. Just a few inches, not all the way. It was a window on the first floor to the left of the front door. He said to Folin, 'Who lives in the big red house over there?'

'It is the mother of Louis.'

'Our host Louis?'

'The same.'

'Someone just opened a shutter. They've been closed the whole time I've been in this place.'

Folin joined him at the window. He put the ring-binder on

215

the sill. They watched the house together for a few moments. Nothing happened. Folin's mood had changed. Bright noticed he had kept his hand on the folder. 'What's in that?' he said.

Folin said nothing, just opened the folder.

The forensic report. Bright had seen a thousand of them. Interspersed with the scene-of-crime pictures. The livid whites and purples you only ever see in forensic colour prints. Two to a page. Four to a spread.

'What's it say?'

'The cause of death was strangulation.'

'With the rope?'

'No. Hands round the throat, it seems. Severe bruising and laceration to the vagina and surrounding area, vagina wall broken, torn through to rectum. No semen or other human samples in the pubic area.'

'So they raped her with a foreign object, like I said.'

'They?'

'Or he. Or she. Or it. Before death, or there wouldn't be all that blood.'

'Yes.'

'How long before death?'

'Of course the pathologist is not able to give accurate times, but not too long. Less than a half-hour.'

'Any idea what it was – the rape-tool? Broken bottle? Hunting knife? Any idea?'

'They have found – splinters? – of wood, tree-wood – bark? in the vagina, and in the thigh lacerations also.'

'A branch off a *tree*?'

'This is probable.'

'Some branch, from what I saw. Opportunist then. Grab whatever's to hand. Sudden rage, not careful planning.'

'But the act may have been contemplated for some time.'

'A-ha.' Bright turned a page to look at another spread of four pictures. 'She was trussed up after death or before?'

'From the coagulation in certain areas it appears that she

216

was roped to the tree after. But the wrists were tied before.'

'Tie her hands. Rape her, kill her, *then* lash her to a tree? That's weird. They sure?'

'As certain as possible. From the bruising and also the amount of bleeding.' Folin turned the page. The next spread showed the body face-down. 'You see her back? Here. And here. Traces of leaves and soil. But not – bark? – of the tree to which she was tied.'

'They can tell if she was throttled in a prone position?'

'Yes, from the areas of coagulation. She was prone when strangled.'

'He can't throttle her while he's doing it with a tree branch. Can he?'

'More than two hands would be needed.'

'Maybe more than two hands were used.'

'It is an unpleasant scenario to contemplate.'

'They see worse on the Internet, they're watching it from the age of five.'

'We must not make assumptions, Inspector.'

'No. First work out how one bastard pervert might do this by him- or her- or itself.' Bright started to ease the pictures out of the plastic wallets. They spread them on the floor, arranging them in an order that told a story. 'Her hands were tied here,' Folin said. 'You see? When she is on the ground. You can see the marks on the wrists. The rope has burned the skin here, you see?' He pointed to Mariela's delicate wristbones, scored with livid scratches where the rope had scraped as she struggled.

'She was on her back when these marks were made?'

'Yes, these marks have been made when she is on the earth.'

'And is the earth in the lacerations the same earth where she was found?'

'It is. The same. The vegetation—'

'Yeah, yeah. So the tree bark here on the inside of her arms—?'

217

'The tree bark comes after death.'

They both stared at the bleak picture-book story spread on the floor, silent for some time. Then Bright said, 'This is my story, right? He ties her hands, he tries to rape her but he can't get it up, or whatever his problem is. So he goes berserk, tears this bloody great branch off a tree or finds it on the ground maybe and does it with that. Then he throttles her. Either because he's scared shitless or because his blood's up and he can't stop. Whatever gives him his kicks. Then he decides to make it look like a ritual, like a serial thing, right? Or like a sex game gone bad. He trusses her up with the rest of the rope, gets it tight round her neck so it'll look like that killed her. Lashes her to the tree.'

'He needs time to do this.'

'It makes me think there's more than one.'

'Somebody must keep watch?'

'If you're on your own you go to all that trouble with a dead body? You kill her, you get out of there, you don't hang around making a freakin work of art out of her.'

'You think he kills from accident?'

'What? He doesn't mean to, he's at the end of his tether? Ha ha.'

'I'm sorry?'

'Nothing, just a nasty little pun. I dunno, I dunno.'

'Does it start as a game and he goes too far? Or is it intentional from the start?'

'A ritual all along? Humiliation.'

'A necrophile satisfaction.'

'I think it was to make it look like the boys had done it.'

'If they did not do it.'

They stared at the story the pictures did not tell.

One picture showed just the rope. An ordinary tow-rope of an innocent bright blue. 'Who'd have a rope like that in their vehicle?' Bright said.

'Oh everybody in this region. Especially in winter. We

218

have bad, bad winters here. The rains can be very bad. Very bad. And the snows worse. Without rope the car is . . .' Folin gestured.

'Stuck.'

'Stuck. Yes. In fields, in the forest, even the roads. The rivers grow very high. They cascade down from the mountains and sometimes deluge the roads.'

'What about motorbikes? They wouldn't need to carry ropes.'

'They are of farming families. It is likely these boys too carry rope.'

'If everyone's got a tow-rope we can't assume intention from the start.'

'No. Is it the boys who have tied her hands? Has she allowed this? Does she believe this is a game?'

'If they did, did they do the nasty stuff as well? Or did that all happen after they'd gone?'

'If they have done it, they will all tell the same story.'

'Yeah, they'll back each other to the hilt.'

'We keep them separate, of course. We can hint that one of them has broken down and told us everything. That way the weakest one may break.'

'If you do that and they've been telling the truth all along, you get to look pretty daft.'

'Yes. I am prepared to look – daft? – to make a break in this *impasse*.'

'The lad who's missing. Franck.'

'None of the boys has yet volunteered one word of him.'

'They've been asked, have they?'

'Of course, Inspector. They each say they have not seen him. On the night in question.'

'If he's done a runner, it's possible he did the nasty stuff.'

'Of course. And if his disappearance is not voluntary—'

'Could be he saw something, watched the whole thing maybe—'

219

'And they discovered him and—'

'Bumped him off as well. Rode his bike off to divert suspicion.'

'This is quite a good reason for them not to mention him to my officers, I agree.'

'That's why you asked me if the river was in spate that night.'

'At this moment the river has given us nothing. No weapon. No body.'

'Have you got anything on any of these lads you can use as the thin end of a wedge?'

'What?'

If Bright had not been so sunk in gloom he'd have laughed at Folin's mystification. 'Use as leverage.'

'Ah yes. We are exploring, of course.'

'Nothing in the records on any of them?'

'No but I have some officers in the field.'

'Asking around.'

'Asking around, yes.'

'No good.' Bright spoke from experience. 'Not in this place. No one'll grass them up. These kids are their own. They're kin. Mariela was an outsider. They all fancied her but they wouldn't lift a hand to help her.'

'You are right. I will hear the truth only if I can find the end of this wedge.'

'Someone you can threaten or bribe.'

'Precisely.' Folin looked at his watch and sighed. 'I must now call the *juge des libertés*.'

'Who's he?'

Folin sighed again. 'It is a new idea. A new level of bureaucracy. To "protect the suspects". He decides whether to send the suspect on remand. He is not part of the case. He knows nothing about the case. But the decision is his.'

'Can you make recommendations?'

'Of course. But he is not obliged to follow.'

Bright shook his head in sympathy. It was the same the whole world over. The prats who made the rules. Folin got through, said a few words, then sat, tapping his pen this way up then that way up, imitating the ritual dance he was going through here. Bright admired the way he kept his cool. He heard him put the same arguments in different ways, he knew the patient tone, the jockeying. Then silence fell at the other end. And Folin let the silence progress. Bright held his breath. This was hard to do – let a silence stretch, resist the temptation to fill it, to jump in with reiterated arguments, pleas. Let 'em stew. Just wait. And in the end he heard the voice on the other end give in. Folin raised his hand in the air with the thumb cocked and the index finger pointing. Bright started to collect up the pictures, replacing them in the binder. The voice at the other end of the phone rolled on, laying out conditions. Folin gravely agreed, thanking the bureaucratic ankle-biter, saying good-humoured goodbyes. He put down the phone and shook his head.

'Tiring, innit, mate? What you get?'

'All the boys on remand. For one week pending review.'

'Big deal.'

'I am informed so. Many times. That I am a lucky man.' He rubbed his eyes with the heel of both hands. 'Tshshsh.'

'Where will they be held?'

'At Lons-le-Saunier. They will be fearful, so long, so far away from home, in a strange place.'

'How can you hold them on so little evidence?'

'The *juge des libertés* could put you yourself on remand also on such little evidence. They admit they were with the victim, by the river, playing sexy games. They do not admit the rope, or forcing her, and especially they repudiate the charge of killing her. But it is enough for the moment.'

Bright put the last picture back into the folder. He got up, stiff from kneeling so long on the floor, and went again to watch the street from the window. His car might come over the crossroads down there and swing into the car park opposite and pull up and the door would open and Jude would get out and . . . 'Judge?'

His tone brought Folin to the window.

The landlord Louis had come out of the hotel. He was crossing the road to the big red house. He opened the gate with a key and locked it behind him. He loped up the drive with long loopy strides. He stopped at the steps to the terrace but did not go up: he turned and looked behind him. He scanned the hotel windows. He did not see Bright or Folin who had drawn back. When they looked again he was just disappearing down the side of the house.

'I have asked him not to leave the hotel.'

'We better go get him then, hadn't we?'

'Hands on?' Folin said. 'This is the correct name for you.'

'You got it.'

'You no more than I. Let us go.'

As they went down the stairs Bright saw Jude, trussed up like Mariela, that rope wound tight round her neck, her face blackened, her strong hands tied, helpless, behind her back. Folin turned to see why he had hesitated on the stair and saw his white face. 'Are you okay, Inspector?'

'A-ha. Yup. I'm okay. Let's go.'

'Do not imagine or think. Try simply to watch and to listen.'

'Listen with mother,' Bright said.

22

Listen with Mother

They too walked round the side of the house to the back. Did none of these people use the front entrance? Folin opened the back door without knocking and they both stepped, silent, into a stone room with an earth floor, empty but for a long manger, just like the one in the teacher's *cave*, where animals must once have come to feed, a row of iron rings set into the stone wall above, to tether the beasts. Again Bright saw rope and images of tying. Tying and dying.

Open stairs went up the side wall. They climbed, quiet and quick, coming out into a kitchen, a big room that stretched from the front to the back of the house. No one there. A door was open to a large entrance hall with a graceful wide main staircase going to the floor above. They looked into the big dining room on the other side of the hall, uncomfortably furnished in shiny reddish wood. No one there either. They went up these stairs, quieter and quicker. A voice came from the first floor, maybe from the room where Bright had seen the shutter open? Sound reverberated off these hard surfaces, terracotta, stone. The echo made it hard to tell.

Double doors, Folin turns the handles, slow and silent. The room is a bedroom. The shutters in here are closed, making it dark, but they have small heart-shaped holes through which light creeps, two long fingers of light, stroking the tiled floor, the crucifix on the wall over the head of the bed, a bed where generations have given birth and died, faded wallpaper a hundred years old, wisteria leaves and flowers, crawling all over the room. The fingers touch a patch of black and mushroomy damp up in the corner where wall and ceiling meet. It's not a cheerful atmosphere. The room has an antique upright sofa and two matching chairs. It has a grand fireplace in cracked marble. It was once some kind of *salon* maybe, what people used to call a morning room. A mourning room: Bright associated that bed with death rather than birth. It was the smell – of trapped air where an old person sleeps. It filled his nostrils with panic. But the voice had not come from this room.

They crossed the landing on silent feet and stopped at the door. The voice had not ceased. Was it male or female? The timbre was deep, but the tone harsh and grating, associated from time immemorial with the cliché of strident mothers-in-law, nagging wives, grinding on, laying down the law. If Louis was in there, he wasn't making a sound: the voice left no room for interruption. Folin stood relaxed, arms folded, head cocked, listening. All the time in the world. Then someone let out this cry: the howl of an animal with its leg in a trap. Folin opened the door.

A woman sat in a stiff armchair, her flesh spilling over its edges, her face and neck a continuous broad mass of folded warty flesh, her sparse hair cut short. One leg rested on a stool. The foot was bandaged, showing swollen purple toes. Louis was kneeling on the floor, his head lowered, his hands over his ears, his upper body rocking to the rhythm of his crying, the high-pitched squealing of a child, outside his control.

Folin gave a perfunctory tap on the door and strolled into the room. Bright followed. The air in here, though not as thick as in the bedroom, was not anything you wanted inside you. Bright took shallow breaths so as not to contaminate his lungs.

'Bonjour. Madame Barbe? Je suis juge Auguste Folin, Madame. Je vous présente l'inspecteur John Bright de Londres.' He said to Bright, 'Louis and I attended the same

224

class at school. But Madame I have not met before, I believe.'

'I think you'd remember if you had,' Bright said.

Louis lifted his head. His howling stopped. His face was wet, water running from his droopy eyes, his nose and mouth. The woman hardly moved, her little eyes glittering at Folin from between the folds of flesh.

One shutter was still open a crack and a beam of light cut a path across the room. This was the *salon* proper. The wallpaper, dark red roses on thorny dark green stems, was grubby and faded but had once been grand. The big marble fireplace had a small electric fire crammed into the grate, but it wasn't on; the air was chill as well as stale. Folin went to the window and opened the other shutter. The light widened and spread, filling the room. He tried to open a window but it wouldn't budge. 'Louis?' he said. 'S'il vous plaît?'

Louis fumbled his way off his knees and opened the window. The handle was stiff that locked the vertical bar that kept the windows shut. He had to use both hands. Then both sides of the window came loose. Bright needed to be in contact with outdoors now, all the time. Not just to breathe but also to check developments. He didn't specify what developments. He just needed to see Jude. Every black car that appeared was his, before he had to admit it was just another Renault or Peugeot or Citroën, that there was nothing yet out there for him. He took up his favourite position: to those inside he was a silhouette; to him they were vivid in the setting sun.

Louis sat now with his mouth hanging open. He wore his apron from the kitchen. It was stained with blood. He kept rubbing his neck with one hand like it itched or was sore. His Adam's apple moved constantly as he swallowed, trying to moisten his mouth.

The mother was giving Folin the benefit of her opinion of being walked in on by the law without prior appointment. She was doing a good job of it, considering she had only

225

one leg to stand on. When she paused to draw breath, Folin's reasonable voice told her this was a murder investigation and his son's fiancée was the victim. Bright didn't need translation; he knew the score. He was watching, with the same frustration but the same detachment as he'd watch a movie without subtitles, picking up the gist, watching the body language because he had little else. He was an audience.

He appreciated how cleverly Folin was using him: he's an experienced observer, so make him the audience at the foreign movie, while he waits to be eliminated from suspicion, and for news of Jude. Waste not, want not: this way they both get something out of the sorry mess. Investigator was his natural role. Observer was not. But it sure as hell beat sitting in a cell in the basement of the préfecture in Lons-le-Sauna or whatever they called it. He leaned back on the window frame and folded his arms. He could breathe here anyway, the air clear and pure, with a hint of the chill of the mountains, now that the sun was nearly gone. Then he heard Folin say *Mariela*, and his concentration narrowed.

The Toad's wide lipless mouth made a downward curve. She took no trouble to pretend that she was sorry for the girl. Bright could have written her script: Mariela was no better than she ought to be, she was a cheap tart and fortun-hunter and she deserved whatever she got.

Folin explained with gestures, and with graphic description in his quiet smooth voice, what had been done to Mariela; Bright recognised *victime*, and *corde*. Either the woman had already heard or the details gave her satisfaction. She listened impassive, the mouth in its downward curve, the hairless eyebrows raised. Bright began to see this woman ordering the killing as she might a meal, the meat extra rare, the ingredients arranged just so on the plate. It was far-fetched but, standing in this room watching her, he could almost believe it.

Louis was abject in her presence. Not the world's most

dynamic male at the best of times, he'd had to go to Mauritius to find himself a bride. Why? Bright asked himself for the first time. A bloke with all his limbs in order, no beauty but not absolutely repulsive, a good business – the hotel obviously doing well, plenty to inherit, if this house were anything to go by – why hadn't Louis been able to find a wife from round here? Because any woman who met the Toad would run a mile. The children might inherit these genes. What woman would risk burdening a kid with such a curse? Or the world with a replica of this?

Her voice was a thin nasal wheeze with a kind of low-pitched gurgle in it, like her lungs were full of water. It was horrible to listen to, it made Bright gag. He loathed her. He'd hesitate to touch her: she might secrete venom like a real toad. He sensed that she did indeed secrete venom, though maybe not of the physical variety. Imagine growing up with this for a mother. Why hadn't Louis stayed in Mauritius where he might have had a chance of happiness? Why had he come back? Because everyone comes back? Everyone comes home?

No. She had the money, that was it. He'd bet Louis didn't own the hotel. He'd bet this creature kept the purse strings in her hands. Her hands, spotted brown and warty like her face, were knotted in her lap and never moved. Never moved. That was interesting. She was lying. Her eyelids drooped over her eyes and opened again in a regular pattern as she talked; her slit of a mouth moved minimally, but her body stayed still.

Bright said to Folin, 'What's the money situation here? Who owns the hotel? She owns it, right?'

The eyes did not even flick in his direction. She stayed impassive, eyelids rising and drooping in their regular rhythm.

Louis didn't look at him either. But Folin did. 'Why do you want to know this?'

'I want to know how much power she's got. And where it comes from. Does she own him in more ways than one?'

Folin asked her: 'Madame, c'est vous qui est la propriétaire de l'Hôtel Sanglier?'

She sat for a while, considering whether to reply or not. Then she spoke. 'Louis,' she said.

She was saying the hotel belonged to Louis? No. She was not; she was issuing instructions.

Louis stood up. But then he was stuck. He looked from the Toad to Folin. He dared not move.

'What's she telling him to do?'

'To telephone their lawyer.'

'She's refusing to answer your questions?'

'Yes. Who owns the hotel is not relevant to my enquiry. In her opinion.'

'Why's Louis not phoning then?'

'I do not know.'

'He needs permission.'

'He has his mother's.'

'He needs yours.'

'Louis?' Folin graciously waved him to the phone on the other side of the room, went with him and had a quiet word. 'I have told him that his lawyer will probably advise him to answer all our questions frankly.'

'Is that true?'

'No.'

'A-ha.'

'But I must allow him to call. It is the law.'

Louis spoke quietly into the phone. It struck Bright that this was the first time he'd heard the miserable sod speak, except for the mumble when he had first shown them to their room in the hotel. Speech did not come easy to Louis: he spoke back in his throat, swallowing his words as though they were dangerous animals that must not escape. He was scared of the words; he was scared of his voice. In this house, in the presence of the Toad, he was a small boy trying to make himself invisible. To escape her wrath? Or to escape her love? Bright could have felt sorry for the guy but stopped himself. This was the coward who'd driven Mariela to such frantic measures. This might be the bastard who'd violated her body with a torn-off tree branch, then strangled her. Pity was out of order.

Louis brought the phone to the Toad. She gurgled orders into it then handed it to Louis to put back on the table in the corner. Then she told Folin where to get off. And then she told Louis to help her out of the room. Louis hauled her, wheezing and grunting, out of the chair. He took her across the landing into the airless bedroom and shut the double doors on her.

Folin said, 'When her lawyer arrives we will continue the interview.'

'With her or with Louis?'

'With both. But Louis will accompany us now, back to the hotel.'

'Be a pleasure to get out of here.'

'I agree.'

Louis drooped ahead of them down the main staircase. Bright fought the impulse to kick him up the arse, to goose him into some sort of life. The sad drip's demeanour was the same now as before the murder. Could nothing change it? Had he been different in Mauritius when he met Mariela? If he'd been like this, why would she have come back to France with him? Even for the life she dreamed of, would she really have married the man they saw here, creeping about like a slug?

It seemed important now to know: had Louis always been like this? As a kid? As an adolescent? It struck him, he could ask Folin. Folin had been at school with the guy. He should know.

But he got no chance to ask. They got back to the incident

229

room. The phone rang. The young cop picked it up. He handed it to Folin. Folin's eyes flicked to Bright and away. After that he avoided eye-contact.

It was bad news.

23

Accidents Will Happen

Arc-lights lit up the night sky. A crowd had gathered on the viewing platform. Gendarmes kept them back from the edge where the fence had been smashed down. They drove past the crowd and on to where the road started the descent into the Cirque. The lights whitened the trees and the sky like snow. The car stopped and they got out. A local cop greeted them, shaking Bright's hand but, like Folin, avoiding his eye. They followed him along a narrow path through trees. Undergrowth had been cut back but brambles still grasped and caught.

The light intensified. The car had ripped the treetops all the way down, had probably turned over once or twice in its descent. It was now the right way up but impaled on the broken trunk of a tree. The windows were at a man's eye-level.

Jude was in the driver's seat, strapped in, her face broken on the right side, her head back. Franck lay in a foetal position, crushed against the edge of the windscreen, blood matting his blond hair. It appeared he had been in the back with no belt and had been thrown over the front seat.

Bright felt Folin's hand gripping his arm above the elbow. He felt the cold air too, and the lights burning his eyes. Icy needles of rain started to fall. He felt those. He watched the scene-of-crime guys, the doctor moving Jude's head. If he could move her head, either rigor had not yet set in or had already worn off. He watched as the firemen used a blow-torch on the car door, the sparks and the glittering rain and the white arc-lights like a football pitch.

The thing was, it looked like Jude, only it was dead so it couldn't be Jude. He thought about Dan and about George who loved her, and he knew that this was his fault, he didn't know quite how, but he knew that he was to blame.

The doors were lifted off by three firemen and laid on a sheet of plastic, pressing down undergrowth. The firemen came back and the doctor instructed them how to get Jude out of the car. Bright tried to go to them to tell them how to handle her but Folin still had hold of his arm. Anyway she hadn't wanted him around. She was leaving him. She was going back home with this lad half her age. She wouldn't want him touching her now. He stayed where he was. He could see from here her eyes were open and he didn't want to see how they looked. He didn't want to have to see that for the rest of his life. He never ever wanted to see that. Never.

They were lifting her. Two of them had her shoulders, one held her head. If he hadn't held it it would have flopped. He held it gently. He lifted a tendril of curly dark red hair from her forehead and smoothed it back. Two more took her hips and her legs, freeing her feet from the metal that had buckled round them. Her feet came out bare. They laid her on plastic sheeting too. Folin moved him round, so's he could see her better. He said, 'I will accept this as a formal identification. This is Jude Craig?'

Bright nodded but didn't speak.

Folin still gripping his arm led him to the rear of the car. The rocky sides of the Cirque were almost vertical but the car had stopped its fall on a ledge. Even the ledge sloped steeply. To move, you had to grab tussocks of grass, trees, branches, anything to hand. The firemen had attached ropes to the trees, cutting off the scene and enabling people to pull themselves up.

The boot of the car had opened and buckled against the back window, a jumble of metal. The boot was empty. There was nothing inside except his tow-rope, shiny blue, coiled

232

like a snake. Exactly the same blue as the rope that had coiled round Mariela. The luggage, if there had been any, had been thrown free.

Folin asked the scene officer some questions, still holding on to Bright. *What's he think I'm gonna do – make a run for it?* But he knew it was Folin's kindness, holding him up, holding him together, an extension of the good manners they went in for round here. He knew this even in the midst of the darkness in the midst of the light. The scene officer lowered himself away, clinging to the rope. Folin said, as though he'd forgotten how to speak English, 'They search for the *bagages* among the trees.'

A fireman came up, easy, hardly touching the rope, carrying Jude's case like it weighed nothing. He proffered it to Folin. Folin told him to put it down. Folin put on his plastic gloves. He let go of Bright to do this. And Bright felt that Folin's grip had been holding him to the ground and that now it had gone he was weightless and might just fly, free-fall, down to where the silver river wound through the bottom of the Cirque, completing the flight begun by Jude. But Folin handed him a pair of plastic gloves. The scene officer hauled himself back up and gave Folin permission to open the bag.

Just her clothes. That blue dress that he'd first seen her in, over a year ago. A deep but vibrant blue like cornflowers or gentians. He'd watched his own hands touching it this morning. He watched the latex fingers examine the rest. It was just her clothes.

Folin said, 'No papers. No passport etcetera.'

'They'd be in her shoulder-bag. Or her pocket.'

'Of course, yes.'

'The hat,' Bright said. The hat was evidence. The hat had been seen. The hat had been noticed when Jude had not.

'The *chapeau de paille de dame*. Yes. I have instructed that they search.'

233

They hauled themselves down again. The boy was being laid, Bright was glad to see, on a separate sheet of plastic. He was badly broken, bones sticking out of the skin of one arm and one leg, one side of his face no longer a face. But his left side was unmarked. He wore jeans and a check shirt. He had been wearing those clothes the last time Bright had seen him, after changing out of his serving gear, to charge off on his *vélo* after Mariela and her band of merry boys. Bright could have had a son his age. Yet this lad had run off with Bright's girl.

But why? This boy was in love with Mariela. This boy was dying of love for Mariela. But you can fall in obsessive love and out and in again as fast as light. In adolescence. And after. He knew. He'd done it himself. There was no rhyme or reason to falling in love. *But Jude wanted a bloke to take care of her.* Something curled and cramped inside of him. *I did not take care of her.* He skimmed his thoughts over the surface of that, like a stone across deep water. Don't go there. Keep away. *I'll never know. I'm a detective because I can't stand not knowing. And the one thing I know about this is that I'll never know.*

The doctor was murmuring to his pocket recorder. Bright didn't need a translation. The kid was pulp, his bones splintered like matchsticks. His parents wouldn't see him like this: they'd see him in the mortuary neatly sewn back together and covered with a sheet, cleaned up. *Yes, that's our son, he was missing two nights and a day and we never noticed he'd gone.* A neglected child. They might as well have thrown him down the Cirque with their bare hands. He felt rage against them and knew it was rage against himself. Wherever they'd failed, they didn't deserve this.

He glanced over at Jude. They were just zipping her into the body-bag. One fireman held down her springy hair to stop it catching in the zip. The zip closed off her face as he watched. They picked up the ends of the stretcher and set

234

off along the little path, just two firemen, one in front, one behind, only little guys, but broad, strong. He needed to go with them, follow her, go with her where she was going. Only she wasn't going anywhere. She had already gone.

But he said to Folin, 'Can I?'

Folin said, 'Yes.'

'Where?'

'Lons-le-Saunier. I will join you there.'

'Thanks.'

'*De rien.*'

He stumbled along after the firemen. Her pall-bearers. Oh Jesus, he would have to tell Dan. *Only with her two minutes and I can't manage to keep her alive. Can't manage to keep her, alive or dead.* He doubted his ability to get over this. He doubted his ability to survive. Dan hadn't loved her better but he'd loved her longer. And he too had managed to lose her, before this ultimate loss. He followed the firemen, kept his eyes on them, all lit, day-for-night. They were all acting in this movie to which he had no subtitles to tell him the plot.

They put her in an ambulance on the road. He got in the back too, with one of Folin's officers. All the paraphernalia for resuscitation was pushed to one side, the meter to monitor the heart, the electrodes to bring the dead back to life. He wondered whether if someone had got there sooner— But no. Her neck was broken. He knew a broken neck when he saw it. He'd seen plenty. A fragile thing, a neck. Jude didn't look fragile. She was strong, what his ma called strapping, a strapping lass, and flexible. He'd even imagined having kids with her. He'd never done that before, imagined long-term. He kept reminding himself, that had not been going to happen anyway: Jude had fallen out of love with him. But that wasn't the end of the story. It was a phase, that's all, a transition, a blip, in the course of their – the passage of their – a rite of passage, that was it – to a better understanding, a more complete, a more total union. He'd told her it wasn't the end, it couldn't be the end. She hadn't believed him then, but she would have, she would, when he came back and they talked and worked it out. He put his hands over his face. He shivered. He still had the latex gloves on. That was how he felt, latex-gloved all over, a thin skin of latex, white, translucent, tight-fitting, between him and the air, him and the rest of the world, him and the rest of life.

He carefully unzipped the top of the bag and revealed her face. The French cop didn't stop him, he even looked away. Her eyes were still open, would be till after the autopsy. They were not looking at him, that was for sure; it was okay, he could look at her without worrying. So he sat there looking at her. He didn't seem to have any thoughts now. He was just eyes, no thoughts. He'd better not touch her, even with the gloves. Never contaminate a crime scene, it was in his blood. But he did. He touched her hair. Touched her face. He leaned over and put his mouth over her mouth. Kissed her on her mouth, rubbed his lips lightly side to side on her lips, like he did when they were alive. Then he zipped her up again, careful with her hair as the fireman had been, not to entangle its strands in the metal teeth.

24

Night for Day

The fog that surrounded the rest of the day was the merciful dulling that nature sometimes provides to those in deep shock. There is only so much we can handle; beyond that we're numb. Bright went through the formalities and was led round like a dog on a lead by Folin or whoever Folin deputed. He was aware that he was never alone but was aware of nothing much else. Until they did leave him alone at last, in his room at the hotel. Then he lay on the bed in his clothes. He sat up and took off his shoes and then lay down again. On his back. He lay with his eyes open and stared at the ceiling. The ceiling was smooth and white and cool-looking. If his eyes closed he saw a car going over a cliff. Or he drove a car over a cliff. Or Jude drove and he sat by her side. Or he drove and she sat by his side. Sometimes she wasn't in a car and nor was he. She just fell and fell. Or he did. And woke with a wild jump and remembered it wasn't just a dream. The dream where you fall and wake on landing, Jude wouldn't wake from and nor would he.

He couldn't tell if he slept or not. It didn't feel like sleep. The car drove at speed along the road then swerved to the right, a distance of eight or ten metres across the grass at the top of the Cirque where the viewing platform was, then crashed through the fence and embarked on its fall. Faster and faster it fell, bouncing and turning and breaking the trees without breaking its fall and he woke with a lurch. He was sweating. He sat on the edge of the bed. He went into the little shower room and ran cold water into the little

237

plastic toothglass. He drank and filled the glass and drank again. He peed, holding the wall with his free hand, his arm stretched out straight in front of him. He watched the stream of urine splashing into the toilet bowl. You drink and you piss – you're alive. You sleep and dream and wake – you're alive.

His last dream had been packed with detail. He was in the car. He was driving. He was driving over the grass and through the fence. The car was moving that way, out of his control. He tried to steer but it was no use – the steering did not respond, the car kept going of its own accord. Staring down as the stream of urine diminished to a trickle he suddenly got what the dream had been telling him. So deep in shock that Jude was dead, that fact so unbeliev-able that anything was possible, he had not engaged his brain. Now he clearly perceived what the shock had hidden from him.

He thought and he paced and he sat and he wrote. He did that all night. He looked at his watch. Not time yet. He wrote some more, sentences and question marks and cross-ings-out and more sentences and more question marks. He looked at his watch again. Six-thirty a.m. It must be dawn. He opened the shutters and the sun, level with his eyes, blinded him and he was driving along a road in Normandy and he heard Jude say, How many dawns have you seen in your life? Another hour at least before anyone else would be awake. He went back to his notes and tidied them up. He checked his watch.

It was seven-thirty. He couldn't wait any longer.

Folin opened his door already dressed.

Bright said, 'It was not an accident. It was a crime scene.'

'I know this,' Folin said.

'I've made some notes.' Bright held the papers up in front of him.

'Come in my room. I will go down to the kitchen and ask for some coffee.'

'I have to tell you what I've got.'

'Sit down.'

Bright went to the window. It looked out at the back of the hotel. Much the same view as from his and Jude's room the first night: the yard, the Petite Rue, the *chambres d'hôte*. It was deep blue, back here, the sky, hardly touched by the blaze on the other side. He could hear trucks grinding along the main road. The day beginning like any other day.

The door rattled and Bright opened it. Folin stood there with a tray. A coffee pot, two cups, a basket of bread, butter, a small dish of jam. He put it on the table by the window. He poured the coffee and added a stream of hot milk. He gave the cup to Bright. He broke off four inches of bread, tore it in two with his hands, buttered one half and gave that to Bright also. Bright started to speak.

Folin said, 'Eat the bread, drink the coffee. This is a command. After, I will talk with you.' He poured and drank his coffee and ate a chunk of bread. 'Good, it is bread from yesterday but not too bad. When I was a boy we were not able to eat the bread on the second day, but now? The bread preserves itself better but it is not so good bread.' He watched Bright try to eat but fail. 'The coffee however is absolutely better. It's good, no?'

Bright drank and drained his cup and put the cup down. 'Jude did not drive over that cliff on purpose. And she's a good driver. She once drove sixty-odd miles in the dark with one arm out of action. So something very weird happened.'

'I agree. But what? A mechanical failure? We must wait for reports to tell us this.'

'How soon?'

'It is priority, of course.'

'And if it wasn't mechanical, okay? We need to know several things.' He referred to his notes. 'Can they tell if she was driving?'

'She was in the driver's seat.'

'She could have been already— dead. When the car went over.'

'How?'

'If he killed her. Will they be able to tell if she took the fatal injury before it fell?'

'Perhaps.'

'If he was in the back seat, stabbed or hit her with something, strangled her, I don't know, and the car goes haywire, she can't control it. She met him in the teacher's house. He forces her into the car. He hides in the back. He makes her drive.'

'Why does he do this?'

'He's hiding out in the teacher's carve. She realises he killed Mariela. Why else would he be hiding?'

'She appears a strong woman, your Jude.'

'Yes, she's strong.'

'But not strong enough to fight this boy?'

'He's armed. Or he takes her by surprise. Or maybe she even drives him away out of compassion, she's a sympathetic— she cares about the underdog, she—'

'Very well, very well, yes, yes. So, one way or another way, she drives him or is driven by him.'

'The sightings said a woman was driving.'

'A woman in a hat, Inspector.'

'He was driving? Wearing her hat? Christ—'

'If, as you suggest, she was already dead. If he panicked in the house and injured her, fatally perhaps, and—'

'And thought he'd better make it look like an accident, and then, on the way, he decides to take himself with her?'

'It is possible.'

'No, mate. What's he got to lose? No one – except maybe

240

the teacher – knows where he is. If he gets far enough in my car he can disappear somewhere.'

'Not for long. He will be found. He will be questioned. We carry identity cards here.'

'He can buy one.'

'Does he seem to you the sort of boy that—?'

'It's easy. The street kids in cities sell everything. He can go to Switzerland, it's only a few miles, the border's not that well policed, I bet.'

'We have had an alert out for him at all the border points.'

Bright breathed out as though he'd done a hundred-yard sprint, and ate the bread without noticing. He ate walking about the room, then he sat down. He said, 'I have to let people know. She has a sister in Australia or somewhere, a teacher, and a brother who works for Renault or something, an accountant, I don't know where. I don't have their numbers but I know someone who will.'

'Her parents?'

'Her mother's dead. Years ago. Cancer. Her dad walked out when she was a kid. She never knew where.'

Folin said, 'Use the telephone in the office.'

The room got the same blast of light as his own but some of the intensity was gone from the sun, now it was higher in the sky. He noticed his hand shake, punching the numbers.

Niki Cato, one hour behind, sounded bewildered. 'It's the middle of the night, boss! What's up?'

'Jude.'

'You've found her?'

'A car crash.'

'Is she—?'

'Yup.'

'John. Christ.'

'Listen, I can't inform her next-of-kin. I don't know their whereabouts. The only person I can think of is— is Dan.'

'Dan, her husband Dan?'

'Yup.'

'I'll get his number for you and call you back.'

'Cato, I— I can't talk to him.'

'Oh, right, okay, boss. I'll do it. You better give me some details. Christ.'

'The car seems to have gone out of control. It was found in this place – there's a few of them round here, a big deep circle thing, like it's been cut out of the rock. It rolled down a hundred feet or more, I don't know.'

'Was she badly—?'

'No. Not a mark on her. Broke her— Her neck was— She was wearing a belt. The air-bag worked. But the—'

'Yes, okay, guv, just so's I've got something to tell the husband.'

'Thanks.'

'Guv, you want me to come out there?'

'No, Cat. Thanks but— I'll let you know if I change my mind.'

'Okay. Boss? Is this connected to the— you know — the other thing?'

'Too soon to say. Waiting on reports.'

'How do you see it?'

'I don't believe in coincidence.'

'No signs at the accident scene?'

'I wasn't in my right mind but I can't believe I was present at an accident scene. Unless she was drunk or something went wrong with the steering, how on earth did she manage to drive the car off the road and through a fence and over the edge of a precipice? No way.'

'Have you rung your mother yet, guv?'

'Ah Christ.'

'Want me to do it?'

'No. It's tempting, believe me. But no. I'll do that.'

'Okay, guv. You off the hook now then?'

'What?'

'Well, if this wasn't an accident, they've had you in custody over the time in question, haven't they? And if it's connected to the other death – well – this means you're off the hook for that as well. Doesn't it?'

25

Dead Centre

'That the deaths may be connected, Inspector – this is a hypothesis, among hypotheses. And this hypothesis is terribly – convenient – for you, no?' Folin handed him another cup of coffee.

Bright held it in both hands, and saw Jude's hands doing the same. In the teacher's house. Yesterday morning. Just before she accused him of being a cop all the time, treating the whole human race as a suspect. Well, he was a cop. That's what he did. And he hadn't been able to protect her. So maybe she'd got what she wanted: maybe he'd give it up. But not till he'd nailed whoever did this to her. For now, that was the only thing holding him together. Keeping him perpendicular. He handed the empty cup back to Folin.

Folin said, 'Therefore, until we have some answers about the – accident – you will remain a suspect. You understand that?'

'I understand it. But if it turns out not to be an accident, you gotta let me off the hook. I gotta be free. I gotta be able to investigate this.'

'This is the death of a British national. The Metropolitan Police will not permit you: you have personal involvement. They will send whom they choose to investigate, no?'

'That's just official. I'm not talking about official. You think they can stop me?'

'With my help, naturally they can stop you.'

'But they won't get your help, will they? Not on this?' He was pushing it, no question. But he had to know where he stood.

'I reserve the right not to decide at this point. I reserve the right to decide at any point on the route. If you make difficulties for me, you will force me to terminate our – association.' He paused. 'But until that time . . .'

'Sure. I got it. Say no more.'

'We did not have this conversation, Inspector.'

'What conversation, Judge?'

'Precisely. Thank you.'

Bright had an urge to hug the guy. He realised this was partly his need for human contact. The night before last he'd slept next to Jude's warm body. He wanted that now. The warmth of her . . . He shut his eyes and opened them again fast. He had been asleep, or something close to sleep. On his feet.

Folin said, 'Sit down. Do you want something to help you to sleep?'

'No, I gotta—'

'When the incident reports come, I will wake you. Until then there is nothing you can do.'

'I can think.'

'You can do that also in your sleep. You may even perhaps think better in your sleep.'

'You swear you'll wake me?'

'I give you my word as a judge. Is that sufficient for you?'

They exchanged a look. Folin knew how he felt about judges. The guy hadn't lost his sense of humour.

'In that case I'll just lie down. I won't sleep.' Bright took off his shoes and swung his legs on to the bed. He lay on his back and looked at the patterns on the ceiling, leaves tossing in and out of sunlight across the window bars in a random complicated dance. Sleep didn't come. Only thoughts. He swung his legs back down. Put his shoes back on. 'I need to make another call.'

'To whom, please? I must ask.'

'My mother.'

* * *

Lily could only say, 'Oh, John, oh, John,' over and over again.

Bright said, 'How's George?'

'Ach, he's fine. Sleeps on my bed and everything. Making the best of things, you know.'

'You might have him longer than you thought.'

'Don't be daft, that's fine by me, don't you be worrying about him.'

'I'll be here till this business is sorted out,' he said.

'Are you thinking it wasn't an accident?'

'I don't know, Ma.'

'If it was an accident, you think she was running away with the boy?'

'Ma—'

'No, no. I just want to say, what I saw of Jude, she wouldn't be doing that, John. And she wouldn't go off without telling you, either. She was a good person. So don't you go thinking that, okay?'

'I'll be looking at the evidence, Ma. Like usual.' But he felt grateful just the same.

When he came back Folin had the reports. In three different folders.

'That was quick.'

'Preliminary only. I requested priority. I hinted at pressure from the Metropolitan Police.'

'And was there any? Pressure.'

'You are an officer of the Metropolitan Police, are you not?' Folin opened the top folder and handed Bright a single sheet. He had photographs, which he did not pass to him. He turned the photos face down.

Bright said, 'It's in English.'

'I requested a translation.' Folin didn't catch his eye when he said that.

Bright's chest felt something swelling inside it. He'd never

246

had a best mate since he was at school in South Norwood. Not a bloke best mate. All his trust relationships had been with women. He'd never given this much thought – just accepted that that was how it was. But at this moment he thought no one had ever done as much for him as this guy in his cool urbane way. He'd better get a grip. He was a suspect in Folin's case, remember. He'd better not turn the man into his security blanket. 'Thanks,' he said.

The report was brief. It stressed that this was a special preliminary summary, not the final summation. Most of it was stuff Bright already knew. He'd seen for himself that the deceased was a white female in her thirties and that she had a broken neck. He shut his eyes a second. Point number six mentioned marks on the wrists and ankles. He stared at this sentence for some time. He held out his hand. 'The path. report on the boy, please.'

He took the piece of paper and his breath stopped moving through his body. He skimmed down the first few points. There it was: marks on the ankles and wrists. His breath started up again. 'These marks—'

'Yes. It is interesting.'

'Did you notice them at the scene?'

'No.'

'Why didn't I?'

Folin gave a minimal shrug.

'Okay, don't answer that. Are these marks indicative of—?'

'I have not yet spoken with the pathologist.'

'Is there any indication of what—?'

'I said. When you and I have talked, I will speak with the lab. Read on. You will find something else of significance.'

Bright read on. At the bottom of the report on the boy it said, 'No immediate cause of death apparent.' He went back through the list of points, through the boy's injuries. His face badly mashed, his left shoulder dislocated, his collar-bone smashed, his left arm broken in several places. None of these injuries, not even all of them together, added up to a cause of death? He went back to Jude's report. Again, it did not state a cause of death. A broken neck? He had made an assumption. He, a hardened experienced cop who knew not to accept anything at face value. His suggestion, that she was already dead when the neck was broken, already dead when the car went over the cliff, this report was substantiating?

He stood up and walked about. He tried to speak but couldn't get his voice in order. At last he said, '"No cause of death immediately apparent".'

'Yes.'

'Marks on wrists and ankles.'

'They have both been tied,' Folin said. 'Yes.'

'But not when they were found.'

'No. The implication is that they were untied again before the car went over.'

'That they were dead when the car went over.'

'Yes. But we do not know – were they dead already when the car has left the prof's house this morning?'

'Or were they alive then, tied up in the boot, and killed later?' Bright tried not to see this as he said it.

'And if this is so, who was driving, yes? When the car was seen yesterday morning? This woman in the hat—'

Bright corrected him. 'Person in the hat.'

'Yes.'

'But why? Why Jude? The boy, yeah, I've had it wrong – I had him as Mariela's killer and the schoolteacher's hiding him and helping him to get away. Then I had Jude helping him to get away as well. He persuades her, or forces her, God knows how, to drive him off somewhere. That's how I had it. Okay, now I'm getting it different. What if it's the teacher who did Mariela? If the boy saw *him*. If the boy's a *prisoner* in the teacher's house, not a refugee? Jude finds the boy? The teacher comes back from the school— But,

248

Christ, Jude's fit and strong, the lad's a strapping sixteen-year-old. How does a shambling middle-aged schoolteacher get them both tied up and into the car? And then he can't be the woman in the hat because every kid for miles around knows him, and even if he— Nah.'

'No, Inspector. He was truly in the school. All his times are verified. I promise you.'

'Okay then, not him, but whoever—'

'Yes, I am following you—'

'How does – whoever – overpower two strong, fit, young people and tie them up?'

'I can only imagine a narcotic, perhaps.'

'But if you've got a narcotic handy why tie them at all?

'Perhaps the narcotic effect may not last?'

'Your pathologist'll look for stuff like that, will he?'

'She. Yes. Of course. The French forensic scientists are quite as good as the British, Inspector, believe me.'

'Yeah, sorry, Judge. Sure. But forget narcotics. It's too far-fetched. Look—'

Folin saw where he was going, and stopped him. 'Of course. There were perhaps more than one, no?'

'That's it, yeah. Has to be.'

'Oh mon Dieu.'

'It's the simplest explanation.'

'So it is not the prof—'

'And it's not the boys; they were in custody—'

'– on *garde à vue* at the préfecture in Lons-le-Saunier—'

'So Franck saw – whoever – kill Mariela. And they saw him. He ran off, took refuge with the teacher, but the killers couldn't leave him, a loose cannon, they're looking for him, and they find him in the house with Jude. Maybe Jude tries to save him, that would be like her, so they take her too. There's more than one of them.'

'Two could perhaps do it if they separate Jude from Franck—'

'—Yeah. Jump them one at a time, the boy in one room and she's in another.'

Folin thought for a moment, then collected up the papers and went to the door. Bright followed. On the landing he said, 'The report on the car?' Folin took the third folder from his sheaf of papers and handed it behind him, on the move. In the investigation room Bright sat and read it through while Folin made his phone calls.

Mechanical failure was ruled out. Nothing wrong with engine or brakes or steering. The car was low on fuel but had enough in the tank to last another twenty miles. Wheels good, tyres good, both axles damaged, most likely in the fall, not before. No fingerprints on the steering-wheel. *No fingerprints on the steering-wheel.* Fingerprints had been wiped off before the car was sent over the cliff. That confirmed someone else, not Jude, had driven the car.

He shut his eyes. Rope. Used in both deaths. Would the marks on wrists and ankles reveal what kind of rope? Would they get fibres? He felt the foreigner's fear that the boffins wouldn't be as good here as they were at home. He tried to swallow this fear, though it was strong in him. Folin had assured him that they were good. But they did do things differently here. For instance, he'd never have got the experts at home to part with a preliminary report like this, not so soon. 'Don't quote me.' That was the watchword at home now, no one wanted to be caught on the hop, no one prepared to put his bollocks through the wringer. Not for anyone. Not for anything. All watching their backs. But maybe that meant things were looser here, more lax? Details might get by them? But surely now that the case included a foreign national as victim, a foreign police-force in on the investigation, they'd have to get it solid, wouldn't they? They'd have to get it good.

As soon as Folin was off the phone Bright started: bam,

bam, bam, question after question. Folin held up his hands in a hey-cool-it gesture. 'Just a moment. I will tell you what is happening and then you may ask me what you want. Okay?'

'Shoot.'

'First, we are taking a different line of questioning, in the light of this new case, with all the boys. Then we will meet again with the parents of the victim Franck. I must go with them to the morgue for formal identification of their son. Meanwhile I have invited Professeur Breton to come here to speak to me. I think now he must tell what he knows.'

'About Franck?'

'Certainly.'

'And what about our friend Louis?'

'Louis? Ye-es, but he is not – I don't know how to say it in English -'

'He doesn't seem the type? He doesn't have what it takes? You can't see him having the balls, or the energy, or the enterprise, or even the sheer bloody rage for this.'

'Exactly. No. But—'

'That's right. You never know. He had no alibi for the time of Mariela's death. Maybe he hasn't got one for this either.'

'Inspector, like you, he has been here in the hotel during two days under the eye of my officers.'

'He got out and went over to his mother's house. If I hadn't been looking out the window we'd have missed that.'

'Oh yes.' Folin looked shocked. 'This is true.'

'We gotta check his movements for the time in question. Christ, what is the time in question? Do we have an esti-mated time of death?'

'We do not yet have the complete report.'

'They know the car – accident – was not the cause of death.'

'They know only that death has taken place between perhaps eght thirty yesterday morning and the time that the car was found – around eight at night. And the questions of body temperature, ambient temperature etcetera, these are all . . .' Folin's English ran out.

'Yeah, yeah. Imponderables. Unless they get some fibres, something to connect with a place of death, somewhere other than the prof's house – the car, the car boot.'

'We must hope not simply somewhere in the country-side.'

'The rope?'

'Yes, we will enquire.'

'My tow-rope was still in the boot. Was that used to tie them up? Tying up is the one thing these two cases have in common.'

'I do not agree.'

'Why?'

'It is different tying up. A different motive.'

'Maybe. You can't be sure.'

'Tying up for sexy games and—'

'Don't assume that, Judge. Mariela was tied up after death. To make it look like a game that went too far. To make it look that way.'

'The report suggests this certainly—'

'You haven't got the final report on that yet either.'

'No.' Folin reached for the phone again.

Bright's brain was turning like a lathe. He knew he was spinning close to the edge of control. But he knew he had to keep it spinning because the spin of his brain was the only thing he had, to nail the bastard that did this. Three good people. Three people in their youth and their prime, two lovely women and a kid on the brink of his life. The kid had been tied like Jude. So he hadn't killed Jude. If he hadn't killed Jude the chances were he hadn't killed Mariela either. The person who killed Mariela killed all three. The

252

people who killed Mariela? It came back to more than one. It kept coming back there. There was something bothering him. Something wrong. But Folin had hit the target dead centre: it hinged on this sex-game business. Real or fake?

26

Boys Will Be Boys

The boys were brought in together. Gérard the ring leader, defiant, lounging, hands in his pockets; Pierre – Pipi – rigid with skin-trembling terror; Robert – Robo – belligerent and mulish, stupefied with anxiety.

Bright said, 'Do they know about the new – developments?'

'No.'

'Keep it that way. Till you need it.'

'I think you may trust me to know my job.'

'Christ, I'm sorry, Judge. I'm used to being in charge, I didn't mean—'

'You understand I cannot allow you to question them.'

'But I can question you?'

'Yes, certainly you may. Also I will translate for you, unless I think the statement insignificant.'

'Unless my arse. Everything is significant until proved otherwise.'

'Yes, yes. This is true.'

'Every word then?'

'Every word. And you will now no doubt advise me to separate the boys?' Folin flashed Bright a smile with daggers in it and then sent Pipi and Robo outside the room to wait.

Gérard sat back in his chair and drawled something at Folin. Folin said, 'Gérard tells us he is waiting for his *avocat* – his lawyer. He called him already. And he tells us that he himself understands English very well also so that he will understand what we say.'

'Well, tell him we're quaking in our boots.'

'We do not need to tell him because he understands English. You can see that he does. *C'est vrai, Gérard, vous comprenez bien, non?*'

Bright's South London vernacular would be hard on those whose English was indeed good. But Gérard kept up his defiant sneer in spite of his total mystification. He sighed heavily at The silly Law's silly jokes.

Bright didn't know how he was holding himself together. These lads – it was like they didn't understand the difference between life and death. Forget right and wrong – that's sophisticated, that's philosophy; no – just life and death, like little kids who pull the legs off insects and then wonder why they don't run around any more. He could tear this kid apart with his bare hands till he was bits on the floor. Just as well he wasn't sitting in Folin's chair. He caught Gérard's eye and held still. The kid stopped sighing and squirming, sat trapped an instant in Bright's gaze, then looked away.

In that instant Bright knew he was innocent. A window of dropped bravado, adolescent swank, through to the scared hollow heart where the kid wished he'd never gone off with Mariela, never started the whole thing. He let them carry on a bit, then, getting his breath back, he said to Folin, 'He's gonna give you what you want.'

A frisson of irritation crossed the judge's face. 'Yes, I think I may have decided that already. Thank you.'

'You gonna tell him about the other – developments now?'

'Inspector—'

'Sorry, sorry. Stumm. I'm stumm.'

Gérard had stopped pretending to understand. He was bored again, Really bored, looking at his hand which was picking at the side seam of his jeans just above his bony knee.

'Gérard.'

He looked up sideways at Folin – James Dean brooding under the eyebrows. But he was already responding to the

255

change in Folin's tone. Bright heard 'Franck' and 'mort'. He was telling Gérard Franck had been found dead.

He could see what Folin was up to – the old trick. Gently, gently. For a bloke who wasn't a cop he was doing well: *Look, we don't think you killed Mariela, and maybe you had nothing to do with Franck's death either. If you tell us what you know we'll go easy on you. But if you continue to lie to us, we don't want to, of course, but we'll have to charge you.* Trust me, I'm a judge.

Gérard's eyes were all over the place, his body lost its assurance, there was no will in his limbs any more, he didn't know where to put himself. Franck was dead! His head turned from side to side looking for enlightenment. Why had they changed their tone? Treating him so gently, like a prisoner before execution. His eyes locked on Bright again. He sat up and put his hands on his knees, big farm boy's hands he had yet to grow into. His lawyer came in.

Folin filled the lawyer in and the lawyer nodded a lot then filled the boy in, even though the boy had already heard it all. The lawyer too told the boy to trust the judge. Again the boy's eyes slid around like he was bound and gagged. He put his face into the overgrown hands. Bright no longer saw them as strangler's hands. Though they might have tried it on, round Mariela's neck. His elbows on his knees, the hands now knotted themselves together under his chin, propping up his head, keeping things in place. Gérard was thinking. It was hard for him: any muscle you haven't used in a while, it hurts when you exercise it. Then the hands came down and gripped the front of the chair next to each bony thigh. He took a deep breath. 'Okay,' he said. He flicked a glance at Bright: *This shows I can speak English.* Folin switched on the tape.

Strange, afterwards, the boy no longer there, just his thin voice on the tape, pauses, hesitations, corrections, and Folin translating. Bright heard the difference in accents between

256

the boy and the judge, the rough with the smooth, even though he didn't know the words. Folin translated as it went along: '"*I never did it with Mariela. Not – you know – all the way? She – teased me. She was always promising, she was always saying, You are a man, I need a real man, not Louis. You and I we'll teach Louis a lesson, yes? And I will teach you a lesson. Me, you understand? She would teach me. But the other boys always came too and she would never send them away and I was getting angry with her, real angry, like she had me on heat all the time. I told the lads to leave us alone but she always said, No let's all go, and that night I got mad. I'd drunk beer in the bar. One of the older guys was buying – his wife had had a baby, he was celebrating – so I had more than usual. We went to the river. Yes, we had been there before, a lot of times. And Pipi was drunk, he can't hold his drink, and Mariela was really fooling around with him, she was letting him kiss her and touch her. He got his hand up her skirt and I went for him and I pulled him off her and he fell down and Mariela was laughing and I got mad and I put my hands round her throat like this and she was still laughing and I held her up against the tree and Robo held her too round the shoulders. She was kicking and laughing and I – I got my – you know – I got my prick out and I got her skirts up and I was pulling her panties. She stopped laughing and she started shouting and screaming, she was struggling and kicking and we couldn't hold her and Pipi got the tow rope out of his bike carrier—*"'

'Why did he have a tow rope in his carrier?' Bright said.

'He had been helping his father's truck out of the mud up in the field.'

'Okay.'

'Here I tell Gérard, "Yes, continue."' Folin restarted the tape.

'"*Pipi – well – we, we started tying her up. She was kicking out and we were all laughing—*'

257

Bright said, 'Was his dick still out?'

Folin paused the tape. 'It is a pretty picture, no?' And started it up again.

'"*They tried to wrap the rope around her while I held on to her. She was trying to scratch my face. I told them, tie her hands, tie her hands together. I wouldn't have – I wouldn't have done anything to her. Not really. It was just – you know – playing around. And she wasn't tied – the rope was just – it was just her hands were tied.*" Now I ask him—' Folin said. '"*Sure I had a hard-on, man. She was asking for it.*"'

'"She was asking for it",' Bright said.

'Yes.' Folin stopped the tape. They stood with their arms folded, looking at the floor. After a moment Folin started the tape again. Gérard repeated their story that they heard a car coming, and Folin interrupted him. 'I ask him here about Franck. I ask, did they see him?'

Bright listened to a long pause on the tape. Then Folin prompting the boy: 'You know that Franck is dead now?' Then a sigh, close to the mike, shocking in its spontaneity, as though Gérard had leaned over, and all the force of his breath and his regret were in the sound. He said the one word. '*Oui.*' It had the sound of every suspect Bright had ever heard, reaching the point of confession. He moved closer to the recorder to hear the authentic voice, straining for the sounds of falsification, elision. But, now the boy was telling it, it seemed he was telling it true.

'"*Yes, we heard something in the bushes.*" This was before or after the car? "*Before.*" How long before? "*I don't know! Ten minutes? I can't say. We were pissed.*" Very well, you heard someone. "*Robo crept round to see and he saw Franck. Franck was in the bushes and he was crying and shaking, you know. Robo didn't speak to him. He didn't know we'd seen him.*"'

Bright said, 'That's when miladdo got his dick out. Bet

258

you anything. Decides to show Franck how a real man does the business.'

'Perhaps, yes. I ask him then, Is this why you tied her up? To put on a show for Franck? He answers no. Then he says, Yes, maybe, partly.'

The tape started again: '"*Okay, yes! Everyone knew Franck was crazy about Mariela, following her about, pestering her. But he's a coward, he wouldn't challenge me for her. So, yes, I suppose we decided to show him how it's done but we didn't—*" Here I interrupt to tell him, Just tell your story please.'

Bright heard another sigh on the tape.

'"*Well, Franck came out of the bushes with a big stick and he was roaring and swinging this big stick around, a big heavy branch, and Pipi and Robo were running around him and laughing and I was still holding on to Mariela. And they took the stick off Franck, they had him on the ground. And they rolled him into the river, and then we heard a car and then we ran away.*" I ask him which way they went. "*Through the woods back to the village. Then we went home.*" What time? "*I was in bed at midnight.*" And both the other boys were with you all the way back? "*Yes, we came back through the forest along the path by Louis' mother's house and came out opposite the hotel here.*" Were there lights in the hotel? In the bar? "*No. It was closed. Dark.*" And Franck – you have seen him again? "*No, sir. No. But he can swim, he's a good swimmer and the river is not so deep there and not so fast because of the dam up by the château. He wouldn't have drowned, sir.*"'

'Suddenly he's calling you sir.'

'Yes because he is really afraid about Franck, that they have killed him.'

'Yup. What about this car they heard? Lads this age know all about cars. And a place this small, they know the sound of different engines. They know who it was. They gotta know.'

'If there was a car.'

'Course there's a car. You still think they kill Mariela, then discover Franck and realise they've been seen and they're afraid they killed him too, so they invent this story about the car to get themselves off? That's bollocks. They didn't kill Franck.'

'They are afraid that they did.'

'That's right! That's why Gérard's got every reason now to say whose car it was, if he knows. It's the car of the killer, that's why. And it's the sound of him too, Gérard; it sounds right: what he's saying, the way he's saying it. We gotta find out about the car. Whose was it? Why was it there? Who was driving? What were they up to? No tyre tracks I suppose?'

'You have seen the road surface.'

'Yeah. So who was it? Someone from the bar, come out to have a look? The boys had been there before with Mariela. Probably the whole village knew about the place. Any number of pathetic old peeping Toms.'

'Let us assume for a moment it was Louis.'

'Out looking for his beloved. Sure.'

'And when he finds her, tied up, underwear gone—'

'—he grabs the stick Franck was waving around and uses it. Then he strangles her.'

'I suppose that the rape with the branch may have been done before, by the boys.'

'I don't. Lads that age? They don't have poor old Louis' problems, do they? Waste an opportunity like that to get your leg over? No chance.' His head felt heavy as a house. But he couldn't close his eyes because of the things he saw in the dark.

His mobile rang. It was Cato, saying he'd called Jude's husband, Dan. 'He took it bad, boss. Howled like a banshee.'

'Is he coming out here?'

'I gave him the details, how to get there, so he might. You want me to come? Bit of moral support?'

'No. Thanks, though, Cat.'

Then he sat through the questioning of Pipi and Robo. Now that they knew Gérard had broken the deal, had talked, had grassed them up, they spewed it out. Pipi cried. They tried to say Gérard had helped throw Franck in the water but their stories differed. Folin persistently manoeuvred them into the truth: they had thrown Franck in and then they'd heard the car and they'd fled without thinking what had become of him. But they said what Gérard had said: '*He can swim, he swims well. He's got medals. It's the only sport he does.*' It was right – he hadn't died of drowning. Folin told them Franck was dead now, by means unknown, and wouldn't be swimming any more. They froze where they sat. But they didn't change their story.

All through the questioning of the boys, Bright's mind flowed round Jude and Franck and the wreck. The wreck. He kept his eyes open only because the whingeing little thugs in front of him were better to look at than the inside of his own head, not because he hoped for anything new.

Folin could not get them to say whose car had scared them off. They did not notice, they said, they were already on their bikes and away.

'Hypnotise them,' Bright said. 'If they don't recall under hypnosis, then it's likely it was a stranger's car. At least that tells us something.'

'A negative is better than a nothing?'

'A-ha.'

'We may try this.'

'Yeah, get their parents and their lawyers to agree.'

'You are tired. You should sleep.'

'Don't think so, Judge. Thanks all the same.' Sleep? He could have laughed.

Folin went to speak with Gérard's lawyer and the parents of the other boys. Bright lingered at the window for a while, reluctant to return to his room. Emile the drunk stood opposite, on the wasteland car-park, hands in his pockets, shoulders up. His face had that pallor that drunks on the wagon get. So Emile had stopped drinking? He was shaking. Was it the tremor of alcohol withdrawal or was he just chilled in his old sweater and no jacket? Why was he there? Trying to cross the road to talk to Folin? Trying not to cross the road to beg a drink? He was hovering anyway, that was certain, in the no man's land between intention and action. Had Folin talked to him? Bright put his name at the top of his To Question list. He gestured to Folin's man: come to the window. Then pointed out the drunk trembling on the brink. He spoke English, slow and clear, and helped out his words with gestures. 'He was crazy about Mariela. She was good to him. Has anyone talked to him?'

The man didn't know.

'You should. He's a drunk but he's not a moron. Get him over here. Talk to him.'

The lad didn't understand.

Bright said, 'Judge Folin.' He scribbled Folin's name and, Talk to Emile the drunk. He said to the lad, 'For Folin – okay?'

The lad nodded. 'Okay.'

Bright looked out of the window again. A truck was going by, shaking the hotel. Emile walked out in front of it.

27

Uureliable Reports

He'd been thrown ahead of the truck, and bounced off the bumper on to the road. The driver had hit the brakes but had driven over his legs. Emile had exchanged one form of crippledom for another. If he got lucky. Either way he couldn't speak to anyone. Not yet. Maybe not ever. Poor sod.

'Let me out,' Bright said. 'I got to get out in the open air, I got to go walkabout. I'm going mad in here. For Christ's sake, I've got an alibi for Jude. And if I didn't do that I didn't do Mariela. Come on!'

'I must repeat: it is not yet established that the two cases are connected.'

'Yeah, it's just coincidence that you get two violent suspicious deaths in a village this size in three days, right? The kid was pushed over that cliff because he knows who killed Mariela, and Jude was with him so she got it too. It's as clear as the nose on your face, man. Let me go!'

But Folin said no.

Bright crashed out of the murder room down the stairs to the bar. Louis wasn't there. The place was empty. He was tempted to pick up a bottle of Scotch. But if he started to drink he'd never stop. He needed a coffee. No chance. No cooks on the Marie Céleste. Maybe in the kitchen? He went through the door into the big dining room. The kitchen door opened and a woman came through.

Tall, dark, the same shape all the way up, but with sloping shoulders and a hard, strong face, she had to be related to Louis. One of the relations who didn't like Mariela. Come to help out Louis in his hour of need.

'Bonjour, M'sieu, je peux vous aider?' Her mouth hardly moved when she spoke. Her voice had the charm of a pneumatic drill.

'Bonjoor. Caffee, see voo play. Shomber four.' He held up four fingers.

'Oui, M'sieu, cinq minutes.'

'Thanks.' Did she know who he was? He was gagging to talk to her. 'You speak English?' he said.

She shook her head. She understood that much then. 'You Louis' sister?' he said.

She stood like a carving, staring at him. You'd have to hold her upside down and shake her to get anything out of her.

'You,' he gestured and scrabbled in his mind for the words, 'voo – soor – de – Louis?'

'Oui.'

That was it. She didn't elaborate. Wouldn't have been any use to him if she had. 'Come to give him a helping hand, hn?'

She stared at him. Charm was not an attribute of this family. Louis was Cary Grant compared with the mother and this one. So the family was gathering. Louis was well protected.

'Did you know she was here?'

'No.' Folin was busy, bashing away at his laptop.

'Did you know she was coming?'

'No.'

'Where's she come from? When did she arrive? Who told her what was going on? The mother? Or Louis? Which one of them asked her to come?'

Folin put his head in his hands. Just for a moment. He took his hands away and sighed at Bright. 'Yes. Yes. Yes. I must write my report. Like you, I must write my report. If I do not, we will not have a case. Please will you write your

264

report? Later we will compare. But please, just for now, allow me to be alone.' His face repented before he was done. He made a small movement of apology with his head.

Bright left.

His head pounded, an iron fist punching in regular rhythm. If he could just review the case, get it straight, as he'd do with any murder inquiry at this stage. He was a professional, wasn't he? Always a cop, Jude had said. Only this time he was no cop: he was victim. Victim, suspect and next-of-kin. Nevertheless . . . *Okay, okay, let's do it. Let's review the bloody case. Let's do that.* He started to write. A sheet for each person. Showing their movements. As far as he knew them. Including his own. And times. As far as he knew them.

How close they all were. Moving around in this heaving darkness of activity. The boys. Mariela. Franck. Louis. The unknown car. And him. And the question: who was the man who had come through the gate from the path that led from the woods and passed him in the car park?

He comes to the crucial moments: the car arriving, the boys fleeing, Franck in the water, Mariela gagged with soil and tied up. Lashed to the tree? Alive or dead? He's not sure. Sexually violated yet? He's not sure. But he tends to believe the boys, so assume she's alive and not yet raped, and someone arrives in the car and gets out of the car and rapes her with the branch and strangles her and Franck sees that, watching and not helping her, too scared to go to her aid. *Or the car is nothing.* It goes on by, and Franck does all that to Mariela because she has betrayed him with the louts. But no. That won't do. Two reasons:

1. The driver of the car – if there was one – has not come forward; and:

2. Franck would have to be some sort of psychopath and that doesn't wash either. Also, Franck ends up dead.

So the mythical car stops, the driver – and here he always sees Louis, he can't help it. In the pursuit of disinterested investigation he tries to make the car-driver faceless, but there it is, Louis keeps coming back, so fuck it, he'll go with that.

Louis gets out of the car, sees Mariela roughed up as she already is, and he goes wild and decides to rough her up a little more. He's impotent so he violates her with this ugly great stick. Then he knows this is bad trouble so he throttles her and leaves her there dead or dying. Why? It's clear why he'd kill her, but why does he leave her there? The river is just by him. Why doesn't he throw her in, like the lads did to Franck? And what about Franck? He's still in the water, watching all this? Now, why does Franck have to go into hiding if he didn't kill her? Because the guy saw him? Did Franck try to intervene at some point? That's why the guy has to leave Mariela there? But Franck gets away from the guy and decides to lie low at the teacher's place? Because if the guy finds him, he's had it. Franck did go to the teacher's house. Otherwise how did he meet Jude? The teacher was hiding him.

Central to the case is that car. Who got out of that car? He has to get rid of the image of Louis. Yes, Louis is the most likely and nine times out of ten it's the husband – not that Louis was her husband, that was the whole problem – but try to put some other images there in his place. Any of the men here will do: they're all crazy for her. Put the teacher. Put the teacher in that car. Put the teacher in that picture. Can't. Can't do it. The teacher is a nutcase of a sort but not of that sort. There's something wrong with the teacher, but it's not that.

Try Emile. Driving? He could barely stand or walk. But he could get that mad with jealousy of Mariela. And drunks can do things you wouldn't expect. Bright had done things himself with more Scotch inside him than anyone would believe – managed to drive in a straight line even; now and then gone berserk. Okay, leave Emile in the picture. But he's so sorry for a run-over cat and yet could do that to Mariela? The Hitler-loved-his-dog syndrome? It's possible. Just. And he did walk under the wheels of a juggernaut. So something's getting to him? Leave him in.

Right. He's got Louis. Franck. Himself if he looks at it objectively but he knows it wasn't him so he leaves himself out just for now because his presence clouds the picture. The boys, only he believes what they say – they ran before the real fun started. Also they're in custody when the second killings happen. So he leaves them out too. Just for now. Just as a working hypothesis. So he's left with any bloke in the vicinity, from another village, even another region. The driver of the car, if he exists, could be a complete stranger. Not likely. Franck's the only one they actually know was there. And he can't talk. Not any more. And the only one who knows any more about that, if we believe the boys, is the schoolteacher. *We have to talk to the schoolteacher.*

See, that's how they get to the second case. The one he's trying to screw his mind to, only it keeps veering off. The boy is in the teacher's house. And Jude is in the teacher's house. And somehow Jude and Franck end up in Bright's car. Dead. We don't know who drove the car. We don't know if they were dead when the car set off, we think they were dead when the car arrived at the Cirque, dead when it went over the edge. *Please God let her have been dead when it went over.* She feared heights. She had a lot of courage, God knows. But she feared heights. A sheer drop like that was hell to her. *So just let her be dead when it goes over that cliff.* If he lets any other picture in, it will be hell for him too for the rest of his life. Hell, it'll be hell anyway, what's the difference.

He stands up and there's a knock. He opens his door. It's the totem pole, Louis' sister, with the coffee. He'd forgotten he ordered it. She brings it in without saying a word and waits while he moves the papers away. She has small brown eyeballs in long eyes. They move as quick as mice, like policemen's eyes, over his papers. She doesn't understand English, right? But she's seen Louis' name on the top sheet of paper in big bold letters. She knows he's suspect numero uno anyway. They all know that. So she flicks her eyes across his eyes just to show him she knows, and then, ramrod up the backside, straight as a shotgun, she leaves.

'She is his sister, yes. She lives in Orléans. She's a civil servant there. Some government department, she has been there fifteen years.'

'She married?'

'Unmarried.'

'She come home much?'

'Just for special occasions.'

'This counts as one.'

'I believe so.'

'She'd have had to get leave.'

'Yes.' Folin looked up from his laptop. Stopped typing a moment. 'Yes?'

'When did she apply? When did her leave start? You asked her?'

'No . . . Are you suggesting—? She is his only sister. She has come to give him help and support in a difficult time.'

'I'm not saying she hasn't. I'm just saying—'

'Yes, I will ask Javet to find out.'

'I've written out some stuff for you.'

'Yes?'

'Two people got the answer to all this. One's Franck. Too late to ask him. The other is the schoolteacher. He knows about Franck. Knows what Franck knew.'

Folin stood up and made a gesture that swept all his papers on to the floor. He cursed and stooped to pick them up. Bright got down there to help. 'Look, I'm sorry. Judge, but—'

Folin hit the papers on the floor with the side of his fist. 'From the beginning you have believed Professeur Breton to be involved in this matter. The Gendarmerie have questioned him. The police have questioned him. The Prosecutor at Lons has questioned him. And I have questioned him. We have searched his house. We have discovered nothing to connect him in any way with Mariela or in any way with Franck. No evidence. You are an inspector of police, not a clairvoyant. It is *evidence* on which we must base our suspicions. He is a man trusted and regarded with affection and gratitude by everyone who knows him.' Folin stopped speaking and went back to picking up his papers.

Bright said, 'I don't suspect the guy of killing Mariela. Or anybody else. I don't accuse him either. I *suspect* him of hiding Franck. The kid was in his house. He left his house, dead or alive, in my car. With— with – Jude. You accuse me of prejudice. Okay, I accuse you of prejudice in the other direction. I accuse you of ignoring the evidence. You can't sit here and wait for the guy to come to you. You've got to talk to him again. One way or another. Formal or informal. He's the only one who can tell us—'

'He cannot tell us anything about the disappearance of your Jude or of Franck. He was not there. He was at the school. Every moment of his time during Mariela's killing and during the morning of the second killings is accounted for.' Folin spoke clearly and slowly with emphasis on each word and exasperation whirring under the control.

Bright said, 'Okay, then, you gotta find out more about Franck.'

'Franck is dead.'

'I know Franck is dead.' Bright stopped and took a breath. 'Why is he dead? That's the question. Because he saw what happened? We gotta know what he saw or we can't move on. Writing it down – it's sorted my head out a bit. The whole thing hangs on Franck. *And the whole Franck question hangs on the schoolteacher.* Because the schoolteacher is the only one who might be able to tell us *what Franck saw.*' He held out his sheets of paper to Folin.

Folin sighed, hesitated, then took them. He rubbed his forehead. He said, 'I apologise to you. I should not have come back here to do this case myself. It is a mistake. Normally I would stay in Lons, collating and assessing the evidence, while a competent lieutenant or captain or adjutant of the judicial police would run the investigation here. I am out of practice, I think you say.'

'Well, I'm not.'

'I know this. This is the reason for my— You have caused me to feel incompetent. I should not allow this to influence me.'

'Listen, Judge, you're doing great. I'm just trying to help. I can't sit here doing bugger-all, I'm going out my head. I'm a f— I'm a prisoner here.'

'And also, since I am confessing, I am guilty because of – because of Jude. And Franck. I am the cause of these deaths because I have not found the killer of Mariela sooner. You must feel this.'

'Jesus. No. No.' Bright put out a hand and touched Folin's arm. Folin flinched and Bright took his hand away. They both stood up. The papers stayed on the floor, except Bright's report, which Folin held. After a pause Bright said, 'I was gonna leave myself out of the report – I know I'm innocent, you know? But I've put my movements in because of one thing: the bloke who came out of the woods with a bag and passed me when I was at my car. He's never come forward to speak to you, has he? Who was he? What was he doing there? Is he anything to do with it? Did he see anything else apart from me? He came from the direction of the crime scene. He could have been a witness. He could have been the—'

'It was Emile. Who now may die.'

'It was Emile? How long have you known? Don't answer that. Doesn't matter now. I see. He saw what happened to Mariela, saw who did it. That's why he stopped drinking. Ah shit. I might have guessed.'

Folin looked tired. He turned away, placed Bright's sheets of paper on his desk, arms straight, clenched fists either side of the papers, staring down at the papers, not seeing them. Silence in the room. Neither of them spoke. The two guilty men. The sin-eaters. Trucks shook the place, trundling by outside. Dogs barked. Apart from that, the village was silent too. At last, Folin said, 'I will read your report. Thank you.'

'Okay, mate.' Bright felt they'd both aged ten years. 'Okay. I'll leave you to it then.' He wanted to ask permission to go out but now was not the time to push his luck. He went to the door. He said, 'How *is* Emile?'

'Still unconscious after the surgical intervention. He has not spoken yet. He has not said why he decided at that point to cross the road.'

'Maybe somebody in the hotel, in a doorway maybe, called him across.'

Folin looked at him steadily. 'Yes.'

Bright left the room.

Downstairs the same strange silence lurked. The few men in the bar drank without speaking. The young guy in glasses read a newspaper. No kids played bar billiards. The machines were silent. Only the solo darts-player, the addict, still threw his darts, and the scoreboard lit up and he went to retrieve his darts and returned to his position and started throwing again.

They looked at Bright when he came in. No one said *bonjour* but most nodded, expressions in their faces of sympathy or suspicion or both. The man in specs gave him a long stare. Of resentment or curiosity? Bright couldn't tell, partly because of the specs and partly because of the man's desire to betray nothing. There was no one behind the bar. He didn't know where Louis was hanging out. And he didn't know how to ask. He retreated, and overheard some low conversation when they thought he'd gone.

He made for the dining room. A sudden hunger roared inside him. He had not eaten since he had seen Jude in his car hanging on the cliff. The Cirque de Ladoye. The Circle of Death. He sat at a table in a dim corner. No light, no light.

She came out of the kitchen, the sister. 'Bonjour, M'sieu. Pour manger?'

'A-ha. See voo play.'

'Vous désirez?'

He touched his nose then gestured towards the kitchen with his chin. 'Whatever it is I can smell.'

She got it – the mime. 'Ragôut de rognons d'agneau au vin rouge.'

He had no idea what that was, apart from the *vin rouge* part. 'Sounds good. Boon. Wee. Mercy.'

When she went back to the kitchen the guy in specs came into the dining room. He passed Bright's table then stopped and came back. He stood opposite, put a hand to the chair. 'May I sit here?'

'Sure.'

He pulled out the chair and settled himself, looking closely at everything he did as though he might have to give a description of his actions later. Bright attributed this to his short sight. The careful way he did everything made him appear almost blind. Seated at last he joined his hands, sliding his fingers together up to the knuckles and clasping them tight. Again he watched what his hands did. Then he raised his eyes and regarded Bright. The glasses magnified his eyes to curious effect, like a character in a cartoon. His face without the lenses was handsome in a characterless way.

Bright said nothing. The man said nothing. The sister came back with bread and a carafe of water. The man ordered his lunch, still looking at Bright, not at her. When she'd gone Bright said, 'You know her?'

'She is the sister of Louis.'

'Older or younger?'

'Two years older.'

'Are they close?'

'Close?' He didn't understand.

Bright imitated the man's gesture, clasping his hands to mime closeness.

'Ah. Close. Yes. They are close since – always.'

'Who are you?'

'Ah. Claude Grandet.'

'John Bright.'

'Inspector of police of London?'

'Right. You?'

'Teacher. Of mathematic.'

'A-ha.' Bright inwardly sat up. 'At the local school?'

'Now not.'

'Why's that?'

'The prof has dismissed me.'

'When?'

'Since one year.'

'What for?'

'I'm sorry?'

'What did you do? To get dismissed.'

'Ah. I questioned his – conduct?'

'What conduct was this?'

'His relation with one boy.'

'What boy?'

'Franck de Genares.'

Yes. 'What – relation?'

'Too – close? Too much attention. Because Franck is star student, etcetera. And more. Like a – son? A – *tendresse*?

273

All note this – relation. The other student mock of Franck. No other teacher will speak with the prof. But I. I protest to him. He is angry and he finish me at end of semester.'

'You got another job now? At a different school?'

'No. And now my wife, she – we have baby. Since three days.'

So this was the guy who'd bought the beer that had made the boys drunk. *Christ.*

The Totem brought the food to the two men who were sitting in silence, a silence so deep that no word seemed ever to have broken it. The plât du jour was kidneys, their glossy backs nestling in a rich red-brown sauce with an aroma of wine and garlic and thyme, with small smooth potatoes, scattered with parsley. Bright slowly lifted his fork.

They ate in silence too. Other people had come in to eat, some of the good old boys from the bar, others strangers, to Bright at least. When they got down to mopping the juice from their plates with bread, Bright said, 'You haven't told the judge, Folin, what you just told me?'

'No.'

'Why not?'

'I – people will know.'

'People will know you've talked to me.'

'But not of what I have talked.'

'Do they all know? About this – relationship.'

'I have never talked of it.'

'You're kidding. After he dismissed you?'

'I may have been wrong. He said – the prof said – I have a disease imagination. I am not suitable to teach more.'

'So why you telling me?'

'Because the boy is dead. Because perhaps he was at the house of the prof. Because your *amie* is also dead. I don't know.'

'You have to talk to Folin.'

'No.'

274

The Totem came back to present the choice of dessert or cheese. Both men declined and Bright ordered coffee. 'You?'

But the man was on his feet. He held out a hand. 'Thank you. Goodbye.' Bright shook his hand, and Grandet left the table, first settling his chair precisely as it had been before he sat in it. In the whole conversation, though his magnified eyes had never left Bright's face, they had never appeared to focus on him. But the eyes of all the good old boys from the bar focused on him as he left the dining room.

28

Private Griefs

The coffee mainlined straight to his veins. His heartbeat quickened. The little maths man had given his mind a focus too, moved him on. He had needed just this – a word to suggest that the prof as they called him was not Mr Perfect, that underneath the trustworthy, noble, humane surface, maybe a few little earthworms crawled. The story would have to be checked. Just now it was only hearsay. The prof had sacked this bloke, so he carried a grievance, a life blow had been dealt him; it could be he was hitting back. How to check? Who could Bright check with, and not give him away to his village mates? He went back up to Folin, taking the stairs two at a time.

'I will find a way.'

'The lunch'll help. Kidney ragôut in red wine sauce. Wouldn't think she could cook, to look at her.'

'Perhaps Louis is doing it.'

'Is he still in the hotel?'

'I permitted him to visit with his mother and her lawyer.'

'Would you permit me to visit with the prof?'

'Only if I accompany you.'

'Why's that?'

'Because I think you want to shake the information out of him like he is a bottle of ketchup.' Folin made a gesture, short and violent. 'I wish to protect not only him but you also from yourself.'

Bright, about to protest, shut his mouth. 'Okay. Enjoy your lunch.'

*   *   *

He stayed in the office, adding to his own report. Wondering about Emile. What had got to him? Bad conscience? For what? Because he'd killed Mariela or because he saw who did and hadn't stopped it, and then hadn't come forward afterwards? Why wouldn't he come forward if he knew something? *Who* had got to him was maybe the question to ask.

But then it wasn't just Emile. The little maths teacher had not come forward either. Till now. This was a close community. Loyalties were fierce. You didn't grass up your friends. Your family. That was the thing – he had to think of this community as a family. They might fight among themselves but they presented a united front to the world. Fortress-family.

But to throw yourself under a truck? That was something more than bad conscience. There are easier ways of killing yourself. Bright had seen him step out. If he hadn't seen him he'd have put it down to drink: Emile, perpetually sozzled, out of control, fuddled, not knowing what he was doing. But Bright had seen, and more and more he wondered if someone had called him across the road. Wait, wait, wait. Speculation could drive you round the bend. He'd be crawling the walls if this went on. He had to do something.

Folin's list of the names of those he had questioned was printed out on the desk. Bright went through it. And came to 'de Genares, M. & Mme'. The parents of Franck, the posh pair from Château-les-Mînes. They had to be allies now. Didn't they? The phone number was printed next to their name. He rang it.

'Why have they come?' Folin said.

Bright shrugged. 'They must have something else to tell you.'

Javet, the young *flic*, showed them in. They looked the same as before, tall, elegant, aristocratically slim. Streamlined as the horses they bred. Dressed in their stiff cream riding macs with their shiny boots. It was only when Bright saw their eyes he found he was looking at the walking wounded. They'd been shot through the heart, the bullet had gone right through; they had the dazed look of those who would wake later to be told the wound was mortal. Bright recognised the condition. A current passed between him and them. They shook hands with him. They simultaneously murmured condolences. The secret society of the newly bereaved.

Folin said, 'You requested to see me.'

They looked at each other and agreed tacitly that the husband should speak. He cleared his throat. 'Yes. We do not wish to implicate any person. But our son—' His hand finished the sentence in a gesture. 'Just less than one year ago, the teacher of mathematic at the school, Claude Grandet, was elected to speak, to remonstrate, with Professeur Breton.' He paused.

'Yes?'

'It was a question of – Franck. It was – the appearance was – that Breton – that he and Franck became too –'

'Too close,' his wife said.

'Yes. Franck is the best student in the school. Breton gives him special attention, extra –'

'Coaching?' his wife said.

'Yes, coaching, in certain subjects, sometimes evenings, often at his house. The other students have observed this and have begin to – to mock – and even to ostracise Franck. We ourselves observed that Franck is not so happy, is quite sad. We enquired of him what happens. He has refused to say. Oh no, everything is okay with him, nothing is wrong. We do not wish to intrude in his affairs and so we do nothing. But Franck is not the same happy boy and we are concerned. We go to Breton and ask him what is with Franck that make him so unhappy. Breton says us quite openly the

278

special, the extra, attention of him, has caused his friends to abandon him, but if he stops, Franck's future, his bac etcetera, will be perhaps damage. He is open. He presents to us the choice.' He looked at his wife.

She continued, 'I have approached Franck. I say to him what we have done. He was angry. Very angry, furious to me. We should not interfere. We should ask to him first, not go right away to the prof, and so on, you can imagine, a typical adolescent. But later I again asked him. We were riding.' She looked towards the window, out there, up in the hills, riding with her dead son. 'We rested under a tree. I said again, Shall we ask the prof to cease the extra – coaching and so on? He said no, it is okay. It is very important for him. For him. For the prof, you understand? Not for Franck. I said, But is it so important for you? He said in one year he would be away from here and these boys would not be of importance to him, he was okay, and please in future speak to him before interference in his life. I felt we had been wrong and I said this to Franck and this I think healed the – the wound? – a little, between us.' The woman had trouble going on. She swallowed and tried but couldn't speak.

The husband took over. 'But Franck became more secretive and then took this – work – in the evenings at the hotel. When we saw the young woman Mariela, we understood his reason. We were not anxious. If there had been an – improper – relation between him and Breton, he was now growing up to be a man.'

'We were relieved we had a good heterosexual son.' The woman spoke with bitter irony.

'You did not tell me of this when I asked you earlier.'

The pair gazed at Folin. What could they say? Again they tacitly agreed the husband should speak. 'We did not wish to implicate – anybody. We ourselves spoke to the— to Breton. He assured us there has been nothing improper

279

between himself and Franck, only a teacher's honest desire to help a boy with such great promise. And he says he has not seen Franck since the – terrible incident – the killing of Mariela. He has appeared absolutely sincere. We believed him.'

'We have recently received information from another person on this matter. You know that Professeur Breton dismissed the young mathematic teacher from his position?'

The pair looked at each other and then at Folin. 'But surely, Maître, the law protects an employee in such a situation. This is not a reason to dismiss.'

Bright and Folin now looked at each other. Bright felt a fool. Why hadn't he thought of that? He'd been so excited to get any ammunition against the prof, the obvious had escaped him. Always check out a statement before acting on it.

Folin said, 'I will explore this further. Perhaps he was dismissed for another reason and now sees a way of revenge on the prof. I will question the young man, Grandet. I will discover more.'

'Thank you,' they murmured.

Bright said, 'Can you talk about Franck? I don't think he had anything to do with what happened to Mariela. Nothing. I mean that. Believe me. Believe me. But I want to know what sort of boy he was. Was he easy-going, relaxed – I mean until this business at school – or did he have – you know – tantrums?'

They looked blank.

'Er – rages, tempers. Was he ever—' These were the kid's parents, he was their flesh and blood, closer than Jude was to him. He had no kids, he couldn't imagine, but he knew they'd do anything to preserve his image and his good name. He didn't want to use the word violent. 'Was he ever out of control?' he said.

They weren't fazed by the question. The mother said,

'Like any boy. Any young man. He would – you say lose the temper – over trifles, small matters. But in a short time would be good-humoured again. He was a nice boy. Eager to please.' It was clear she could not say any more. The husband made a movement, very slight, indicative that he was there to protect her. She nodded as though in agreement with him.

The husband said, 'If we believed it to be possible that Franck has killed this young woman, believe me, we would say it. But we do not believe it. Not because he is our son. But because we know him. And we know it is not possible.'

They all stood. Folin shook their hands. 'Merci pour être venus. Je comprend votre difficulté. Merci.'

Again, shaking hands, sympathy passed between them and Bright, without words. He watched them go to the door and he didn't want them to disappear. He wanted more from them. He got to the door first, opened it and, with a flick of the eye to Folin, followed them out. Folin couldn't follow them without looking like either a spy or an idiot. Bright shut the door behind him. 'I'm not allowed off the premises but I'll see you out?'

'Not allowed?'

'I'm a suspect.'

'You?' They stopped on the landing and stared at him. They reviewed their communications with him in the light of this. Monsieur de Genares said at last, 'We have understood that you are helping Maître Folin.'

'In England we have an expression helping the police with their enquiries. It means you're a suspect but there's not enough evidence yet to bring a charge. Judge Folin's a good man. He's letting me help in both ways. He's making use of me. I don't mind. I like to be useful.'

'We wish to say to you . . .' Madame spoke slowly. 'It is difficult. But we must say . . . we do not know what has happened but believe that your – fiancée – what happen to her, if it has happen because of our son – we want to tell you we feel much sorry – sorrow. She was a tourist, your – *amie* – she was not a part of the story. If she had not encountered Franck, perhaps . . .'

Bright shut his ears. He knew all this. He knew it and wouldn't think about it because to think about it was to invite an eruption of rage so volcanic it would spill over and fry everything in its path. He accepted the words with a nod. He said, 'Franck was crazy about Mariela. He went off after the boys. The boys tell us he came out of hiding to stop them doing – what they were doing with her. They overpowered him and threw him in the river. They heard a car approaching and they all ran. So when this car arrives Franck is in the river or is climbing out. Now, we don't know what happened after that. Did the car stop? We don't know. Whose car was it? Who was driving? We don't know. Where Franck went after that? We don't know. I believe the prof – Breton – was hiding him in his carve. Or somewhere on his premises. But he denies it. And they all believe him. In spite of the fact that Franck ends up in the car with my – with Jude. Jude was at the house. Where else would she have come across Franck? He thumbed a lift from her – you know, hitchhiked – on the road? Not likely, is it? See, I agree with you – Jude stumbled into this – maybe trying to help Franck, save him from – what? who? The prof or someone else? Folin won't let me see the prof, question him, because he thinks – well, he knows – I'm prejudiced. But you know Professor Breton. You could talk to him. He's not telling the truth. That's what I think. But if you talk to him . . .' He spilled this out, quiet and quick, begging them. *Taking advantage? So what. Out of order? So what.* 'I'm not in charge here. I'm used to being in charge, running the show. Sorry if I've—'

'No, no . . .' They murmured together, then Monsieur De Genares spoke for them, with his customary dignity: 'Thank

282

you for this information. We can not promise to speak with Breton. But we will not abuse your confidence.'

Bright nodded. 'Okay. Well, thanks. It was worth a try, eh?'

He watched them start down the stairs. Hope descending.

29

And Reliable Reports

'Well?'

'Let me speak to Breton.'

'No.'

'Let me come with you when you speak to him.'

'No.'

'If I just go on the run, what's the worst you can do to me?'

'Put you in prison in Lons-le-Saunier.'

'For how long?'

'It would depend, I suppose, on what you do during your escape. If you kill someone, naturally you will stay for the rest of your life.'

'I need to talk to him. I can't talk to him on my own. I need a witness.'

'You need a guard to restrain you.'

'Why are you giving him the free ride? What is your strategy? I can't believe you really think the guy's not involved. So what are you up to?'

'The car that arrived at the scene? It was not his car. His car has been in the garage in the village since three days.'

'Why?'

'For *service annuelle*. The *garagiste* confirms this. Even so, we have examined the car forensically. There is nothing. In his house, as I said, there is nothing.'

'He's had time, he could've—'

'Yes, of course, naturally he can clean and so on. It is not suspicion, it is fact! It is fact that we lack.'

'Are you going to question him about the dismissal of the

maths teacher? Are you going to question him about the rumours of something funny between him and Franck?'

'When I have completed my enquiry to a colleague in employment law, yes.'

'How long will that take?'

'It will take as long as it takes.'

'You know something? Sometimes your English is too good.'

'He promises to telephone me before the end of today.'

'A-ha?' Bright rubbed his face all over with the palm of his hand and his hand felt surprise to find his face still the same to the touch, when everything inside and in the surrounding world had so fundamentally changed.

'And your lawyer?'

'A-ha. He promises too. Before the end of the day.'

'If he does not telephone. Or even perhaps if he does. I think you must take a sedative. I think you must sleep a little.'

'Yeah?' The floor rocked under his feet. He knew the signs of extreme fatigue. The earth became a rocking raft. This sensation came over him in sudden short upward thrusts, through the soles of his feet up through his body into his head. The expression 'air-head' just about described it. At these moments he could lie down and sleep anywhere, but immediately his mind took over again and forced his body to attention. The red danger light was on and wouldn't go off. He knew he must sleep. He knew what sleep deprivation could do even to the sane and normal: turn anyone into a loony in forty-eight hours. But he feared that, once asleep, he wouldn't wake. The solution would get away. 'I can't sleep until I've talked to the schoolteacher again.'

Folin sighed and went back to his laptop and Bright went back to his window. A bloke could get sick of this view. 'What's the French law on bail?'

'Bail?'

'You know what bail is!'

'It is not relevant until we have brought a charge.'

'So bring a charge.'

'Against whom?'

'Me! Bring a charge. Charge me with perverting the course of justice or something. Charge me! And then release me on bail. Come on!'

Folin gave a short laugh. 'You have yet to pervert the course of justice. And please! Please do not make my work more complex than it is now. Please. You are the *juge des libertés'* chief suspect. He will put you on remand the moment you step out of line. And then you will be completely powerless. And I will be powerless to help you.'

So that was it. Folin had put himself in the firing line for him. It was out in the open now: if Bright put a foot wrong, it would reflect on Folin. He gazed at the guy and sighed, shaking his head.

Louis and his sister appeared below. They crossed the road to their mother's house. They were the same height but they walked like different animals, she with a ramrod-straight military stride, Louis with bent legs and drooping head like an ape. She held his upper arm as they crossed the road. Scared that he too would take advantage of a conveniently passing truck? Or keeping him upright? Or frogmarching him to another interview with their charming parent against his will? That seemed most likely.

How did she get on with Mother Toad? She lived a long way off and didn't visit often. Was that just chance? Or had she got out and stayed out – put plenty of distance between them and kept it there? 'When did she arrive, the sister? Did Javet check her out?'

'Ah yes. Here.' Folin found the paper. 'She is on annual leave of two weeks.'

'Why now?'

'Why are you on annual leave now? Because it suits your

plans, because it is not tourist season, because—'

'A-ha. Okay.' He took the paper. He couldn't understand the French but he could understand the numbers. Her leave had started on the Sunday, two days before Mariela's murder. Was that coincidence? 'When did she apply for this annual leave?'

Folin pointed out another date on the report. 'Three weeks ago.'

'Do you believe in coincidence?'

'Coincidence is normal.'

'Has anyone questioned her neighbours in Nogent? Do we know when she took off for here?'

'We wait to hear this.'

'We wait.'

The brother and sister were just disappearing round the side of the house. He'd give a lot to overhear their conversation, to have a direct line to that first-floor room.

Folin's phone rang. 'Folin . . . Ah, Javet. Oui?'

He saw himself small and distinct as though looking down from a great height. A little figure imprisoned in a big room with gibberish talked all round, a code he couldn't break, scurrying about, searching for something he'd lost. He shut his eyes a moment and swayed. This was sleep deprivation all right, and it was getting worse.

'A tout á l'heure, Javet, et merci.' Folin put down his phone. 'Mademoiselle Agnès Barbe? Her neighbours saw her on Sunday but not after. They thought she was going to her office as usual. She did not inform them that she intended to go away.'

'Would she normally tell them?'

'No. They are not friends, just neighbours.'

'What about her car? They see that?'

Folin checked the report again. 'She garages her car around the corner. They would not know if it was there or not.'

'Great. And no one sees her here either till today. Four days – and nights – since she was seen. Three days – and two nights – since the murder. We don't know when she set off. Or how long she was on the road. Do we know yet when she arrived here?'

'No.'

Bright made an impatient movement, turning to the window again.

'Javet is below. He will request Mamselle Agnès to visit me here when she returns from her mother's house.'

'About time.'

'I will endeavour not to understand that.'

'Sorry, mate, I know you're doing your best, but, Christ . . .'

When she came in, the temperature dropped. She sat down without bending her back, just angled her knees and made a sideways shift of her lower body. She wore a deep green sweater, looked like cashmere, and a narrow black skirt to mid-calf. Her legs were as straight-up-and-down as the rest of her. Nevertheless, in the way of French women of a certain age, she looked elegant, even if severe. She wore no jewellery but a watch, practical, not expensive, a man's watch.

She didn't speak or make any social noises. Having sat when Folin asked her to, she waited. She wasn't insolent or wary. Bright didn't get any whiff of fear off her, or the resentment she'd shown when she'd brought his coffee earlier. Maybe the visit to Mother Toad had calmed her down? Or maybe what he was getting off her was simple exhaustion? No. She was neutral. That was it. Neutral. And that was weird, wasn't it? Her brother's girlfriend that she and her family disapproved of has been raped and murdered and now an English woman and a young boy are also dead, possibly because one of them was a witness to that murder. Her brother, although there is no tangible evidence against

288

him, is yet in a very difficult position, and she sits here in front of the judge, idling in neutral.

Folin asked her in English if she spoke English. She said, also in English, 'Not enough.' As with Bright earlier, she was indicating that she spoke enough to get by but did not care to try in these circumstances. Folin said, 'I shall translate for Inspector Bright. You understand?'

She nodded. She did not look at Bright. But Bright never took his eyes off her.

Folin began speaking, to her in French then to him in English. 'When did you begin your journey?'

'Early Wednesday morning.'

'And when did you arrive here?'

'Yesterday.'

'At what time?'

'I'm not sure. Around noon.'

'Was your visit here planned in advance?'

'No. Louis reached me on my portable – mobile – yesterday morning. I was intending to go farther south for the sun.'

'Ah, like Inspector Bright and his fiancée.'

She made no response to this. But she didn't look the type to whom the sun would much appeal.

'Where in particular were you going?'

'To Marseille.'

'Had you booked an hôtel?'

'No. It is always possible to find a room. Near the airport if nowhere else.'

'Why Marseille? From Orléans for a short break by the sea one would expect you to visit – La Rochelle perhaps.'

'We used to go to Marseille as children. My father liked the Calanques.'

Folin explained. 'The Calanques are many small inlets, along the coast to the east of Marseille. They are only approachable by walking along the cliffs of sand with pine forest, behind and above. Or from the sea. They are very private, very charming, but difficult to access.' Again she didn't change her posture, move her head or even her eyes. 'You always visit Marseille for your vacation?'

'Once a year at this time.'

'Where were you when Louis phoned you?'

'I was between Nevers and Autun.'

'Not so very far from here in fact.'

'Well, yes.' She showed no sign of worry at Folin's insinuation. 'Perhaps a hundred and fifty kilometres.'

'Is that perhaps a slightly odd route to take, Mademoiselle, for Marseille?'

'I like to drive through this region. I like to use small roads. And I like to take the route by Gap and Sisteron. Any route is more amusing than the motorway through Lyon.'

She didn't strike Bright as a woman who did anything for amusement, but you never can tell: maybe she was a raver under that severe armour she wore. Like hell.

'So you took a route through this region without intending to visit your brother, or your mother, even for a day.'

'I was intending to visit my youngest brother who works in the dental hospital in Geneva.'

'He didn't tell us you were intending to visit him.'

'No, I had not told him.'

'Why not?'

'Because I might change my mind. As you see, I did change my mind. He is very busy always, he works long hours, he is very dedicated to his work. It is better if I do not interrupt him, but just arrive. I do not like him to make elaborate preparations for me.'

This was more voluble than she had been so far. Why? Lying? Or was there something about this younger brother? Bright got the first hint of warmth from somewhere in that monotonously glacial tone. He spoke for the first time. 'How much younger is that brother?'

She replied, in English, without glancing at him, 'He is nine years younger than I.'

'Does he have a girlfriend, live with anyone?'

This time she waited for Folin to translate.

'He has lived with a person for some years but has recently separated and now lives alone.'

'How long since she visited him?'

Folin again translated. 'Three years.'

'That the same length of time he's lived with this – person?'

'Yes.'

'And is this person male or female?'

This time he got a reaction. Her body stiffened, her eyelids closed, briefly, indicating irritation. Her shoulders rose. She breathed in and held it. She was going to refuse to answer, tell them to mind their own business. But that would have betrayed her feelings. So she spoke. One word. 'Male.'

So her little brother, the one she idolises, is queer, and she doesn't like to admit that. Bright started to see the life of these three siblings as kids growing up. That grotesque mother, probably an emasculated father who died young. This Agnès must have been the refuge and strength of those two brothers, a buffer between them and the mother, but imbibing her ways just the same. Their protector, but feared probably almost as much as the monster herself. After all, if Agnès removed her protection, they were vulnerable as hell. She had that threat to hold over them if they displeased her. He heard Mariela say, 'His family not want he marry me.' He said to Folin, 'Ask her about Mariela. Ask about her attitude to Mariela.'

'Louis' fiancée, Mariela . . .' Folin let it hang.

She made no reaction.

'You have met her?' he said.

'Yes.'

'How many times?'

291

'Once.'

'Only once? She has been in France many months.'

'Once was enough.'

'You did not approve?'

'She was not the right wife for Louis.'

Bright said, 'Would anyone have been the right wife for Louis?'

Her eyes flicked sideways to him and away. None of his business. Family affair.

Folin said, 'So, Mademoiselle Barbe, there is no one who can say where you were on Tuesday night when the murder of Mariela takes place and you are not far away also when the fiancée of Inspector Bright and the boy Franck de Genares are killed.'

'I understood they died in a car accident.'

'Who told you this?'

'It is what people are saying.'

'We are not yet certain. Elements of the deaths appear suspicious.'

She raised an eyebrow. That was all. Couldn't care less, that was the implication. None of her business. She was good. Bright couldn't tell if it was superb control or the truth.

'We wait for reports. Then we will know whether to investigate these deaths as murder or accept them as accident.'

No reaction again. Nothing to do with her.

'How long do you intend to stay here, Mademoiselle?'

'I have requested more leave. I will stay while Louis needs me.'

'You understand that he is a suspect?'

'Yes.'

'Has he spoken to you about the situation he is in?'

'He is upset, naturally, both by the death and by being suspected.'

'And what do you think, Mademoiselle?'

'Me?'

'You have known him all your life.'

'For the last fifteen years I have lived in Nogent.'

'Would you say he was capable of such a violent act?'

'I am not a psychiatrist, Monsieur. I have simply advised him to contact our family lawyer. My mother has done so. Louis and my mother will meet him later over there at the house. I trust this is allowed.'

'Yes, this is your right as a citizen of France. It is even the right of a British citizen in this country. Inspector Bright too awaits his lawyer.'

'She'd better spell out her movements to the lawyer, as well as old Louis'. She's got no alibi at all, far as I can see. What's her car? Did she stop anywhere for petrol? Food? She speak to anyone who can vouch for her whereabouts? You setting up enquiries along her alleged route?'

He'd got her attention all right. If she were a cat her ears would be twitching. She understood every word, no question. He could tell. Her spine tightened, and the muscles in the back of her neck. Barely visible to the naked eye, but flashing in neon lights to him. Folin translated just the same. She calmly replied that she would supply him with a list of places she had stopped at on the journey, she had nothing to hide.

'Did you pass a night somewhere, Mademoiselle?'

'I slept for a few hours in an *aire* at the side of the road. It was enough.'

'And in the *aire*, there were other vehicles? Other drivers sleeping?'

'One truck. As I arrived it departed.'

'At what time was that?'

'I did not check the time. It was dark but well before midnight, I believe.'

'And what time did you leave the *aire*, yourself?'

'It was dawn. There were no other vehicles there when I woke.'

'You will have receipts for your petrol and other purchases on the journey?'

'No.'

'No?'

'This was not a business trip for which I would claim expenses. I do not clutter up my life with useless pieces of paper. So, no.'

'Very convenient,' Bright said.

'My English colleague is naturally frustrated, and is bereaved, as is your brother.'

It was clever of Folin to remind her of Bright's bereavement. Most people, even in her shoes, would have offered formal condolence – sorry for your loss, or the equivalent. She turned to look at him but said nothing. The small brown eyeballs in the long eyes were opaque. She turned back to Folin. 'He has no right to question me, has he?'

Folin was taken aback. It showed in his voice as he translated. 'No. But he has the privileges that I as the *juge d'instruction* accord him.'

'Is that all? May I go now? Louis is not capable just now of managing the hotel. My help is needed below.'

'You may go, but I will need to speak with you again. And you will please provide an account of your journey here to my colleagues in the room next door?'

'If you wish.' She left the room as she had entered it, upright, contained, expressionless. The door closed and Folin let out a sigh. Bright said, 'Her alibi will be no alibi. There'll be enough to tell you she was actually on the road. It'll be possible for her to have got here from wherever she was. But it won't be possible for you to place her anywhere in particular. You might as well not bother trying.'

'I must try.' Folin sounded whacked out.

'Yes, you gotta.'

The phone rang. Folin had a brief conversation. 'The pathologist is going to fax his report on Jude and Franck.

294

He wanted to be sure I was here to receive it. Do you want to be here also?'

The fax machine began to warble before Bright could answer. He couldn't speak anyway. The pages tongued out of the slit, spilling in folds onto the floor. He stayed at the window, like his back was stuck there. He couldn't move. The pages stopped reeling out. Folin was already reading. Bright prised himself off the window sill, helped him tear the pages. His hands shook.

Folin sat to read. He made notes here and there. He got to the end and looked up. 'The cause of death? Carbon-monoxide poisoning with a level of eighty-five per cent saturation in the blood. Of both victims. Bruising to the wrists and ankles indicate both were bound before death occurred. But the death itself would obviously have been painless and had occurred before the car went over the cliff.' The last comment was not in the report. It was Folin's offering.

Bright found himself sitting on the floor, his hands in his hair clutching his scalp, his knees bent up, his elbows either side of his knees. He wasn't sure how long he'd been there – a minute or an hour. Folin was offering him coffee. With a sense of endless repetition, he took his hands out of his hair and accepted the cup. The hot liquid hurt his throat and his chest. The light was leaving the sky outside the window. Folin said, 'I have made a rough translation of the concluding page.' He gave this to Bright.

Bright studied it. He straightened out his legs. Stiff as an arthritic old man. Let his head fall back against the wall. Shut his eyes. Opened them again. Shutting your eyes was out. Tears were out. Screaming was out. This made it real. Down here in black and white. They'd been left in the car with a hose to the exhaust, bound and gagged, Franck uncon-scious, probably, from a blow to the head, Jude, he hoped, or did he? – unconscious too, until they were dead, taken

295

in the car to the top of the Cirque de Ladoye, the car set in motion to crash through the fence and go over the edge. All over. Done and dusted. Problem solved.

He starts to see it in his head. When the car first sets off from Neufchâtel driven by someone in Jude's straw hat, where are the bodies? In the car covered up or in the boot? Most likely the boot. And when the car gets to the Cirque? It's dark, got to be. Too dangerous to do in daylight. Where was the car all that time. Could've been anywhere. All this forest. All this space. The driver gets out of the car and manoeuvres Jude into the driver's seat. A dead body is a dead weight. Jude is not small, she's what in the old days they'd have called a fine figure of a woman. 'There were two of them,' he said to Folin. 'There's got to be two. One couldn't manage alone. *And there's got to've been another car.* How does the perpetrator get back where he came from after he's pushed my car over the edge? Someone helps him. Someone helps him to do the whole thing. My car was driven from Nerfshattle but the other one wasn't. No one saw another car. Or if they did it was just some ordinary French car that no one would notice.'

'They rendezvoused en route.'

'Or at the Cirque.'

'But to drive back to here is dangerous.'

'The whole thing is dangerous. It's dangerous to be seen driving back here together but they could have been seen at any time, at the Cirque or anywhere. Emile could have seen them and put two and two together.'

'Emile was not pushed under that truck, he walked.'

'Yeah. Yeah.'

'You yourself saw him.'

'Yeah.' A breath rasped out of Bright's throat. 'I dunno.' His mobile rang. He didn't recognise it at first. He located it at last in his pocket. 'Bright here.'

'Monsieur l'inspecteur?'

Franck's father. 'A-ha. Yes?'

'We have gone to Professeur Breton as you asked. He is sick, very sick. He cannot speak to us. We believe he needs a doctor. The juge d'instruction, Maître Folin, perhaps he will bring a doctor to see him?'

'What are you saying? You think he knows something?'

'He is much affected by the – incidents. He needs medication or may do something violent, dangerous, fatal perhaps to himself. He refuse to have a doctor visit to him, you understand. We are not able to persuade. We are desolated, Monsieur.'

'Okay, that's okay, thanks for calling me, Mushoo de Jenner. I'll call you back, soon as I can. Thanks. Thanks. Orvwah.' He came up off the floor like a spring. He grabbed his jacket and Folin's. 'We gotta go, Folin. Now.'

30

Walking Away

Hardly anyone in the bar. Just the two old guys with their shopping-bags, the Buchon brothers, Breton's alibi. A young lad serving. They watched the judge and the Brit policeman out of the door.

The sun was going. Shreds of grey cloud across pale yellow sky. Grey air, no shadows. They crossed the road fast and went through the wasteland car park, the picket gate, along the shadowed path with the stream in the undergrowth. It was dark in here, the way muddy and narrow. Five minutes and they were out the other end, the river curving away to their left and running straight to their right, on the other side of the lane. No cars.

They turned left on the road, their feet making a small clatter in the loose gravel. Soon they passed the little house, steep roof, three dormer windows, no lights on, where the brothers lived. Those two in the bar. Jacques and Olivier Buchon. Funny old codgers. They'd been in the bar when it was all happening down here. They knew nothing. Oh yeah? Bright would take bets they knew all there was to know, and would never tell.

The road curved to the right, across the ancient stone bridge. The river continued straight, through a small clump of trees, parting from the road which curved left again after the bridge. The high wall of the teacher's garden rose up ahead, and then the gates. The high wrought iron gates, backed with sheet metal for privacy. They were locked. They had never been locked before.

Folin pressed the bell, an old one set in a big brass circle on the gatepost. But Bright didn't wait for an answer. He grabbed the iron bars and walked his feet up to a foothold. The top of the gate curved up to the middle. He chose the hinge end, levered himself, scrabbling with his toes till his arms supported him, to get a knee on top of the gatepost, then swung over and dropped.

He ran up the drive. Heard Folin drop into the grass behind him. He left the front door for Folin. He ran round the side of the house through the garden of shadows to the back entrances. The *cave* door first. It wasn't locked. He pushed it and went in. He thought he heard something but wasn't sure. The garden room was empty but he bolted the door behind him to cut off escape. He listened. No breathing, no movement. He took the stairs a few at a time, flowing up like a cat. It was dark but this cellar was printed on his memory; he didn't need light. The door at the top was not locked. He turned the handle with extreme care and opened it a crack. The kitchen was dark too. He loped through into the dining room and through there to the living room where he saw a tall figure beating the hell out of Folin in a frenzy with an iron-headed mallet. The schoolteacher slumped in a chair, tied to the chair, his head hanging, blood dripping from a pulpy gash in the back of his head.

Bright ran at the tall figure, one hand to a shoulder, the other at the waist. He got a grip and pulled. The attacker was beyond noticing, but Folin knew now that he had help. He ducked, and butted the attacker in the guts. The attacker was gasping and panting and now gasped harder and sharper but lifted the hammer again. Bright thrust his right knee between the attacker's legs from behind then kicked back hard at the ankle to break his balance. Folin grabbed the legs too, in a rugby tackle, and brought him down. But the frenzy didn't stop, the attacker kicked like a felled mule, screaming, still gripping the hammer. When Bright knew Folin had got him and wouldn't let go, he went for the hammer. He leaped on top of the guy, stamping on the wrists as hard as he could. The scream modulated from rage to pain. Bright went on stamping till he heard bone crack and the crazy's grip on the hammer loosed. Bright kicked it away. The crazy was sobbing now but still struggling to get free of Folin who was hanging on to the flailing legs for dear life.

Bright desperately searched for something to restrain the crazy. He could see nothing. The heavy curtains were shut and the darkness thick. He undid his own belt and dragged it out of its loops. He got the flailing arms, sat on the creature's back, and said, 'I'll break your bloody collar-bone as well as your wrist if you don't keep still, you mad bugger.' With the end of the belt between his teeth he managed to wind the leather round the good wrist and then in a figure of eight round the broken useless one. He pulled tight and the crazy screamed like a frightened horse. He said to Folin, 'Use your belt on the ankles.' But Folin had already got the idea. The crazy was still bucking like a mule. Bright sat astride its back, holding the thighs and the back of the knees while Folin, panting, wound his belt round the ankles twice.

They turned the trussed-up bucking screaming thing over. It was Agnès. Folin was astounded. But Bright already knew. He left her, and Folin on his mobile, to attend to the teacher. The man was conscious but only just, floating in and out on waves of pain. He was tied to the chair with clothes-line. Bright unwound it and threw it to Folin to secure mad Agnès with. 'Where's her brother? Where's Louis? I thought I heard something. Is he still in the house?'

Folin asked her. Her mouth was set now in a tight line of pain. She'd determined not to speak. He tied her to the cold iron stove, the rope round and round her and it, no way she could break free. He ran up the stairs to search above. Bright shouted, 'Have you called an ambulance?'

'Yes, the *pompiers* will arrange everything.'

Bright ran out to the gates, pulling back the great bolts, shutting out the picture of his car here in the drive behind these gates and Jude dying in it. He pulled, and the gate creaked open, one side, then the other. No electronically controlled mod-cons here. He ran back in. He gave the teacher water from the jug on the table. The man swallowed and his eyes opened.

'Can you talk?'

Breton nodded.

'Gonna tell us what happened?'

His head lolled again. Bright lifted it. 'The ambulance is on its way. You've got a bad gash in the back of your head, but you're conscious and you're not concussed, you know what I'm saying. You gotta tell me. You owe me. Before they come. Were you harbouring Franck?'

'Yes'. The man spoke in harsh gasps. 'He sees Louis attack Mariela. He is afraid to fight Louis. Louis runs. Franck comes out of river, to help Mariela. He sees Mariela is dead. He runs but hears a man run after him. He knows Louis has seen him. He runs to here and hides himself in my *cave*. I find him next morning. He refuse to tell me what happen but then next day all the world knows. I believed Franck has killed Mariela, because she has made him crazy. Yes, I hide him. He is—' The man broke down, liquid rolling out of his eyes and his nose, his body heaving. Bright gave him more water and a napkin off the dining table. He mopped himself up while Bright used another napkin to mop the back of his neck where the blood was hardening over a wound open to the pale-blue bone of the skull.

'Okay, I know why you harboured him. What happened here with Jude and him? What happened here?'

'I do not know! I was not here! I was in the school! I cannot stay here because I do not want to make suspicion here. I tell Franck stay in the garden hut. Do not come into the house. I will come at night with food. I do not know

301

what will happen.' He made a high-pitched moaning sound. 'If I had told the *juge*, Franck and Jude would not be dead now.'

'So you go to school and our friendly local innkeeper phones his big sister and they come round here and hit Franck over the head and Jude gets involved and they get them both in my car and turn on the ignition and use it as a gas chamber. You stupid bastard. I'd like to do the same to you, only it would be too slow and too merciful. Get me away from him.'

Bright was crying now, an awful squealing coming out of him, like a trapped animal. Only this was a trap he might never get out of, stuck here in this horrible house for ever, seeing Jude passing out, in the dumb-cluck London police-man's car, in broad daylight, in the good French headmaster's driveway behind his big privacy-sealed iron gates.

Folin took him by the shoulders and an ambulance man helped to lead him out of the house. He crouched in the dark outside with his back against the wall, howls coming out of him like gobs of vomit, and didn't know how to stop.

He didn't see crazy Agnès being manhandled out to the ambulance, he just heard her voice. She screamed out in the dark, 'Louis! Louis! Ne parles pas! Ferme la!' He heard only *Louis!* and he was up off his haunches and off through the garden and round the back of the house.

Undergrowth and no moon and no other light and only memory to guide him and his skill as a hunter, of the nocturnal predator known as the criminal. Only he's an urban hunter, the country an alien place where it's hard for him to pick up the spore. Too many scents and sounds and unfamiliar obstacles. He tripped and fell headlong, hands first to break his fall, lucky to hit only newly dug soil and nothing lethal.

He hears something behind him and swings round, and

Folin's voice whispers out of the dark, 'Police are surrounding the garden. They search the house.'

Bright says nothing but makes over to the left or what he hopes is his left and leaves Folin behind, and his outstretched hand touches stone and, feeling upwards, recognises the garden wall. *Okay.* The stones are rough and not newly mortared. Only small protrusions to grip but it's enough. He's on the top and over and down the other side and away into the woods. No sign of a gendarme or any kind of cop. Fat lot of use surrounding the garden.

The woods bring him out to the bank of the river. He runs along it, as best he can in the pitch dark. He can see a bit now but not enough to put on any speed, keeps tripping and nearly pitching into the water. But hits the bridge and clambers up the bank, on to the stone parapet and over it into the lane. Now he can go fast – he wasn't his school champion sprinter for nothing. But that was a lot of years ago and he starts to feel how many, has to slow a bit on the path alongside the garden of Louis' mother's house.

He stops to suck breath into his lungs and to think. Where would Louis go? To his mother the Toad? Never. Agnès his big sister has always protected him from the maternal venom. They must have had a plan, a contingency plan, what to do if they're interrupted. So Bright starts running again, his breath grinding in his chest and a dull ache in his legs but keeping speed, keeping going. And comes out opposite the hotel. There it is, all lit up and welcoming. Hôtel Sanglier, so cosy, always a welcome at the inn. And when he crashes the door back on its hinges and sees Louis behind the bar he gets his second wind. A brief flash of astounded faces, all the good ol' boys, and he's round the bar and lifts the flap and Louis's raising his arm with something in his hand, God knows what, a bottle probably, but Bright's smaller, with a lower centre of gravity, and he's gone for the waist and grabbed the other arm and thrown the bastard sideways and Louis's hit the deck in the cramped space and none of the good ol' boys is lifting a finger to help him, or to help Bright either, perched on their high stools, not taking sides, sitting on the fence. He's got Louis by the ankles and he's pulling, and the guy's a dead weight like a corpse, in fact he wonders if he is a corpse, knocked his head on something and died stone dead. He hopes so but, knowing Louis, thinks he's just playing dead, as he has done all his lousy life.

He keeps dragging and the long soft body bumps and bangs along the floor, Louis grabbing for a handhold but not getting a grip. And Bright's thinking all the time, where the hell to take him where they won't be interrupted, and can only come up, on the spur of the moment, with one place.

Louis tries to hang on to the swing door but Bright kicks him between the legs and Louis' hands forget saving his life and go to save his bollocks. What for? They've been no use to him up to now and no use to anyone else either, but now they're more important to Louis than his life, the selfish-gene theory in living proof, and Louis long enough distracted by pain and protection of his genital organs to enable Bright to get him inside the single cubicle in the gents' and the door bolted behind them.

He pushes Louis into the space between the pan and the wall. It's a tight squeeze. He jams a knee on him to keep him there. And when his hands go round the man's throat and his thumbs are pressing his windpipe, all he can think is that this loser, this useless tosser that the world would have been better off without, has robbed him of a person that mattered, has robbed him of her last hours, is the reason she spent her last hours not with him who loved her but with a golden lad she was trying to protect.

I know you, you bastard. You couldn't even do it yourself. You ring up your bloody sister and she comes running

304

and the pair of you go for Franck and then Jude gets in the way. It would take two of you to get her. She wouldn't go willing. And you'd have to take her by surprise, and even if you told me how, I wouldn't understand a fucking word you say, and he's banging the guy's head back against the wall and this noise is coming out of him and, going by the stink, he's shat himself, in an appropriate place, and a pool of urine is leaking its way out of him towards Bright's feet on the mosaic floor, and it's these physical manifestations of what he's doing that make him see his hands on the man's throat and hear the failing breath, and then he woke to the fact that someone was beating on the door and rattling it and shouting his name: *John! John! Stop!* And he does. He stops. The man's head lolls into the corner and at that moment he doesn't care whether he's killed him or not.

Next day Ted Adams arrived. Bright, a sedative forced on him by the chief of the ambulance crew, was asleep and he slept till evening when he woke to find Adams sitting in the chair in his room. Reading. Bright watched him for some time, getting his bearings. And then remembering. But only up to the point when he'd opened the cubicle door and let them in. 'Did I kill him?' he said.

'Jesus, John.' Adams jumped an inch out of the chair. 'If you mean the landlord, no, you didn't. He's in hospital in Lons-le-Saunier being treated for a bruised neck and windpipe and a slightly damaged scrotum.'

'Has he talked?'

'Physically incapable at the moment apparently.'

'He won't even when he is capable.'

'Nor has the sister.'

'She won't either.'

'Is there any evidence against them?'

'They'll get her for GBH or whatever they call it here

against the schoolteacher. And against the judge. There'll be no evidence against either of them for . . . Only hearsay – what the teacher says Franck told him.'

'I'm so sorry, John.'

'Is Emile still alive?'

'Is he compos mentis?'

'He is.'

'Then don't be sorry. He's the witness. That's all Folin needs. Folin won't let it go. Nor will I. I know how it happened, every step of it, Janet and John Go Murdering. They were going for Franck because he'd seen Louis destroying Mariela. They got Jude because she was there and they couldn't leave a witness. How did they get her? They must have given her some bull about Franck: if she struggled he'd get it or something. She's a big strong girl, I mean—'

'I know, I know. She must have thought she could save Franck, I agree.'

'I mean, even that evil pair, the Start-rite Psychopaths, even mad as a couple of monkeys on crack, they'd have a job overpowering Jude. Anyway, they got her and Franck in the car with the hosepipe from the exhaust, and that was that. I don't know how long it takes, carbon monoxide. I hope it's quick. I hope it's peaceful. God help me, I hope it didn't hurt—'

'John—'

'Don't worry, I'm not gonna break down again, I've done that. They releasing her body to take back?'

'Yes. By Eurotunnel. Going back with us. I've made all the arrangements. Jude's brother and sister—'

'Jesus.'

'Yeah. They just want a simple do. The brother lives up north but the sister's coming from New Zealand. They'll have it in London because that's where Jude's friends are.'

They both sat, seeing the possibilities of the social interactions involved. Jude's nearest and dearest that Bright has never met, and will they want him there, and how will he dare, how will it be possible to face them, or to face anyone come to that, or to face himself ever again?

'They want you there, in case you were wondering.'

'And Dan? Her husband?'

'He's been sedated ever since he got the news. I went to see him and his girlfriend in the posh loft in Southwark. The girlfriend's taking good care of him. He's like a baby with its nanny. She'll hold him together. He'll be okay.'

Bright had his doubts but didn't bother to say. 'My ma will keep George,' he said.

'George?'

Bright didn't speak for a while, then just one word, looking at the window where he saw from the light that it must be evening already. 'Cat,' he said. And then, 'Jude's cat.'

The funeral took place in the little chapel at Golders Green. Not the first time Bright had stood here witnessing the transition from dust back to dust. But the first time for someone he loved. Kate Creech came with him. For support. And because she was Jude's friend too: 'I liked her a lot, I'd be going anyway,' pretending she wasn't doing it primarily for him.

He didn't even know where to sit. 'I don't know what connection I am. She was leaving me. It was over anyway. For her.'

But where to sit wasn't a problem. In the left front pew sat Dan with a woman older than Jude, the red hair going grey, but unmistakably her sister, with two teenage kids, a girl and a boy. In the pew behind them sat a bloke, a bit overweight, receding ginger hair, younger than Jude but with a look of her: her brother, had to be, with his wife and a little red-haired boy with freckles and innocent blue eyes that could have been Jude as a kid. Dan's girlfriend – what was her name? Oh yeah, Lina. Leaner – Jude's name for her – sat two pews behind on the other side. Bright and Kate sat two pews behind her, more separated from Dan and the family than even Leaner was. Weird how people reclaim their dead. Easy to see why. Wanting to cling on.

He stood at a distance for the burial too. Not to intrude. He and Kate.

Leaner had rejoined Dan, standing close to him, holding his hand. After it was done and Jude had been lowered back into the earth she had loved and worked and grown things in all her life, the little group dispersed. Kate left his side to go and drop a handful of soil and have a last word with the relatives. Dan looked around, searching, saw Bright and made straight for him.

Dan was a big man and now, slimmed down and with his head shaved, looked more dangerous than he had in Jude's day. But Bright didn't flinch. Some things override even a momentary spurt of fear.

Dan speeded up. This close, his face was shiny with running tears. He thrust out his hands. He grabbed Bright by the upper arms. He swallowed the tears that reached his mouth, licking them in as a cat laps milk. He shook Bright back and forth, not hard, just while he got himself ready to speak. He took his hands away and just stood. 'It was me,' he said.

'You? You what?'

'It's my fault.'

Bright felt a surge of – what? – jealousy? This guy claiming to be the cause of her behaviour still, even though they'd split up and she'd been living with Bright for more than six months? But his voice stayed quiet. 'How come it's your fault?'

'I sent the letter.'

'What letter?'

'The letter threatening her.'

Bright's chest felt tight. The death threats they'd gone all the way to the Jura to get away from? 'You?'

'I knew you'd been getting threats. I wanted you to leave her. It seemed a way to get you away from her.'

'You?'

'I thought you'd leave her, you see, so that you'd no longer be a danger to her. But you took her away instead.'

The speed the mind works at, faster than light, deeper than darkness, downhill racing, through the months, the weeks, the last days. If only I'd known. If only I'd said. If only I had. If only I hadn't. *If only*. The only words that remain after a death, any death. If only if only if only.

Dan took the folded hankie out of his pocket, blew his nose and wiped his face. Bright came back from eternity to rejoin his body in the cemetery. Couldn't tell how long he'd been elsewhere. Minutes? Hours? Days? Years? Everything looked the same. People walking away from the grave. Earth dropping from Kate's fingers. Leaner waiting patiently for Dan to come back to her. As she always would, poor kid. And Dan waiting there to be blamed. The old masochist-sadist joke: 'Hit me hit me!' 'No.'

'Thanks for telling me,' Bright said. And walked away.